THE RING

The Legend of the Niebelungenlied:
The Volsungr Saga
The Saga of Ragnar Lodbrokr

THE RING

The Legend of the Niebelungenlied:
The Volsungr Saga
The Saga of Ragnar Lodbrokr

Heilan Yvette Grimes

HOLLOW EARTH PUBLISHING
HOLLOWEARTHPUBLISHING.COM

The Ring:
The Legend of the Niebelungenlied:
The Volsungr Saga and The Saga of Ragnar Lodbrokr

ISBN-10: 1879196069   ISBN-13: 978-1-879196-06-3

First Print Edition March 2012.

10   9   8   7   6   5   4   3   2   1

HOLLOW EARTH PUBLISHING • HOLLOWeaRTHPUBLISHING@GMAIL.COM

Colophon: The Cover is set in Desdemona. The Half Title, Title, are set in Desdemona and Aller Display. Section/Chapter Openings are all set in Fertigo Pro. The text is set in 10/12 Bembo/30 and 10/12 Bembo/28.

Francesco Griffo (1450-1518) was a typeface designer working for Aldus Manutius. One of his innovations was the italic font, which he designed around 1502.

Griffo's is a sad story. It was the custom in this era that towns, royalty, or central governments controlled the printing concession for an area. The Venetian government gave Aldus Manutius the printing concession for the city Venice and environs. After many years, and designing some of the most successful typefaces of the era, Griffo decided to go out on his own, taking all the matrices and punches he had cut for his typefaces with him so he could create sets of typefaces to sell to other printers. However, Manutius claimed all rights to Griffo's lifetime of work and the Venetian government backed him up. Since Manutius was the only printer in the area, Griffo had no hope of employment. He couldn't create sets of fonts from the typefaces he had designed because he didn't have the matrices or punches. He couldn't create new faces because he didn't have the tools, or a concession to give him the legal right to do so. In 1516 Griffo returned to his hometown of Bologna, a broken man. Sometime thereafter he was accused of beating his son-in-law to death with an iron bar. Nothing further is known of him.

Bembo is a typeface designed by Griffo around 1495 for Petro Bembo, the humanist poet, later a Cardinal and private secretary to Pope Leo X. The typeface was designed specifically for Bembo's 60-page book Petri Bembi de Ætna Angelum Chalabrilem liber, about his trip to Mount Aetna, published in February 1496.

The version of Bembo used in this book was designed in 1929 by Stanley Morison for the Monotype Corporation based on Griffo's original font. Special characters and accented characters were created by the author, Heilan Yvette Grimes, using Fontographer.

Cover: Rackham, Arthur (illus) (1924-August) [1911]. *Siegfried & The Twilight of the Gods* (New Impression ed.). p. p. 22. London, United Kingdom: William Heinemann. Retrieved on 22 June 2011.

for

MaryAnne

who is quite legendary herself

CONTENTS

Part Two: The Saga of Ragnar Lodbrokr

Glossary

Genealogy

This version of the ring saga has it all: greed, gruesome deaths, vengeance. It's a family saga and families do have their problems.

CURSED RINGS

There are many cultures in which a cursed ring is a dominant force in stories and legends. The cursed ring is passed from person to person, resulting in death and destruction to those who wear the ring. Where have we read stories or legends before? Turns out lots of times.

The cursed or magical ring has been an archetype in literature for thousands of years in just about every country and culture. The ring can imbue the wearer with magical properties, can sometimes grant wishes, enhance talents, give the wearer invisibility, immortality, etc. Many rings are cursed because one shouldn't morally get something for nothing. You always have to give up something. Usually it's your life. You might initially profit from a cursed ring, but ultimately it will turn out badly for you. Especially if the ring is stolen or has come into the wearer's possession by foul means.

Rings make a great archetype. They are circular so can represent a circular story. Rings can be used to bless a marriage with the married couple wearing matching rings. Rings can have a pattern that can act as a seal to add legitimacy to a document such as a treaty between Kings or nations, or certify a marriage. Rings can represent a friendship and pledge of defense between Kings. Families are brought together by rings, and are torn apart because of greed. People always covet what they don't have. They always covet the ring.

Rings also frequently represent a sun sign and can have magical properties. Though the ring in this book is unadorned, many saga rings carry inscriptions or have magical stones set in them.

Rings are easy to steal and then give all their legitimacy and power to the thief. But, again, magical rings don't like to give longterm goodwill to people who

have acquired the ring by dubious means. The ring points the long arc of the story towards justice. Ring thieves die.

The Ring is a retelling of the Norse *Ring of the Niebelungenlied,* which is itself a version of the German *Der Ring des Nibelungen (The Ring of the Nibelung).* This saga is the greatest family saga in history. Versions of the ring saga have been told in many cultures. This saga has it all: greed, vengeance, betrayal, mighty battles, great passions, and gruesome deaths. It's a family saga and families do have their problems.

My version of the ring saga incorporates two Scandinavian Sagas: *The Volsungr Saga* and *The Saga of Ragnar Lodbrokr. The Volsungr Saga* tells the story of the Volsungs and their doom. The story is about generations in a family, a stolen cursed ring, a dragon, the grand doomed passions of the two main characters (Sigurdr and Brynhildr), wars, Kingdoms, glory, and defeat. The Volsungs are cursed and it will not be lifted until the last Volsung is dead. Most versions of this myth conclude with the events after Sigurdr and Brynhildr's death and the eventual return of the ring to its source to break the curse. They ignore the daughter Sigurdr and Brynhildr had. She and her descendants are really the last of the Volsungrs. Her saga is told in *The Saga of Ragnar Lodbrokr.* When the last of her line is dead, then the Curse of the Volsungrs will finally be over.

RINGS COME IN MANY SHAPES

Neck Rings, Arm Rings, Finger Rings

There are several types of rings: neck rings, arm rings, and finger rings. But no matter what shape all rings in a legend have their own personality: some can be mischievous; some can attempt to change the wearer to a darker person; other rings want only to lead the wearer to adventure.

Neck Rings

These are not as prevalent in myths, but are prevalent in many ancient ceremonies and folk lore in just about every society on Earth. Padaung women wear them from babyhood onward, adding rings, in order to stretch their necks. Ceremonial priests of various cultures wear them during sacrifices. They are meant to imbue the wearer with metaphysical powers. They provide protection and prevent the soul being sucked up through the neck and out the mouth. They also prevent demon spirits from entering the body through the mouth. They are a force for good for the wearer.

Arm Rings

There aren't that many Arm Rings in legends. Probably the most famous is the Norse ring Draupnir.

Draupnir: Draupnir means "the dripper". It is a red-golden arm ring forged by the dvergar Sindri and his brother Brokkr and given to Odin as part of three gifts given to the Æsir to win a wager against Loki. Draupnir was shaped like a snake holding its tail in its mouth. Many people assume the snake is Midgardrsormr, the world serpent. However, this can't be since the ring was forged before Midgardrsormr was born. Every nine days Draupnir magically produced (dripped) nine more arm rings equally as valuable.

At Baldr's funeral Odin laid Draupnir on Baldr's chest before his ship was sent to Helheimr. Hermodr later journeyed to Helheimr to convince Hela to release Baldr and his wife Nanna back up to Asgardr. She refused. As Hermodr was leaving Baldr gave Draupnir to him to give back to his father, Odin. Draupnir in this instance meant death and hoped for resurrection.

Finger Rings

By far the most common ring in legends and folk tales is the finger ring. Finger rings are portable and can be easily passed from character to character. Since people come in many shapes and sizes many rings fortunately have the ability to shrink or expand to fit the wearer. This solves the problem of having to cut the ring to fit a different wearer. Many times rings are impervious to change and can't be resized unless they do it themselves. However some rings remain the same size which means they can slip off a finger and get lost. If they're too small for a wearer the ring can be hung on a gold (usually it's gold) chain and worn around the neck where they can be snatched away. Frodo in Tolkein's *The Lord of the Rings* wore his ring on a chain around his neck.

Rings can be concealed and are easily stolen. They are ornamental and can be worn. If they have magical properties the finger wearing the ring can point and aim the ring's concentrated magical powers at a specific person or object. In some legends rings can be rubbed to release magical power. Sometimes, as in Tolkien's *The Lord of the Rings,* the ring attempts to change the wearer, for the worse and has to be destroyed which leads to a journey and quest to destroy the ring. Along the journey there are many who try to steal the ring. But, ultimately, good conquers evil and the ring is destroyed.

THIS TOO SHALL PASS

Persian Fables

According to several fables by Persian Sufi Poets "This Too Shall Pass" is inscribed on a ring imbued with magical powers. The ring supposedly has the ability to change one's feelings to the opposite of what they are. If the wearer is happy, then the happiness will pass and the wearer will become morose. If the wearer is sad, then the sadness will pass and they will become happy.

Jewish Parable: King Solomon's Ring

Legend has it that King Solomon (known in Arabic versions of the story as Prophet Sulayman) had heard of a magical ring and sent one of his trusted ministers, Benaiah ben Yehoyada, to find it in time for Sukkot which was six months away. Benaiah agreed to find it but wanted to know why it was so special. Solomon explained that the ring would make a sad man happy and a happy man sad. Now for Solomon the ring was a myth that really didn't exist. but he wanted to teach Benaiah a lesson in humility in sending him to find something that was nonexistent.

Benaiah went on his way. The seasons passed, first spring and then summer. Benaiah had been searching fruitlessly and had returned to Jerusalem without the ring. Sukkot was the next morning. So, Benaiah went walking through Jerusalem and found himself in the poorest section of town. At first he came across a poor merchant setting out his wares on a well-worn carpet. Thinking he had nothing to lose he asked him if he'd heard of the ring, "Good sir, I am looking for a ring that makes a sad man happy, and a happy man sad. Have you ever heard of such a thing?"

The merchant searched amongst his wares and found a simple gold ring. He took a knife and quickly inscribed a phrase on the ring and gave it to Benaiah. Benaiah read the inscription and smiled. His search was over.

Sukkot arrived and there were feasts and celebrations all over the city. Solomon sent for Benaiah ben Yehoyada knowing he must have failed since Solomon had made up the ring, "I have heard that you have been searching all over many lands and have just returned here. But, you have not come to give me the ring, and today is the day you were to give it to me. I can only think you have failed." His other advisors looked on and smiled since they too knew the ring had been a joke.

Benaiah confidently stepped forward and held up a ring, "Yes, I have found the ring and I humbly give it to you."

Solomon was much surprised and took the ring and read the inscription. He stopped smiling and showed the ring to his other advisors. They too stopped smiling. Solomon realized that life was transitory. What we gain and what we lose in life matters little for it will all waste away. Great buildings make great ruins. Great lives become dust.

The inscription read: *This too shall pass.*

Solomon's Other Ring

This was not the only magical ring King Solomon had. There was the Ring of Aandaleeb (also known as the Seal of Solomon). A demon named Ornias was harassing a young boy employed by King Solomon. Ornias was stealing his salary and sucking his thumb and draining him of his life-force. Solomon prayed for help and the Archangel Michael appeared and gave Solomon a ring that was half brass and half iron, the Ring of Aandaleeb. It was inscribed with a Star of David and gave Solomon the power to enslave Jinns/demons. King Solomon could use the ring to call forth good and evil Jinns. He sealed his commands to the evil jinns with the iron part of the ring. He sealed his commands to the good jinns with the brass part of the rings.

King Solomon used the ring to call forth and enslave Ornias. Solomon forced Ornias to build his temple.

Additionally The Seal of Solomon also imbued King Solomon with the power to understand the language of animals and speak with them.

PHILOSOPHY

380 BC The Republic by Plato

Plato mentions the Ring of Gyges in Book Two of his *Republic*. It gave the wearer the power of invisibility whenever they called on it through the ring. Plato uses the ring's powers to provoke a discussion about morality. If one can suffer no consequences from an action (i.e., being invisible when you do something immoral) how many people would choose to follow the moral course?

RINGS IN LITERATURE

The following are just a few stories that use rings as plot devices. There are many more. This list is just to show you how prominently rings have been used in literature. I was able to find almost all of these stories free online to download and read.

1485 Le Morte d'Arthur by Thomas Malory

Thomas Malory in his *Le Morte d'Arthur* gives the name of Nimue to the second Lady of the Lake in the Arthurian legend. She enchants Merlin by giving him a finger ring. The ring makes Merlin fall in love with her. She takes advantage of his besottedness and imprisons him. While he's imprisoned she becomes Arthur's chief advisor and gives him the sword Excaliber. She will be one of the four Queenly pall bearers who carry a wounded King Arthur to Avalon.

1516 Orlando Furioso (The Frenzy of Orlando)

Orlando Furioso (The Frenzy of Orlando), is an epic poem written by Ludovico Ariosto in 1516, and made into an opera in 1727 by Antonio Vivaldi (many other operatic versions have been composed). The poem is 38,736 lines long, one of the longest poems in literature. Set amid the war between Charlemagne and his Christian paladin army (including Orlando, his most famous warrior), and King Agramante and his Saracens who invade Europe to avenge his father's (Traiano) death. Princess Angelica owns a magic ring that gives the wearer invisibility. Brunello is a dvergar who steals the ring and gives it to King Agramente and is given a Kingdom for his efforts. Throughout the story people struggle to gain the ring. Orlando goes mad (his frenzy) and begins killing just about everyone in sight. In addition to the ring there's a hippogriff, ridden by an English knight named Astolfo, who flies to the moon hoping to find something to cure Orlando's madness.

1709 One Thousand and One Nights by Antoine Galland (French Translator)

A sorcerer named Maghreb gives Aladdin a magic ring that when he rubs it a jinni (genie) appears. Many people are aware of a more powerful genie Aladdin calls forth when he rubs his magic lamp. The genie of the lamp has to do the bidding of whomever is in possession of the lamp. Though Maghreb eventually reclaims the lamp, Aladdin still has the ring. The genie of the ring is not as powerful as the genie of the lamp.

1854 The Rose and the Ring by William Makepeace Thackeray

William Makepeace Thackeray's *The Rose and the Ring,* published in 1854, is a satire exploring how beauty can affect someone, both in how people act towards them, and how they react to the sudden attention because of their great beauty. In the story a magical ring and a magical rose from a fairy named Blackstick can embue the owner with beauty. During the course of the story the ring and rose endow four royal cousins with great beauty. Two of them are female and two are male. Each in turn are thought of as a great beauty. Thackeray explores how this sudden "beauty" affects their lives, which is not for the good.

1870 Story of the Volsungs and Niblungs by William Morris and Eirikr Magússon

Englishman William Morris became fascinated with Norse Mythology and Scandinavian Sagas. He wrote his own version of The Volsunga Saga, which he translated from the Old Icelandic with the help of Eirikr Magússon.

1907 Edith Nesbit's The Enchanted Castle

Three children discover an enchanted castle. On the castle grounds there is a rose garden with a giant maze. The children go through the maze and come upon a sleeping Princess, who is not really a Princess. She's just pretending to be one. She is actually the niece of Mabel, the housekeeper. She awakens and informs the children the castle is filled with magic all around. She takes them and shows them a magic ring of invisibility.

1937 The Hobbit and The Lord of the Rings by J.R.R. Tolkien

J.R.R. Tolkien was a Norse Scholar and Professor at Oxford University, England. He based his books on ideas and characters (at least their names) in many Norse and Old English texts. So, it's no surprise that a series of rings form the basis of the plots of *The Hobbit* and *The Lord of the Rings*. The Rings are forged by Sauron and the Elves of Eregion under his instructions. The elves receive three rings, the dvergar receive seven, men receive nine. However, Sauron, at Mount Doom, forges the One Ring that rules them all. It is the quest to find and destroy the One Ring that makes up the plot to *The Hobbit* and *The Lord of the Rings*.

1955 C.S. Lewis's The Magician's Nephew

This is one of C.S. Lewis' *Narnia* novels. In London in 1900 Digory Kirke and Polly Plummer live side by side and one day meet and decide to explore the attic their

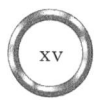
houses have in common. They run into Digory's Ungle Andrew who shows Polly a magic yellow ring. She touches it and vanishes to the "Other World." He gives a second yellow ring to Digory along with two green rings they can use to bring them back to this world. Polly and Digory explore various places and meet with Queen Charn who will reappear as The White Witch in C.S. Lewis' *The Lion, the Witch and the Wardrobe*.

1968 The Zero Stone by Andre Norton

When I was a kid I read everything Andre Norton wrote. *The Zero Stone* was one of my favorite novels. There's murder, an apprentice gemologist, a stolen interstellar ring, and a pregnant cat named Valcyr (she communicates by telepahy, and her newborn will not be a kitten). Andre Norton liked cats.

1974-1976 Dancers at the End of Time by Michael Moorcock

The Dancers at the End of Time is a series of science fiction novels and short stories written by Michael Moorcock. The immortal decadents (people in the books) use power rings. They alter time and matter with the rings. *The End of All Songs* is one of the books in the series where power rings figure prominently in the plot.

1977- 2010 (New novel released 2013) The Chronicles of Thomas Covenant, the Unbeliever by Stephen R. Donaldson

Stephen R, Donaldson's fantasy series, *The Chronicles of Thomas Covenant, the Unbeliever,* tells the story of Thomas Covenant. In this world Thomas Covenant is a writer who keeps to himself because he has leprosy. In an alternate world, The Land, he is a hero who saves the world. He is the possessor of a magic white gold ring, originally his wedding ring. The ring gives Covenant power over "wild magic". There is an epic struggle throughout all the Chronicles of good versus evil. This series is influenced by *The Legend of the Niebelungnlied* and other Ring epics.

1989 Roger Zelazny's Knight of Shadows

Merlin is the central character. However, he is not the Merlin of Arthurian legend. This Merlin is the heir of Prince Corwin. The 9th book in Zelazny's *Amber saga, The Chronicles of Amber.* Merlin finds the magical Spikard Ring and steals it. It also appears in the next book in the series, Prince of Chaos (1991).

1997 Harry Potter by J.R. Rowling

Marvolo Gaunt's ring in Harry Potter is made of gold and cursed because it had a bit of Lord Voldemort's soul in it. The stone setting in the ring was a black stone known as The Resurrection Stone and gave the wearer the ability to communicate with the dead. The ring was one of the Deathly Hollows and a Horcrux. It had passed through the House of Gaunt until it was stolen by Tom Riddle. Riddle wore the ring as a student at Hogworts and made it the second Horcrux. Somewhere between the fifth and sixth *Harry Potter* books Aldus Dumbledore journeyed to the remains of the House of the Gaunts, found the ring and recognized it as a Horcrux. The

temptation to communicate with the dead was too great and he put it on a finger on his right hand and immediately began to be overtaken by the ring's curse. He managed to destroy the ring (and that part of Lord Voldemort's soul). But the curse continued working it's way through his body so he hastens back to Hogwarts where Sevarus Snape manages to temporarily halt the spread of the curse in Dumbledore's hand. Dumbledore knows eventually as the curse slowly spreads through his body Draco Malfoy will kill him. He makes Snape promise to kill him when the curse starts to engulf him. Snape agrees but hesitates when the time comes for him to kill Dumbledore. He overcomes his reluctance and eventually kills Dumbledore.

2012 The Ring by Heilan Yvette Grimes

The Ring, based on the Norse version of *The Ring of the Niebelungenlied* and *The Volsung Saga,* corrects a lot of the discrepancies in the German version. There is motivation and reason for what happens. And it's a lot gorier.

The Ring is a tragic family saga with many villains and heroes, including the doomed lovers Sigurdr and Brynhildr. There are not one, but two dragons, with the legendary Fafnir being the most famous of the two. There are Gods, Valkyries, Kings, Queens, Princesses, Princes, dvergar, shapechangers, and Adventurers.

The dvergar Andvari has a magical ring called the Andvaranautr. Andvari has used it to produce a huge hoard of gold which he keeps hidden in a cave behind the Andvarafors, a waterfall which feeds a mighty river. Andvari's Hoard along with the ring are stolen. Andvari curses the ring and therefore the wearer of the ring with tragedy. The curse can only be broken when the ring is returned to the river at the Andvarafors. Many people come under the ring's spell. They covet the ring and must have it even if they have to steal and kill for it. There's greed, gruesome deaths, and vengeance. Families do have their problems.

In the meantime follow the ring. Nothing good happens to whomever wears the ring.

OPERA

1848-1874 Der Ring des Nibelungen (The Ring of the Nibelung) by Richard Wagner

Richard Wagner's Ring Cycle comprises four operas which Wagner wrote from 1848 to 1874. They are *Das Rheingold (The Rhine Gold), Die Walküre (The Valkyrie), Siegfried,* and *Götterdämmerung (Twilight of the Gods).* They are the Teutonic version of the Norse *Legend of the Niebelungenlied.* The Teutonic version has a flawed plot and does not make as much sense as the Norse version, nor is there as much blood or gore. In Wagner's version Fafner is a giant, not a fire-breathing poison-spewing dragon.

TRADING CARD GAMES, ROLE-PLAYING GAMES, VIDEO GAMES

Trading Card Games

1996-2004 Yu-Gi-Oh! (King of Games)

This is a Japanese manga by Kazuki Takahashi. In the Trading Card version of the game there is a Cursed Ring card.

ROLE-PLAYING GAMES, VIDEO GAMES

Magic rings play major parts in many role-playing games like Dungeons & Dragons. Many video games include a quest usually with a ring.

COMIC BOOKS

1940 Green Lantern

The most famous ring in comic books is Green Lantern's power ring which he had to charge up using his magic Green Lantern. The power ring is not all powerful. It has a flaw. It can't affect wood.

Originally there was only one power ring, the green one, worn by Alan Scott, the first Green Lantern. Later more power rings and lanterns of different colors were added (Blue, Indigo, Star Sapphire, Red, Orange, Black). Each ring had its own power lantern and required its own oath to be spoken to recharge that ring. The most famous oath, of course, was the original Green Lantern's oath (supposedly written by the Science Fiction writer Alfred Bester):

> *In brightest day, in blackest night,*
> *No evil shall escape my sight.*
> *Let those who worship evil's might,*
> *Beware my power... Green Lantern's light!"*

I once won a tote bag and a rather gaudy ring with a huge green glass setting, at the tradeshow Book Expo America, by being the only person in the audience able to recite Green Lantern's oath. Knowledge is power.

The above are just a few examples of thousands in history, legend, and folklore. Now, enjoy this book about what I think is the best ring saga of all.

Heilan Yvette Grimes
yvettegr@hotmail.com

ACKNOWLEDGEMENTS

As much as some authors hate to admit it, no book is born by itself. There are many others who contribute, sometimes not even realizing they've done so. Some of these people I've also thanked before in other books.

Thanks to MaryAnne who has been a true friend to me.

Thanks go to Lin Haire-Sargeant and Sage Green, for encouraging me to keep writing. Lin, especially gets multiple thanks for her sainted reading and editing of this book in more permutations than friendship requires; and without once complaining when I presented her with a yet another manuscript saying there were just a few more changes I'd like her to look at and tell me what she thought. Her suggestions were always insightful and spot on. This book contains a lot fewer "that's" and a lot more commas than it would have had without her help.

Thank you to my father, James Grimes, and grandfather, Ernest "Tony" Gullett. They always believed I could do amazing things, even when circumstances seemed to indicate otherwise. They never faltered in their belief in me. Other writers should be so lucky to have that kind of support.

I've always been interested in Ring Sagas and give homage to all that have come before and have inspired my effort. My advice though, would be to make certain any jewlery you wear, particularly rings, isn't cursed. Don't know quite how to do that. But, if you put your beautiful ancient ring under a microscope and there seem to be flecks of blood, beware.

Next, in sixth grade my friend Debby Wood taught me to draw an arcane linking chain symbol. When I asked what it meant, she wouldn't tell me then, but said when we grew up she would tell me. As a hint she told me it was very mysterious and all powerful. It was important for me never to forget it. In the meantime while waiting to grow up I scoured libraries trying to find out what the symbol meant. The closest I came were some Nordic linked chains. I figured it meant I was supposed to learn what I could about Norse Mythology and Scandinavian Sagas. So, I proceeded to do so. Many many years later at a school reunion I ran into Debby and asked now that we were grown up, could she tell me the secret mystery to the linking chain symbol. I'd been waiting all these decades to find out what it meant. I had started studying Norse Mythology and Scandinavian Sagas because I thought that's what it meant. I drew the symbol on a napkin, exactly as she had taught me. I asked if it had anything to do with Norse Mythology or Sagas, which I had spent years studying? Debby looked puzzled, and said she had no idea what I was talking about. Didn't remember any of it. Probably something her brother drew one evening and she just passed it on to me. The mysterious knowledge saved for adulthood was probably her brother's joke. So, in a way, this book is the result of Debby Wood's older brother's joke. Be careful what you base your life on.

Of course, I had to do research when I was a kid. I began with the Lane Public Library in Hamilton, Ohio, and soon exhausted their resources. I started frequent trips to the Cincinnati Public Library, which because of the German influence, was a treasure trove of information. Even though I lived in a different town, they gave me a library card and let me take out books. And, I hope I don't get anyone in trouble at this late date, but even non-circulating books from the 19th century. Several books seemed to never have been read. I found one from the mid-1800's with uncut pages. But, I eventually exhausted their resources, too.

On a whim I wrote to King Frederick IX of Denmark telling him I was rewriting The Norse Myths and all the Sagas in English, but was having difficulty finding sources. Could he suggest anything? Every day I check the mail. Nothing happened. Weeks turned to months. Nothing. So I continued organizing everything I had. Typing out stories and sagas, filling notebooks, searching for any new bits of information. I had begun going to old bookstores and buying whatever old books on Norse Mythology and Scandinavian Sagas I could find.

Then one day when I got home from school my Grandmother told me there was a huge box in the living room for me. It was from the National Museum of Denmark (Nationalmuseet) in Copenhagen. Inside were photocopies of all the Sagas. Hundreds of years of sagas. Apparently the King had asked them to photocopy from their collection or any others in Denmark. I was awed. I didn't need other sources. I had copies of the originals. So a huge thank you to King Frederick IX and the National Museum of Denmark. I can truly say that this book (and future volumes of Sagas) would not have been possible without you.

As I started pulling out manuscripts I came to the realization that they were not in English. They were in Old Iceland and Old Norse. So, my next thank you goes to The News Depot in Hamilton, Ohio. I frequently used them to order books. I requested that they find out what was available and order any Old Norse or Old Icelandic dictionaries, which they did.

Now my thanks take a short jump across the ocean to England. Thank you to the legendary Foyle's Bookstore (W & G Foyle Ltd.) in London. The greatest bookstore in the world, exasperating as it was. On my first trip to London one of the first places I visited was Foyle's and bought a copy of every book they had about Norse Mythology and Scandinavian Sagas, including every dictionary, or grammar book we could find at that time.

Find is the operative word. Enormous thanks to the sales staff because I browsed the shelves and couldn't find anything. I climbed ladders, got down on my hands and knees for bottom shelves, looked in boxes, moved piles of books. Nothing made any sense. And I was getting tired because there are 30 miles of shelves in the store.

I spoke to Miss Foyle herself who explained the books were sorted and shelved by publisher as if that were obviously the best way to do it. Well, that explained why nothing made any sense. And it added to the problem because I had no idea what I wanted, or whom had published anything. My foolish plan had been to go to Foyle's, find the Norse and Scandinavian Saga section, and buy things. I mentioned this to Miss Foyle but she didn't seem to grasp the concept of "by author" or "by topic". Seemed rather disdainful, in fact.

Miss Foyle did order her staff to help me find what they could while I was there. They couldn't find a lot, though they all assured me they had seen lots of books on the topic, but they didn't know just where they had seen them. The solution was that they'd keep my name and address on a list. Every time they came across a Norse/Scandinavian Saga book, while looking for someone else's book, they'd pull it out and put it in a box with my name on it. If something new (actually quite old) came in, they'd hold it for me and not even put it on the shelves.

After they'd accumulated several books they started "the correspondence ritual". I had told them just send me a bill, and I'd buy everything I didn't already have. They had a list of what I had so they could just compare everything to that list. But, there was a process they insisted they had to go through. I asked if we could streamline the process so I could buy books in a few weeks rather than half a year. But, they doggedly stuck to their procedure.

They'd send a polite note to me in the United States inquiring whether or not I wanted the books on an enclosed list. If not, they'd release them into the store. I would then write back saying I wanted the books, and they could assume I'd want every book they ever acquired on Norse Mythology and Scandinavian Sagas that I didn't already have (I kept their list of my books updated).

In response to this they'd send me an invoice. But, I wasn't to pay it immediately. Before they'd accept payment, I had to confirm the invoice was correct and I was willing to pay the amounts on the invoice. I'd write back assuring them I agreed to the amounts on the invoice and that they were fair and acceptable.

Then, they sent me the invoice again with instructions to pay it. I'd pay it. Next came a confirming receipt saying I had paid and my check had cleared. Did I still want the books or would I prefer a refund? I'd send back that confirming receipt writing that everything appeared to be in order and that I indeed still wanted the books and there was no need to cancel the order or issue a refund.

Then I'd receive another letter asking if I wanted the books shipped by air or by boat with prices for each. And, they always pointed out that shipping by boat was cheaper, though it took longer, and many times the package never arrived at all. In view of the fact we were already at the half-year mark and I would be extremely upset if the package were lost at sea, I always opted to have everything shipped by air and would respond with those instruction and another check for shipping costs. It was at this point they'd finally ship the books to me.

This was the procedure for every book I ever ordered from Foyle's, bless their hearts. I loved their eccentricity. I once told someone about my experiences with Foyle's and they didn't seem surprised. They told me a famous quote about Foyle's which, after my delightfully eccentric experience with them, seemed all too true: "Imagine Kafka had gone into the book trade."

Apparently, I'm not the only one who has had to navigate the labyrinthine world of Foyle's. I can only hope and dream that somewhere, (and who knows where?), there's a copy of this book lost forever on one of their shelves.

This also brings me to the British Library which was always kind and helpful with the research I did there, sometimes, letting me go back into the bowels of the library and just search amongst the stacks. I hope no one ever got in trouble for that. I was always respectful of the books.

Finally, thank you to Hermann Pálsson, Professor of Icelandic Studies at Edinburgh University. When I was a kid and started struggling through those Icelandic Sagas in the original Icelandic I was filled with questions. I noticed the Penguin Books paperback Njal's Saga. It had been edited by Magnus Magnusson and Hermann Pálsson. Indeed, Mr. Pálsson seemed to have written all of Penguin Book's Norse and Saga books I had in my library. I wrote to him care of Penguin Books with pages and pages of questions about Old Icelandic. They forwarded my letter to him. He wrote back an equally long letter answering all my questions in detail, and inviting me to send any further questions I might have directly to him at Edinburgh University. Thus began years of correspondence and an education in Norse Mythology and Scandinavian Sagas that I am blessed to have received. Thank you dear Hermann.

If anyone reading this book has any comments, questions, answers, has sanquinely found mistakes, and would like to contact me, don't hesitate to do so. I'm rather friendly, and don't bite.

Heilan Yvette Grimes
March 21, 2012
yvettegr@hotmail.com

PART 1
THE
VOLSUNGR
SAGA

HEILAN YVETTE GRIMES

CHAPTER 1
SIGI, RERIR
AND
VOLSUNGR

This saga begins with Sigi, who was a great man of tall and noble bearing, thought by many to be the son of Odin, a claim that Sigi did not deny. Skadi was one of his friends, though not as well born, powerful, or as wealthy. Still, he was well regarded in the Kingdom. Skadi's servant, Bredi, though low born, had improved himself until he was thought of as better than many of those who were higher born and more powerful than he. Bredi was skilled in the things a servant should know, and had observed and learned the ways of those better born than he. Because of this, and his good nature, he was often asked to journey about with those above him in class, almost as an equal.

Sigi Goes Hunting

Such was the case one day as Sigi prepared to go hunting and invited Bredi to accompany him, "I would like you to go hunting for deer with me, Bredi. I've found my luck is better when you're along and the hunt more successful. My aim seems more true when I have your advice to rely on."

Bredi happily agreed for there was nothing he liked better than hunting, and he was quite good at it. However, this skill proved his ill luck on this day. He and Sigi hunted until evening, at which time they gathered their prey together into two piles. Sigi saw Bredi's pile was much larger, and was jealous Bredi was still the more skilled hunter. Usually this didn't bother Sigi, but for some reason today it irked him that a mere thrall had bested him again at his favorite sport, for he had never beaten Bredi at the hunt.

Bredi was standing next to him and casually remarked, "The hunt was very successful today. You're improving. Your pile is almost as high as mine. I'm sure you'll beat me at the next hunt."

Bredi was trying to be complimentary, but Sigi didn't take it that way. And a mere servant was speaking to him like that! There would be no next hunt. Unexpectedly Sigi wheeled around and attacked Bredi, who had no time to defend himself, dying instantly from the blow. Bredi was the better fighter of the two. Had he had even an inkling Sigi was going to attack him he could have easily fended him off. But the blow was struck so quickly, and with such force, he had no time to react. He was dead before he hit the ground.

Sigi stood staring at Bredi's still body, horrified and ashamed at what he had done. Instead of bearing Bredi's body back to the Hall for an honorable funeral, confessing his unheroic deed, and offering to pay weregild to Bredi's family to make up for the cruel injustice, actions which might have brought him forgiveness, he buried Bredi's body some distance away in a snowdrift.

Sigi moved both of the piles together to form one, marked it, and hurried back to the Hall where he was met by Skadi who was wondering where his best servant was, "I had hoped he would return with you since I have some important matters to discuss with him. Perhaps he has stayed with what you've slain until you send others back to fetch the rewards of your hunt?"

Sigi forced the lie from his throat, "It was very strange. No sooner had we left this morning than he headed off by himself saying he wanted to hunt alone. I haven't seen him since."

Skadi responded, "That's very unlike him. I wonder what he must have been thinking?"

Sigi turned to hurry off, "I'm sure I don't know. Excuse me while I send some of my servants to fetch home what I've killed. I've marked the spot but am afraid poachers might find the pile and then all my work today will have been in vain. It has certainly been the most successful hunting day I've ever had. Maybe not having Bredi along helped me concentrate on my own skills rather than holding back so I didn't insult Bredi?" Skadi stared at Sigi, curious why he would be so solicitous of a servant's feelings.

Later that evening the servants arrived with the pile of animal carcasses. Too many, some thought, for one man to have killed in a single day. Skadi was standing beside Sigi as each deer was piled into a heap in the courtyard, after which he said, "I think you've really outdone yourself. I also think that not everything you've killed today has been brought back."

He left Sigi, went to his servants and bid them accompany him back in to the forest. There they searched through the night until they found the snowdrift where Bredi had been buried.

"No honor has come by this death," said Skadi as Bredi's stiff, frozen body was pulled from the drift. He further proclaimed, "So Bredi can have the honor his life would have eventually brought, it is hereby ordered all large snowdrifts bear his name and be known as Bredi's Drifts. In this way Bredi's memory will not be entirely forgotten."

Sigi had been respected and liked until the discovery of Bredi's murder. A Thing was held during which Sigi tried to offer a defense for his actions. His inadequate arguments fell on deaf ears. He was judged an outlaw and exiled.

Skadi pronounced the judgement, "You are now banished from our land for not less than three years. And even at that time, if we still feel ill towards you about this horrible deed and you come into the sight of any person dwelling in this land, that person will have every right to slay you, even if you provide no provocation. From this moment on until you have righted your wrong, you will be as a wolf in the holy places, and will no longer be permitted to stay in the land of your father."

Sigi left the land. Though those in his Kingdom had deserted him, his father had not. Odin saw to it he had an army and many ships with which to fight in other lands and gain victories and renown. Odin sided with Sigi in battle, promising him he would never forsake him in combat and victory would always be his.

Such was the success of Sigi's conquests it was not long before he conquered all of Hunland and had become King of that noble land. His reputation extended across borders until now he was thought to be one of the greatest warriors in the world.

After settling in his new Kingdom and having brought some order there, he decided it was time to find a suitable wife and marry. The woman he found was noble in bearing, pleasing of appearance, intelligent of word, and good of deed. They had a son whom they named Rerir. He grew to manhood possessed of a powerful build and skilled in warrior ways.

Sigi's life thereafter was blessed into old age. But at one point for unknown reasons Odin forgot his promise and did forsake his son. Not every man will be blessed all his life, and many will never be blessed. Sigi's time had come to an end. His enemies hated him, his friends envied him. Soon it was hard to tell one from the other. Both groups had a single thought in mind: Hunland.

There came a day when many of Sigi's friends, his brothers, as well as his wife's brothers set upon him while he was protected by just a few warriors. Though Sigi and those loyal to him fought bravely, they were outnumbered and all were slain.

o   o   o   o

Rerir loved his father and had had no part in Sigi's slaying. Despite his grief he gathered together a great army so he could avenge his father's death and win his rightful inheritance back from those who had stolen it. He proved to be a worthy leader and soon regained the throne and what was rightfully his.

After bringing order to his Kingdom, his first thoughts were to ignore those who had tried to usurp his inheritance since they had been unsuccessful and he had easily won back his lands. However, honor demanded his father's death be avenged even if it meant the death of his own kinsmen. His first act as King was to order the execution of all his uncles, and all the others who had plotted and slain his father.

o   o   o   o

Rerir ruled wisely. Such was the prosperity in his Kingdom he was beset by Kings from other Kingdoms wanting to join his and live under his rule and protection. Although some of his conquests came from wars, many came from peace. It was not long before he was better thought of than his father. He was certainly more powerful, his Kingdom larger, and his wealth from the taxes of the realm far greater.

Rerir also married a noble and proper wife. They lived together in great happiness for a long while. Yet the increased joy of children had not yet come to them. There was no heir to the Kingdom. Rerir and his wife were both devout and prayed to Odin and his wife Frigg for help.

Odin listened to their prayers and sought Frigg's aid in the matter. "See what you can do to insure my grandson has a son to inherit the Kingdom his father has secured."

Frigg was usually able to attend to such matters without difficulty. She called Gna, her casket-bearing maid to her. Gna, the daughter of the jotun Hrimnir, lived in Asgardr as one of the Æsir.

Frigg gave Gna orders on what to do, "Take this apple and give it to Rerir so his prayers might be answered."

Gna donned her crow-guise and flew off to Rerir's Kingdom, landing at the edge of the wood close to where Rerir sat on a mound under a fir tree. She could hear him bemoaning his sad lot at not having a son and praying to Odin for help. Flying around overhead, speaking all the while, she dropped the apple into his lap,

> *"Take the apple, take the apple.*
> *Your prayers have been answered.*
> *Your wife shall eat the fruit and bear fruit from it.*
> *Blessed be Odin and Frigg who have answered your prayers."*

Gna flew back to Asgardr.

Rerir ran back to the Hall and excitedly told his wife what had happened. He gave her the apple, which she ate. Soon she was with child.

The months passed and her waiting with child was easy. But the dark thoughts on Rerir's mind were not. Wars brewing in far-off lands were threatening his own realm. He thought about how he might avoid wars with Kings he'd never met, Kings anxious to make their reputation by defeating him. He had mighty warriors in his army and could send the best of them to lead his army. But, then, he'd lose the respect of the warriors who thought they would be following him to win glory and honor. Wars are won by leaders inspiring those following them. If he were too cowardly to lead his men, he would not be able to inspire them. He was the best warrior in his land. It fell to him to lead. If he assigned the task to others and they lost his Kingdom because they couldn't inspire his warriors to victory, then he would have no one to blame but himself. Leading his army was his duty.

o   o   o   o

The preparations were made and the day finally came for him to lead his army. It was with great reluctance he bid his wife goodbye and led his army off to the edges of his Kingdom's boundaries and offered protection to his subjects who had been set upon by the invaders.

The might of his army frightened the invaders so they immediately surrendered and offered him their allegiance. He had conquered his enemy without a battle, without drawing blood, without any loss of his followers, while increasing the might of his army at the same time.

He put in place protections so his subjects would never have to fear invasion again.

Now that his borders were once more secure he could return home. However, the Norns had already woven his wyrd, and the final threads had been added. His tapestry was finished. It was not his lot to return to his wife, or see his child born. He became ill and died away from home at the edge of his realm. He died a hero.

His wife mourned Rerir. And somehow this mourning caused her to remain with child for six years, which was not natural, and she knew it. One day she realized the Norns had finished weaving her wyrd and her time to die had come. Yet her child had still not been born. Fearing his death would accompany hers; she ordered the child cut from her so it would live. Immediately upon being cut from his mother he stood and kissed her. He was a fine young son, very large of appearance. With her last words she named him Volsungr.

Volsungr told his dying mother of his vows, "While still unborn I made vows that I would never retreat from fire or sword because of fear. I vow to you I will be a wise and just ruler of Hunland, worthy to carry on as my father and grandfather's successor."

As his father before him, and his father's father before him, Volsungr became a great warrior and wise ruler. His fame spread throughout many lands and even into other worlds.

In the meantime Gna had returned to live with her father, the Jotun Hrimnir, in Jotunheimr, and had returned to being called by her Jotun name, Hljod.

Over the years Volsungr's legend grew, even reaching the ears of those in Jotunheimr. Hrimnir, a father of only daughters, was always on the lookout for suitable husband material, the main criteria being wealth, fame, and hopefully a Kingdom or two. Volsungr more than fit the bill. He sent his daughter Hlojod to Volsungr hoping the young, handsome (not that that mattered to Hrimnir), landed King would have her as his wife. This was the same daughter who had been called Gna amongst the Æsir and while serving Frigg had given the apple to Rerir so his wife would become pregnant with Volsungr.

Her appearance was pleasing and she was gifted with great wisdom. Volsungr immediately fell in love with Hljod and asked her to be his wife. She accepted.

Their life together was long and fruitful. Their first-born had been twins, a son and daughter, whom they named Sigmundr and Signy. In all they were blessed over the years with ten sons and one daughter.

Volsungr's father and grandfather had only had one child each. So their Hall didn't need to be large. Volsungr with his eleven children and wife needed something larger.

Volsungr oversaw the building of a huge Hall built to accommodate and honor his children. He constructed the entire structure around an enormous, powerful oak tree called Branstokk, whose name meant the stem of the children. Branstokk's trunk stood in the middle of the Hall. The limbs and top of the tree grew through a hole in the ceiling and overreached the entire roof of the Hall shading it from the sun. Some said the tree had been blessed by Odin himself. And surely such a blessing would accrue to Volsungr's children, particularly Sigmundr and Signy.

Sigmundr and Signy were the fairest and best of Volsungr and Hljod's children, and also their favorites. But all their children brought fame, glory and good fortune to the Volsungr name and happiness to their father and mother. Signy grew to be a great beauty and stories of her charm and intelligence spread throughout all the Worlds of the Tree. As she reached marriageable age many suitors sent word of their interest in her.

One of these suitors was Siggeir, who was of the Siklingar. He was a powerful King who ruled over the Goths in Gautland.

CHAPTER 2
SIGGEIR AND SIGNY'S WEDDING FEAST AND THE SWORD GRAMR

The message Siggeir received from Volsungr and Hljod concerning his inquiries about marrying Signy, and uniting the Kingdoms of Hunland and Gautland in the process, was so encouraging that Siggeir decided to journey to Hunland and formally request her hand.

Once in Hunland he met with Volsungr and Volsungr's sons, "I'm glad your sons are here, Volsungr, so they can hear my offer." Volsungr's sons nodded towards Siggeir in acknowledgement. Volsungr had already confided what Siggeir's intentions were to his sons.

Siggeir continued, "We are both powerful rulers of vast Kingdoms, yet there are other lands larger and more powerful. If we should join our Kingdoms together, which would be accomplished by my marrying your only daughter Signy, then our united Kingdoms would be the most powerful in the world. Our bonds of kinship could work to bring further glory to each of our families. What do you say to my request?"

Volsungr and his sons went off to discuss the offer, whispering amongst themselves in a far corner of the room. Siggeir looked on anxiously, but he thought they seemed well disposed to his offer.

Volsungr and his sons walked over to Siggeir and gave him the good news. "Those in Asgardr smile down on all of us now as we join our realms and create a more powerful Kingdom. We would be honored to welcome you into our family. Let's discuss the matter of the dowry and how things might be arranged."

Eventually a bargain was struck and a dowry settled on. It was arranged that Siggeir would return to his land and make whatever preparations he needed for the wedding and return as soon as possible. The wedding feast would be held in Volsungr's great Hall. Siggeir would be allowed to bring as many wedding guests as he wished.

After Siggeir departed for Gautland, Volsungr had the difficult task of informing Signy of the arrangements determining her future that he and her brothers had agreed to, without consulting her. This would be the first she would hear of the arrangements. He sent for his daughter, hoping for the best but expecting the worst. She could be strong-willed.

Volsungr spoke first breaking the news of her engagement to Siggeir putting what he thought was the best possible spin on it, "Just think what an enormous advantage such an alliance, er, marriage would be for us, er, you?" Signy not only seemed unmoved by his pitch, but downright hostile. Volsungr continued, "Just think how powerful Hunland and Gautland will be once our Kingdoms are united? We'll never have to worry about invasions from without."

Signy responded to that remark, "But I'll have to worry about invasions from within. I'm not a piece of property to be bargained over." Signy was known to speak her mind, "I've never even met Siggeir. What if he's not to my tastes? How come I wasn't informed about all this while he was visiting here? Looking back on all the domestic tasks you've given me the last few days it would seem you deliberately kept me out of the way. I feel I should have some say in this matter since the fulfillment of the marriage agreement lies with me."

Volsungr continued trying to persuade her while her brothers looked on and nodded in agreement with their father's words, "Siggeir is a great King. He is intelligent and has a fine countenance, though he is a bit short."

Signy interrupted, "A bit short? He barely comes up to my waist. Why would I want that thing crawling all over me at night like a bug inspecting a piece of cake?"

Volsungr continued, trying not to picture the troll-like Siggeir enjoying his husbandly rights with his beautiful daughter, most likely against her will, "He enjoys hunting and warring. What more could you want in a husband? Besides, just think what this union will bring to our family?"

Signy shook her head no, and looked at her father and each of her brother's as she replied, "If your idea of a mate is how well he hunts and wars, and you feel this union is such a good idea, then why don't one of you marry him? He doesn't sound as if he would be to my liking, but it seems as if any of you would get on quite well with him."

Her brothers and father had no idea what to say to that.

Signy continued, "You and my brothers gain a Kingdom. What do I gain? How is this marriage to my advantage? The marriage of Kingdoms births lands and warriors to all of you. The marriage gives me all the responsibility and none of the joy. It will be a loveless marriage I'm trapped in. This is not something I sought, nor is it anything I want."

Signy turned to leave. Volsungr followed her into an anteroom and spoke, "You've always given me every reason to be proud of you. Now you disobey me. I remind you that I am your King as well as your father. If I command you to do this, then it must be done."

Reluctantly Signy agreed to the betrothal, "You may command me to marriage, but you cannot command my heart to love. There will be no smiles during the

marriage feast. I will endure it, and will make no pretense other than this marriage is a land deal and I'm the payment."

○   ○   ○   ○

Volsungr's household prepared an elaborate celebration. The main Hall was magnificent. It had been built around a great oak tree called Branstokk, which lived in the center of the Hall. Its top grew out through a hole cut in the ceiling, overarching the outside of the Hall.

Fires burned the length of the main Hall; golden shields hung on the walls reflecting the flames lighting the Hall. Everything was bathed in the golden glow of the shields. Decorations hung from the ceiling, walls, and even the doors. Everyone was excited—everyone, that is, except Signy. Everyone else went to the wedding in celebration of a great event with an even greater feast to be had. She went as if she were one of the courses served along with the other slaughtered animals.

Siggeir arrived bearing magnificent gifts. Accompanying him were many great warriors from his land, to remind Volsungr of his might.

Siggeir presented fine swords to Siggeir and his sons, "I present you and your sons with the best swords of our land so that we can fight together, side-by-side rather than opposite and opposing."

Sigmundr noticed the swords they were presented did not seem quite as long, thick, or sharp, as the ones Siggeir and his warriors wore. The embellishments were not as grand. And the scabbards seemed to be of plain cloth rather than tooled leather.

Siggeir presented fine cloth and threads to Signy, "Here are fabrics that you might sew new clothing befitting your station as my wife."

Signy looked at the bolts of fabric, enough to provide her with a lifetime of sewing, "I see you bring me fabric and threads but no means. Where is a fine sword I can use to cut the fabric? Where is a dagger I can use to cut holes in the fabric and thread rope thick enough for hanging?"

Siggeir stepped back a bit. Clearly his wife was not entering the marriage in the same spirit he was, "You will have needle, thread, and scissors. That and your skills at needlework should suffice. Leave the ropes for those who might have reason enough to use them in the future."

Signy tossed the bolts of fabric and thread behind her, "Hmmph! Perhaps I'll first weave a tapestry telling the tales of the greatest heroes the world has known." Siggeir puffed up at this, thinking she was talking about him. She noticed and continued, "Don't worry Siggeir your name will be mentioned down in one small section. I'm sure I can find a blank bit of fabric about the size of my hand to weave words of your great deeds and wyrd:

> *"And on a terrible feast day in which angry winds blew outside the Hall, did*
> *Siggeir wed Signy the Great-Granddaughter of Sigi, the son of Odin. This*
> *was the crowning moment of Siggeir's life. Never before or after had he*
> *engaged in such a battle. A battle he would one day give his life for."*

Signy's father and brothers noticed she referred her lineage back to Sigi, not Volsungr. Signy was getting angrier and angrier. So much so that Volsungr suggested she leave for a few moments, "You have had a tiring day. Perhaps you should retire briefly so you can compose yourself? Rejoin us after you've done so." Signy rose to leave the table. Volsungr continued, "Don't forget the fine gifts Siggeir has brought you. Take them to your bedchamber. Rest a bit then return for your wedding so that we may begin the feast." Signy did as she was told.

o o o o

Eventually Signy returned and Siggeir used that moment to awkwardly hand her another gift, a magnificent jeweled necklace. She stood there holding it. Her brothers thought she had been overcome by his thoughtfulness in giving her a more appropriate wedding gift. Only Sigmundr could see the way she truly felt. Her eyes met Sigmundr's and then she turned and left the Hall with Volsungr and Sigmundr following quickly after her.

They argued just outside the Hall, loudly enough so the guests heard. Everyone shifted uncomfortably in their seats. Even more so when they realized there might not be a feast served anytime soon. Many of the guests had not yet eaten that day, saving themselves for the expected enormous wedding feast.

"I'll not be wedded to that monster. He's repulsive." Signy threw Siggeir's gift to the ground. The fittings broke and the jewels scattered on the floor, an ill omen for the start of a marriage.

Volsungr gathered the gift up and tried to hand the jewels back to her. She turned to walk away. He gave the remnants of the necklace to one of her brothers. "Siggeir isn't so bad. Most of the world fears him, yet to you he is thoughtful enough to think of bringing many gifts."

"Yes, gifts to bind me as his slave for life." She brushed her father's arm aside.

He continued, more insistent, "It's too late to back out now. It'll be a great dishonor to all of us if you do."

Signy looked at Sigmundr, who shook his head as he spoke, "I'm afraid I have to agree with father. Treaties have been signed, commitments have been made. He has honored every part of our bargain. In exchange he has had only one request, your hand in marriage. You'll have to go through with it."

"Ill it bodes this family to force me into this marriage. In the future you should consult those in whose hands you place your wyrd. But I see that I am forced into this. I don't enter into this marriage happily. Only grief shall come out of all this."

Volsungr, Sigmundr, and her other brothers, returned to the Hall, relieved Signy was going to go through with the marriage. Now they had to reassure Siggeir.

Siggeir seemed concerned when he saw Signy was not with King Sigmundr and his brothers when they returned to the hall. He whispered to Volsungr, "There will be ill will towards you and your family if there is no wedding tonight."

Moments later Signy entered and it seemed as if the Hall lit up even more, such was the radiance of her beauty. Siggeir was spellbound and pleased. Unfortunately she did not have the same reaction upon being re-introduced to her betrothed. She looked at the dark, twisted, puny figure who would be her husband and glanced at her tall handsome brothers, especially Sigmundr.

Signy took her place next to Siggeir. The two stood on the dais facing the assembled guests. Volsungr stood behind them. Once Siggeir realized the marriage ceremony was starting he grabbed Siggeir's hand, in an attempt at tradition. After all the bride and groom being bound together in marriage should at least be touching each other.

The guests were somewhat confused. There was no procession down the Hall and kneeling before Volsungr for his blessing. Instead he just stood behind the two, placed his hands over their heads and quickly said words of marriage binding them together, "And with these words I bind Siggeir and my beloved Signy together forever as one, our Kingdoms joined as one. May they be as happy years from now as they are tonight. Now let us celebrate the expansion of my Kingdom and my new son-in-law."

Volsungr spoke the words quickly finishing before Signy had a chance to change her mind. He left out the part about anyone objecting to the marriage should speak up because he was afraid the bride would speak up.

The odd ceremony was performed with few words from Volsungr, and over quickly. The speediest wedding ceremony any of the invited guests had ever witnessed. No one objected because the relieved guests knew now they'd be fed.

They were several courses into the meal when Volsungr began to relax. He thought to himself that the wedding feast was going quite well. So far Signy had managed not to kill her husband during one of the main courses. However, dessert remained. At this point Volsungr didn't much care. Gautland had been ceded to him upon the marriage of Signy and Siggeir. After that property transaction it mattered little what happened to the groom. In fact, the groom meeting with an unfortunate accident, or beset by thieves in the night, worked to his advantage.

Things were working out well for Volsungr's Kingdom. He settled down to eating and listening to the entertainment.

The Uninvited Guest at the Wedding Banquet

The courses kept coming and the evening wore on in the great Hall. Volsungr and his sons were seated on the dais facing the length of the Hall. Sigmundr was seated to Volsungr's left, while Siggeir was seated to his right. Signy was seated to Siggeir's right.

The plates were covered with food, and when even a smidgen of plate showed more food was piled on. The mead horns were refilled without asking. Revelry continued throughout the night. Gradually people slowed down, their bellies full, their heads dizzy and light from the continuously flowing sweet honeyed mead.

At near the darkest hour a stranger appeared in the Hall standing in front of the dais with his back to the mighty oak Branstokk. No one knew where he had come from or how he had gotten past the guards. He was tall, and though middle-aged, seemed much more ancient in his manner. He wore a spotted, hooded cloak, the cowl of which he pulled back to reveal a broad-brimmed hat pulled low over his forehead to hide his missing right eye. The stranger was barefoot, and wore skintight knit leggings laced at the knee. In his right hand he carried a shining long sword carved on the blade and hilt with magic runes. He raised the sword, prompting guards to move in front of the dais in case he intended to do harm to any who sat there. The stranger whirled around and threw the sword half the length of the Hall towards Branstokk where it lodged to the hilt in the trunk of the tree and wavered left to right for a bit as it settled into the trunk.

Everyone in the Hall was silent, too surprised to speak. The stranger's voice thundered throughout the Hall, "Only one of you here is deserving of that sword. And that is the one who can draw it from the tree—a simple task indeed. And whosoever accomplishes that task will have the sword as a present from me. Gramr is a good and glorious sword that will win victory for its owner in every battle, save one. Much blood will flow from its blade for it is thirsty for the blood of those it vanquishes."

The old man walked out through a hallway. Volsungr signaled for him to be stopped and brought back. A guard ran after the stranger, but returned alone, "He has disappeared. The guard attending to the outer door says the stranger did not pass through it. Yet I was at the entrance to the Hall and know he did not come back this way."

There was a murmuring in the Hall that the visitor had been Odin himself, and the sword was a gift from the Æsir. People scrambled from the banquet tables to get in line to have a chance at drawing the sword from Branstokk. Everyone tried to situate themselves according to their rank so they would be as close to the front of the line as possible, fearing that if they were too far back the sword would be drawn out before their turn came. Volsungr was placed at the head of the line but gave up his spot to Siggeir who gladly made the first attempt.

Siggeir anxiously tugged and strained at the sword. He braced his feet against the tree trunk and pulled, making several tries, turning purple in the face with veins bulging from his neck with the last one. Yet the sword still held as firmly as ever. Finally he gave up and took his chair.

Next came Volsungr's sons, all except Sigmundr. Each in their turn tried with all their might until all nine had had a chance. Then one by one the others in the Hall had their turn, down to the lowliest servant. None could loose it. Despite all their efforts Gramr had not budged an inch. Several went on to a second round of trying, with the same results. Finally, one of the guests pointed out that Sigmundr had not yet tried. He was urged to do so. Slowly Sigmundr walked up to the tree, grasped the hilt of the sword in his right hand and pulled. It slid out as easily as if it were a knife being drawn through warm butter. The sword appeared not to have been held to the tree at all since his effort had been so slight. Some witnesses said they thought the sword hilt had jumped into his hand even before he touched it.

Siggeir's eyes shown with envy as he gazed at the sword. He wanted it more than anything. "That sword would make an excellent wedding present to bind our families," he suggested looking back and forth between Volsungr and Sigmundr.

However, Sigmundr, though he had encouraged his sister to marry Seiggeir because of the alliances their father had made, was personally very much against the marriage. He certainly had no intention of parting with the sword Gramr, and certainly not as a wedding present for a marriage he opposed. "You already have taken my sister to bind our families. Don't press your luck. I may give you the sword in a way you would not like."

Siggeir would not be dissuaded. If he couldn't have it as a gift, then he would make an offer to purchase the sword from Sigmundr, "That sword is the finest I've ever seen. If you do not want to give it to me, then I'll buy it from you. I'll offer you three times its weight in gold and precious gems. Surely no one could resist such a price?"

Sigmundr managed to do so saying, "You might have had it a lot cheaper if it had been fated for you to own it. You merely had to pull it out of the tree as I did. But since I have gained it, never shall it leave my hands except that it has been broken or is taken from me by the one who gave it to me tonight." Seeing that Siggeir was preparing to make another offer, Sigmundr continued, "Even though you offer me all of the gold and precious jewels in your Kingdom, and ours, you shall never have this sword."

Siggeir was offended by the insult but pretended he had not heard it. Siggeir was wont to deal with those he disliked when it was to his advantage. He could wait to make Sigmundr pay for the insult. In fact he determined in his mind to rid the joined Kingdoms of all the Volsungrs and inherit the sword for himself. This might take a lifetime to do, but he was a patient man. Already, he was family. He plotted in his mind to go from being the newest member of the family to being the only member of the family, and by default the head of the family and owner of all the wealth of the family, including the sword Gramr.

That evening his marriage to Signy was consummated in a rather perfunctory manner. The grunting and groaning of Kingdoms merging, stained red. And with most mergers one side was satisfied, the other wasn't. One slept, the other stared at the ceiling plotting a way out. A wedding night in which one of the two involved does not notice the anger, hatred, and resentment of the other does not presage a happy marriage.

∘ ∘ ∘ ∘

The next morning Siggeir decided it was a good time to leave, since the sea was calm and the weather was fair with a good breeze. He sent word to Volsungr that he feared a storm might be approaching and wanted to leave rather than wait it out. Volsungr and his sons made no attempt to stop him.

Signy went to have one last talk with her father. "I don't want to leave with Siggeir. I don't love him. He is a rough, uncouth man. My home is here. This is where I belong. I know we have nothing but trouble ahead of us unless this marriage is annulled."

Volsungr was adamant in his refusal, "Although you'll always be my daughter, and first in my thoughts, your duty is now to your husband. He is your first kinsman. You owe your loyalty to him before any loyalty to me, your brothers, or the rest of our family. It would be dishonorable to break the marriage at this point, especially since Siggeir is blameless in the matter. Those who deal with him know he can be cunning. If this marriage is ended he will repay us in double the evil what he expected in happiness from you. You must go through with it.'

Volsungr accompanied Signy to Siggeir's boat to say goodbye, and make certain she boarded.

Siggeir offered to make amends for departing the wedding feast so soon, so his leaving would not be thought an insult. He spoke loudly enough so those waiting to see Signy off could hear, "Volsungr, you and your sons must come to Gautland and visit your new lands which have been won by this marriage. Accept this invitation to come and stay for a long while so that we may get to know each other better, and you may be reunited with your beloved Signy."

Volsungr thought this would make Signy happy and immediately gave his word and accepted the invitation. Signy shook her head no, but he paid her no heed.

Siggeir yelled to Volsungr as his ship drew away from the port, "Three months hence bring your sons and as many of your household as you wish to Gautland. We'll be ready for you by then. I promise I'll give you the greatest hospitality and show you the finest of times. It will certainly be a visit you'll never forget."

CHAPTER 3
THE SLAYING
OF
VOLSUNGR

Three months later Volsungr and his sons journeyed to Gautland in three ships, completely crewed and fully provisioned. Their journey met with good weather and an even breeze. Their voyage was fair and uneventful and they arrived in Gautland at eventide.

Signy learned of their arrival and met her father and brothers aboard her father's ship for a private talk. "You must leave this land at once without stepping ashore. There is no good for you here."

Volsungr scoffed at her warning, "We have been invited here and in good faith have we come. Siggeir is now a member of our family, therefore he could have no ill feelings towards us. Harming us would be like harming himself. He is now our brother and we are his. He would never go against his brothers."

Signy replied, "And I am your sister and I'm telling you he is not your brother. He is your rival. I don't think a wound to you will cause him any pain. Not all Kings are as honorable as you. During the last three months he has sent messengers throughout Gautland summoning the greatest warriors he could find to join him here. Contests have been held in all manner of war games, and the winners have been assembled here as Siggeir's army."

Volsungr looked around. "I see no army waiting to attack us. I do see porters anxious to unload our goods and help us to Siggeir's Hall. I'm sure we can fight against them and prevail."

Signy continued, trying to persuade her father of the danger, "Siggeir has raised an army that no other army could match. He intends to do evil to you. Blinded by your trust for him you have foolishly come virtually unarmed and with few warriors. Depart to your own land and gather together your greatest warriors and return. Then you might have a chance against him since the greater King will lead your army. I beseech you; don't go to Siggeir now in such a disadvantaged state. He will charm you and convince you he means you no harm. And false words than those have never been spoken."

Volsungr answered, "It is told throughout all the lands of the vow I spoke when not yet born. A vow that I would never retreat from fire or sword because of fear. I have ever kept that vow. Would you have me break it now? Never shall women be able to make fun of my sons at sport and yell to them that they are cowards afraid of death because they are born of my blood. There comes a time when a man must die, be he King or commoner. If this is my time then the greatest army in the land following behind me will be of no use. None can escape a fate that waits around the corner for him, though he alters his route. Fate can alter its path to fulfill its duty. The Norns are cunning and will meet him, nevertheless, around a different corner. If there is a fight then we will do the best we can." He motioned for the crew to start carrying off their baggage. Putting his arm around his daughter he continued speaking while walking with her towards the plank, "I've fought one-hundred-and-twenty fights, sometimes with the greater army, sometimes the lesser, and I've never lost in battle. The size of the army behind you matters not. Only your wyrd will determine whether or not you walk away from the battlefield pink and rosy hued, or are carried off grey and lifeless. Never has it been said that I was a coward and ran from a fight or sued for peace in fear of my own weakness."

Signy began to cry and begged her father's permission that she might leave Siggeir and remain onboard the ship. They stopped while Volsungr answered her, "You will go back to your husband and stay with him no matter what happens between our two countries which have been united by your marriage. It is your duty as my daughter to obey me, and your duty as his wife to stand beside him."

Signy returned to the Hall while Volsungr and his sons stayed onboard ship that night. The next morning Volsungr commanded his men to get up and go onto the land and be prepared for a battle, just in case his daughter's warnings were justified. Once ashore they started for the Hall and were immediately set upon by Siggeir's army attacking full force, save for their leader who had hung back in a cowardly manner.

Volsungr's men fought with heroic courage. Eight times they broke through Siggeir's lines, but on the ninth assault Siggeir's superior numbers finally put them down. Volsungr was slain along with all his men except for his ten sons who were captured, bound, and brought before Siggeir.

The ten sons of Volsungr stood in chains before Siggeir. Sigmundr had been forced to relinquish his sword Gramr to Siggeir, who motioned with it for them to be taken away. "I'll send orders on how they are to be disposed of later." He finally had the prizes he sought the night he had married Signy. Volsungr, his partner and enemy was dead. He now ruled the united Kingdoms of Hunland and Gautland as his own. He was married to Volsungr's daughter, one of the most beautiful women in the world, though not as happily as he had wanted. Volsungr's ten sons were his prisoners. And the prized sword Gramr was his. He could not have felt any better at that moment.

When Signy learned her father had been slain and her brothers were being held captive and had been condemned to death, she went to Siggeir to see what she could do. "I realize you intend to kill my brothers and nothing I say will alter that.

However, grant me the favor that they not be killed quickly. Let them be held in stocks as long as possible, for I remember the saying, the eye rejoices in what it sees. I cannot hope for more than this from you."

Siggeir answered, "You must be mad to wish such a fate for your brothers. Instead you should be begging me to kill them as quickly as possible to save their suffering. However, I'll do as you wish and they will stay alive as long as they can under the circumstances they are in. The longer they live the greater will be their suffering, and the better will be my revenge."

Signy turned to leave, but Siggeir signaled for the guards to stop her, "I have granted your request. However, I don't think its wise for you to be going about while they are still alive. It would be too painful for you to see them confined in chains. You might want to visit them, perhaps with some implement to cut their chains." He commanded she be taken and locked in her room.

∘ ∘ ∘ ∘

The ten brothers were dragged to a certain part of the wildwood where their chains were linked together. Siggeir's men began chopping down a tall oak, planning its fall well, causing it to land across the legs of the ten brothers. The tree crushed the legs of those brothers nearest the heavier part of the trunk.

At midnight of the first night the brothers heard animal steps behind them. The sound moved through the trees until it was to their left. Each brother stared into the forest. Two huge glowing red eyes met their gazes. The eyes came closer followed by the form of a giant she-wolf. She walked among the chained brothers sniffing at each of them for the smell of the most cowardly. Suddenly she stopped and bit the head off of the brother closet to the trunk of the fallen tree, and continued eating him until there was nothing left, neither flesh nor bone, nor even the chain binding him. Then she licked up all the blood before it could seep into the ground. Now, well fed, she departed.

The next morning Signy sent her most trusted servant into the woods to find out what had happened to her brothers during the night. He reported to her upon his return, "I have bad tidings. One of your brothers has been eaten by a she-wolf and there is nothing left of him to report. I tried to free the others but the oak was too heavy for one man to lift. I fear the fate of the she-wolf will befall your other brothers, too."

Signy set to thinking what she could do. Meanwhile darkness came again, and once more at midnight the she-wolf appeared and did as she had done the night before. Now there were eight brothers left. And so it continued seven more days until nine of the brothers had been eaten, all save for Sigmundr.

On the tenth day Signy sent for her servant. She gave him a cloth full of honey she had been secreting away each day during her morning meal, along with instructions on how it was to be used, "Smear it until it covers Sigmundr's face and head, then put what is left in his mouth. He'll know what to do after that."

The servant did as he was commanded. At midnight the she-wolf returned and sniffed all about as had become her habit. What she smelled on the wind this time was not fear, it was the sweet smell of honey. Instead of biting off Sigmundr's head she began licking at it. She licked all over until the honey was gone. However, the odd thing was she still smelled it. Sigmundr opened his mouth and the smell became stronger. She greedily thrust her tongue inside his mouth hoping to lick up every last drop of the golden sweet heavy liquid. As she did so Sigmundr bit down on her tongue and held his jaws shut tighter than any vise. The startled she-wolf jumped back and began pulling, tugging desperately trying to free herself. Sigmundr would not let go. She braced herself against the oak tree and pushed as hard as she could. Sigmundr held fast, his mouth a vice. Enraged the she-wolf pushed even harder with her forepaws and pulled with her head until the oak tree burst just as her tongue was torn out by its roots. The she-wolf shook her head back and forth splattering blood every which way, trying to shake away the pain. Sigmundr leapt up and grabbed her around the neck. As he choked her he yelled out, "Here, let me stop the blood for you by applying a firm tourniquet."

Slowly the life went out of the she-wolf. There were many who later said the she-wolf had been Siggeir's mother who had changed herself into the wehr-shape of a wolf by sorcery and trollcraft. Whether or not this was true, it was at this time Siggeir's mother disappeared and was never seen again.

CHAPTER 4
THE BIRTH
OF
SINFJOTLI

Sigmundr retreated into the forest and waited until morning for the arrival of Signy's messenger. Together they buried the she-wolf. "We must make certain Siggeir suspects nothing. The discovery of his mother's death would certainly let him know I'm alive. Return to Siggeir's Hall and tell Signy I'll wait for her in the deepest part of the wildwood."

Shortly after Signy's messenger left, Siggeir's messenger arrived and saw the burst oak and the blood all around. He hurried back to the Hall and reported the news to Siggeir. "Sigmundr is nowhere to be seen, but there's blood everywhere. He must have put up more of a struggle than the others."

Siggeir was pleased and went to Signy's room and ordered her released. Immediately she rushed past him into the corridor, anxious to run out to the wildwood and search for Sigmundr. But Siggeir wasn't going to let this moment pass. He ran after her catching her by the arm to stop her, "Where are you going in such a rush? I thought we might forget what has happened and have a meal together to celebrate."

Signy looked at him in surprise. She had no time for this and made up an excuse to leave. "I've been kept in my room so long that I yearn for the open air. I would like to be alone today so I can think about what has happened and plan what I am to do. I seem to have only a few options."

In Siggeir's mind those few options only included being with him, so, he let her go.

Signy left the Hall and headed into the woods. She passed by the spot where her brothers had been murdered and continued into the forest. Soon she found Sigmundr who comforted her in her grief, vowing to avenge the wrongs done to the Volsungrs. "If you can get me a sword and some armor I'll go now to Siggeir and avenge our family."

Signy was more practical having had a long time locked up to dwell on vengeance. "How can you alone avenge these deaths? Even with my help it would only lead to disaster for both of us. My husband has no fewer warriors than he did when you first fought him and he defeated you then. And you have fewer fighting with you than you did eleven days ago. I counsel you to wait. Patience will win us the vengeance we seek. It matters little whether these deaths are avenged now or even twenty years from now, as long as they are avenged. We can afford to bide our time and strike when the time is right so we'll have victory."

Sigmundr realized Signy had always been smarter and a better strategist than he or his brothers, the proof being that his brothers were now dead and he was in hiding and only by his sister's cunning was he still alive. If only he and his brothers had listened to her advice sooner. There would be a lot more Volsungr's around. Sigmundr listened to her now, but with suspicion. Why didn't she want to take immediate action? "Have you any plans on what we should do? We're the last of the noble Volsungrs and it's our duty to kill Siggeir to avenge our family. And the sooner the better. Perhaps your marriage is happier than I suspected."

Signy drew herself away from him at those remarks, "I have even greater reason than you for wanting Siggeir dead. Whereas you will live here in the forest while we plot our revenge, I must live in the Hall with Siggeir. I assure you my lot is the more difficult of the two of us. Come let's swear a solemn oath on Ullr's Ring, by the goddess Var, and on the river Leiptr, and then make plans for your immediate needs."

This was done, after which Signy returned to Siggeir's Hall.

o   o   o   o

Later that day Signy journeyed back into the forest with her servant bringing other helpful things for Sigmundr. The three constructed an earthhouse, completely underground, except for its entrance that was concealed from above. Signy, her servant, and Sigmundr were the only three who knew it existed. Over time Sigmundr improved the earthhouse until it became quite comfortable for him. Signy sent him enough food to be stored and other supplies so that after a while he was entirely self-sufficient. At night he hunted for meat. He found it much easier to kill a sleeping deer than one that will run away at the sound of a footfall breaking a twig. Why had no one thought to hunt while their prey slept? Then he answered his own question, "Because there is no honor in killing without a challenge. The prey is just as dead by the one who sneaks, but without honor it's a deed that can't be shouted about."

Sigmundr waited patiently while the time passed, honing his warrior skills as best he could fighting shadows. His hatred of Siggeir grew with each passing day. Some might say as the years passed he became slightly unhinged. As he became more self-sufficient Signy visited less and less, fearing Siggeir might be having her followed. So Sigmundr's contact with real people was very rare. He spoke with his brothers a lot. Though someone watching from afar would think they resembled a stand of nine trees near his earthhouse. And they might think it a bit more than passing strange as he sat eating his meals laughing and joking with the trees, occasionally splashing them with ale from his tankard as he gestured reenacting many of the great battles the brothers had fought. The glory of their past lived on in the forest.

The Fate of Signy and Siggeir's Two Sons

Eventually Signy had two sons by Siggeir. When the eldest reached ten years of age Signy sent word to Sigmundr that she would be sending him her eldest son and he could use him as he wanted in seeking revenge for the deaths of Volsungr and their brothers.

Before she sent him away from the Hall she took her young son to her bower to test him. Her young son looked trustingly at her. He was dressed for a day in the woods, with a small package of food, and not much else. Instead of giving him advice about being in the woods, she stood him in front of one of the tapestries she had been weaving. It showed the last battle of the Volsungrs, and their defeat by Siggeir.

Her son remarked, "That is my father besting the Volsungrs. You don't seem to have made him very mighty. He is a lot smaller than the Volsungrs who seem to tower over everything. Perhaps you can unravel it and reweave it properly. After all, my father did beat and kill the Volsungrs."

He had been so indoctrinated by Siggeir that he no longer realized those in the tapestry whom he spoke against were also his relatives.

Signy did not hold out much hope for her son. As he stared at the tapestry she walked up to him, took needle and thread, and began sewing his garments to him, sewing through his flesh. Her son screamed out in pain and started crying before Signy could even finish one sleeve. She ripped the sewn sleeve from his arm. He cried out even more and ran from the bower into the woods leaving behind the packet of food Signy had prepared for him.

Signy motioned for her servant to run after him and report back to her. Soon the servant was so fearful of the forest he returned to the Hall telling Signy he had lost track of the young lad.

o   o   o   o

Sigmundr came upon the boy wandering in the forest late in the evening. "You seem to be lost? Is there anything I can do for you?" He saw that the puny and bent boy did not resemble Signy in the least. His father's blood certainly flowed in his veins.

The trembling boy looked at the wild man standing before him whose matted greasy hair had not been washed in a long time, nor his beard trimmed, and whose eyes continually darted from side-to-side, senses heightened and watchful for things that might harm him. Despite the man's appearance the young lad found the towering trees in the forest, the strange sounds, and the darkness, even at midday, scarier. He answered, "I've lost my way and no matter which way I go I keep ending up in this spot. I came into the forest from Siggeir's Hall with my mother's servant, but now he seems to have disappeared. I'm hungry too, and I didn't bring any food with me."

Sigmundr motioned for the boy to follow him, "Come with me. You can bake some bread at my house while I fetch some firewood. It'll be too cold for you to return to Siggeir's Hall tonight. You can do so tomorrow morning, if you want too."

After arriving at the earthhouse Sigmundr gave the boy a bag of meal and some instructions on how to make the bread. He went off into the forest leaving the boy alone. Later, when he returned he asked if the bread was ready, "I don't smell anything in the air. Where's the bread?"

The boy was huddled in the corner of the earthhouse, afraid, "When I took the bag and placed it on the table I felt something wriggling around in the bottom. I was too afraid to stick my hand in and feel what it was. I'm not all that hungry anymore." Although the growling of his stomach seemed to belie his statement.

Sigmundr looked at the scared child and saw how cowardly he was. It was hard to believe this boy was his nephew. He was not brave enough to help him avenge the kith and kin of the Volsungrs.

The next morning Signy went into the forest and came to the earthhouse whereupon her son upon spying his mother, ran to her, so glad to see her despite her strange behavior the day before. A familiar face, even unfriendly, in an unfamiliar environment, is still looked on with relief. He threw his arms around her neck. Now he felt safe, "I've been so afraid here in the forest. I'm so glad you've come for me."

However, her reception of him wasn't as friendly. She pried his fingers one-by-one from her neck and brusquely set him aside, and went to talk with Sigmundr, "Will he do for our purposes?"

Sigmundr shook his head no, "I'm sorry, but if I were ever in need in battle the child would be too cowardly to help me."

Signy looked at the boy in disgust. There was no mother love. The child, though scared, felt safer now that his mother was here. Signy agreed with Sigmundr, "Then he's of no use to me either. Why should he live, eating food meant for those braver than he? Take him and kill him." Sigmundr did as he was instructed. The last image the boy saw was his mother turning her back on him and leaving the forest. Sigmundr buried him amongst the nine trees/uncles to keep watch over the child, lest he escape his grave in some otherworldly form.

That evening Siggeir remarked he had not seen his son in several days. Signy truthfully responded, "He went into the forest the other day and ran off away from the servant he was with. I went searching for him today, but could not find him. I believe, perhaps, the forest has swallowed him up as it is known to do."

Many children met their fates in the woods, so Siggeir accepted this.

o o o o

Winter passed, then Spring, Summer and Fall came and went. Soon the next winter was upon them again. Signy took her youngest son, who was now ten-years-old, to her bower. He stared at the tapestries making identical remarks to what his brother had said. He even yelped in pain when Signy began sewing his clothing to him. Though she did get through the first sleeve and was starting on the second when he drew back. She pulled the sleeve from his arm, ripping out the stitches. He ran from the bower into the forest.

The child ran through the dark woods, until he ran straight into a wild man. Sigmundr could see Signy's resemblance in the boy. He was alike to his older brother as if the two had been twins.

Sigmundr also gave him some meal and the task of baking some bread while he went out into the woods. The young lad could see Sigmundr amongst a stand of trees standing over a burial cairn. He seemed to be arguing and pointing to the burial cairn underfoot.

The child reached into the meal to scoop out a few handfuls to make bread. Instead he felt a squirmy thing, threw down the bag, which spilled all over the floor. He saw a small worm slither from the bag and down a hole in the earthen floor.

Sigmundr returned to the earthhouse and saw the lad backed into a corner of the room trembling. He pointed to the bag of spilt flour, "There was something nasty and squirmy in the bag. It ran down that hole." Pointing at the hole he noticed for the first time there were many holes in the earth floor. He realized the house was probably overrun with squirmy creatures.

Sigmundr was too disgusted with the boy to stay with him in the earthhouse and went outside where he saw Signy approaching.

Signy had followed her son into the woods and came to the earthhouse where she saw her son standing in the doorway. He had that same soppy look of happiness and relief her first son had had upon seeing her. He couldn't contain himself and ran to hug her. She stepped back as he threw his arms at her, grasping empty air. "Stay here, I must talk with this man."

Once again Sigmundr asked Signy what he was to do with the cowardly, trembling, scared child. She replied, "Like follows like. A second cowardly brother follows the fate of the first." She left without even looking at her son.

The last thing her son saw was his mother leaving without saying goodbye or even looking at him. His eyes glistened with tears, and then they saw nothing. They stared out into the world blankly. Sigmundr slew the second son.

Once again Siggeir accepted the disappearance of his second son as a natural order of events and tried to comfort his wife, though she had exhibited no need for comforting. "Signy, these things happen to young rambunctious boys who run into the woods. Don't fret about it, we'll have more sons. At least we have each other." He seemed oblivious to the fact his wife didn't seem upset. He also mistakenly thought he and Signy had worked through their problems over the years and their marriage was now fine. However, marital problems that included slaying most of your wife's family are something the other partner can seldom get over. Signy smiled at Siggeir, occasionally did her wifely duties, but silently plotted.

o   o   o   o

Signy found a storehouse, little more than a shed really, just outside the Hall, and had it converted into a bower where she thereafter spent most of her time weaving tapestries telling of the heroic deeds of the Volsungrs. But she also wove plots in her mind. Plots that had to do with the death of Siggeir and his entire household. None would be spared. In her own way she had become just as unhinged as her brother. He lived with his madness in a hole in the ground, she lived with hers in a shed apart from her household.

By keeping to her bower she also hoped to avoid the advances of her wretched husband who longed for a son to replace the two who had mysteriously disappeared in the woods.

o   o   o   o

One day Signy heard there was a witch wife in town and sent for her. She paid the witch wife to temporarily change guises with her. By use of chants and necromancy the witch wife was able to bring about their transformations. Signy then left her bower in the witch wife's form and journeyed into the forest.

The witch wife, in her guise as Signy, went to the Hall and stayed with Siggeir. Her impersonation was such that the King was none the wiser that the next three days he spent with someone other than Signy. In fact he should have been suspicious that "Signy" was much friendlier to him and seemed to enjoy his affections.

o   o   o   o

Once in the forest Signy headed to Sigmundr's earthhouse, consciously changing her manner of walk and gesture. She knew even at a distance people can recognize others not by their looks, but by how they move.

Sigmundr was fooled. To him she was just a lost woman in the woods. She asked for shelter telling him it was too late to travel any further that night and she was tired from being lost all day. "I have money enough to make it worth your while if you'll let me spend the night here. I won't trouble you at all. I know many stories of heroic adventures with which I can entertain you."

Sigmundr had been in the forest alone for several years now and longed for company, especially female company. He welcomed her inside and offered her food, "It's been a long time since I've had a visitor. You're welcome to stay as long as you like. Tell me of the lands where you have traveled. What news do you hear of King Siggeir and his wife Signy?"

She answered, "Nothing much on that account. He has quieted down lately and does not stray too far from his home. Certainly, it's a lucky thing for him. He was never a great warrior. I remember watching as he fought against King Volsungr. Now there was a warrior." She stared at Sigmundr, then continued, "You have the bearing and looks of a Volsungr. I thought they were all dead?"

Sigmundr was taken aback by her words. He had long since stopped worrying about Siggeir finding him. Yet here was a woman who immediately linked him with the Volsungrs, and had guessed his secret. He decided to try and keep her at his earthhouse as long as possible so she would be unable to spread the word around about him.

They were both silent while they ate their evening meal. Sigmundr kept staring at her. Finally he said, "You're very comely to look at and though I can't quite put it together, you seem to remind me of someone. Have we met before?"

She lied, "No, I've only recently arrived here."

She realized the error of her lie almost immediately. If she were only recently arrived, how then could she have watched Siggeir fight King Volsungr? But, Sigmundr had been too long without company, or those who actually spoke back when he spoke with them, for the "tree" brothers he spoke with never responded to his questions or stories. He did not catch her in the lie.

Instead he had other ideas, having been alone for many years now. "I've already offered you my hospitality for the night. If you like, I have a mind to be even friendlier and have us share only one bed. It's been a long time since I've had company here in the woods. Especially the company of a beautiful woman such as yourself."

Normally this was not the type of pickup line that would work with a woman. It did this time because his visitor had come there with exactly that purpose in mind.

She nodded in agreement. "It's rare that a woman finds a man such as you nowadays. What you suggest would be greatly to my liking."

It never even occurred to Sigmundr, being possessed of a healthy male ego, that a woman meeting a wild, unkempt man, who rarely bathed and had a distinct odor about him, and was possessed of twitches, tics, and wild eyes, would even hesitate to accept an offer of his bed and company. He had no mirrors so in his mind he was that handsome warrior who had so much promise so many years ago.

She stayed for three days and three nights and they enjoyed each other's company. Volsungr tried to persuade her to stay longer, but she refused. "I have important business other where. But I'll keep the secret of your whereabouts safe. Have no fears on that score. I have always been a friend to the Volsungrs. So much a friend, one might even think I were one of them." Still he did not guess her identity. Before she left, he embraced her and took her to his bed one last time. And this was the time Sinfjotli was conceived.

She left. Sigmundr never saw her again.

The Birth of Sinfjotli

Signy hurried back to Siggeir's Hall and regained her own form from the witch wife, whom she paid and sent on her way. And the pay was quite handsome. The small fortune the witch wife received also required she leave the area, set up house as far away as possible, and never contact either her or Siggeir again. If she did she would forfeit the money she had been given. The witch wife was very logical about the payment. She now had enough money to spend the rest of her life in luxury. What did it matter where that was? She left the area, never to be seen again.

Nine months later Signy gave birth to a son whom she named Sinfjotli. Siggeir was beside himself with joy. He didn't suspect Sinfjotli was not his son, since Signy (actually the witch wife) had made love to him more in those few days nine months before than she had during all the years of their marriage. He knew those days were when Sinfjotli had been conceived. Certainly, not after since Signy had rarely left her bower in the last nine months. She just stayed there eating and weaving. And, he never suspected, she was plotting vengeance with the son who had been growing inside her. A son who was 100% Volsungr.

No one in the Hall even suspected Sinfjotli was other than Siggeir's son, even though none cooed at the baby telling it how much it looked like Siggeir. Rather they would say, "How unlike your father you are, you're strong and shapely." However, everyone was discrete and these words were never uttered while Siggeir was around.

Sinfjotli grew tall and strong and became skilled in warrior ways. At a distance many said he looked like Volsungr himself. It was bandied about in the hallways that Signy was prepotent and Siggeir impotent, and the result was Sinfjotli who was entirely of the Volsungr kin. Little did they know how close they were to the truth.

When Sinfjotli reached the age of ten Signy decided to send him to Sigmundr as she had done with her two other sons. Before doing so she put him through the same test she had put her other sons through. After he was dressed and ready to go into the woods Signy took him to her bower and stood him in front of the tapestry she was working on. Her son looked at the weaving and noticed the warrior in it looked a great deal like him. While he was staring at the tapestry Signy took a needle and thread and sewed his garments to him, sewing through his flesh. Sinfjotli did not so much as bat an eyelash. Her other sons had screamed out in pain and had started crying before Signy could even finish one sleeve. Instead, Sinfjotli asked to be told the story of the brave warrior in the tapestry.

"He was a great man who should have been King," spoke Signy as she continued her sewing. "But his Kingdom was stolen from him by Siggeir."

"My father cheated him out of his land? That hardly seems an honorable thing to do. We should right this wrong." Sinfjotli ran his hand over the tapestry.

Signy continued, "I didn't say your father cheated the man out of his Kingdom, I said Siggeir did."

Sinfjotli pointed to another tapestry, "Who is that noble warrior? He looks brave and strong."

Signy smiled and answered, "That's Volsungr, your grandfather. He vowed never to retreat from fire or sword because of fear. And he never did. He suffered greatly in battle yet never was a coward. His valiant blood flows through your veins."

Signy pulled the garments off her son, tearing away parts of his flesh as the threads were ripped out. Her other sons had screamed out loudly, even though their clothes had not been sewn on as completely. She asked Sinfjotli if it had hurt. He replied, "It is unlikely Volsungr would have yelled out. What he could bear I can also bear."

Signy smiled at her son, proud of his bravery. She sent him into the forest.

When Sigmundr met Sinfjotli in the forest he did as he had done with Signy's other sons. He took him back to the earthhouse and gave him some meal to use to make bread while he went to fetch firewood. Later, when he returned carrying the cords of wood, he found Sinfjotli had finished the baking. Sigmundr inquired about the meal, "Was there anything odd about the meal I gave you?"

Sinfjotli replied, "At first I thought there were things living in the meal, so I kneaded it all together so whatever was moving in the bag was destroyed."

Sigmundr laughed, took the bread and threw it out. "I'll not let you eat this bread, for poisonous serpents were in the bag of meal I gave you. The taste of poison will not harm me and so eating this bread would bring me no hurt. Although you seem to be able to tolerate the touch of a snake's poison, I doubt you could swallow it without harm. Instead, let's eat some other food and talk. I think we have a great deal to discuss.

Back at the Hall Siggeir, still with pleasant memories of the witch woman disguised as Signy, insisted she perform her wifely duties. And from his forceful efforts she bore him two more sons who took after their father's cowardly nature. With these two sons he forgot about Sinfjotli whom he assumed had been lost in the woods like his two elder sons.

CHAPTER 5
VOLSUNGR'S DEATH IS AVENGED

Over the years Sigmundr and Sinfjotli grew to know each other, and Sigmundr was amazed at how much Sinfjotli took after the Volsungrs, and how little he took after Siggeir. He had no idea Sinfjotli was his son by his sister Signy. Because he thought Sinfjotli was Siggeir and Signy's son, he remained wary of him. He might have the manner of the Volsungrs, Sigmundr thought, but he still might have Siggeir's evil heart.

The day came when Sigmundr told Sinfjotli who he was and of the great wrongs perpetrated on the Volsungr family. "Your grandfather and great-uncles journeyed to this country in trust and honor, but Siggeir tricked them and has been the bane of our family."

Sinfjotli answered, "We must avenge these deaths. Let's get our swords and go to Siggeir's Hall and kill him now." He rose to get their weapons.

Sigmundr cautioned against the plan, "No, we must wait until you're older. Stay with me and I'll raise you as my foster-son and teach you warrior skills."

Throughout the long winter Sigmundr taught Sinfjotli the history of their family and told him of the glorious battles won by Volsungr, Rerir, and Sigi, and how Odin had always favored them. That summer the two went about the woods harrying innocent men passing through the forest, and stealing their wealth. Often Sinfjotli announced he was ready for them to seek vengeance, but Sigmundr always said, "Not yet. Be patient. A time will come, but it is not now."

o   o   o   o

Once while hunting through the woods for someone to rob and slay they came upon a cottage. They crept up silently to a window and peered in. They saw two men asleep, sprawled on two chairs, each wearing costly gold rings and clothing that showed their wealth. Sigmundr explained who the two men were, "They have come into this forest for years. Their father owns this cottage and keeps it for his two sons. He is a great King, and the two men you see before you are both Princes, although you'd never know it by looking at them lolling about like that. When they were young they were wont to get into mischief. Unfortunately one person they tried to play a trick on was a sorcerer who, instead, played a cruel trick on them. Using magical incantations he turned them into unwilling shapechangers. You can see their wolf-guises over in the corner. For ten half days they must go about in those wehr-shapes as wehr-wolves. They are permitted to remove them for only a half day. Usually they are so tired from going about as wehr-wolves they do nothing but sleep once they assume their regular shapes. We have come upon them on the fifth day and see them as their mother would like to always see them. Such is not their wyrd. When they awaken they'll again put on the wolf-guises and prowl the woods."

Sinfjotli was intrigued by what he saw. "What would happen if we stole their wolf-guises and wore them instead?"

Sigmundr also was curious. "I don't know. But I do know a way to find out."

They both went to the front door. Sigmundr tried the handle and found it unlocked. This was going to be easy. They quietly entered and soon realized the Princes were so exhausted it didn't matter how much noise they made. Sigmundr grabbed both wolf-guises and threw one to Sinfjotli. They quickly put them on and ran from the cottage on all fours. It would be ten half days before they could come out of the guises.

The two found they had the same nature as before, although perhaps a bit wilder. When they spoke to one another they could hear the howling of wolves, and yet they understood each other. They ran off into the wildwood. Before separating from each other Sigmundr suggested what they should do, "If you're attacked howl like a wolf as loudly as you can. I'll come running to your side, and you'll do likewise in the event you hear me howling. I feel we are both strong enough that we could fend off seven men each. If one of us finds he has been set upon by more than seven men then he is to howl and the other will come running. Heed this rule, Sinfjotli. You're young and overly courageous without realizing the danger you may be in. Men, on the other hand, will see your fine young coat and think you are a good catch."

Sinfjotli thought Sigmundr was being overly cautious, but nodded in agreement, nevertheless. Each left the other and went his own way.

Soon Sigmundr was set upon by nine men and howled for Sinfjotli, who came running. They easily killed the entire hunting party and parted once again and did not see each other for several days.

All this time their natures were becoming more and more feral and wolf-like. Sigmundr found he liked rolling in piles of leaves or chasing after rabbits and other small animals.

Sinfjotli found a new treat. He began stalking a farmer and his family who lived at the forest edge. There was a pile of garbage in the back of their house where the leftover meals were discarded. Sinfjotli discovered he liked the rancid meat that had been lying about for several days. However, best of all was if it was old enough to have a tinge of green to it and be covered over with crawling maggots. One day he found a piece of pork that had become all slimy and smelly with age. After dragging it under an oak tree he began gnawing and licking at it. He was so intent on this feast he didn't notice the farmer and ten other men sneaking up on him. Fortunately for him, one of the farmers tripped over a stone and cried out as he fell. Sinfjotli immediately sprung up and growled at them with slaver running from the sides of his mouth. The farmers attacked, but Sinfjotli fought fiercely and one by one he killed all the farmers with very little injury to himself. Sigmundr heard the fighting and came running to Sinfjotli's side. By the time he reached him Sinfjotli was back on his haunches under the oak tree eating the rest of the pork.

Sigmundr was furious, "Why didn't you howl for me? It was only by chance I heard the trouble you were in."

Sinfjotli answered, "What trouble? It was only eleven farmers. I can certainly handle that, as you can see by their bloody bodies. I know the meat is fresh and not particularly putrid, but help yourself"

Sigmundr persisted, "Why didn't you call for my help? We agreed if either was set upon by seven or more then the other would be called."

Sinfjotli was getting bored with the conversation and wanted to continue his gnawing, "That was a rule you made. I never agreed to follow it. Leave me in peace so I can continue eating my meal. It's a lazy day and I've already done enough killing and fighting. Besides, why should I call you just for eleven men? I helped you when the nine attacked you because you're old and needed my help. I'm young and can easily handle twice what I've killed today."

Sigmundr had been becoming more wolfish the last few days, so when he was insulted he did what his nature told him to do. He rushed at Sinfjotli and bit him in the throat, biting his windpipe in two. Sinfjotli was so startled he made no effort to defend himself. He fell to the ground gasping for air, and then was still.

Sigmundr immediately realized what he had done, but it was too late. He threw Sinfjotli over his back and ran off to the earthhouse cursing the wolf-guises all the way since it was not a day they he could come out of them and assume their human forms. "I could help Sinfjotli if I had hands to stitch up his wound. My paws will only be good for digging his grave and burying him as I would a bone. I curse these wolf-guises and wish I could throw them where the trolls could have them."

Sigmundr walked out of the earthhouse trying to think what to do. It was then he remembered that once he had been walking in the forest and had seen two weasels fighting. One had bit the other in the throat much as he had bitten Sinfjotli. Then seeing what he had done the weasel ran into the copse and grabbed a leaf from a herb growing near the edge of the thicket. When he returned he laid it across the throat of the other weasel. The wounded weasel immediately jumped up clean and whole again. Sigmundr began looking around for the herb, but without any luck. Suddenly he saw a raven flying overhead and in its beak it carried a leaf from that same herb. The raven circled around coming ever closer until it landed on Sigmundr's shoulder. Sigmundr took the blade and the raven flew off.

He ran back to the earthhouse and put the herb on Sinfjotli's throat. Sinfjotli jumped up whole and well as if he had never been hurt.

The two remained in the earthhouse until it was time to come out of their wolf-guises. As soon as they were back in their own shapes Sigmundr grabbed both wehr-shapes and cast them into the fire, breaking the spell forever, except for the poor unfortunate Princes who ever after had the forms of men but the natures of wolves.

Finally, Volsungr's Death is Avenged

The years passed during which Sigmundr and Sinfjotli grew strong from their many adventures. Finally the time came to avenge Volsungr's death.

Sigmundr began thinking on this matter and how the vengeance could be accomplished.

One day Sigmundr sent word to Signy that he and Sinfjotli would come that evening to avenge Volsungr's death. He told her where to meet them.

That evening he and Sinfjotli went to Siggeir's Hall and hid in a storeroom behind several tuns of ale and casks of beer. The storeroom was at the front of the house just off the porch, near Signy's bower. Signy met them there where they plotted Siggeir's final solution.

Signy and Siggeir had two young sons who chose at this moment to play on the porch with a golden toy, bowling it along the porch while they ran after it. As it happened a ring fell off the toy and rolled into the storeroom where Sigmundr, Sinfjotli, and Signy were holding counsel. One of the children went to search for the ring and was startled when he came upon Sigmundr and Sinfjotli. Both were helmeted and dressed for battle wearing white byrnies. The boy gasped when he saw the two fully armed warriors and ran to tell his father. Sigmundr and Sinfjotli dared not chase after him lest they lose the element of surprise and be confronted by an army of Siggeir's warriors. Their hope was the child would not be believed and scolded for making up fanciful tales.

o o o o

The child was breathless with fright as he related what had happened, "Father, they were as white as ghosts and as big as jotuns. They both had fierce angry faces. I was awfully frightened." The child jumped as his mother entered the room. He pointed at her, "And she was in the room talking with them. They were whispering in low voices, so I didn't hear what they were talking about."

Signy shook her head at Siggeir as if to say, boys will be boys. "It must have been that ghost story I was reading him earlier. You know how impressionable children are?"

Her son looked puzzled because his mother hadn't read to him in years. "But father, she hasn't . . . She wasn't . . ."

Unfortunately Siggeir believed his wife and shushed his son and shooed him away, "Be quiet. Don't make up stories about ghosts. You've made me very angry.

Now go play with your brother and don't bother me the rest of the evening. For some reason I feel uneasy tonight and prefer to be alone. And no dinner for you tonight. You can think about how lying and telling tall tales has made you hungry as you watch your brother eat"

Signy took her son from the room. "Go play with your brother and don't bother your father anymore this evening."

Her son now had thoughts of being read to since Signy had mentioned reading to him, "Will you read me a story tonight?"

Signy pushed him away, "That's such a silly idea. Where on earth did you think of it? Though, I will tell you sagas will be written about the legend of tonight. Perhaps I'll read them to you one day, if you're still around. Now go find your brother."

The boy went off to find his brother and tell him what he had seen. Maybe his brother would believe him about the ghosts.

A short while later Signy found them back playing on the porch. "My two wonderful sons, how nice to see you."

Her two wonderful sons looked at her puzzled. She was hardly ever this friendly towards them.

"Come with me and I'll feed you." Her sons walked towards the door reveling in the attention their mother was showing them. "No, not in the house, your father would notice. Come with me."

"But, Mother, I thought you had said I was not to have dinner tonight?"

Signy answered, "What kind of nonsense are you babbling. Of course you can have dinner tonight."

She took them both into the storeroom and presented them to Sigmundr. "Here are my sons. One has already betrayed you to Siggeir, and the other will soon betray you. Kill them for their interference."

Her sons shook with fear at their mother's betrayal.

Sigmundr looked at the two boys. "Never will I kill someone for telling the truth."

Signy looked over at Sinfjotli whose thinking was far more in line with hers. Without a thought to it he drew his sword and slew his two half-brothers. Then he and Sigmundr each picked up a body and carried both children into the Hall where they threw the lifeless forms at Siggeir's feet. Sinfjotli spoke, "Here are your two younger sons, cast at your feet by the faux son you thought you had lost years ago. Look on Sinfjotli standing before you, who has become a mighty warrior, and has come to avenge the deaths of the noble Volsungrs."

Siggeir leaped up and called for his guards to capture the intruders. Guards entered from every door attacking the two. Sigmundr and Sinfjotli fought bravely and killed many of Siggeir's best warriors, Eventually, though, the strength of Siggeir's forces overcame them and they were subdued, bound into fetters, thrown into a chamber and kept there under guard throughout the night.

Siggeir spent the night trying to devise a suitable punishment, a long and tortuous death. At dawn he had several servants dig a deep pit and build a structure of loose stones and turf inside it, A large flat stone was set in the middle of the pit, dividing the damp earthen room into two compartments.

Early that morning Sigmundr and Sinfjotli were thrown into the pit, one on each side of the center stone. After the tomb was sealed they would be able to hear but not see each other, and slowly each would starve to death hearing the dying moans of the other. Perhaps each even hearing the other eating parts of themselves as they died of hunger.

Signy came to the edge of the pit carrying a bundle of straw. Workmen were busy sealing the top. Siggeir signaled for one of the guards to stop her. She spoke to her husband. "I've only brought some meat wrapped in straw, thinking it would help them."

Siggeir responded, "No doubt it will. You have my permission to toss it into Sinfjotli's side of the barrow. Thus will his suffering be prolonged, and his punishment be made greater for having killed my sons."

She threw the meat to Sinfjotli and before he could say anything the workmen sealed the barrow so tightly even air could not get in.

Sinfjotli yelled through the wall to Sigmundr, "I will not touch the meat so we might die nobly together."

Sigmundr encouraged him to eat it, "As long as a warrior lives and has strength there is always hope. I don't begrudge you the food. You bring no dishonor to yourself by eating it."

Sinfjotli refused, only to have Sigmundr order him to eat the meat.

Sinfjotli felt in the straw. Instead of meat he felt a hard shape and recognized it as the sword Gramr. He yelled out in excitement loud enough for those standing over the barrow to hear. Fortunately Siggeir had ordered everyone to leave them to die alone. Signy was dragged back to the Hall, for she had wanted to sit vigil until they had died. However, Siggeir was wise enough to know someone might tire of sitting vigil and work out a way to remove the covering stone.

When Sinfjotli yelled out his discovery, only Sigmundr could hear the good news, "Sigmundr, Signy has saved our lives. I've found something better than meat in the straw. My fingers have felt the hilt of your mighty sword, Gramr."

Sigmundr responded, "Gramr is so sharp it can cut through anything without its edge being dulled."

Sinfjotli understood and thrust the sword through the rock wall dividing them. Sigmundr grasped the other end and they sawed back and forth for hours and hours until they had cut the stone in two. Sigmundr pushed one of the rocks aside and walked into Sinfjotli's side of the barrow. "Stand on my shoulders and cut a hole through the ceiling." This was easier since the ceiling was a thin rock covered over with dirt. Siggier had not thought it necessary to put a heavy rock over the barrow. That would have taken reinforcing pillars to hold it up. He felt the thinner rock was quicker and quite sufficient. He was wrong.

It was night when the two emerged from their grave.

The two resurrected men had only one goal. They made their way to Siggeir's Hall. It was still the middle of the night and all was quiet. Siggeir had dismissed all the guards, satisfied the Hall was safe since Sigmundr and Sinfjotli were buried away in their tomb.

Sigmundr and Sinfjotli stealthily sealed all the exits save one and piled kindling and wood throughout the Hall and set it afire. Those inside awoke to a raging inferno. Many died, mostly from the smoke, some not making it further than the ends of their beds. Those who got further, ran from exit to exit, disheartedly finding them all blocked. Burnt rafters began falling blocking people and trapping Siggeir in his room. Some finally found the open way. Sigmundr and Sinfjotli allowed the women out, but cut down all the men as they ran through the exit.

All still living could hear Siggeir trapped in his bower yelling out, "Who has lit this fire in which I now burn?"

Sigmundr yelled back in triumph, "Sigmundr and Sinfjotli, Signy's brother and son have. Know you now that it's impossible to kill all the Volsungrs."

Then to his horror Sigmundr saw his sister Signy at another window. "Are you trapped? Sinfjotli and I will rescue you."

Signy yelled back, "I am only trapped by my bad deeds."

Sigmundr called out to Signy, "Get away and make your way to the side door and we'll help you. But first take what you want from the Hall so you can be repaid for all the humiliation you've had to suffer these years. You've been the bravest Volsungr of all, and have suffered the most. This is not the night of your death we will save you."

Signy left the window and moments later came out the side door and stood in front of her brother and son. She knew her death was upon her, and it would be honorable. First, though, Sigmundr and Sinfjotli needed to know the truth.

"I've ever sought the vengeance on Siggeir that he is now receiving. To bring this about I've caused the slaying of four of my sons whom I deemed worthless. Only one has lived to manhood and that is Sinfjotli who is more a Volsungr than anyone realizes. Many years ago, Sigmundr, I journeyed to your earthhouse in the guise of a witch wife. We slept together. So now look upon the son of that union, Sinfjotli, your son and my son. The blood of the Volsungrs flows double in his veins. He is no kin to Siggeir. So now for all I have done it is my fate to burn with Siggeir. Our family's honor has been reclaimed, so I am happy to die with him even though I was loathe to live with him." She kissed Sigmundr, her brother and beloved, and Sinfjotli, her son, and turned and walked back through the flames.

Some of the women began pointing at Siggeir's window. The King was climbing out and preparing to jump. Some women had positioned themselves so they could break his fall. Sigmundr and Sinfjotli ran over and pushed the women aside. They held Gramr between them. Sigmundr yelled up to Siggeir, "No women will catch you if you jump. It will be Gramr's fearsome edge that will catch and cleve you in two. Have no concerns about your burial for there's a recently deserted barrow nearby separated into two parts by a stone. That will hold your duplicitous self quite nicely."

Siggeir climbed back into his room being helped inside by Signy. The flames fed more and more by the tables, chairs, and beds in the Hall, as well as tapestries of the glories of Siggeir's false exploits, flared up and through all the windows. Sigmundr and Sinfjotli watched as the biggest funeral pyre in history lit the night sky. They watched as Signy perished with Siggeir and all his men.

The next day Sigmundr, feeling there was no further reason for him to remain in Gautland decided to raise an army and reclaim the throne of Hunland. Siggeir had paid little attention to Hunland and the throne had been usurped by a pretender. Volsungr's fame was such that men clamored to be in his army so they could receive the glory and bounty of warring and conquering.

Eventually Sigmundr set sail with Sinfjotli at his side back to Hunland. The two easily drove out the King who reigned there. That evening Sigmundr sat down in Volsungr's Hall and rested his head against Branstokk, the tree that had always brought him luck. His father's death and those of his uncles' had finally been avenged. Yet there was sadness in him because he had lost his sister, Signy, his other, who had saved him so many times and made his life and glory possible.

CHAPTER 6
THE BIRTH
OF
HELGI

Sigmundr's rule was strong and just, and his fame spread throughout many lands. Eventually he married Borghildr, sometimes known as Borgny, and built a Hall in Bralundi, a secured part of his Kingdom, so that they might have a peaceful, comfortable life together. After a while he felt life was becoming too settled, so he gathered together his army and went off to war, as is the nature of Kings who gain their Kingdom from conquering.

While he was away adventuring Borghildr discovered she was with child. Praying to both Frigg and Freya, she asked that her child might be born healthy and grow up strong and whole. Both the Æsir and Vanir looked on the birth with favor and sent their blessings, "May your son grow strong and healthy and bring honor to the Volsungrs." What they didn't realize was she was to be delivered of twins, and they had each sent one blessing to her firstborn.

Borghildr's belly grew and grew until she felt her swollen belly was about to burst. Everyone commented the birth would be soon and the signs portended a great warrior being born, though one born of tumult.

At one point the storms outside raged so fiercely that the streams in the mountains filled with the added rain and surged down the mountainsides, causing rivers they flowed into to swell and overflow their banks.

Borghildr was uneasy at the violence heralding her son's birth.

The next day, though, was as calm as the previous day had been raging. On the day of Helgi's birth the cloud-laden dawn sky had cleared and warmed the land till nothing remained but a fine misty dew glistening on the fields. However, if you looked closely you could also see dew covered spider's webs in the field making them glisten in the rising sun.

o   o   o   o

Borghildr looked out from her bower window knowing today her son would be born. The sky was beautiful, but she saw a troubling vision in the field, a vision of shadowy warriors ready for battle. Instead of being cohesive and ready to fight together, they seemed to lack discipline as if they were being pulled by two sides. The two ravens in the trees screeched in anticipation of the battlefield meals they would have because of the battles that would be won by Helgi. One raven was heard to yell, "Now will come war. Which side for me?" The other raven responded, "Whichever you chose, then the other side for me. We will not fight side-by-side, but opposite."

Then the mist cleared and Borghildr realized she was just looking at a distant field of waving grass. Yet the vision had been so real to her that she was troubled it happened before her son's birth.

o   o   o   o

Helgi was born with the sound of a rumbling sky trying to darken the day. Everyone agreed the signs portended the fact a great warrior had been born into the world. Many gathered outside Sigmundr's Hall, rejoicing in the hero's birth. He would be a leader destined to surpass even his father in greatness.

After Helgi had been severed from Borghildr, she reached out her arms to hold him. "Let me have my son, Helgi."

Then her back arched in pain.

The mid-wife said, surprised, "There's another one."

His birth was harder on Borghildr. He was large and the birth difficult. He did not slide out as Helgi had. Instead Borghildr had to push and push to try to eject him. Finally, the mid-wife reached inside and pulled him out by his legs for he had been turned around inside. An omen of a world upside down for him. He was pulled from his mother, arms failing, feet kicking. Borghildr named him Hamund. While he was being cleaned she held and cuddled his brother Helgi who immediately began nursing. When Hamund was brought to her, she waved him off until Helgi had finished eating and had fallen asleep in her arms. Only then, did she exchange Helgi for Hamund. By this time she was tired and her milk almost gone and her nipples were sore. She asked that Hamund be taken away while she slept. She was small and did not have enough milk left for her second son. Thus began Hamund's life of being second best.

However, so he wouldn't starve a nursing woman who had also just given birth was brought from the village to take care of Hamund's needs. The nursing woman had extra milk, having birthed many children. She made certain her new son, and other nursing children were fed first. Hamund spent his babyhood always hungry, never quite fully fed. He would be hungry for everything in life ever after.

○ ○ ○ ○

A few days later some Norns from Asgardr arrived. Borghildr had been alerted to the Norn's visit so she had had time to prepare Helgi. He was presented to the Norns clad in a byrny and a flowing white robe. Even though he was only a few days old his eyes flashed with the might of a warrior. And though small, he looked the part.

The Norns stood at the foot of Helgi's cradle to pronounce blessings on him. One of them spoke, "Here is born Helgi, the greatest of the Budlings. He will be the best of Kings and a mighty warrior, for he has been born in the midst of a storm, yet the sky has cleared for him. Though he will fight many battles, the paths through his enemies will be cleared and he will gain fame and fortune. He will rule over his father's Kingdom which he will have increased many times over. When he dies he will live as a leader of the Einherjar in Valhalla where Bragi will sing songs of praise describing his battles."

The Norns secured his golden wyrd-threads to the middle of the heavens and then strung them out to the east and west until they covered the world and were tied to the corners of the sky. Neri's sister, one of the Norns attending Helgi's birth, secured the northern thread so it could never be cut loose.

Then almost as an afterthought Borghildr remembered her second son, Hamund. He was with the nursing woman in a room near the stables. Borghildr sent a servant to fetch him. The servant arrived at the stable door and yelled for the nursing woman to bring Hamund quickly to Borghildr's rooms, "Be quick about it because there's no time, the Norns are about to leave."

The nursing woman protested, "But I haven't had time to get him ready."

The servant who had always looked with pity on Hamund's lot in life was determined he receive a blessing from the Norns as his brother had. His life was going to be difficult enough and she was determined he have at least this. The nurse was dawdling so the servant threw some swaddling over the child and grabbed the nurse's hand to drag him along, "Come quickly, there's no time to spare or he'll miss a blessing from the Norns. Even a rushed, afterthought blessing, is still a blessing from the Norns. And very few receive a blessing at all. So be quick about it."

The nurse protested, "Have you no sense of smell? His diaper needs changing."

And thus Hamund's presence would be discerned well before he entered the presence of the Norns.

The Norns waited and waited then left despite Borghildr's entreaties to wait just a few moments more. But a moment to a Norn can irretrievably affect someone's life. Giving up they left and passed Hamund in the hallway, glancing only briefly at the smelly child. They mistook him for the son of the servant woman holding him out to the Norns. He received no blessings or fateful golden threads strung from the heavens portending a great future.

Such was his fate that he was forgotten by all, including his mother. After he was too old to nurse, the nursing woman, the only maternal figure in his life, went back to the village while Hamund stayed around the Hall with nothing to do. And no one noticed him. He ate in silence in the corner of the kitchen from plates filled with scraps that had been set aside to be thrown into the garbage. Scraps so bad and rotten they weren't even thought fit for the dogs.

o o o o

Sigmundr had just returned from warring in far off lands. Hearing of Helgi's birth (servants forgot to tell him about Hamund's birth) he hurried to his wife's side. A few days later at his son's natal feast he presented the baby with a leek for luck and officially named him Helgi before the assemblage.

Sigmundr spoke, "I've recently returned from battle and have conquered new lands which I now give to my son as his own. He shall have the lands known as Solfjoll, Snjofjoll, Hatan, Himinvanga, Sigarsvoll, Hringstadir, and Hringstod, the harbor in that land." Next Sigmundr took a shining long sword, carved all over with runes, and laid it across his son's blanket and continued, "You will be a great King. Be just, but do not hesitate to use this sword if might is needed to bring about your plans."

As was the custom of northern Kings, soon after his birth, Helgi was sent to be raised foster-parents. His foster-father was by Hagal. This was so he could grow up unspoiled by the flattery that would attend him if he grew up in Sigmundr's household. He was to be treated as Hagal treated his own sons, no worse and no better.

Meanwhile Hamund grew up forgotten. No one sent him off to be raised and skilled in warrior ways. He gained his knowledge from listening, standing unobserved against walls or in corners. He slept in unclean stalls, and took clothing discarded to be burned. He had no dreams because his life was a nightmare. He just existed, one day blending into the next. Birthdays were nonexistent. When on rare occasions someone noticed him they thought he was one of the many beggars who hung around the Hall. He was a ghost, living an unlucky and unblessed life. His existence was the opposite of his twin brother's.

o o o o

Helgi had just reached his fifteenth birthday when Sigmundr became embroiled in a bitter dispute with King Hunding, who ruled in Hunland. Sigmundr sent word to Hagal to send his son back that he had a mission for him. They met and Sigmundr gave him instructions on how he could help them fight against Hunding. "I'm sending you on your first mission. Travel to King Hunding's land as a common laborer and gain a position in his court. Look about and remember all you can. Count the number of men he has, assess how powerful they are, and take note of the methods of battle they use. After you've learned all this return to me and report what you've found out."

Helgi did as he was bidden and journeyed to Hunding's Hall. He traveled using the name of Hagal's son Hamal as his own. Hunding was away when Helgi began his spying. News of a mighty victory against King Sigmundr reached the Hall before the King's triumphant return. Helgi heard this and went to Heming, one of Hunding's sons, and revealed his identity. "Though you have thought me to be Hamal, son of Hagal, I have really been a wolf in disguise. I am none other than King Sigmundr's son. Tell your father when you see him that I have labored in his Hall and seen the cowardly deeds he has done. Even the lowliest milkmaid would make a greater warrior King than Hunding." At those words Helgi fled the Hall

Heming ran to his father and told him what had happened. Hunding ordered warriors after Helgi. They followed him to Hagal's estate, but after looking around could find no trace of him. Helgi had ridden hard and reached Hagal's before the King's men. He searched but found no good hiding places on the estate. So, he put on the clothing of a milkmaid and busied himself with the cows, filling pail after pail as if he had milked cows all his life.

When Hunding's men passed by, Helgi kept his head bent low. But this unaccustomed modesty in a milkmaid caught the attention of one of the soldiers. He looked at her admiringly. This was just the type of woman he had hoped for all his life, tall and well built, not like the small thin things at Hunding's Hall. He began questioning her, thinking he might be able to work his will with her, "Miss, you are certainly brawny and tall, a fine strong maiden to roll in the hay with."

Hagal saw the attention being paid to Helgi and interrupted the soldier, "She's my best bondwoman and more than she seems, for once she was a shieldmaiden and rode to battle as a Valkyrie. She is Sigar's sister. I came upon her many years ago bathing in a lake, her swan-guise carelessly left on the shore. I stole it and now she must stay here as my servant. She has performed many tasks for me which have strengthened her so her arms have become muscled from milking the cows and churning the milk into butter day in and day out as she sang sweet butter charms to make the milk transform into butter. She is a maiden of many talents and surprises. However, as a captured swan maiden you may not have her. I alone know where her guise is, thus she stays with me."

The soldier continued eyeing the milkmaid. Helgi was becoming angry, trying to keep himself from attacking the guard. He looked up and his fierce eyes stared at the soldier who could not hold their gaze. "Her eyes seem to burn right through me."

Hagal answered, "She hasn't gotten much sleep the last few days, and has been up since early morning carrying on with her milking. Her eyes burn red with tiredness and perhaps from a little too much liquor last evening."

The soldier was satisfied and departed with the rest of Hunding's men.

o   o   o   o

King Hunding was furious when he learned Helgi had escaped, "This news is not to my liking. It's never wise to let a foe's son remain alive. Keep searching until you find him."

○ ○ ○ ○

Meanwhile Helgi had joined with Sinfjotli, and together they had raised a mighty army so they could battle Hunding with a better chance of defeating him. They saw the war as their own just cause and a chance for them to gain a Kingdom.

The two armies met. Helgi and Sinfjotli were victorious. Helgi slew Hunding with his own sword. Later Hunding's sons, Alf, Eyjolf, Hervardr, and Hagbardr gathered another army and sought Helgi and Sinfjotli so they might avenge their father's death. The battle took place on Logafjollum. Helgi's army was easily victorious and he slew all of Hunding's sons beneath the area known as Eagle Rock, winning for himself even greater glory.

As Helgi headed home from the Battle of Eagle Rock he came upon a group of women all beautiful to look upon. He could tell by their clothing and manner they were nobly born. There was one in the group who far exceeded the others in beauty. Helgi drew aside one of the women and asked the identity of the woman he was interested in. The woman replied, "She's the daughter of King Hogni."

Helgi remembered the stories he had heard of Hogni. Supposedly a dvergar had slept with his mother and she had subsequently given birth to him. That explained why he was pale, having the grey pallor of the dead, had coarse black hair, and was small and stooped. Fortunately Sigrunr had taken after her mother's side of the family. Helgi asked to be introduced to her.

Upon hearing Sigrunr speak Helgi lost his heart to her and offered her shelter, "Return with me to my Kingdom and I'll protect you from the dangers that can so often beset beautiful women alone on the highway. I'll prepare a great feast for you and a good welcome."

Sigrunr answered, "That cannot be, for there are other plans in store for my attendants and me."

Helgi answered, "What plans? Perhaps I can help so the deed will be done faster and then you can journey to my Kingdom."

Sigrunr sighed and answered, "My father is King Hogni, and he has given me in marriage to Hoddbrodr, a vile despicable warrior who was a coward when he slew Isung. He is the son of King Granmar of Svarinshaug. It's all against my wishes and I've vowed never to be wed to him. Hoddbrodr and his brothers Gudmundr and Starkadr are searching for me to fetch me to their land where I will be forced to become Hoddbrodr's wife."

Helgi listened to her story and then spoke, "Is there anything I can do?"

Sigrunr could hardly believe her ears, "If you are truly making such an offer then you are a noble and kind warrior. I vow here in front of my attendants that if you can rescue me from the fate awaiting me, I will gladly stay with you. I look at you and see a handsome warrior, brave in spirit. I've longed for one such as you all my life and will gladly share your hearth and home if you can bring it about."

Helgi was pleased. "Smile, for your troubles are over. Hoddbrodr will not take you without a fight. Nor will he have you while I'm yet alive, this I vow before the river Leiptr.

Helgi sent messengers to his father's Kingdom, laden with gold to raise a new army so he might rescue Sigrunr. He waited for the men to assemble at Raudabjarg. It wasn't long before he was met by a great assembly of warriors who had traveled from Hedinsey and Brand Isle. Others came from Norvasund, born along in powerful ships captained by Hjorleifr. This group included Sinfjotli who had arrived with more men so he might fight alongside Helgi.

Helgi turned to Hjorleifr and asked, "Have you counted how many will fight for our cause?"

Hjorleifr answered, "It's hard to know for certain. Of the ships that sailed out of Tronu Strand and are now harbored in Norvasund, they carry about 12,000 men. And 7,000 more again await at Sogn in Hatun Sound. But the greatest army is in a place known as Grindur where there are 15,000 men."

Helgi thought for a moment and then gave Hjorleifr a command, "It's wise then we sail for Varinsfjord so we can command them better from there."

They sailed out of the east, starting at midday. By nightfall a terrible storm had come upon them. Instead of seeking shelter and lowering the sails Helgi commanded that they sail on, "Have no fear and do not lower the sails. Instead hoist them as high as you can. Odin sends a mighty wind to carry us faster. We are safe under Odin's protection."

The men did as they were commanded. The ship tossed and turned in the sea, many times nearly capsizing. It was all the crew could do to hold onto the storm ropes lest they be thrown overboard. The waves sounded as if mountains were being thrown against each other. Lightening flashed in the sky, sometimes striking the masts of some of the ships and traveling down their lengths to the decks. Many of the men thought the Valkyries must be riding overhead to a battle somewhere, the hooves of their horses striking the clouds and causing the lightening. Then out of the sky they saw Sigrunr in the garb of a Valkyrie leading her attendants. Sigrunr stilled the storm and guided Helgi's ships to safety. Odin had smiled on them. None of Helgi's men were lost that night.

The next morning Sigrunr returned and gave Helgi directions where they could find a safe harbor. They sailed on until they reached Gnipalund and that evening anchored their ships in Una Bay.

Their arrival had not gone unnoticed by others. Gudmundr, King Hogni's son, had seen them and leaping on his horse Sveipud had ridden down to the shore. He came upon Helgi and his men busy lowering their sails and inquired as to their identity, "Who has lordship over this fleet?"

Wearing a shining helm upon his head and a snow white byrny, and carrying a gold-striped red war shield in one hand and a spear draped with a red banner fringed with gold in the other, Sinfjotli stepped forward to answer, "Come back to us after you've finished feeding your pigs and hounds. Tonight when you've returned to your farms, tell your wives the Volsungrs have come from the east and they can finally have something to look forward to at night. Helgi, Sigmundr's son, is leading us. Tell Hoddbrodr Helgi awaits him in battle, if he's not too cowardly to fight."

Granmar answered, "The words you speak are false. You seem to have forgotten whom it was you once fought. Why do you insult those who have never done you harm? Perhaps eating too much wolf-meat, or sucking the flesh from cold corpses, or killing your two half-brothers has affected your judgment? I'm surprised you think good and true men would follow your lead."

Sinfjotli replied, "Your memory has grown dim with age. It seems you've forgotten when you lived as a witch wife on Varinsey and yearned for a man, and chose me from everyone to fulfill your desires. Then there was the time when you rode as a Valkyrie from Asgardr, and brought men to battle against each other. Don't forget I begat nine wolf whelps upon you in Laganess."

Granmar answered, "How well you lie. How could you father wolves, when everyone knows a jotun's daughter did cut and geld you as if you were a horse at Thorsness near Gnipa Grove. Your heritage bespeaks your life. You began as a bastard stepson of Siggeir and from there you and Sigmundr lived in the forest in the guise of wolves committing obscene acts. However, the worst deed you've done was to kill your two innocent half-brothers, and that act has followed you wherever you've gone."

Sinfjotli began to speak but was cut off by Granmar, who continued, "I'm not finished with your evil deeds yet. Indeed, I'll cut them short so we don't spend the night here. However, I would be remiss if I didn't mention when the stallion Grani had you as his mare on Bravoll Field, and I did ride you at a gallop across that field. And don't forget when you were a goatherd for the jotun Golnir."

Helgi had heard enough and stopped the battle of words. "You're both dishonoring yourselves speaking of these disreputable acts. It would bring more honor to you if you fought with swords rather than words. It's even foul for us to listen to the accusations you hurl at each other." Helgi turned to Sinfjotli and continued. "Although I could hardly be thought of as Granmar and his sons' champion, yet I know they are brave men. I've heard of their battle in Moinsheim where they brought great honor to their name."

Granmar spoke to Helgi, "Hoddbrodr and I will meet you at Frekastein in Solfjoll, a land falsely given to you by your father at your natal feast. I ride now to Solheimr Hall to summon Hoddbrodr."

o o o o

Granmar and his men rode off to Solheimr where they met Hoddbrodr waiting for him at his Hall gate. He too was wearing a byrny and helmet ready for battle. Sitting on his horse Sveggjud he asked, "What news do you have of the army that has landed? I thought my bride Sigrunr would have landed instead. Why do you look so upset?"

"A great army led by Helgi and Sinfjotli has landed on our shores. Helgi also desires Sigrunr as his wife. So, if you would have her as your wife you will have to fight for her."

Hoddbrodr asked about the army rallied against him. Granmar answered, "They are scattered in several positions, some offshore, some to the end of our

Kingdom, and some to our side. In all there are about 34,000 men waiting to fight us."

Hoddbrodr thought for a moment and then said, "I'll send for warriors throughout the land."

The rider of Sportvitnir carried the news to Sparinsheidi. The horses Melnir and Mylnir were sent to the dark, ominous Myrkvidr Forest. Soon many warriors were gathered under Granmar and Hoddbrodr's banner hoping to bring glory and wealth to their family names.

o o o o

The two armies met at Frekastein. Helgi was the more aggressive of the two leaders. He led his men charging through the ranks of Granmar's army. Many were killed with each assault.

The battle raged on throughout the day, the once green field now turned red. Odin watched from Hlidskjalf in his Hall Valaskjalf, and saw the battle coming to an end. It was time to send his Valkyries to the battle to gather up the bravest warriors for Valhalla.

o o o o

Lightening flashed in the sky as the shield-maidens hovered above the battlefield. When Helgi looked up he saw Sigrunr leading the women he had first met attending her. Helgi then ran at Hoddbrodr, attacked and slew him beneath the King's banner.

Odin smiled on Helgi and victory was his that day. After the battle he and Sigrunr walked throughout the bloody field. Hrollaug's sons lay where they had died at Hle Fells. All the sons of Granmar had been slain. They came upon Hoddbrodr, who had not yet died, but was near to sdoing so. Sigrunr touched him and he died. She smiled at Helgi and said, "I am grateful for your bravery in slaying my tormentor. Now we'll live and rule this land together. Great honor and legend will attend your name for the slaying of such a worthy and mighty foe as Hoddbrodr. My heart is glad at your success."

They continued searching Frekastein, and made a grim discovery. Sigrunr came across the dead bodies of Hogni, her father, and her brother Bragi. Starkadr's body was found at Styr Cliffs. The only one of her kin remaining alive was her brother Dagr. Helgi was upset at having caused the death of Sigrunr's father and brothers, but she forgave him, "We're both saddened by what has happened, but none may escape their wyrd woven by the Norns. And such was the wyrd of my kin." She looked out over the battlefield.

Helgi turned and spoke to Dagr, who was being held by several soldiers, "To make up for Sigrunr's losses I will spare your life. I've always been taught that it is wise to take the life of all living kinsmen of foes I have killed so they could not avenge the deaths of their family. However, if you will swear fealty to me and the Volsungr kin, and vow not to seek vengeance on me, then I will treat you as if you were my own brother."

After the battle Helgi and Sigrunr were wed and took up residence at Sevafell, hoping to live a long life together.

Dagr journeyed to far off lands hoping to win a name for himself. Yet he never forgot the wrongs done to him. It was in his mind to break his vows and seek vengeance against Helgi.

CHAPTER 7
THE DEATH
OF
HELGI

Dagr made sacrifices and prayed to Odin for help avenging his kinsmen's deaths. Odin agreed that it was only right such vengeance be granted and appeared to Dagr to lend him his spear Gungnir to do the deed. Once thrown it was never known to miss its mark.

Dagr rode towards Fjotur Grove and saw Helgi standing there off in the distance. He continued riding towards him and yelled out as he approached, "Helgi, I have waited too long for this moment. You've dishonored my sister and slain my father and brothers. Now you shall be given the same gift you gave them."

Helgi looked up and walked forward to greet his brother-in-law who was yelling something to him in the distance. Unfortunately the wind was blowing away from him and he never heard the words Dagr spoke. He was startled to see Dagr's arm raised aloft. Then Dagr heaved Gungnir which flew through the air, its shaft glistening in the sunlight. Disbelief shown on Helgi's face as he yelled out, "You've dishonored yourself by breaking your vows." Then Gungnir drove straight through his heart and off into the distance, disappearing without landing, returning to Odin.

Dagr watched Helgi fall and then geed his horse and rode to Sevafells where he found Sigrunr and told her the news, "I have bad news for you. This morning I slew Helgi in Fjotur Grove. His followers showed fear when they were slain in battle. However, Helgi stood and confronted his death valiantly. For that I'm certain he will be among the honored in Valhalla, if not their leader."

Sigrunr did not answer with praise, as Dagr expected, "Have you forgotten you swore sacred oaths of allegiance to Helgi? Killing him brings you great dishonor, for you have broken those vows that you swore by the river Leiptr and on Unn's frozen altar. This bodes ill for you. Naught good will come of it. I curse you myself. May your ship be hindered even though there is a strong breeze and your sails are filled and bursting away from their masts. May your horse have trouble with its pace and not be able to out race the horse of your enemy. And may the sword you draw harm no one unless the flesh it cuts is yours. Be careful as you swing it over your head and around your shoulders, lest it loose the one from the other. I would have Helgi's death avenged. I wish you were transformed into a wolf and had to roam the fields eating the maggot-ridden carrion that lies there. And even that wouldn't be a fit punishment for you, since it wouldn't be severe enough. What's the weregild you're willing to pay for Helgi's death?"

Dagr was angered by her words, "I don't understand you speaking such madness to wish these fates upon your brother. The vengeance I sought was in your behalf, too. Don't forget those Helgi slew were also your relatives. Perhaps it's Odin causing this split between us?" He failed to mention Odin had blessed the killing by giving him his sword Gungnir to do the deed.

Sigrunr answered, "Don't blame this on Odin. He didn't kill Helgi. It's entirely your fault. What should I have cared about the killings already done? Has your killing my husband brought back our father or brothers? All you've done is make me a widow."

Dagr tried to placate his sister, "Since I've caused you this injury I'll offer you weregild for Helgi's death. I'll give you red-gold rings as well as the steads of Vandil and the land called Vigdale. Additionally, you may have half my Kingdom if you'll do away with your sorrow."

Sigrunr turned from him, responding, "How can I ever be happy again since you've slain my beloved? How can I live here at Sevafell when I know Helgi's memory will haunt me here? I'll never be happy again until Helgi rides back to me, which is something that will never happen."

She left Dagr, returned to the Hall and ordered a great funeral barrow be constructed and Helgi's body should be retrieved from the field where it lay, taken to it and prepared with highest honors.

In the meanwhile Helgi was making his way to Valhalla, where Odin himself met him at the door. There he was given command of the Einherjar. Among those serving him in Valhalla were Hunding, who was commanded to draw Helgi's footbath and light up the fire in his room. Helgi gave him further orders, "Make certain my dogs are safely bound. Stable the horses, and wash out where the pigs have lolled all day. After you've done all of that to my satisfaction then you may go to bed. If you work at these tasks and show you have a flair for them, then I'll show you warrior weapons and train you in their use, certainly a training you lacked on Midgardr."

Back in Sevafells Sigrunr had still not accepted Helgi's death and was sad with grief.

○   ○   ○   ○

One night a serving woman was walking near Helgi's burial cairn and saw a host of warriors on horseback riding towards it. Even though the group was large, silence accompanied them. They were as quiet as dead men. The serving woman fell to her knees and chanted as the sight passed by her, "I see wonderful bewitching things. Before me do dead men kick their heels and spur their horses on as they ride overhead? How can dead warriors head for home? Or, perhaps, it is Ragnarokr that has come and the end is near for all of us?"

The dead answered in unison, "You do not see wonderful bewitching things, for your eyes deceive you. Nor are we the ill doing of all things. Watch as we jab our spurs into our horses' sides and ride off, proving that dead warriors can head home."

The serving woman rushed to the Hall to find Sigrunr and reported what she had seen, "Helgi's cairn has been burst open and within I heard moans, though I dared not venture in to look."

Sigrunr jumped up and questioned the serving maid further, "What else did you see? What did you hear?"

The serving maid was trembling as she answered, "I saw nothing else since it was dark. However, I heard a voice from within saying his wounds still bled and he could not yet find peace. He said only a visit from his wife would help him find peace. Then his voice began chanting 'Sigrunr, Sigrunr,' over and over again."

Sigrunr, heedless of the hour, ran to the burial cairn and without a moment's hesitation entered. There she met Helgi who spoke to her as if he were still alive, "I'm happy you've come, as are Huginn and Muninn, Odin's ravens."

She saw Helgi's body sitting up with the funeral shroud hanging limply from him, soaked with his blood. Helgi's hair was covered with rime and an unnatural chill filled the room. She reached over and caressed his cheek with her hand, "Why do your wounds still bleed, even though you are lifeless? Why are you so cold to the touch?"

Helgi answered, "It has been impossible for me to find peace so long as you weep for my death. Your grief has been a torture to me, for every tear you have shed has been a drop of cold blood I have bled."

Sigrunr vowed to weep no more so that he might find some comfort, "I didn't realize I was making you suffer. However, henceforth you'll have nothing further to worry about on that score. Is there anything else I can do for you?"

Helgi answered, "No. Now I must ride back over Bifrost and return to Valhalla."

Sigrunr piled together some hay on a platform within the cairn and made a comfortable bed for herself. "I'm tired and would lie here with you Helgi, my husband, kinsman of the Ylfings, as we were wont to lie while you were still alive. Hold me in your arms so that I may remember your touch."

Helgi gladly did as he was asked, "Truly there is nothing in this world that can't be granted when it is possible for a dead man to still lie with his wife and think lustful thoughts about her."

Sigrunr shifted her position slightly while Helgi continued to speak, "I fear I can't remain here long. Soon I must leave you among the living. There's only one way we two can be together again and share our love as we are wont to do even now."

However, he didn't mention the solution to their problems. Instead he held her closer to him, hoping the warmth from her body might warm and quicken his. Then he spoke for a final time, "I must prepare to leave since I must be in Valhalla before Salgofnir the cock crows to awaken the Einherjar. I must be there to drill them in their practice so they'll be fit and ready when the final battle comes."

Helgi left before dawn and never again returned to his funeral barrow. Sigrunr kept her promise and mourned for him no more. The next night she visited the cairn again with her serving maid hoping to find Helgi there once more. But Helgi didn't return.

The serving maid spoke to Sigrunr, "Don't wait here for the dead, nor stay here alone at night. The dead are more to be feared in the dark than by the light of day. If you must come here by yourself do so while Sol guides Arvakr and Alsvin across the sky."

However, it was not long before Sigrunr went to Asgardr to join her husband. The grief and sorrow of being apart from him was more than she could bear and her heart burst asunder from the grief she felt. Once more she put on the garb of a Valkyrie and joined her husband. But it was spoken of by many that both lovers were reborn and their story repeated. Helgi Hundingsbane came to life again as Helgi Haddingjaskati, while Sigrunr lived once more as the Valkyrie Kara, the daughter of that great King Halfdan.

CHAPTER 8
THE DEATH
OF
SINFJOTLI

Shortly after the defeat of Hoddbrodr and Granmar, Sinfjotli and the company of men who chose to follow him, separated from Helgi and decided to return to Borghildr's land in Denmark, the land Sigmundr had settled in after marrying Borghildr. On their return journey Sinfjotli and his warriors engaged in further battles and won much wealth and acclaim for themselves. They arrived home just before winter, laden down with gold and other booty, their fame having preceded them. The tales of their glorious victories were well known throughout the countryside and they were welcomed home as heroes. Once in Hunland they rested for a while, healing their wounds.

However, the peaceful life was not for Sinfjotli. He soon became restless and desired the warrior's life once more. He gathered together another army and went about conquering new lands. While in one of the lands bordering Hunland he caught sight of a beautiful woman, whom he found fairer than any other he had ever seen. His heart went out to her and he desired above all things to have her as his wife. He asked around to find out more about her. But what he found out upset him greatly. She was already betrothed, as it turned out, to his stepmother Borghildr's brother.

Sinfjotli sought out his stepuncle whom he found lazing about in the courtyard of his Hall, located near Sigmundr and Borghildr's Hall. He tried to persuade his stepuncle to give up the maiden so instead he could marry her, "What's she to you? She has no wealth to speak of. There is no advantage to your marrying her."

Sinfjotli's stepuncle had had no particular interest in the marriage that had been arranged for him until he realized his famous stepnephew was smitten with her. There was nothing he liked better than bringing some misery to the charmed life Sinfjotli apparently lead.

As the two discussed the matter their words became more heated until finally blows were exchanged. Sinfjotli was the greater warrior and slew his kinsman.

Sinfjotli went to his father and confessed what he had done. Sigmundr answered, "I've already heard about the incident from witnesses. All of their testimony is agree it was a fair fight. They even agree Borghildr's brother cast the first blow. Neither you nor the young lady would be dishonored if you asked for her hand in marriage."

At that moment Borghildr entered the room greatly distressed, having just learned about her brother's death at the hands of her stepson. Then Sigmundr told her Sinfjotli wanted to marry her brother's betrothed. Borghildr and Sigmundr began arguing. She saw things differently than he did, "What Sinfjotli has done dishonors your name. It would be best if he left this land at once and never set foot here again."

Sinfjotli looked at his father for instructions, ready to obey him if that was his command. Sigmundr responded, "Borghildr, I cannot order my son away when he has done nothing wrong. Although I've never believed in offering weregild for an honorable death, in this instance I think it is right so that some peace may be bought for this family. It's difficult to justify the death of a brother to his sister. Accept the weregild Sinfjotli offers you so this matter can be put out of our minds."

Sinfjotli spoke to his stepmother, "I've recently returned from battles bringing great coffers of gold home with me. I offer all of this wealth to you as payment for your brother's death."

Borghildr saw it was hopeless to pursue the matter, so she accepted the weregild. However, dark thoughts grew in her mind. She intended to have vengeance. "I'll accept the weregild if you will let me arrange a large burial feast for my brother. It is my wish that all of the greatest warriors in the land attend and pay homage to his memory. And it is my request Sinfjotli sit at my side on the dais and speak to everyone there of the glorious deeds my brother was known for. If this is done, then I will feel my brother's death has been paid for."

Sinfjotli agreed in order to keep peace in the family. However, it would be a hard speech. Not because he didn't want to praise his stepuncle, but because his stepuncle had never gone to war and there were no glorious deeds to speak of, unless wrestling a maiden in the straw could be talked about as a great battle. And he had lost those engagements more often than he had won.

Finally Sinfjotli wrote his speech substituting the names of cities and far-off lands in place of the serving maids his stepuncle had conquered. And in this manner he was able to speak the truth in his funeral speech.

Borghildr asked Sigmundr for his help with the funeral feast, since Sigmundr had attended a great many that he had been responsible for. She wanted her brother's to be the best ever given and talked about long after the dirt had settled on his funeral barrow.

○ ○ ○ ○

All the arrangements had been made and soon the guests began arriving and were put up at the Hall. Unfortunately so many had been invited they had to share two and sometimes three to a room, which made for crowded conditions considering the armor and great swords they wore. Tempers were short.

On the first night of the feast there was much revelry and praise for the memory of Borghildr's brother. Although many could be heard asking whom he was and what exactly had he done, since they had never heard of any of the places Sinfjotli had mentioned in his speech. However, the mead flowed copiously and they were ready to toast his memory over and over again, summoning serving maids to fill their tankards with each toast.

Borghildr carried drinks to everyone in the Hall, accepting the condolences of the warriors as she handed them tankard after tankard of mead. As the evening wore on and more and more tankards had been drunk the thoughts expressed about her brother became more heartfelt and sentimental until many of the warriors were crying at their tables as they remembered riding into battle with Borghildr's brother at their side bravely hewing and hacking at bodies as they cut their way through enemy lines.

The tales of single combat were amazing. One warrior insisted he and Borghildr's brother had both slain one hundred berserkrs in a battle. He had slain sixty-five while Borghildr's brother had slain thirty-five. He motioned at a skald with his sword, indicating he wanted the deed recorded in the verses the skald had been ordered to keep of the valiant deeds done by Borghildr's brother, "And make certain you credit me with my part. Many are the deeds I've done which have ended up in verses about Volsungr."

And so the evening progressed with grand braggadocio as plentiful as the mead.

Borghildr was sitting by Sigmundr and noticed Sinfjotli had not been drinking to the memory of his stepuncle. She fetched a special horn she had had made, ornately covered with scenes of her brother's fake warlike deeds. Handing it to Sinfjotli she encouraged him to drink a toast to honor her brother, "Here, Sinfjotli, drink to the memory of your stepuncle. That was a fine speech you gave about him, although I'm not too certain about the geography of his deeds. Yet the names did seem familiar." She handed him the cup and smiled, though to some it looked more like a grimace.

Sinfjotli held the cup and looked at the drink. It seemed as if scum was floating on the top. "I can't drink this. It seems muddied, and it's my belief that it's charmed, or worse."

Sigmundr looked on and saw the insult Sinfjotli had given to his wife's honor. He took the drink from his son's hands. "Let me see." He inspected the drink. "The drink looks fine to me. In fact, if you don't mind." He then drank it down in one gulp.

Borghildr gasped and ran to his side. Then she remembered Sigmundr was immune to poison. It could be spread all over him, or put into his drink, without effect. Unfortunately everyone else also forgot this fact. Sinfjotli was only partially blessed. He could be covered with poison without any effect. However, drinking a draught of it was just as deadly for him as for anyone else.

Borghildr looked at Sinfjotli and insulted him, "Are you so young that others must drink your mead for you?" She handed him another cup of mead. It too looked suspicious.

Sinfjotli again looked at the mead and spoke, "Deceit and trickery swims in this drink."

Sigmundr took the cup and once more drank it down with one gulp, with no apparent ill effects.

For the third time Borghildr offered Sinfjotli a drink, "Do you have the heart of a Volsungr, or of a chicken? Perhaps Sigmundr isn't your father after all? Maybe the twisted ugly Siggeir begat you upon a serving wench. That's your true heritage."

Sinfjotli refused to fall for her taunts. He took the drink and stared at it, "There is poison in this drink. I'll not imbibe from this cup."

Now Sigmundr had been drinking all evening, and in a short space of time he had downed two large tankards full of mead. The effect of all this was beginning to show. He wiped his forearm across his lips and spake slurred words that Sinfjotli misinterpreted with disastrous results, "If the cup contains poison then strain it through your beard. Are you born a Volsungr, and my son, or not?" Sigmundr had meant that Sinfjotli should pretend to drink the drink, and instead to pour it into his beard.

Sinfjotli hoisted the cup, looked at his father for the last time, and drank the mead quickly. So quickly much of the drink slopped over his mouth and fell through his beard. But he drank enough for Borghildr's deadly purpose. Sinfjotli immediately fell to the ground, dead, poisoned.

Sigmundr was dumfounded, speechless with grief, realizing his son had been doing his bidding in drinking the mead. His senses cleared immediately. He went over to his son's body, picked it up and carried it from the Hall. He walked through the wood and down to the riverbank until he came to a long and narrow firth. There a ferryman was waiting to take passengers across the river. The one-eyed man spoke to Sigmundr, "Do you wish to cross the river? If so, I can only take one of you at a time since my boat is so small."

Sigmundr nodded, still too overcome to speak. He reverently placed his sons' body on the boat. The ferryman shoved off westward across the river. Upon reaching the center of the river the ferry vanished from Sigmundr's sight. For in truth the ferryman had been Odin gathering up another warrior for Valhalla. Sinfjotli was now reunited with his brother Helgi.

Sigmundr returned to the Hall and ordered all his belongings be packed. That same evening he and his army departed southwards for Frankland, one of his other Kingdoms. He never saw Borghildr again. She died soon after the feast, some say by suspicious means.

Sigmundr was well thought of by his subjects, although deeds of war had not crossed his path in many a year. His glory had been great, his victories many, but now it was time for a new hero.

CHAPTER 9
THE DEATH OF SIGMUNDR BREAKING OF GRAMR

Hjordis was the daughter of a powerful King named Eylimi. She was fair and beautiful, and thought by many to be one of the most intelligent women in the world. She was gifted in the arts as well as in healing. News of her pleasing attributes traveled throughout many lands resulting in interest for her hand in marriage from two powerful Kings.

King Sigmundr was interested in her after hearing reports of her great beauty and gifts. He desired her to be his wife since Borghildr was now dead and he was free to marry.

King Lyngvi, the son of King Hunding, heard of Hjordis' grace and beauty and wouldn't be put off from wooing her at the same time as Sigmundr. He had been at the battle of Frekastein and fought against King Helgi, barely escaping with his life.

Eylimi was quite shrewd and knew his daughter was more valuable if there were two Kings vying for her. With this in mind he invited both Lyngvi and Sigmundr to visit at the same time to make their cases why each thought they would make the better match. Eylimi didn't care which one would be the better husband; he was interested in which marriage would bring the most benefit to him. Messengers were sent back and forth from Eylimi to Sigmundr and Lyngvi.

First it was arranged that Sigmundr would visit Hjordis to see whether or not they were agreeable to each other. Sigmundr made extensive preparations for the journey and now finally satisfied the preparations were perfect, started on his way accompanied by a large retinue.

Eylimi made certain Lyngvi knew Sigmundr had been invited to meet with Hjordis, and was already on his way. He did not extend an immediate invitation to Lyngvi. He wanted Lyngvi to ask for the honor.

Eylimi's plan worked. Lyngvi looked forward to winning Hjordis away from Sigmundr, his enemy's father. His correspondence with Hjordis was just as extensive as Sigmundr's. After he learned Sigmundr was going to visit Hjordis he also asked for permission to visit pointing out the advantages of marrying Hjordis to him, "I am every bit as powerful as Sigmundr. But, I have the advantage of youth. I am younger and more potent. I can give your daughter sons and you grandsons." There was no proof he was more likely to give Eylimi grandsons or that he was more potent than Sigmundr, but the fact of mentioning such a thing pleased Lyngvi. He sent Lyngvi the invitation he was always going to send him anyway.

Within the week Eylimi's messengers traveled on ahead and reported details of the two King's progress.

Lyngvi was travelling with a small entourage and making very quick time. Eylimi was pleased. Lyngvi did not appear to be a threat, though it was still an army

Things were much different with Sigmundr. Messengers reported a large army was accompanying Sigmundr. These reports worried Eylimi so he sent a messenger to Sigmundr to gain his assurances his intentions were peaceful. After a few more exchanges between the two Eylimi was reassured and gave orders for a huge feast to be prepared to honor and welcome King Sigmundr and King Lyngvi.

Once Sigmundr reached Eylimi's realm he found waystations and fairs had been set up along his route so his journey would be as interesting and as comfortable as possible. He thought he was being accorded special honors for the visit. But Lyngvi was also given the same treatment.

o   o   o   o

Sigmundr and Lyngvi arrived within hours of each other and were put up on opposite sides of the Hall. Each was scheduled for a first meeting with Hjordis at different times that afternoon, before the feast. Eylimi hoped his daughter would be able to make a choice before the feast so that one of the Kings would leave and make things easier for him. He went to Hjordis to discuss the matter with her.

"I hear Sigmundr is to meet with you first?" She nodded yes and Eylimi continued, "I feel uneasy having such great warriors here, especially since both have brought their armies with them, and one of them will be disappointed before the evening is over."

Hjordis interrupted him, "It might be they both will be disappointed. I may not fancy either one of them."

This thought had never occurred to Eylimi. Now he had more to worry about, "I know you have many suitors to choose from and have always vowed the choice of whom you marry would be yours. However, I want you to make the decision tonight. Hopefully, it'll be either Sigmundr or Lyngvi. You have good judgement so I'm going to leave the matter entirely up to you." Actually Eylimi wanted nothing to do with the decision and was praying the rejected suitor wouldn't be too mad, or blame him. With luck he might get through the evening without a major war taking place in his dining Hall. Or, on the other hand, he might not even have a Hall by the morning. These thoughts troubled him greatly.

Hjordis answered, "I've been thinking on the matter and can agree to narrow down my choice between these two Kings. The songs sung about them have impressed me. I've seen them both from my window and can tell you now that I am leaning towards one over the other, and after my meetings this afternoon I'll be able to make the announcement tonight at dinner."

The thought of a public rejection of one of the suitors troubled Eylimi, but he could not persuade his daughter otherwise. He tried to change her mind but had to leave their meeting content with the fact that by tomorrow morning everything would be arranged, one way or the other. He thought once more that if he had had sons it would have been a lot easier.

At the feast that night Hjordis motioned for silence and stood up to speak. Seated on either side of her were Lyngvi and Sigmundr. "I've always vowed to follow my own counsel in matters concerning my life. As such, the decision tonight is mine and mine alone. This decision has been very difficult. However, it has always been my intention to marry the King with the greatest fame attendant on his name. And with that consideration my decision has been narrowed down to one, and he can be none other than Sigmundr. Many of you may find this surprising since Sigmundr is considerably older than I am. However, I'm convinced we will be happy together."

She sat down. Lyngvi left the table and signaled for all his men to follow after him. The Hall emptied rapidly.

The marriage ceremony was held that night, after which it was consummated. The wedding feast and attendant celebrations continued for several days, each day better than the day before. Finally it came to an end and Sigmundr departed for Hunland with Hjordis, having decided to live there now that Borghildr was dead. The couple extended an invitation to Eylimi to return with them and stay for a while, which he agreed to do.

o   o   o   o

All the while Lyngvi had been brooding on the insult cast on him by Hjordis. Now more than ever he wanted her as his wife, so that he might tame her tongue. The only way to bring this about was to slay Sigmundr and Eylimi. Thus he would gain rule over the Kingdom of the Volsungrs as well as Eylimi's lands, as well as take his enemy's beautiful wife as his own, and rue her, too.

Lyngvi led his army to Hunland and stationed them on a field near Sigmundr's Hall. He sent word to Sigmundr that he had led his army in the open and wished an honorable fight, providing Sigmundr and Eylimi weren't too cowardly for such an engagement. Sigmundr and Eylimi dispatched messengers throughout their lands so their armies would reassemble. Within a week's time they led them to the field and stood ready, opposite Lyngvi.

Just before the battle began Hjordis and her bondmaid took their valuables, including the wealth of the Volsungrs, into the forest with them and hid, awaiting the outcome of the fight.

Both Sigmundr and Eylimi were amazed at the size of Lyngvi's army. It was much larger than their combined forces. However, size is not often a determining factor if the warriors are skilled and positioned wisely. Sigmundr's army was much better trained and fought more fiercely since they were led by the better King.

Sigmundr urged his men on, riding at the forefront of the attack. His arm flailed about with Gramr in it, hewing a wide path through Lyngvi's men. Gramr cut through the strongest shields and byrnies, and separated many heads from their bodies.

As the battle progressed it was hard to tell who was winning or losing, although it appeared Sigmundr's forces now held a slight advantage. The arrows and spears rained down on both sides, with each side suffering heavy losses. However, Sigmundr's spæwights protected him well and deflected any arrows and spears heading his way. Sigmundr met with such success that day that his arms were red up to his shoulders with the blood of his enemies.

The battle raged throughout the afternoon. During the evening a one-eyed figure wearing a blue mantle and slouched hat came striding onto the battlefield, oblivious to the fighting going on around him. All fighting ceased. The silence was sudden and eerie. The stranger walked up to Sigmundr and raised his spear, holding it out horizontally with both hands. Sigmundr held Gramr over his head and smote down on the spear shaft with all his might. The shaft did not break, nor was it marred in any way. However, Gramr burst into two pieces. The stranger hurled his spear towards Sigmundr's army. Everyone now realized the stranger was Odin and the spear he had thrown was Gungnir, a spear that never missed its mark once hurled. Sigmundr's spæwights left him.

The battle now turned against Sigmundr and Eylimi in favor of Lyngvi who would be proclaimed the victor before darkness was upon them. It now seemed Lyngvi's men could not miss with their arrows. They fought with renewed strength, while Sigmundr and Eylimi's men fought as fatigued warriors barely able to hold their shields in front of them as they staggered about trying to protect themselves. However, Sigmundr fought with renewed courage and tried to lead his men to victory. But his losses were mounting and his army growing smaller and smaller. It came to pass that Sigmundr and Eylimi died honorable deaths leading their armies. The battlefield was littered with the dead. It had been a costly battle. Now all the known Volsungrs were dead save for Hjordis who was hiding in the woods.

CHAPTER 10
THE BIRTH OF SIGURDR SIGMUNDRSON

Lyngvi rode from the battlefield to Sigmundr's Hall intending to take Hjordis as his wife and claim the lands and wealth of the Volsungrs as his own. However, nothing and no one awaited him at the Hall. He searched everywhere but could find neither the wealth of the Volsungrs nor Hjordis. In his mind the wealth would have been sufficient. Therefore, he decided to secure what he did have. He journeyed throughout the land setting up representatives to take up positions of power so he could consolidate his grip on the Kingdom. He accomplished this within a few days and could walk throughout the land with confidence thinking he had killed all the Volsungrs and had nothing to fear of revenge since there were no kinsmen left to do the deed.

The evening after the battle Hjordis ventured from the woods to the battlefield. She searched among the injured and slain for Sigmundr and found him wounded and dying, "Is there anything I can do for you to ease your pain and make your suffering less?"

He answered, "There are many men who have lived even though all thought of their doing so had been given up by others. But all hope and luck has left me by the will of Odin. My body will not work against such a power as his. Odin himself has split Gramr in two and commanded I never draw that wonderful sword again. I've only fought while he desired me to do so and victory was always mine. Now he is against me, a battle that I can't fight. I must die."

Hjordis tried to persuade him he should live, that great deeds were yet before him, "Who will avenge your kinsmen's deaths if you die?"

Sigmundr slumped forward a little, but raised himself up again, "The vengeance of which you speak will have to come from another. You are presently with child. When he is born name him Sigurdr Sigmundrson. Raise him to be a strong warrior and teach him the legends of the kin of the Volsungrs. When he has grown to manhood he will be the greatest hero of all. Take my sword Gramr and keep it as his heritage, my gift to him. When it's time, give it to him so that he might work wondrous deeds with it, deeds that will be mightier than the father's ever were. His name will be remembered as long as the world shall endure. Let this be enough fulfillment for my life." Sigmundr grabbed at his side and lurched forward. Blood was running from the corner of his mouth. He continued, his voice softening, "Teach him to be brave, yet kind. Now I'm tired and ill of my wounds and must rest. My journey to Valhalla has started. Don't weep for me for soon I'll be eating and fighting with the best warriors that have ever been. And many of them shall be my own kin. Odin himself will welcome me at the gates of Valhalla."

Hjordis sat with Sigmundr's body throughout the night. At dawn, as the sun flooded the morning sky in orange and red Sigmundr died. Hjordis, weeping, held Sigmundr's now lifeless body in her arms. But her grief was interrupted by the approach of her handmaiden, "Mistress, there are warriors in the distance. They've landed in huge warships and now approach on horseback through the woods onto the battlefield."

Hjordis grabbed her servant's hand and pulled her behind her running into the woods, "Quick let's change garments. Henceforth you'll be Sigmundr's wife, overcome with grief, and I'll be your serving maid. If asked I'll name you as Hjordis, daughter of Eylimi, and wife of the noble Sigmundr. We must do this in order to protect my and Sigmundr's unborn child."

The Vikings looked out over the battlefield and beheld the carnage before them. Already ravens and beasts of the forest were feasting on the flesh of the dead heroes. One of the men pointed out to his leader the figures of two women on the other side of the field fleeing into the woods. Alfr, their leader, son of Hjalprekr, King of Thjod, spoke, "Send two men after them and bring them to me so we might learn the story of the brave heroes who have fallen in this battle."

Shortly thereafter the two women were brought to him, "Gentlewomen, we mean you no harm and will honor you with the respect due you. Tell us what has happened here? Who was the leader of this army that has fallen?"

Hjordis, dressed as the serving maid, answered for both of them. She told of the battle and the deaths of King Eylimi and King Sigmundr, and the many other men who had died bravely in battle for his cause. She ended scornfully with, "Their bane was brought about by Lyngvi who has dishonorably won, or many would say taken, their Kingdoms."

Alfr was visibly moved by the story and filled with admiration for Sigmundr. He ordered Sigmundr and Eylimi's bodies be found and given the burial befitting heroes and Kings. He continued questioning the two women, "Where is the wealth of the Volsungrs? We'll protect it for his son who has yet to be born, since you tell me the Queen is with child. It would be an evil thing indeed if Lyngvi should also gain the wealth of the Volsungrs."

The serving maid answered, "We'll take you where it has been buried."

King Alfr, along with several of his men, followed the two women into the forest. There his men dug up the gold and jewels. They were amazed at how much there was. Never had they before beheld such wealth piled all in one place. Carts were brought from the ship so the treasure could be transported easily. It took the better part of the day for this to be done.

After the wealth was safely stored aboard ship, Alfr offered them his protection, which they gratefully accepted. They accompanied him to the ship and soon they set sail for Hjalprekr's Kingdom.

o   o   o   o

Later that day Hjordis and her serving maid were sitting on deck near the quarterdeck, their identities still changed. Alfr sat at the tiller of the ship and spoke with them. Invariably their conversation led back to Sigmundr and how great he had been. Over the next few days Alfr had many conversations with them and grew to respect their counsel. What puzzled him though, was why he seemed to like the serving maid better than the Queen.

The trip to Thjod was uneventful. At the Hall Hjordis and her serving maid were given a suite of rooms and treated with honor and respect.

o   o   o   o

One morning, shortly after their arrival, Alfr was talking with his mother. She asked him about the two women, "How come when I look at them I see the fairest and most comely of the two has the fewer rings and is not dressed as well? How come when they speak the Queen seems coarse and frequently unintelligible? What do you know of these women? She whom we should think the least of is certainly the nobler of the two."

Alfr responded, nodding his head, "I've also doubted myself and thought her movements and actions are not those of a serving maid. When I first beheld them walking towards me from a distance I prepared to address the one who was on the left since her bearing was so noble. However, when she came closer I could see she was dressed as the serving maid. She certainly had the mien of a Queen, if not the clothing of such."

His mother returned to her needlework, but before doing so said, "You should look into the matter further."

Alfr turned to leave. "I'll test them to see whether or not they've been tricking me."

That evening after dinner, Alfr sought out the two women's company to talk with them. He spoke first to the serving maid thinking it was Hjordis, "What method do you use to tell the time when it is night or early morning if there are no stars to help you?"

She answered, "When I was younger I had a habit of drinking milk while I fed the cows at a certain time each night and in the morning. Now I become thirsty at those same times and can reckon the hour by that method."

Alfr laughed, "Truly what odd activities for the daughter of a King." He turned to Hjordis in the garb of the serving maid, "And what of you? Do you slop the pigs at a certain hour, and become hungry at that time now because of that?"

Hjordis answered differently. "When I was young my father gave me a gift of a ring. The band was gold, but the stone in it was of such a nature that it grew cold at dawn as the sun was rising and warm in the evening as the sun was setting. By such means was I able to tell the time."

Alfr was surprised, "How can it be that the father of a serving maid would have such a gift to give to his daughter? I think you've hidden the truth from me long enough. Haven't my actions proven I intend no harm to you or your child? I offer you hospitality and friendship. Will you continue to reward my gifts with lies?"

Hjordis now answered, "You've guessed correctly. I'm the Queen, Sigmundr's wife and Eylimi's daughter. I ordered my serving maid to wear my clothes. However, now we'll change and have no more tricks with you. Understand that I did it only for protection and to protect the life of my unborn son. When we first met I didn't know whether you would be a friend or foe of my husband's. If a friend, then you would understand and forgive my actions later; if a foe, then you would have cut the child from me before its time."

Alfr took her hand, "It's true you couldn't have known whether or not I would do you wrong. But now I wish to do things very right for you. I would that you be my wife. Your son will be born and given the honor due the son of a great King. I'll raise him as my own and treat him with all respect. When he has become of age his wealth will be returned to him, hopefully greatly increased, and I'll supply him with an army so he can regain his Kingdom. After you have borne me a child of my own I'll give you a great marriage dowry."

Alfr's mother and father gave their blessings to the wedding. A great feast was held and there was much rejoicing. Some months later Hjordis gave birth to Sigurdr Sigmundrson. Alfr was true to his word. At the natal feast he sprinkled the child with water and named him, "At this feast I sprinkle water on a great warrior who will follow in his father's footsteps. I name him Sigurdr Sigmundrson in honor of Sigmundr. Though he is my step-son I will raise him as truly as if he were my own blood, and tell him of his father's great deeds that he will grow up honoring the memory of Sigmundr. He will be educated in the ways of the warrior and trained in all warrior skills. When the time comes I will provide him with ships and an army and help him regain his Kingdom and become a King in his own right."

At the feast Sigurdr was presented to Hjalprekr. He took the baby in his arms and stared into its eyes. Sigurdr held the King's gaze. "This child will be a great warrior. There are few who will ever achieve his greatness, nor will many be able to hold his gaze."

o o o o

Sigurdr's youth was spent learning many skills, including music and good manners. He learned the ways of fairness and goodness from Hjalprekr's household. Sigurdr was ambitious, brave and had grown to be a tall, strong warrior. Hjordis had told him about the Volsungrs and that it would one day be his duty to avenge their deaths and regain the Kingdom that was rightfully his.

Sigurdr was also raised by a foster-father whose name was Regin. Regin was beardless and short in stature, pale, wan and exceedingly old. He had taken up residence in the Kingdom so long ago that none now living could remember a time when he hadn't been there amongst them. It seemed he had always been there.

Regin was the most renowned smith in the land and taught Sigurdr all he knew of the art. However, this was not the limit of his knowledge. He taught him the skills of rune cutting and how to read them, as well as how to play Hnefetafl, and speak many languages, things which Sigurdr eventually surpassed his teacher in ability. But warrior skills were the most important lessons Sigurdr learned from Regin.

Regin had become Sigurdr's foster-father not entirely unselfishly. He had often been asked to be foster-father to many great men's sons, but had always refused. At Sigurdr's birth he had cast his rune stones and what he read augured well. He knew Sigurdr was the warrior who would be able to do the deed that he had been seeking someone to do ever since he first arrived in this land. You see, Regin was much more than he seemed.

o o o o

One day Sigurdr and Regin sat talking, "Sigurdr, are you aware Alfr holds a great deal of your gold in his treasure chamber? Do you really trust that when you become of age he will return it to you peacefully?"

Sigurdr answered, "Alfr has always treated me well and honored my mother. I'm sure when the time comes and I ask for my inheritance he'll give it to me freely and in good faith. Right now it is best it remain in his care. I've not the force behind me to protect it from those who might steal it."

And on yet another day Regin again spoke to Sigurdr about his trust in Alfr, "You're treated as if you were a stable squire by those in the Hall. You run at his will and fetch for him as a common servant does."

Sigurdr answered, "That's not true. I do Alfr's bidding out of friendliness and love for him. I'm his sworn liegeman until the day he dies. What I want to do for myself, I do. And whatever I want Alfr would give me without hesitation. I've merely to ask for it."

Regin prompted him, "If such is the case then it's about time you asked for a horse. How can you be a great warrior if you walk to the battles? They'll be over with before you arrive on the field."

That evening Sigurdr spoke to Alfr on the matter, "Father, I feel I have need of my own horse so he and I can get to know each other and eventually ride as one to battles."

Alfr thought this was an excellent idea, "Go to Gripir the stud-keeper, and tell him you are to be allowed to choose any horse, even my own, amongst those in the royal stables. Also, choose from amongst all I own whatever else you think you'll need. You are as my son, and as such you may have whatever I have that you desire."

The next day Sigurdr went to Gripir so he might make his choice. Gripir gave him instructions on where the horses were, "They're in the high meadow grazing now, since the grass is longest there. Go through the woods and continue up the path until you reach it. Here's rope and some fine oats so you might lure the horse of your choice to you and capture it. It is always best that a horse know whom his master is from the beginning."

Sigurdr began walking through the woods. There he came upon a one-eyed old man, wearing a blue cloak and broad-brimmed hat pulled low over his face to conceal his missing eye, "Where are you going, lad? It's often dangerous walking through the woods alone."

Sigurdr was startled by the appearance of the old man. He had been looking straight ahead and could have sworn that moments before no one had been in front of him. It must have been a trick of the sun shining through the trees. "My father has given my permission to choose a horse from amongst his herd. I'm on my way to the high meadow to do so and have been thinking on the matter while I was walking. That's why I jumped when you came upon me."

The old man spoke, "I know a bit about horses. Would you like me to help you choose the best one?"

Sigurdr accepted the offer. They walked further until eventually they reached the high meadow.

"First," said the old man, "we must drive them over the meadow down into that far valley. There's a swift-moving river called Busiltjorn that cuts through the valley. We'll select the horse who is brave and strong enough to cross that river."

Sigurdr was thankful for the old man's advice. They both ran at the horses to stampede them down the side of the mountain into the river. Many of the horses turned, shying away from the river and running along it. Some ran into the river, though fearful of drowning returned to shore. Only one horse unhesitatingly ran into the river, crossed it and made it to the far shore. And that was the horse Sigurdr chose to be his own. It was a huge grey stallion, muscular, strong and only a couple of years old. He was quite wild since no one had ever dared to even try to ride him.

Sigurdr stared across the river at the horse and then called to him. "Grani, for that shall be your name, come over to this side once more. Surely you are the greatest horse there is."

The old man commented as the horse swam back across the river and stood nuzzling Sigurdr, "This horse was born of Sleipnir's kin. Guard and feed him well and he'll grow to be the best of all horses. Never will he tire in battle or lack the courage to carry you charging at your enemies, no matter how heavy and fast the spears and arrows fly. His legs are good and strong. He'll be a jumper and unafraid of fire, which may come in handy for you some day." The stranger then vanished before Sigurdr's disbelieving eyes.

Sigurdr patted the horse on the forehead and neck to calm him. Then he reached round, grabbed Grani's mane and swung himself lightly onto the horse's back. Grani jostled back and forth a bit but did not try to buck the young warrior off. They rode back to Regin's smith and Sigurdr showed off his new horse.

Regin seemed impressed, "That's certainly a fine horse. However, I've been thinking about the wealth of the Volsungrs and the treasure that is held in trust for you. Would it not be a great thing if you were to more than double it with a brave act? And in the process you'd win fame and honor, all before you have come into your inheritance."

Sigurdr was interested, "It would certainly prove to all my blood is that of a true Volsungr. Where might I find such a treasure? No one is giving them away that I'm aware of."

Regin moved over to a chair, sat down, and answered, "There's one treasure greater than all the others. The Treasure of the Volsungrs is a mere pittance compared to it. I speak of Fafnir's Hoard."

Sigurdr also took a seat, "Where might I find this treasure? I've heard the name, but can't place where."

Regin smiled, glad Sigurdr was interested. Maybe this was the warrior he had been waiting for. "A short distance from here is a place called Gnitaheidr where the miser Fafnir, in the form of a dragon, lies over his Hoard, guarding it. Your eyes will be bedazzled to see such a gleaming treasure all in one place." Regin swallowed for his mouth had begun watering at the thought of all that gold, while his hands were twitching opening and closing trying to grasp it, but instead holding nothing firmer than air.

Regin continued, "This Hoard is so rich even the most miserly King would be more than satisfied with it. Win it and the glory of the Hoard will follow you the rest of your days. A young warrior as strong as you, and riding such a goodly steed, should have no difficulty with the task."

Sigurdr thought for a moment and then responded, "If it's as you say then many a fine young warrior would have already gained the treasure. Even though I'm young I can see what you tell me is not entirely true. Now I seem to remember about Fafnir. He's large and totally evil. His aspect and manner is most fearsome. He'll not welcome me, nor will he relinquish his treasure lightly. In order to gain the hoard I'll have to slay him. A poison-spitting worm such as he is beyond my ability."

Regin had been only half listening, dreaming instead of what he would do with the gold once it was won. However, he did hear the last sentence, "Would that you would believe the tall tales of others? I tell you I know this Fafnir and know that everything about him has been exaggerated. His size is not nearly so great, and his poison not nearly so deadly. It has always been said the Volsungr's can handle a little poison. Fafnir is a mere lingworm, a small worm who likes to crawl about in the heather eating his fill."

"But what is his fill? Is it those tilling the field? I don't think it would do me any good to fight Fafnir and lose my life at such a young age." Sigurdr turned to leave.

Regin rushed over to Sigurdr and put out his hand to stop him. "Wait. Let me tell you Fafnir's story, and then you can judge whether or not you want to become part of its legend. Perhaps, all you're good for is listening to tales. The other Volsungrs have caused great legends to spring up around their memory. Maybe the stories of Sigmundr's battles will be the last ones told about the Volsungrs?"

Sigurdr answered, "At the moment I'm not the equal of Sigmundr, Sinfjotli, Helgi, Volsungr, Rerir, or Sigi. But their blood flows through my veins and I'll prove myself, but only after I'm ready, which is the mark of a good warrior. Never have I given anyone a case to lay the name of coward to me. Why are you so interested that I fight Fafnir and win his Hoard of gold?"

Regin sat back down in the chair. "Listen and I'll tell you the story of Fafnir and his kin. Though not about heroes and warriors, as are the tales of the Volsungrs, it may prove interesting to you."

Sigurdr sat down to listen.

CHAPTER 11
REGIN'S STORY
REFORGING OF
GRAMR

My father was Hreidmar who was a successful farmer and had a great deal of wealth, though many said the wealth was gained not by the toil of the field, but by magical arts. He had two daughters named Lyngheidr and Lofnheidr, as well as three sons, Fafnir, the eldest, Otr, and then me, Regin, the youngest.

My brothers became good at whatever they attempted. Fafnir was the strongest of us and used his strength in a greedy manner to gain whatever he wanted. Ever since we were young children he claimed the greater portion of everything for himself. He chose first at mealtime and kept the best for himself. He always took the legs when we had chicken. My other brother, Otr, was different. He loved to share with others. He was a great hunter and always provided us with enough food for our meals. He particularly liked to fish. He fished, not in the usual manner, with bait, rod and tackle, but in the form of an otter. For he, like my brother Fafnir, was a shapechanger. At first he'd change into an otter only occasionally. However, as he got older he went about in the form more and more until he remained in that shape almost exclusively. It just felt more comfortable to him. He'd return home with the fish he'd caught, give most of the catch to my father to cook, and take his share over by the hearth and lay on the floor eating alone. Then drowsy from the meal, he'd sleep until the next morning when he would arise and go fishing again. This was the life he settled on and loved the best.

I was the least skilled of Hreidmar's sons. My talent lay in building things, and working with metal. While still young I built a great Hall for our family. It was constructed using a heavy framework of iron. This was so the gold and jewels used throughout the Hall wouldn't weigh it down. The Hall was magnificent and shown for miles around. I also built all our furniture, and helped out around the house. I always thought my contribution to the family had been greater than my brothers'. Unfortunately, Hreidmar didn't think so.

But to continue the story...Because it was such a valuable house, with valuable things inside, Fafnir was stationed in front to guard it. He wore a Helmet of Terror on his head that had originally belonged to our father. Anyone looking at him couldn't help but look at the helmet too, which transfixed and frightened them so much they ran away never to return.

A great river ran near our house, the same river in which Otr fished every morning. Living at the river's edge was one of the svartalfr, a dvergar named Andvari, which is why the river was sometimes known as the Andvarafors. He was the son of Oinn. He too was a shapechanger.

Once while creeping around at night near the forest's edge he saw a glow emanating from deep in the forest. He was wary of going into the forest at night. Out in the meadow he had light enough from the stars and moon. In the forest, even during the day it was dark because very little sunlight broke through the trees. At night the blackness engulfed everything in the forest. He thought to himself that he should wait until morning when he'd be able to see better. But the ring seemed to read his thoughts and glowed a little brighter. He stared at the glow, transfixed. He looked down and suddenly the ring was on his finger and he felt powerful. He had never been powerful. He didn't work in the mines like other svartalfar. He hadn't been strong enough. He had been encouraged to go above and leave the mines since he was useless there. So, his life had been lived skulking around at night trying to steal whatever he could to live. Now he had a powerful ring. None of the svartalfar in the mines had a ring like this. Someone more powerful than the svartalfar had made this ring. He was certain of it.

He looked again. There was no ring on his finger. He had been certain of the chimera. It had been real. It had been on his finger. Then he again saw the glow off in the forest. He determined to follow it. That would be the light that would guide him through the darkness.

He began making his way to the glowing ring. The forest darkness engulfed him. The tree cover blocked out the stars and moon until he was in pitch-blackness. Even though he was one of dvergue who worked underground and could see well at night, he would have been lost except for the glow of the ring pulling him towards it. And the closer he got the greater its force. Pulling and pulling him. At one point he tried to go back, but he was already in its thrall. He could only move forward, towards the ring. As he got closer he could see behind the glow was a Norn sleeping beneath a tree. The ring was on her finger.

Andvari stared at the ring. It was magnificent. He was used to seeing wondrous gems and golden objects. The svartalfar worked deep in Midgardr collecting gold and making fine objects from them. They made weapons of war, and other objects just for their beauty. He recognized the ring as the work of the svartalfar. Despite not knowing how the Norn had come by the ring, in Andvari's mind since he was of the svartalfar it meant the ring rightfully belonged to him. Thus with that logic he determined to take the ring.

Stealing the ring was easier than he thought it would be. The Norns made up the lives of many and spent a lot of time dreaming dreams for some and nightmares for others. Andvari found the Norn was in a deep sleep dreaming of the destinies

she could weave for others. She dreamed of magnificent futures for some and great tragedies for others.

One object she dreamed was a magical ring that had the power to find gold. If worn on the first finger it caused the wearer's hand to point in the direction where there was gold. However, she knew gifts of gold should never come about easily. So, the ring bore a curse. The one who next wore the ring would be cursed with greed. He would hoard away the gold he found. Then he would be filled with fear that someone might steal his hoard of gold. After that his life was set. He would have no choice but to spend his life protecting his hoard of gold. He would be wealthy, but never able to enjoy his wealth. He would ever be fearful that he would spend some of his gold and perhaps never have enough for his future. No matter how much gold he acquired it would never be enough. His life was given to his hoard. He could never spend it and he would live in fear it would be taken from him.

Andvari crept up and stole the ring. It was easy. She did not awaken, but merely sighed. From then on the ring was named after its new owner and was known as the Andvaranautr.

Eventually Andvari gathered together a great hoard of gold. Until this time he hadn't been concerned too much with wealth. But now that he had it he felt he had to guard it, lest he lose it, or it be stolen from him. So he hid his hoard in a cave behind a waterfall at the Andvarafors. That evening he went back to an underground cave he called home. He tried to rest but it was a fitful sleep filled with dreams of the many ways people were plotting to steal his gold. He awoke, unable to sleep, worrying about his gold. What if someone should take it while he was in his cave? What if someone were taking it right now? He hurried back to the Andvarafors and shapechanged into a pike and swam around in front of the waterfall keeping guard so no one could steal his gold. And that's where he would stay. He could change back into a dvergar and go up behind the waterfall and count his gold, lay on it, even play with it. Then he could swim around in front of it to guard it. This made him happy.

The Andvarafors was the water where Otr fished. One day after Andvari had first shapechanged himself into a pike to guard his gold Otr had also shapechanged into an otter and was out fishing at the Andvarafors. He recognized the pike swimming in the water near him as a shapechanger. But he didn't try to catch him, knowing he was really a dvergar and as such wouldn't have tasted too good.

o o o o

Now as it happened, one day Otr had a particularly successful day fishing. It wasn't time to go home so he laid his fish out in a row on a rock. He was a little hungry and swallowed one down. With his stomach full, lots of fish caught, and the sun beating down on him the day seemed lazier than ever, so he closed his eyes and took a nap.

Odin, Hoenir, and Loki were walking through the forest adventuring on that day. They came to the Andvarafors and followed it along until they came to a magnificent waterfall set back into the forest. Laying on a rock near the river they saw an otter, half asleep. It occasionally yawned, sniffed at a fish, and obviously deciding that it was full, rolled over and went back to sleep, basking in the sun. The three Æsir stared at this. Loki was feeling hungry and saw a chance for a good meal. He took a stone and flung it at the otter hitting him between the eyes, killing him instantly.

Loki, being of ill conceit and a braggart began boasting about what he'd done, "Did you see that? I've gained an otter for us and gone fishing all with one blow. How many others could do that?"

Loki continued bragging, retelling the story and embellishing the danger of the deed with each enhanced version. At one point as he walked back and forth he thought he had caught the glint of gold behind the waterfall. He kept this knowledge to himself, deciding to come back alone later and investigate the matter. In the meantime Odin and Hoenir had set about skinning the otter. They finished by midevening. The light was getting dim so they decided to try and find a place to stay for the night. They didn't have to walk long before they came to Hreidmar's house. The gate was unlatched so they walked in. The way was unguarded since Fafnir had gone off looking for Otr who should have been home by now.

Once inside the house they came to the central Hall where they found Hreidmar seated in front of the fire. Hreidmar offered them his hospitality. "How do you do? I'm Hreidmar, master of magic. Why have you come to see me? If you come in peace then you're welcome to stay the night."

Odin spoke for the three, "We're not warriors, so you have nothing to fear on that score. We're merely adventurers traveling about for our own pleasure, learning all we can of the world." Odin bowed in greeting and removed his broad-brimmed hat that had been covering his missing eye and continued, "We were walking near here and passed fields filled with corn. They probably belong to you?" Hreidmar nodded that the stranger was correct. "Never have we seen such a harvest. We decided anyone that skilled as a farmer would be interesting to meet and so we've made our way to your home."

Loki always had to add his part, and did so now, "We're not as poor as we seem. If you grant us your hospitality we can provide you with a meal tonight. Look what I carry in my pouch. We have fish enough for everyone here, plus an otter." Hreidmar jumped at the mention of an otter and ran to look at it. Loki continued his boasting, "Although I hate to brag, I must mention that I won all of this for us with one toss of a stone, just a little pebble really. I threw it with such force that it killed the otter before he even knew what had hit him."

Hreidmar yelled out, "Otr is my son. Fafnir, Regin, come quick. I need your help. Your brother has been slain."

Loki immediately took in the situation and changed his story somewhat, "Actually not all the glory is mine. These two urged me on to do the deed because they were hungry. I really was interested in bear tonight." He put in the last hoping Hreidmar didn't have a son called Bear.

Fafnir had just returned and came at his father's calling. I ran in from my smith carrying a large hammer and some iron chain. Between our strength and my father's necromancy, we were able to subdue and bind the strangers. I took Odin's spear, Gungnir, and began looking at how it was crafted. I was impressed. "Ordinary travelers don't carry spears like this," I remarked to my brothers and father.

Fafnir had taken Loki's magical shoes that gave anyone who wore them the power to fly over land and water. Fafnir tried putting them on but his feet were much too big.

I spoke, "Although they look poor at first glance, if you look closely a second time you can see the trappings of great wealth upon them. This spear, for example, is the work of the svartalfar in svartalfheimr. And you know what they charge for treasures. Each one of our prisoners is wearing gold rings."

Odin replied, "It's true. We aren't what we seem. We can offer you weregild even though we're innocent of any dishonorable deed. We didn't know it was your son when he was slain."

Hreidmar answered, "Your lack of knowledge makes no difference now. He's still dead and will remain so. Perhaps if you hadn't skinned him I could have done something about the matter. Let me think a moment on how you three shall die."

Loki then stupidly began to threaten us, which certainly wouldn't have done any good. Odin shushed him and spoke once more, "Don't forget our offer of weregild, which should be accepted since the slaying was accidental. We're not without means." Odin turned and looked at Loki.

Hreidmar, Fafnir, and I talked in the corner amongst ourselves. Loki strained every which way, more with the effort of hearing what we were saying than with trying to break free. I thought we should ask for a fortune from them, "I believe these three are very special and not at all what they seem. Let's ask them for a great treasure. I don't think we'll be disappointed if we do."

We agreed and walked across the room to the three prisoners. Hreidmar spoke, "We agree to your offer of weregild. It shall be thus. Here is Otr's skin. We'll not be satisfied until it's filled completely with gold and then buried all over in red gold on the outside so that not even a hair remains uncovered." I helped Fafnir and my father pull at the skin until it stretched over a good part of the room.

Fafnir laughed as he yelled at the prisoners, "Now, fill that if you can."

Loki motioned for them to be freed, "Let us go and we'll get your gold for you and return immediately."

Hreidmar looked at the three, "Not so fast. You three are strangers to us. Your wealth might just extend to the ends of your fingers, or it might be greater. That's something we can't take your word on. Two of you will remain here as our prisoners. Only one of you will fetch the gold. My sons and I will leave you for a few moments so you can consult amongst yourselves and decide who is to be set free." He turned to leave, but remembered something and spoke to them again, "One other thing. The weregild must be paid this evening. Tomorrow morning one of you will be killed. If the weregild is not paid by the end of that day, then the next one will be killed. So whichever one of you leaves here this evening must return tonight if he is to save both his friends, or within a day to insure he doesn't walk home alone."

Odin made the decision for them, "Loki, you're cunning enough to know where there might be gold at hand. We don't have time for you to return to Asgardr and bring it from our supplies there."

Cunningly Loki answered, for he remembered the glint from behind the waterfall, "I think I'll be able to save you two. I have a way of smelling out gold."

Odin and Hoenir had to put up with his bragging, since he was at this moment their only hope.

My father, Fafnir, and I returned. Odin indicated Loki was to be set free. As Loki headed for the door Hoenir yelled out, "Once you're out of sight don't forget about us and go on your merry way. If you should return to our own land without us ill things will happen to you."

Loki ran off towards the river with that thought in his head. He soon reached the waterfall and called out, "I can see there's gold behind that cascade of water. Whose is it? I mean to have it and would talk with the owner."

There was no reply. Loki looked all around. He noticed the water in front of the waterfall was churned up and a pike was swimming nervously back and forth. "Perhaps he's trying to fool me into thinking he's a mighty sea serpent, perhaps even Midgardrsormr himself, lies guarding this treasure. Still I must be careful even though his size is small. If he can change himself into a pike, then he must be knowledgeable about magic. It would be best not to rush at the pike, lest some spell be cast on me." Loki set to mulling the problem over in his head, "I can't capture him with my hands and he would be too smart to be hooked with bait." Then he remembered Ægir's wife Ran had a net that she cast into the sea, using it to catch drowned sailors. The island on which Ægir and Ran lived was but a short distance away. Loki ran off to visit them. The pike relaxed his swimming, hoping he had scared the stranger away. Perhaps a legend would grow about the sea monster near the waterfall and no one would come near there. Then he would have peace and could bring his gold out in the open where it would shine in the sun and he could look at it. Maybe even touch it. Or, dive up and down in it. A miser's dream fit for a pike, too.

In the meantime Loki came upon Ran standing on the shore looking out to sea hoping to see a ship. "Ho, Ran, lend me your drowning net so I can work some mischief with it. If you do this I can promise you a good story of the deed afterwards. And if I should slay anyone in the venture you're welcome to do with them what you will.'

Ran answered, "You may borrow it now since I've gathered in enough gold and dead sailors for one day." She pointed to the treasure of gold and bodies laying on the beach. 'There don't seem to be any more ships passing by for me to have mischief with. Maybe you'll have better luck. But bring it back soon. I don't want the sea to be too calm. I caution you not to let the Æsir know about this net. It might prove to be your undoing if they remembered there was a means of drawing things from the sea and you happened to be hiding in the sea at the time. In fact, why don't you try it on for size now so I can make it larger if it feels uncomfortable.'

Loki grabbed the net and ran off with Ran's laughter echoing behind him. He didn't appreciate Ran's humor. While the net was in Loki's possession no sailors drowned at sea, no children drowned at play.

Loki returned to the Andvarafors where he cast it into the water and easily drew out his catch and laid it on the shore. Andvari lay gasping, his gills opening and closing rapidly trying to breathe. He wriggled and tried to leap back into the water, but Loki caught him and held him firmly in his hands until Andvari had no other choice but to change his shape back into that of a dvergar or else drown in the air.

Grumpily he spoke to Loki after his transformation, 'What do you want with the son of Oinn? I've never bothered you, why do you treat me like this?"

Loki smiled, "Tell me your story and about the gold you've hidden behind the waterfall."

Andvari answered not the least bit convincingly, "What gold? I have no gold?"

"Don't lie to me. It's an easy enough task to kill you here and now. Tell me your story and I'll spare you, though I fear you've lost your hoard."

Andvari stopped struggling and related his tale, "Once I happened on a beautiful ring which I now call Andvaranautr since I've owned it so long. Shortly after I found it I began wearing it and discovered the hand wearing the ring would raise up and lead me to a spot. If I dug there I'd find precious gems or gold. These I've collected over the years from all the nine Worlds of the Tree, so now my hoard is the most valuable in the world."

Loki spoke, "Dvergues are supposed to be exceedingly cunning and wise. If this be the case and you wish to save your life, then answer these questions for me. Men who tell lies of others and deal falsely with their friends have a painful fate awaiting them. What is it?"

Andvari answered, "They're doomed to wade the waters of Vadgelmir in the deepest part of Hel. The more lies he has spoken the longer will be his bath in those poisonous waters."

Then Loki remembered Odin and Hoenir and decided to hurry things along, "You're trying to trick me into wasting my time asking you silly questions. Bah! Give me your gold immediately or I'll end your days right now."

Andvari reluctantly agreed to give up his hoard, "There it is in the cave. You're welcome to it."

Loki put Andvari down, shoving him towards the cave, "Come then, and help me carry the treasures out."

They worked most of the night carrying the hoard out and piling it on the shore. Even though the sun had long since departed, the area shown as bright as day from the gleam of the gold.

Andvari turned to go, "There now you have my treasure. I'm leaving this land in search of new treasure."

Loki caught the departing dvergar by the back of his collar. If his jacket hadn't been button he might have been able to squirm out of it and run away, but he couldn't. "Wait just one minute. Not so fast. You seem to have forgotten your magic ring. Do you think I'm going to let you keep it?" Loki looked at Andvari's hand and noticed the ring was gone. "Where is it?"

Andvari looked down at his hand. He had secretly put the ring under his arm. "Believe me when I tell you the ring is of no use to you. It's poorly made and the gold has not the quality of the pile you have before you. Let me keep just this one ring from the pile. With it I'll be able to find more precious things and soon my hoard will be as big as this. I'm the only one the ring's magic will work for. Please leave it with me."

Loki was having none of it, "Sorry, but I want that ring. It's not quite so ugly as you say. In fact I rather fancy it myself. Where did you hide it?"

Andvari innocently shrugged his shoulders. The ring fell to the ground. Both made a dive for it, but Andvari being closer to the ground reached it first. He quickly put it on his finger and held his fist closed so tight his knuckles shown white.

Andvari was stubbornly determined to make a fight of it, "I've seen many people wear this ring over the years and have noticed one thing. If it's worn on a finger by one who casually asks it every once-in-a-while to find some gold then it does as it's asked and attracts wealth and happiness to the wearer as if it were a magnet. If it's worn on a finger that greedily points every which way looking for gold then it causes tragedy and attracts the doom of the wearer. I wear it and am its rightful owner. Others wearing it are consumed by greed and are owned by the ring. It works its spell on me a little. Before I gained the curse of ownership I did not lust after wealth as I do now. Nor did I swim about all day in the water in the form of a pike guarding my hoard. I had friends and often visited them and had merry times. Now my time is spent ever watching so no one will take my gold. My time has been wasted all these years. Even though I've been vigilant my gold is still being taken from me. I beg of you, just leave my ring and I'll bless your thievery, take the ring and I'll curse it. I can see the greed and lust for gold will be the death of two brothers, and the source of bad luck for eight athelings. No good will come from your stealing this ring."

"Bah! I've been cursed at by better than you. What do I care if it's cursed? Mores the better since I'm straightway giving it to Hreidmar for weregild. In fact I'll feel a little better knowing he's going to have such ill luck with the hoard." Loki grabbed the struggling dvergar's wrist, pried his fingers open and pulled off the ring. After he had it he picked up the dvergar and heaved him clear across the stream. Andvari landed in the hollow of a tree. Now that he was in his regular dvergar shape his natural fear of water came over him and he was unable to swim back to the other side of the river and fight for his gold. He was so rattled by everything he had temporarily forgotten his shapechanging spells. All he could do was watch as Loki gathered up his gold in Ran's net and prepared to depart.

Andvari yelled after Loki as he walked into the forest, "I now curse that ring and the gold that goes with it. In greed do you take it, so all who wear it will be cursed with greed and will never be satisfied with what they have. The hoard shall be the bane of every man or woman who would own it. Sorrow will come to all who wear the ring. This curse I lay on Andvari's Hoard until all the treasure, including Andvaranautr, is returned to these waters. Death and destruction shall follow all who would possess my ring and my gold. Take that." Andvari shook his fists, but Loki was too distant to see or hear. Andvari suddenly remembered his shapechanging chant, turned himself back into a pike and dove into the river. He swum up and down the stream furiously, mad at having lost his hoard. There's nothing like an angry svartalfar who has turned himself into a pike for churning up a river. However, this only caused the sediment to swirl around and get in his unblinking eyes. "Bah, I'll get them." He swore and swore as he swam about.

Loki returned to Hreidmar's home before the day was over and dropped the gold on the floor. Ran's net had been wound around several times so the gold and treasure wouldn't slip through the holes. It took Loki some time to unwrap the net. All the while Odin and Hoenir stared at the net seeing how useful it was. There would come a time when such knowledge would be useful to them and not so useful to Loki. However, that's another story.

Finally the gold lay gleaming on the floor before Hreidmar, Fafnir and myself. Because of this treasure gold would be known henceforth by many as ottergild. We stood with our mouths gaping at our newly acquired wealth.

Loki spoke, "Here's gold enough to fill Otr's skin, no matter how much you stretch it. Release my two friends since we've kept our part of the bargain."

Odin and Hoenir were released. Hreidmar, Fafnir, and I began filling the otter skin with the gold. Odin and Hoenir ran their hands through it. Even those who came into contact with it peripherally were affected by it. Odin saw Andvaranautr and thought it the most wonderful ring he had ever seen. He removed it from the pile, unseen he thought, and slipped it on his little finger.

Every piece of gold put in the skin seemed to stretch it even more. Eventually, though, it was filled and the skin stood up of its own accord. Hreidmar, Fafnir and I then began piling the remaining gold over top it and around it until the skin was completely hidden. Loki had been helping us hoping, I think, to arrange the gold so some of it would be leftover for him. But such was not the case and it was all needed to cover the otter skin.

Then Loki spoke, "Now let's go. Give me my shoes, and give my friend his spear. We'll depart from you in peace."

Hreidmar motioned for them to stay, "Not so fast. I have to inspect it closely to see if the gold covers all of the skin." He glanced over the top and bent low to inspect the mound of gold. He even crawled along on the floor looking for a chink in the hoard hoping to find a bare patch. When he was nose to nose with the front of the otter skin he noticed a tiny whisker was sticking out. He pointed this out to Loki who tried to move other pieces of gold over to cover the hair. He only succeeded in making matters worse. Finally, he put everything back the way it was. Still the whisker peeked out. Hreidmar looked triumphant. "The weregild has not been paid. You three will remain my prisoners. I've plans for you. I might as well keep the gold you brought since you three won't have any further need of it."

Odin looked down at the ring on his finger, "Not so fast, Hreidmar. Here's a ring that I carelessly slipped on my finger while I was looking at the hoard. It'll just cover the whisker." He placed it on the hoard and continued, "Now set us free. We wish to leave this place, even though it's dark out and we have little chance of finding further accommodations for the night."

Their property was returned to them and they were shown the door. As soon as they were safely outside Loki yelled back to Hreidmar, "The trick's on you. The gold and treasure you have there is cursed. Whoever owns the gold and wears the ring shall have ill luck follow him. This bad luck will be his or her death, and even give death to his or her kinsmen." Hreidmar would never have accepted the weregild if he had known it was cursed.

Odin, Hoenir, and Loki returned to Asgardr. They had met with more adventure than they had bargained for on their trip.

o   o   o   o

In the meantime the gold began to work its spell on Hreidmar, Fafnir and me. Fafnir and I had been speaking amongst ourselves and decided we wanted our share now.

We met with our father and I spoke first, "We had a lot of money that had been left to us by other relatives. But you kept watch over it and after a while thought it was your money and took it all and built this house with it."

Fafnir continued, "Therefore, we don't want you to have access to our share of the ottergild. We want to divide it equally here and now."

Hreidmar retorted, "What makes you think you're entitled to any portion of this treasure?"

I answered, "Otr was our brother, and by tradition we are his nearest relatives, much closer to him than you are. Give us our share."

I guess I had spoken a little more forcefully this time. Fafnir could barely take his eyes away from the gold but did manage to snort his agreement. A change seemed to be coming over him.

Hreidmar was adamant. The weregild would not be shared with them, "Nothing will you have, not even the tiniest bit of dust that has fallen from the smallest nugget. It's all mine and I intend to keep it that way. I don't know where you ever got the idea we were bargaining for gold for you two. If such had been the case then surely we should have asked for more. Perhaps if you run after them you can catch the three again and make them get more of it for you two. They seem to be able to accumulate it quite rapidly."

Hreidmar began carrying the gold into his strongest, most secure room. After it was all in there he shut and locked the door and went up to his bedroom. He yelled at his two sons from the other side of his locked bedroom door, "Now you two will be unable to take the gold from me. Why don't both of you stop worrying and do as I do. I'm going to bed, it's been a long night."

But Fafnir and I were not to be so easily dealt with. We began plotting together on how we might get the gold. First we tried outright to pick the lock on the door. When that didn't work we tried to break it down. Unfortunately Hreidmar had secured it with charms, so brute force was useless. As long as Hreidmar remained

alive the charms would protect the gold room against any unwanted entry. There remained only one way to deal with this problem. Hreidmar being alive was the problem.

Fafnir grabbed a sword and crept up the stairs towards Hreidmar's room. Thinking we would only be interested in the room where the gold was stored our father had neglected to put protective charms around his room. We easily opened the door, he hadn't even locked it, to his bedroom and crept. Fafnir stood over the bed looking down on our father. Then he thrust the sword through Hreidmar's sleeping body. Hreidmar awoke and gripped at the hilt of the sword which extended a little bit above his chest. He called out for his two daughters, "Lyngheidr, Lofnheidr, come here I need you. I've been plotted against by your brothers and run through with a sword. You two are the only others of my kin left. I give you the duty of seeking vengeance on Fafnir and Regin after my death."

Our sisters' room was nearby so they could easily tend to Hreidmar's wants and needs throughout the night. They had been ill-treated by our father all their lives. Now was their chance to let him know. Lyngheidr answered, "Even though you have been dealt a dishonorable blow you should not expect us to spill our brothers' blood on your account. We owe you even less loyalty than they do. Have you ever offered us a portion of your wealth for our inheritance? Have you ever been concerned with our lives? Have you ever put aside anything for dowries for us so that we might marry? The answer to all these questions is no. You've used us as serving maids to do your bidding. You've never intended us to leave here. Our lives were laid out by you to have us do your bidding until you were old and scraggly, drooling in your cups of wine. That was our future with you and if you lived. That is not the future we want for ourselves. Why should you now expect us to avenge your death at considerable risk to ourselves?"

Lofnheidr added her part, "You are dying, Fafnir and Regin are still alive. Your hand grasps no gold. You can only promise to pay is with empty air. Our future is with those who have the gold to pay for our lives and our loyalty. They can toss us gold coins, you can toss us nothing but feathers from your bed. And feathers will neither buy us a meal nor shelter over our head. It will not buy us husbands." The two sisters went back to their room.

Hreidmar tried to rise up, but this only caused the sword to cut deeper into him. He fell back into the pool of his blood that now covered the bed and yelled as loudly as he could after his daughters. "You wolf-hearted women. Thus I give you my instructions. If either of you are born of a son in wedlock then his duty will be to avenge my death. If, however, you are delivered of a girl, if she will not accept the task, which I think she will not having such a cowardly mother, then the first born son to her in wedlock will avenge this most foul act." The sisters never heard this. They were singing and dancing about in their room, planning their futures, full of hope they would be able to marry and have their own families. However, their brothers were their father's sons and the gold overtook took their sibling duty. The sisters would never rise out of their poverty, never have a family, never be happy.

Hreidmar died. Thus was his death brought about for the sake of gold. The curse had begun. Charmed by greed, then death, awaited whomever wore the ring until it is returned to its rightful owner. Fafnir removed Andvaranautr from his father's finger and put it on his own. The evil worked into him immediately. He now thought of the gold as his own, not something to be shared with me.

The next morning I found Fafnir in the gold room rolling on the gold, reveling in it. I suggested we divide it amongst ourselves. "Everything to the left of this center line will belong to one of us, everything to the right to the other. You may have your choice as to which side of the room you claim as your own."

Fafnir stood straddling the line. Throwing his arms out in both directions, heaving gold coins and jewels into the air, he yelled at the top of his lungs, "I recognize no lines of demarcation. The entire room is mine, thus I claim it all as mine. I was the one to force the door to our father's room open, which, of course wasn't true, since it had been unlocked. I was the one to thrust the sword through our father. I am the one for whom the gold is meant. You're not deserving of any of it. Nothing will you have, not even the tiniest bit of dust that has fallen from the smallest nugget. It's all mine and I intend to keep it that way. Leave now in peace, or leave later in pieces." He took the sword Hrotti in his hand and flailed it over his head threateningly.

Since I had been the least in physical abilities of my brothers I knew fighting against Fafnir would be futile. I sought counsel with my sister Lyngheidr, "It's none of my business since neither I nor Lofnheidr have been included in these matters. Do what you will, I don't care who owns the gold."

I saw no other course but to leave Fafnir to the gold. The only thing I took with me when I left was my sword Ridil. As I left the Hall Hreidmar's last words echoed in my mind. 'My life has been forfeit, so your life is owed. This is the law and one day justice will be done. Oh, who will come to avenge my death? I cry with my last breath for an avenger."

Shortly after I left, Lyngheidr and Lofnheidr did likewise. Fafnir was now alone with the gold, which pleased him greatly. Its spell transfixed him. He grew to love the gold. Often he dived into it, throwing gems and treasures into the air and catching them. He never tired of looking at the gold or being near it.

Then Fafnir began worrying someone was plotting to steal the gold from him. He was constantly glancing back over his shoulders trying to catch a glimpse of the shadows of the would-be thieves. He found our father's Helmet of Terror and took to wearing it. But that still didn't seem to be enough. Talking to himself he walked about the Hall trying to figure out what to do. "This place is just too large for me to guard. There are too many entrances which could be exits for some thief with my gold. I could be in one room while someone was robbing me out the back door in another. No, I must find some place that's better, some place that's darker. Maybe even scarier."

He looked around on his father's land and found just the place on Gnitaheidr. It was a deep cave sunken back and partially hidden by trees, with just one entrance. "Perfect. But it'll need a little work." He set about reinforcing the chamber with iron beams he sunk deep into the earth. He was taking no chances the ceiling would fall in and hurt his gold. He put in an iron ceiling, walls and floor. This would make it more difficult for someone to bore into the chamber and rob him. Lastly he installed a large iron gate at the entrance to the lair. It was worked all over with locks and bolts. No one would be able to get in without the proper set of keys. After he had carried the hoard to his lair he went out into the forest and dug a deep hole into which he placed the keys, and then walked away. But what he had done prayed upon his mind. What if someone had seen him? He went back and dug up the keys and waited until the middle of the night, a time when he was certain everyone was asleep. He reburied the keys in a different spot. Now all was safe and ready. He sat in the front of the lair trying to keep awake to prevent anyone from taking his gold. The sword Hrotti lay across his lap. Slowly the days turned into weeks, the weeks into months, the months into seasons and then into years. Gradually his shape changed to that of a more accommodating guardian. His skin turned green and his body lengthened. His arms shrank to little appendages. He was now a fearsome dragon whose very breath exhaled poison. He did not have to unlock the locks anymore, so the keys could remain safely buried. He could slide in through the bars and lay on his gold. Never was he happier than when he lay across the hoard, and no matter which way he turned his head all he could see was the red glistening metal. This was what life was all about."

Regin paused for a moment and then continued his story, "In the meantime I made my way to the court of Hjalprekr of Ty and Thjod, also known as Jutland and Denmark, carrying only the sword Ridil to remind me of my lost inheritance. There have I lived for many years earning my living as a smith, since I have great skill at that work. I gained the King's trust in that time. But never did I forget the wrong done to me or the vengeance I owed my brother. It has always been my plan to find a young lad who showed promise and raise him up to be the strongest warrior there ever was. Then I would ask a favor of him for the knowledge and skills I have given him. This favor, the killing of the dragon Fafnir, would also win great fame and honor for him. Now you have heard my story. Will you help me?"

Sigurdr had listened to the story and agreed a great wrong had been committed. But he remained a bit doubtful about Regin's justification in seeking vengeance. It seemed to him Regin had played almost as big a part in the wrong as his brother had. Finally, after thinking the matter over some more, he came to the conclusion Regin did deserve some kind of justice and agreed to help. "I'll do all I can for you. First, though, I must have a sword to fight with. Use your skills to fashion me the strongest sword known of any warrior. Make it so it will cut deep and true, that I might win glory in the battle I wage with it. If you succeed in smithing such a sword I'll use it to slay Fafnir. I would never consider going against him with anything less."

Regin smiled for the first time in a long while, "Leave it to me. You won't be disappointed. I'll forge a sword for you that will slice through Fafnir's hard skin as if it were melted butter."

Regin worked through the night and forged a long iron sword. The next morning he handed it to Sigurdr. "Try this. It's the best work I've ever done."

Sigurdr hefted it about, "Don't brag about your work yet." He smote down onto the anvil with the sword. It immediately shattered into hundreds of pieces. All that was left in Sigurdr's hands was the hilt, "I think you'll have to work a little harder for your brother's death." Sigurdr left.

That evening Sigurdr returned. Regin had worked all day and had readied another sword. "This one is better than the last. I was able to find some charmed metal and have cut runes into it. Try it."

Sigurdr took up the sword. It was lighter than the first, yet seemed stronger. He hit at the anvil a second time. It too shattered into hundreds of pieces. "Have you been lying to me about your skills? You've given me two swords, both of which have broken with one blow, and without much effort. Perhaps you would send me against Fafnir knowing your swords would fail? That way you can add the treasure of the Volsungr's to your family's ill-gotten gains."

When he was alone Sigurdr thought on the matter. He went to his mother for he remembered being told of the broken sword Gramr that his mother had stored away. "Mother, Sigmundr gave you the sword Gramr before he died. Where is it? I would have it as my own."

"You remember well what I told you when you were just a baby." She walked over to a chest that she opened. Lying under some blankets was a white linen cloth. She took this out and laid it in Sigurdr's lap. Tenderly she unwrapped it. Inside laid the sword Gramr in two pieces, still as shiny as new. "Take this broken sword and win glory for the Volsungr name once you have gotten it forged whole again. Before all other deeds you must avenge your father's death in order to honor your family."

Sigurdr took the broken sword to Regin who was working on a third sword, "Cast aside that sword. Even if it were twice as good as the other two you forged it would not be a portion as good as this sword broken apart. I would that you forge this sword into one piece. Then shall it begin to taste the blood of vengeance. Forge it into one if you are skilled enough to do so."

Regin flinched at the insult but took up the two pieces. He worked through the night forging the sword into one piece. His work was so fine that no matter how closely you examined it, it was impossible to tell the sword had ever been split in two. He took it hot from the forge and presented it to Sigurdr. It seemed as if the edges of the sword burned with fire, "This is the best work I've ever done. If this sword breaks then I'll admit defeat. I'm unable to do better work than this."

Sigurdr took the sword and raised it over his head. He smote down on the anvil with it. The anvil was split in two from top to bottom. And this was done without dulling the edge of the sword in any way. The sword remained unblemished with no mars or nicks to indicate it had just bitten through cast iron. Sigurdr was awed by it. He had not even used his full strength on the anvil, "I'll take it to the river to test it further."

Regin looked on at his cleaved anvil. A smith is only as good as his anvil for it is used to pound the shapes of everything he makes. If the anvil can't take the pounding, then don't expect the object being forged to be strong. Regin's anvil had been charmed with magic to make anything made on it stronger. He was going to have quite a time trying to find another anvil like that. He might never do so, and never be the smith he had been. Then he remember the gold. And that memory started playing in his mind. He wouldn't need an anvil anymore. Once Andvari's Hoard was retrieved and once more in his possession he wouldn't need to work. He could just sit around all day and look at his gold, and protect it. He would have to protect it. He would need an anvil of some sort to forge the iron bars he'd need to protect the gold. He sat on the broken anvil greed starting to overtake his thoughts. In his mind he was building the greatest vault the world had ever known. It would be magnificent. Magnificent enough to match his hoard of gold. Even the thought of Andvari's Hoard was working it's way into his soul, changing him.

Sigurdr watched Regin changing before him. It was of little concern to him. His concern was slaying Fafnir, gaining Andvari's Hoard for his own, and winning great fame and a name for himself. Before his thoughts had been of avenging his father, now maybe it was a little bit more about the gold and slaying Fafnir.

As Sigurdr left the smithy he took a lock of wool from Regin's cloak. At the river he tossed the wool upstream and held the sword on its edge in the water. The wool floated with the current and passed against the sword. The strand of wool was sliced in two. Sigurdr smiled and returned to Regin's smithy.

Regin could see Sigurdr was pleased with Gramr, "Now that you have a sword worthy of your strength you must go against Fafnir as you have promised. Come with me and I'll lead you there."

Sigurdr put up his hand to halt Regin. Being away from Regin and thoughts of Andvari's Hoard had brought Sigurd back to first avenging his father before tackling someone else's vengeance, "Not so fast, master smith. My first duty is to avenge my father. Then I'll attend to your business, for the honor of my kin is more important to me than winning the glory of slaying Fafnir."

Regin disagreed but there was nothing he could do. Sigurdr left and prepared all he would need to bring vengeance to his father's slayers and further honor to the Volsungr name.

CHAPTER 12
GRIFIR'S PROPHECY

Grifir was the son of Eylimi, brother of Hjordis, and uncle of Sigurdr. He ruled over a small Kingdom, not with might but with wisdom since his army was small. He had the gift of prophecy and used his ability to foresee events to prevent attacks on his Kingdom and squash plots that might be brewing against his rule. Because of his wisdom many others sought his counsel. One such was Sigurdr who had arrived at Grifir's Hall after a long day's ride.

Just outside the Hall Sigurdr met a man who barred his way. "Who are you that you can prevent me from seeing my uncle? I've had a tiring journey and don't want to waste my time arguing with you."

The man answered, "My name is Geitir, and I've been ordered to guard the door. There are many who would wish to enter. Grifir doesn't have time to see them all."

Sigurdr walked towards the door. "So Geitir is your name? Doesn't that mean goatherd? Shouldn't you be out in the stables cleaning out the stalls? Go on your way and let me pass. Grifir is my sister's brother. I am Sigurdr the son born of Sigmundr and Hjordis. I wish to see my uncle and have his counsel."

Geitir continued to bar the way. "Wait out here. I'll announce you to Grifir and ask him if he wants to see you."

Geitir went into the Hall, closing the door behind him. He walked up to Grifir and announced Sigurdr, "There is a strong young warrior, tall in stature, and noble of bearing, standing outside who wishes to see you. What shall I tell him?"

Grifir answered, "That sounds like Sigurdr, my nephew. I've been expecting him. I'll go to meet him."

Geitir followed as Grifir went outside the Hall. The King motioned for Geitir to take Grani from Sigurdr, "Take his horse and stable him. Make certain he is rubbed down and well fed."

Grifir motioned for Sigurdr to follow him as he turned and walked back into the Hall. "Tell me about my sister Hjordis. How is she?"

They talked for a while of family matters. Then Sigurdr asked Grifir the question he had journeyed all this way for, "Tell me the course my life will take?"

Grifir answered, "Are you sure you really seek this knowledge? Many people who are given this answer regret having asked the question?"

Sigurdr implored his uncle, "I'm certain I'll perform legendary deeds. However, now I'm confused about what route to take with my life. I need your help."

The two had entered the throneroom and Grifir seated himself on his throne. "Very well, I'll tell you some of your life to come. Your sons and their sons' sons will follow in your legend and be heroes, though not as great as you. Yet, they will be nobly born."

Sigurdr was dissatisfied, "But what of my life? What will happen to me tomorrow after I've left here, for example? I seek more relevant knowledge to my life as it is now, not how great my heirs will be."

"So you would have more recent knowledge? That's dangerous knowledge to acquire. More often than not it will hinder your progress. But as you wish." Sigurdr nodded that he wanted to hear. Grifir continued, "Then you must follow my instructions. First avenge the deaths of your father and King Eylimi. The sons of Hunding must be dealt with above all other concerns, no matter what the pressure is for you to do otherwise. If you ignore this counsel then your life will be a tragedy."

Sigurdr was pleased, "Then it is true that I will perform magnificent acts, my name will live on and Sigurdr's saga be sung in song by the skalds for generations to come?"

Grifir sighed, "This often happens when a fate is learned. Don't be too carried away with your legend before you've performed the deeds that inspire the songs. Remember, no songs will be sung about you if you go out and celebrate now."

Sigurdr was jumping with excitement, "What glorious act will I do after the avenging of Sigmundr and Eylimi?"

Grifir answered, "You'll slay Fafnir. Then ignobly you will slay Regin and a curse will follow your family through generation after generation. If you can hold off slaying Regin you'll prevent a great deal of ill luck for those who follow after you. Heed this advice."

Sigurdr was so excited he didn't pay attention to the last part of Grifir's prophecy. He thought only of the wealth and glory that was to be his. "If I slay Fafnir and Regin then Andvari's Hoard will be mine. Combined with the Treasure of the Volsungrs I'll be the richest King in the world."

Sigurdr was satisfied with the prophecy. He thanked Grifir and returned to Alfr's Hall. There Regin sought him out and urged him once more to keep his promise and slay Fafnir. "You've made a vow to do this for me, so why do you wait?"

Sigurdr replied, "Don't hurry me. I've had wise counsel from my uncle. He has told me that first I must avenge my father and King Eylimi. After that I'll slay Fafnir and gain great glory with the doing of that mighty deed. Don't despair, I'll slay Fafnir, eventually. You've waited all these years, you'll just have to wait a while longer. Now it is my intention to slay my father's killers and nothing you say will dissuade me from that task."

Regin asked to be allowed to go with him, "I ask your permission to accompany you on your journey since I don't think I can stand waiting for you to return. I'll do my fair share. It's always wise to have a smith accompanying an army so broken swords and dented armor can be repaired. If I go with you I'll feel better about the matter."

Sigurdr was surprised, "Your reputation as a smith is well spoken of throughout the land. You have work a plenty here. I'm surprised you would wish to give all that up for a life that will hardly be accommodating? But if it is your wish, I would certainly be honored to have you as the smith to my army."

Sigurdr went to King Hjalprekr and Alfr and thanked them for their help, "I appreciate the kindnesses and love you've shown me over the years. Now it is my fate and duty to leave here and reclaim my own Kingdom. I must seek out the sons of Hunding and let them know there is yet one Volsungr who still lives, and remembers their treachery. In this regard I have just one more favor to ask of you. I'll need an army to help me. Can you grant this last request?"

Alfr responded, "Such was the promise I made to your mother before you were born that when the time came I would help you reclaim your rightful inheritance. So gladly will we give you the best warriors we have and any other help you wish. Your success means our borders will be bounded by a King who is our friend."

Messengers rode throughout King Hjalprekr's Kingdom summoning the greatest warriors in the land. Spears, arrows, and swords were sharpened. Only the most fearless and fearsome horses would be used. Saddles were fitted and readied. Everything was done in a proficient manner so there would be no mistakes that could later prove fatal for the company of men.

Great ships were built to carry the army. Sigurdr chose the best outfitted to captain as his own. It was called the Sea Dragon Keel, and was magnificent to look at, heavily armored yet detailed with finely carved wood.

The fleet set sail on a fine sunny morning. All omens portended a successful venture. Gigantic waves lifted the ships up and carried them out onto the sea. Their sails stretched with the wind. After a few days the wind turned to a storm and the waves became blood red in their fierceness. The seas churned while the ships rocked back and forth, nearly capsizing. Some of the sailors urged Sigurdr to lower the sails. The First Mate sought to give him some helpful advice, "You're inexperienced in sailing. I've been First Mate on many expeditions and can see the winds are too strong for these untried ships. The waters have nearly swamped us. Look to the starboard and you can see one of the ships nearly keeled over. Let's proceed a little more cautiously until the sailors have the feel of the boards under them."

Sigurdr ignored the First Mate's advice, "I'm anxious to seek vengeance. Raise the sails as high as they'll go. None shall be slackened. These ships are well built and will hold against the rages of the sea and the huffing and puffing of a little wind. You need not fear Ran and Ægir will claim us as their own."

Sigurdr's luck held and they weathered the storm with neither injury to ship nor sailor.

As they were leisurely sailing passed the rocks of a promontory one of the sailors pointed out the figure of a man walking on the water towards the Sea Dragon Keel. Regin yelled out to the stranger, "What ho, you do seem to be performing a wondrous feat. Who is it that calms the seas so it can be walked on? Who does this trick for us?"

The stranger, who could now be seen to be an old man wearing a blue cloak and broad-brimmed hat pulled low to conceal a missing eye, answered, "My name was Hnikar when Huginn alit on my shoulder, though some have called me Karl from the Mountains. Others have named me Fengr, and still others have yelled out Fjolnir and I've answered. But if you wish, just remember Hnikar, though you may choose the others if you please."

Regin answered, "Hnikar is certainly apt, since it means wave stiller, does it not?"

The stranger nodded that it did. He continued, "Who commands this armada? He must be a great King to have such fine ships."

Regin replied, "Our leader is Sigurdr Sigmundrson. Though he is young and as yet untitled, he was born of a great King and seeks to reclaim his crown. All who meet him are agreed he is worthy of his heritage and will, no doubt, have little trouble in winning it."

Hnikar seemed impressed, "I've heard of him. He's well spoken of. Will you lower your sail so I might board?"

By now Sigurdr's attention had been caught by what was happening. He signaled the stranger was to be allowed aboard; little realizing it was Odin who was his guest. As soon as the stranger stepped aboard the waves began beating against the ship again and the sails filled with wind. The ships sailed swiftly and safely passed the ness in their way. Soon a storm arose which helped rather than hindered them on their journey.

Sigurdr spoke to the stranger, "Hnikar, one who can walk where ships would sail must surely be knowledgeable in things that are to come. Tell me what fate awaits us in the battle we are shortly to be engaged?"

Hnikar replied, "There are many good signs and omens attending your venture. The black ravens will fly from your camp to the other, where the food will be more plentiful. This is a good sign. Your men will prove their worth as warriors. As for you Sigurdr, you will wield Gramr mightily in the battle."

Sigurdr started at the mention of Gramr. How did the stranger know about Gramr? Hnikar continued speaking without interruption. "If, as you travel abroad, you see two men standing this will be a good sign, for they will be thinking of fame and glory and mentioning your name under their breath. And if under the limbs of an ash you hear wolves howling, this too is a good sign. Have your army go to the battle fully prepared. This means not only are their weapons sharp and their armor whole, but their personal needs have been attended to. A warrior should be well fed and well groomed the morning of a battle. It may be late evening before there will be another chance to eat. A growling stomach will distract a warrior. Follow this advice also. If you see a great number of helmstavers before you, then it is wise that your army keep their faces away from the setting sun. Luck and victory will follow after the army who can see its enemies rather than be blinded by the light. The battle will be won by those who stand fast and fight. It's better to fight during the day than at night when your footing may falter causing you to fall. Ill luck attends those who stumble on the field. The thing you cannot fight against, but should be wary of are the Disir. They fight on both sides. Follow my advice and good luck will attend you."

The storm carried them to the shores of King Hunding's land, ruled over by his sons. As his ships entered the headland, Sigurdr turned to speak to Hnikar. However, the stranger had suddenly vanished and was nowhere to be seen. A search of the ship failed to find the stranger. Some of the crew thought this portended bad rather than good. A disappeared prophet might have vanished, but might also have fallen overboard. Such a death would curse their adventures. The sagas would sing of fate misdirected, not glory achieved. A sense of doom overtook some of the crew.

o o o o

However, their first battle belayed that sense of doom. That day Sigurdr's army met their enemy in a pitched battle that was sung about for generations to come. Fire and sword were loosed against their enemy. They laid waste to the land before them, burning the homes and crops of the people living there. The workers fled in fear. Several ran to King Lyngvi and told him enemies were about in the countryside. No one could ever remember having seen such destruction wrought by a single army.

One farmer spoke rudely to his King, "You're a fool if you think you've nothing to fear from the kin of the Volsungrs. The leader of the armies attacking us claims to be the son and nephew of Sigmundr and Eylimi, whom you slew on that blood-red field many years ago. Help us stop the ravaging about of his army. He is doing great harm to your Kingdom. The people are sore content with your leadership."

King Lyngvi summoned his counselors of war and asked them for their advice. They were all of one mind, "WAR!"

Messengers were sent throughout Lyngvi's realm summoning all strong and able-bodied men to his side for the fight against Sigurdr. He promised the warriors great wealth and honor.

In short order his army was raised and he marched against Sigurdr accompanied in command by his brothers. The two armies engaged in battle on a large field which soon was covered with the blood of the dead. Arrows and swords pierced warriors, while axes crushed down upon helmets and byrnies. Heads were split asunder and bodies hacked to bits. Great carnage was wrought that day.

The battle continued throughout the day with little change in either side's strategy. Sigurdr rode at the head of his army swinging Gramr in all directions, hewing and cutting down many excellent warriors and their horses. He cut a path through the heaviest of the fighting. Soon his arms were covered with blood up to their shoulders. Warriors shrank back from him in fear. The Disir were of one mind

that day and sided with Sigurdr. None could win in a fight against him. No warrior present could remember ever having seen such a hero lead his men on to victory.

Both sides were evenly matched in strength. However, Sigurdr had fate on his side against the sons of Hunding. The slaughter was tremendous. Sigurdr followed by some of his men broke through the main line of defense that had been set up by King Lyngvi. Now the way lay open to the sons of Hunding.

Sigurdr found Lyngvi and hit him a glancing blow that felled him from his horse. He leapt off Grani and before Lyngvi had recovered his senses Sigurdr cut the insulting blodorn rista, blood-eagle, on Lyngvi. He slit down Lyngvi's torso with Gramr and then broke the King's ribs apart. Then he drew forth the lungs of his enemy. Yet Lyngvi still lived and was aware of the pain he felt and what was happening to him. He fainted from pain and horror. Sigurdr slapped him back to consciousness. Sigurdr laid the lungs outside Lyngvi's body. At this point Lyngvi mercifully fainted again. "Just like the coward you are. You hid behind your men, and now at the moment of my greatest glory you faint." Sigurdr stomped his foot down on both of Lyngvi's lungs. A final breath issued without his control from Lyngvi's lips before he met his dishonorable death.

Sigurdr yelled his triumph so all could hear, "Odin gave your first breath and I give you your last. Inbetween you wasted each gulp of air and spoke words of deceit and dishonor. Let everyone know the blodorn rista, what many commonly call the blood-eagle, is the fate awaiting all who lead others against the Volsungrs."

Sigurdr leapt up on Grani and began his search for the other brothers. He came upon Hjorvardr and quickly cut him in two across his stomach. The soldier's arms and upper body flipped and fell forward, while his legs and lower body fell backward causing his head to rest across his toes. The other sons of Hunding met with similar fates, until at last the Volsungrs and King Eylimi were avenged.

Sigurdr returned to King Hjalprekr's realm overland accompanied by most of his men, while the rest of his army sailed the ships back home. The army marched behind him carrying with them the results of their victory, the booty from the battlefield, as well as the wealth of the Volsungrs and great honor. The stories of the battle preceded Sigurdr and his army so that on every step of the return journey they were met by cheering crowds who knew the full story of their encounter with the sons of Hunding. Wherever his army stopped for the night they were honored with feasts and revelry. Every man of them was happy and content.

o   o   o   o

Sigurdr had been home just a little while, still savoring his victory, when Regin approached him, "You've defeated your father's enemies, carved the blood eagle on your father's banesman, reclaimed your throne, and gained great wealth. Yet your recent victory will be forgotten as soon as the news of other battles by other warriors makes its way across the land. One victory does not make for a legend. Many will think maybe you were just lucky that time, or Odin was the real winner. If you add to your acclaim by killing Fafnir everyone will know you are a hero to be reckoned with. Honor your vow and in the process add further fame to your name."

Sigurdr answered, "You are right. It's now time for the slaying of the worm Fafnir. Those were the thoughts I was thinking as you came in. I'll attend to the matter immediately."

CHAPTER 13
THE SLAYING OF FAFNIR AND REGIN

Regin laid out a plan for Sigurdr, "We must ride up to Gnitaheidr at midday. At that time Fafnir is wont to crawl to the edge of the cliff and reach over for a drink from the river cutting its way through the land below."

Sigurdr stared at Regin, "He drinks from over the side of a cliff? How high is the cliff?"

Regin answered, trying to put things in as good a light as he could, "It's a small cliff, a mere thirty fathoms."

Sigurdr calculated and exclaimed, "You want me to slay a dragon that's 180 feet long? I think you've exaggerated slightly about Fafnir being just a little larger than the lingworms in the heather field."

"He may be 180 feet long, but he isn't very wide, perhaps the width of the little finger on my left hand, maybe a little larger. In any event, you've proven yourself valorous in battle and I have no doubt you'll be able to acquit yourself well against Fafnir. Besides, I have a plan that's sure to work." Regin mounted his horse and rode off. Sigurdr followed on Grani.

o o o o

Only Sigurdr and Regin rode to Gnitaheidr. Regin's plan did not call for an army.

At first they found it difficult to find Fafnir's track since they could find no spindly uvulating tracks. The two climbed up on a hill to view the way from the cliff edge back to the woods. Sigurdr started when he realized the furrow they had been standing in was the track. It was clear Regin had been untruthful about Fafnir's size. At his widest he was as wide as Sigurdr's flagship.

"Regin, I can see by Fafnir's track that he's exceptionally wide. If your little finger were that large you'd fall over on your side, pulled down by its weight."

Regin replied, "So he's a little larger than I remembered. I feared if you knew his true size you might have been scared and not have kept your end of the bargain. Skalds do not exclaim sagas of a hero of one battle subsequently eaten by a dragon weeks later. I am giving you a chance to become a legend. But what does it matter now? We're here so let's make the best of it. Here's my plan."

Sigurdr cut him short, "I might have given it a thought or two knowing Fafnir's real size. I also might have brought my army with me. But no matter the method, I would have honored my oath." Sigurdr kept staring at the size of the track. Every time he looked it seemed longer and wider. "At least there are two of us to accomplish the task," Sigurdr wondered aloud.

Regin responded, "But then the glory would attach to both of us. It better becomes a legend to do his single most deed of glory alone. I am here to watch from afar and record the truthfulness of the deed in case you are, for some reason (incapacitated or dead—he added to himself) unable to do so. The skalds do not sing about deeds of bravery and glory unless they know of them.

Regin, hoping to distract Sigurdr from Fafnir's size, for he saw Sigurdr could not tear his gaze from the furrow before them, spoke now of the practical matter of how one man could kill a 180 foot fire-breathing, poison-spouting dragon.

"You should dig a deep hole along Fafnir's track and sit in it. When Fafnir returns to his hoard he'll crawl over you. Thrust up Gramr and cut him lengthwise through the heart and win a place in song and legend with the doing of the deed. Begin digging the hole now while I go hide in the bushes. I'll signal you when I see Fafnir coming." Regin ran off.

Sigurdr yelled after Regin, "What if I'm in front of the blood and venom and it runs into the hole? It's poisonous to the touch and will kill me. What kind of plan is this anyway?"

Regin yelled back over his shoulder, "I've already given you the major part of the plan, you work out the details. You have the brave heart of a Volsungr, use it."

Regin couldn't hear him, but Sigurdr yelled out anyway, "I think you wouldn't be too upset if Fafnir and I were both killed and the entire hoard fell to you."

Sigurdr began digging a pit. He looked up and saw an old man standing over him. The man looked familiar, but he couldn't quite make out his features since he was blinded by the sun shining overhead. The old man spoke, "Why are you digging this hole? Has someone died?"

Sigurdr answered, "I hope I'm not digging my grave. If all is successful, I intend to slay the dragon Fafnir by kneeling in this pit which I've dug in his track and stabbing and slicing him as he crosses over it."

The old man looked out of his one eye at the pit, "You've had very poor advice in your planning. I see a problem. If he spits out poison into the pit, or if his blood flows into it, you could find he has avenged his own death by slaying you also." Sigurdr nodded yes. The old man continued, "If you dug many pits in a circle around the pit you are sitting in, and then linked them together by a series of troughs slanting away from your pit, then the blood and poison will flow away from you and run into the other pits, sparing you from being covered in the dragon's vile liquid. I'll also give you additional advice, though you haven't asked for it. When you first look at Fafnir avoid his head for he wears a Helmet of Terror that will transfix you. Pull your sword from his body and knock the helmet from his head, then you'll be free to gaze on his ugly visage."

Sigurdr looked about the landscape and measured off an equal number of paces between seven markings forming a circle around his pit. He would dig that many more pits. "I feel eight pits should be sufficient protection, what do you think?" He turned around but the old man had disappeared. Nonetheless his counsel was wise and Sigurdr followed it.

Just as Sigurdr was finishing the last pit he felt a rumbling beneath his feet. Then off in the distance he saw a grey puff rising in the air and heard a muted roar. Fafnir was crawling back to his lair breathing poison and venom in his path. Sigurdr scrambled into the center pit and crouched down waiting for the dragon to crawl overhead. He was exceedingly calm considering he might be dead in a few minutes.

Sigurdr first saw the dragon's two buckteeth hanging over his bottom lip. Then his chin passed overhead. Sigurdr waited until the monster's front legs crawled past. He knew the heart lay just behind them. At this moment he thrust his sword up into the dragon just past Fafnir's left shoulder and wrenched Gramr down towards Fafnir's belly as hard as he could. Fafnir rolled on his side. Sigurdr jumped out of the pit and pulled the sword back again, putting a second slice in the dragon's underbelly. As yet he had not looked at Fafnir's head. He followed the old man's advice and flailed blindly at Fafnir's head. He heard the helmet bouncing along the ground and knew it was safe to gaze into Fafnir's eyes. As he looked along the dragon's body he saw it was pale grey from head to foot. He had expected something green. Sigurdr held Gramr in both his hands, raised his magnificent sword and once more plunged it straight down as far into the dragon's body as he could. His arms followed the sword into the wound so he was covered with the blood up to his shoulders. His skin hardened as if it were iron. Sigurdr realized the blood was not poisonous to him. He began rubbing it all over his body. The only spot he couldn't reach was inbetween his shoulder blades. Everyone has just such a spot. It's the spot where if you have an itch you must ask a friend for relief. However, ever after on those spots he had smeared with blood his skin became as hard as iron so swords, arrows, or knives could not pierce his flesh.

Fafnir knew he had suffered his deathwound, yet still he struggled. His tail flailed about knocking down several trees. He tried to bend his head so he could swallow his slayer, but Sigurdr was standing just out of Fafnir's reach. Fafnir gave up and began talking to his slayer trying to learn his identity so he could curse him, "What's your name and whose son are you? What kin are you that you have the courage and power to slay me?"

Sigurdr had been raised to fear the curses uttered by the dying. As long as Fafnir didn't know his name or his kinsmen's name he knew a parting curse could not be uttered on him. He was determined to answer as obliquely as possible, "Unknown would be my kin to you. My name is go fukt dyr, which means noble beast. I've neither father nor mother and have come here alone and unaided."

Fafnir didn't believe him, "By what miracle have you come to be born if you have neither father nor mother? Sigurd did not answer. Fafnir continued, "Very well, if you are ashamed of your family then keep silent about your heritage. No doubt you come from a long line of thieves and tricksters. Probably unmarried. Go away and let me die in peace."

Sigurdr couldn't let the insult to his lineage go unanswered, "You're wrong. I'm Sigurdr Sigmundrson. No doubt you've heard of the great King Sigmundr and the glorious deeds he wrought in battle?"

Fafnir became more curious, "Now I'm truly puzzled. Although I've heard of Sigmundr, as far as I know I had no quarrel with him. I've just been sitting for the last hundred years or so, simply guarding my gold and bothering no one. Who has urged you on to do this foul deed? Where did you find such courage? Had you not heard of my length or of my awful Helmet of Terror that, if you had not struck it from my head, would have caused you to do my bidding once you gazed on it?"

Sigurdr saw no harm in answering his questions now that his identity was known. It might even help. So far Fafnir had forgotten to hurl a curse at him. Maybe if he made him think of Regin, then Regin would be the cursed name that would die on the worm's lips. "There is one you know who has one purpose and one purpose alone. He has plotted your death for many years so he might have his rightful inheritance."

Fafnir's head jerked when he heard the word inheritance. Sigurdr continued his story, "Now do you know of whom I speak?"

Fafnir tried thinking, then spoke, "It seems once, long ago, I was part of a family. It's so hard to remember such things since it was then that I had a form akin to yours, puny and white and I walked on two legs. Could it be a brother I had—was his name Regin?—has brought about my death?"

Sigurdr answered, "You're right. Although he's brought it about, he has really had little part in it. Instead he hides over in the distance trembling."

Fafnir continued taunting Sigurdr, "I could understand your slaying me if I had done harm to your kin. But why should you, a slave taken in war, have the bravery to slay me?"

Sigurdr defended his heritage, "Do you say I'm too weak to carry on the name of Volsungr? Although I was raised in a Hall other than that belonging to my family, yet was I always free. Certainly I was free enough to cause you injury. So keep the word slave for some other. It applies naught to me."

Fafnir heaved up trying to get comfortable, but was unable to do so. He was growing weaker. "You take my words wrong. I didn't mean to insult you. However, to show you I mean you no harm I'll give you some good advice. Andvari's Hoard, which I have guarded all these years, has been the reason for the waste of my life. Pass it by and go on your way. It'll bring nothing but evil to you and your kin. It shall be your death too, for those who win it become trapped by their prize. Surely you're strong enough to leave it where it is, and hide the entrance to the cave so its curse will end with me?"

However, Sigurdr wasn't that strong. Gold blinds both the just and unjust alike. Sigurdr answered, "Gladly do I take lordship of that gold and will keep it until I die. Whether I die rich with the gold, or poor without it, there still will come a day when death stands in front of me and beckons me to follow. It is better then to have lived life with wealth. No, I'll take the gold rather than your advice, since both are as valuable as their worth. And your worth isn't much as you lay before me dying, killed by my sword thrust"

Fafnir continued, "Then let me give you some other advice since you won't follow my urgings concerning the gold. Be cautious before you set out to sea. Make certain your ship is secure, else you will surely drown. Wait to set sail until the sea is calm and the wind is but a fair breeze."

Sigurdr answer, "Great adventures are not the result of a calm sea. Roiling turbulent oceans push a ship faster and harder to battle. Look what the lazy life has begotten you, laying there dying from a deathwound gotten as you slithered back to your sleeping place. Yours will be counted as an ignoble straw death by the Norns."

Fafnir realized this was true. His was not a noble battle death. Slain as his thirst was quenched, his belly full. Off to bed, not off to battle. There was no response he could give Sigurdr to reclaim any glory in his death.

Sigurdr decided to quiz the dragon, "If you would give me wisdom then answer these questions so I might know you are wise. First, who are the Norns?"

Fafnir answered, "There are three main Norns who weave the fates of nations and those in all the worlds. They are known by the names Skuldr, Urdr, and Verdandi. However, there are lesser Norns who are the attendants on individuals. They often appear at the birth of a great warrior and give their blessings to him. Sometimes they appear and utter a curse. Some of these Norns set forth from the Æsir, some from Alfheimr, and others are known as the Daughters of Dvalin when they come from Svartalfrheimr."

Sigurdr was satisfied with that answer and asked his next question, "What is the name of the battlefield where Surtr and the Æsir, and the friends and foes of each other will meet at the last battle, a battle which will be fought with fire and water and mixed all over with blood?"

Fafnir answered, "That's certainly a long question for a simple answer. The unformed field is called Oskopnir on Vigridr Plain, a hundred rosts on each side. But enough of these questions. My thoughts turn now to my brother Regin who I now remember. He has finally won against me and brought about my death as he vowed he would do. Beware, for he will be your bane too, a thought that gladdens my heart. In times past I wore my Helmet of Terror and all who looked at me were afraid. And a long time did I think upon Regin's portion of the gold. I regretted stealing it only a short while, for I grew to love it so much I knew it was best it had stayed with me. Regin could never have loved it as much as I have. Loved it to the exclusion of all else. Loved it to the exclusion of life itself. My life has been a waste lived for gold. Gold I would not spend to increase my comfort. Only gold for my bed. Gold for my life. Regin would never have made the sacrifices I did to protect it. I spewed forth my venom on all who tried to creep up on me hoping to steal just a chunk of the treasure. And after a time I knew I was the most powerful of all, since no one came around to challenge me any longer until this day. They were all afraid of me. Who are you who has no fear of me?"

Sigurdr spoke, "You can only gain victory for so long if you depend on artificial contrivances such as your Helmet of Terror. My power is from my own strength and cunning. And that will win the battle any day."

Fafnir rolled a little more onto his side and laid his head on the ground so he could rest. He could feel the life force draining from him with each beat of his cleaved heart. "Once more I give you advice. Leap upon your horse and ride as far away as you can. Don't follow my track to the lair. Only golden evil wrapped in gilt awaits you there. You've given me a deathwound and if I were of a mind to seek vengeance on you I'd straightway urge you to take the gold. However, that is not my intent. Run from it so the rest of your life can be happy. Learn from the unhappiness of my life. It has all been useless."

Sigurdr shook his head no, "I cannot follow your advice. The gold draws me towards it even as I speak to you. My head keeps following along your track hoping to see the glint of gold in the distance."

Fafnir finally gave up, "All right then, take the gold and may it bring you trouble all the days of your life, which will be a lot shorter than you think. The gold is cursed and brings downfall to everyone and every family who owns it. It will be your death and also the death of many of your kinsmen."

Sigurdr stood up and said, "If I thought your words were true and not a trick, I'd leap on Grani and ride away from here as fast as I could. But death has muddled your senses and you don't know the things of which you speak. Die then so I can be off to the gold."

Fafnir spoke one final time, "Your wish is granted. Now I die, and in the form of a dragon. I had hoped to change back into the puny ugly shape I once wore. Such is not my wyrd. The evil and greed of my life has worked its way clear through my body so my old shape will not come out even though I will it. Such is the wyrd of shapechangers who become too much like the form they assume. It's bad enough to pretend to be a dragon, it's worse to become one." At that he rolled on his back and died.

Regin remained safely at a distance until he saw Fafnir was truly dead. He left his hiding place and went up to Sigurdr who stood wiping the blood from his sword on the grass. Regin decided to make his claim on the hoard, fearful Sigurdr would think he should have it all since he had done the actual slaying. But hadn't he, Regin, told him about Fafnir and given him the idea to dig the pits? And of course, wasn't the gold his weregild by right? It might take some doing, but Sigurdr would receive none of the Hoard. He spoke to the young warrior, "Praise to Sigurdr for you have battled against one larger and stronger than you, yet have you bested him. Long will stories be told of this day and our victory. Many have feared to even look at him. Yet you've not only done that, you've also slain him. And even though he's my brother and by rights you owe me your life or weregild for the doing of the deed, I'll be generous and instead share a portion of Andvari's Hoard with you.

However, I'll only agree to this if you will cut out Fafnir's heart and roast it for me so I might eat it."

Sigurdr didn't know how to answer Regin's speech, "Surely you are joking about this?"

Regin was seemingly overcome with grief. He wiped a dragon tear from his face, "No matter what his faults were, Fafnir was my brother. I'll miss him. I can't forget you killed my brother . . ."

Sigurdr broke in, "At your urging I must remind you."

Regin continued, "I agree, I can hardly be held blameless. I'm as guilty as you are. I stand equal to you as if I had taken the sword and plunged it into Fafnir with my own hands. We share equally in the guilt and . . ."

Sigurdr finished his sentence, " . . . you feel we should share equally in the gold? It seems to me when the sword was plunged into Fafnir you were a safe distance away. While I contended with the might and main of Fafnir you played with yourself in the bushes. No, you had nothing to do with this act. Don't try to take the credit now and change how the deed came about."

Regin answered trying to justify his part, "If I had not welded together the shards of the sword Gramr in such a fine manner, then you would have had no weapon with which to go against Fafnir. Yet would my brother live? No, the blame goes with me, more so than with you."

Sigurdr was beginning to tire of the bandying of words, "I've heard what you say and agree you did forge Gramr into one piece. However, many a warrior has won the battle with a dull edge to his blade. Such would have been the case had I gone against Fafnir with a lesser weapon."

Regin pressed the issue. "Again I say that I share in this deed. I urged you on and prompted your spirit to succeed." Regin reached down and took his sword Ridil and cut out Fafnir's heart. "Do as I urged you to do, and roast this heart for me. I'm tired from all that has happened today and will rest until my meal is ready."

Sigurdr was tired of arguing and grateful he would be left in peace while the heart was cooking. He prepared a fire and spitted the heart on a stick and propped it up so it roasted over the flames. He turned it occasionally so it cooked evenly on all sides. Finally, he thought it was done since he saw the blood bubbling up out of it. He touched the heart with his finger to see if it was hot clear through. He burnt his finger and put it to his lips to suck on and relieve the pain. As soon as he tasted the blood from the heart he was immediately able to understand the speech of the birds in the trees overhead. The nuthatches, tomtits, and woodpeckers were all twittering amongst themselves about what they had witnessed.

And spoke the first, "I can see Sigurdr sitting there cooking Fafnir's heart for another, when he should be eating it himself. For to do so will gain him great wisdom."

And spoke the second, "Cowardly Regin sleeps over there and is safe for now. But when he awakens Sigurdr should beware. The man means him harm."

And spoke the third, "If he were to cut off Regin's head right now then he would have the gold for himself. He wouldn't have to share so much as a nugget of it."

And spoke the fourth, "He would be well advised if he followed your counsel. Strike off Regin's head and then go to the beckoning Hoard and take the treasure. Journey thence to Hindarfjall where Brynhildr sleeps waiting for his awakening touch. Of her he can ask questions and receive true answers in return. He would do well to follow this advice. Kill Regin before it's too late. Where there are wolf's ears, wolf's teeth are close by."

And spoke the fifth, "You're right. He will prove himself stupid if he spares the kin of he whom he has already slain. Regin will work his vengeance somehow. It might have taken him a long time, but he finally bested Fafnir, and will best Sigurdr, too, if he is not slain."

And spoke the sixth, "Slay the brother and win the treasure for himself. That's what he should do."

Sigurdr could stand the twittering no longer and spoke out loud to himself, "Regin will never slay me. I'll not travel about having to cast a glance over my shoulder at every turn, fearful someone's kinsman seeks my death." He drew forth Gramr and separated Regin's head from his body at the neck ending the dreams of gold that had been playing about in Regin's head.

Sigurdr heard the woodpecker in the distance chittering, "The fairest of the fair dwells near here. Clad in byrny and shield she patiently awaits the hero's coming."

And spoke the second again, "Good tidings give the Norns to those who follow the path to Gjuki's Hall. He has a daughter who would be Sigurdr's for the wooing."

And spoke the third again, "But I speak of another meant to be Sigurdr's own true love, though not, perhaps, his wife. The shields of red and gold surround her body, protecting her on Mt. Hindarfjall. The flames shoot up and only the bravest warrior can enter there."

And spoke the fourth again, "Gently she sleeps, with warm breezes blowing over her. Nothing disturbs her rest. Thus does she sleep an unnatural sleep from the sleepthorn caught in her throat, put there for disobeying the bidding of her leader. From the battle did she fare riding Vingskornir. But now he grazes alone in the field while she sleeps on. Who will dislodge the sleepthorn and awaken her?"

Sigurdr tried to shut out the babbling. He ate most of Fafnir's heart and pocketed the rest in a pouch. He drank the blood of the dragon as well as that that flowed from Regin. As he looked over the dragon's body he saw one of its scaly fingers wore a bright shining ring, the Andvaranautr. He pried it from the finger and put it on his own finger. The ring miraculously shrunk to form a perfect fit. Suddenly the longing for the golden hoard grew more insistent. He mounted Grani, and at the last moment remembered Hreidmar's Helmet of Terror. He bent over Grani's shoulder and scooped it up, then rode along the dragon's track until he came to Fafnir's lair.

The iron gate sprung open at his touch. He saw the lair was encased in iron with strong beams sunk deep into the earth. He thought about this for only moments, for his eyes rested on the Hoard. His mouth fairly watered when he saw it. He

calculated it would take three ordinary horses to bear it back to his Kingdom. He would try and put as much as he could on Grani, being careful not to weight the horse down too much. He strapped two large chests to his saddle, one hanging from each side of the horse, and piled as much gold as he could in each chest and found magically they were large enough to hold the entire Hoard. As he placed more in each chest, more space seemed to open up in each chest. The mountain of gold fit completely in the two chests.

Standing back he looked at Grani to see if his back swayed at all under the weight. Grani seemed as strong as ever as he shifted restlessly from foot to foot. Sigurdr searched through the lair to make certain he had every bit of the gold. Then he took the sword Hrotti, a hauberk wrought of gold, many other costly things, and the Helmet of Terror Fafnir had stolen from Hreidmar.

After the treasure was loaded he pulled at Grani's reins, trying to lead the horse away. He didn't mount Grani for fear his added weight would break the animal's back. However, the horse wouldn't budge until Sigurdr had leapt on him and laid his whip to his back and his spurs into Grani's side. Grani trotted along lightly, untroubled by the weight he carried on his back.

They rode along, leaving behind the bodies of Fafnir and Regin for the carrion eaters that had been gathering for a feast. Sigurdr listened to the speech of the birds and followed the directions they sang out as he journeyed towards Brynhildr.

From that day forth he was known as Sigurdr Fafnirsbani, Sigurdr the bane of Fafnir.

CHAPTER 14
SIGURDR FINDS BRYNHILDR ASLAUGR IS BORN

Sigurdr rode long and hard through wild untrodden, cheerless lands. The shield he carried was covered with red gold and the image of a dragon had been painted on it, brown upon the blood-red field. Fafnir's Helmet of Terror, his golden byrny, and Grani's saddle all had like symbols painted on them. All fittings on his clothing and horse were made of gold. As he rode along the sign of the dragon told all who saw that he was Sigurdr and he had slain the dragon the Værings called Fafnir. He was now Sigurdr Fafnirsbani.

He was no longer a young boy venturing out for his first battle. He was now a warrior, brave and bold. He was courteous and helpful to those he met and his legend spread through all the lands north of the Grecian Sea. Fame and glory was his.

Many women saw him and desired him. His hair was red-golden and hung down his shoulders in long curly locks. His red-golden beard was short and neatly cut and suited his wide face. His nose was long and he had high cheekbones. However, the most striking thing about his looks were his piercing eyes. Few could hold his gaze. His body was strong and powerful, with shoulders as broad as two men's. He was tall enough so that when Gramr, seven spans long, hung at his side it did not touch the ground. As he walked through cornfields and wheat fields, the dew shoe of the scabbard cut the ears of corn or grazed the top of the grain. His strength was disproportionate to his size. He had never lost when pitted one-on-one with another warrior. Such was his physical prowess that he could wield Gramr, throw a spear, or bend a bow mightier than any other. He could tame the most savage horse, even those who had thrown hundreds of riders before he came along. He yearned for adventure and knowledge and had become so wise it was not often he heard something he did not already know. He held his tongue until he was certain the words he spoke were true and worth saying, so never was he thought the fool. He traveled through the lands for his own pleasure helping others and taking the wealth from his enemies and giving it to his friends and those in need. All this he did without fear.

Sigurdr rode southward until he reached the land of the Franks, in the Rhineland. Off in the distance he could see Hindarfjall, a mountain reaching high into the sky. A bright light was shining at the top. He urged Grani on.

Even though the path was steep Grani did not falter and soon carried Sigurdr to the shining light that stood at the top of the mountain in Skata Grove. When he reached it he saw it was a fortification made of red and white shields locked together so there was neither entrance nor exit. It was surrounded on all sides by tall protective flames that reached above the height of the shields. A banner unfurled at the top of the shields to reveal a standard Sigurdr did not recognize. He geed Grani at the flames. The horse ran and easily leapt over both flames and shields. Sigurdr was inside the fortification.

Once inside, the flames died away leaving a fine ash on the ground surrounding the shields. He noticed the shields were like glass from this side and he could see out over the landscape. Sigurdr dismounted and walked along cautiously exploring the area. He heard a sound. Sigurdr drew forth Gramr, holding it out, ready for battle if need be.

Sigurdr came to a large Hall. The land shook and the heavens thundered as he entered. In the main room he came upon a great warrior clad in full armor. The warrior appeared to be asleep on a bench. He moved closer, and poked the sleeper with the point of Gramr. The prodding did not rouse him. He tried to remove the helmet from the head of the warrior but it was stuck fast. The byrny and remaining armor was also held close to the skin and would not come off. He took Gramr and easily cut the armor from the collar down the center of the warrior and then across the chest and down both arms. The armor fell away. He could now remove the helmet. What he saw surprised him. It was not a man at all, but a beautiful woman with golden hair flowing over her white linen garments.

Sigurdr was overcome with her beauty and bent down to kiss her. His kiss moved her head and dislodged a sleepthorn that was sticking in her throat. She awoke and saw standing over her a well shaped young warrior, clad in magnificent armor. He had red-golden hair and most pleasing features.

She smiled, "Who are you that you have had a sword strong enough to cut my byrny and dislodge the sleepthorn that has kept me here? Is your name Sigurdr Sigmundrson, now Sigurdr Fafnirsbani? Is it Fafnir's Helmet of Terror you wear on your head?"

Sigurdr removed the Helmet of Terror, "You're right. I am Sigurdr, son of Sigmundr, but now known as Sigurdr Fafnirsbani. How did you know my name? The helm I hold did come from Fafnir, and he got it from his father Hreidmar. I was born with the blood of the Volsungrs flowing through my body. The birds have told me you were the daughter of a great King, and you were more beautiful than all others. I can see they spoke the truth."

She arose and went to fetch horns of mead for them. When she returned she handed one to Sigurdr and motioned for him to sit beside her, "Take this mimis-cup and drink while I tell you my story.

My name is Brynhildr. I am the daughter of King Budli. My brother is Atli Budlason, my sisters are Bekkhildr, who is married to King Heimir of Hlymdale, my brother-in-law who is also my foster-father, and finally Oddrunr."

Sigurdr took the cup of memory and sipped the cool liquid. He was immediately refreshed and his mind was cleared from the monotony of his journey.

Brynhildr began her story, "I was put here to sleep by Odin's will, for I disobeyed him. Before my long sleep, I rode to battle as a Valkyrie and fetched the dead back to Valhalla for Odin."

She sat up and continued her story, "Once there was a battle between two powerful Kings, Hjalmgunnar and Agnar, Audi's brother. Perhaps you've heard of them?"

Sigurdr nodded that he had since they were Kings of renown and legend.

Brynhildr continued her story, "Hjalmgunnar was the older of the two and had fought many battles and always won Odin's blessings. He had been promised victory in this battle. Before the battle my eight sister Valkyries and I were bathing. Agnar had come upon our swan-guises and stolen them. Without them we would be unable to ride to battle. He only agreed to return them if I promised him the victory, which I did. At the battlefield I saw how valiantly Agnar fought and he was the more powerful of the two and deserved the victory, so I kept my word. Disobeying Odin I awarded victory to the younger warrior and struck down Hjalmgunnar. This displeased Odin. When I next met him he told me I would no longer be welcome among the Valkyries, but would have to become a mortal maiden once again and be given in marriage. I asked a favor of him which he granted. I wished to be given to the most powerful warrior in the land. One who knew not the name of fear, for I didn't deserve the fate of being wed to a coward. Odin agreed to my request and placed me here in this shield-laden, fire-protected fortress. I was given a drink containing the sleepthorn. It lodged in my throat as I swallowed the mead. Thus have I slept here unchanged in appearance or youth for twelve years awaiting your arrival. Only the noblest warrior riding a brave steed born of Sleipnir would be able to pass through the flames unharmed and awaken me. Now you have heard my story. Ask if you would know more."

Sigurdr sat for a moment thinking of the story and then asked her for knowledge, "You've been a Valkyrie and have learned the knowledge of the Æsir. Teach it to me."

Brynhildr answered, "Much of what I'll say you probably already know, since it's common knowledge among valiant warriors. However, I'll gladly tell it to you. If there are any other questions you want to know, just ask. Let me refill your cup first so the drink of memory will help you retain the knowledge I'm going to give you."

Brynhildr filled their cups. She held both up and turned towards the night and day, towards the Æsir seeking blessings on the drinks. She gave one of the cups

back to Sigurdr, "Drink this mead for it is mixed throughout with fame, and is full of stories and the knowledge of the runes. Wise and sweet words mingle with the liquid.

"Cut and learn the sig-runes, the runes of victory. Carve them upon the hilt of your sword, and also on the edge and blade. As you do this call out the name of Tyr twice and cut the tyrrune.

"Cut and learn the grimrunar, the runes of the sea. Carve them into the stern of your ship. Also cut them on the rudder blade. Burn them into the oars so they will cut through the water with more force. If you do this your ship will fair well and swiftly across the sea. No matter the nature of the seas or how high the waves break against your ship, you'll always return to port safe and unharmed, even in the worst storms. The brimrunar gives you control over the elements and the power to triumph over wind and waves.

"Cut and learn the malrunar, the runes of speech, and learn them well. Learn them especially if you want to pay back in double the grief you have been given by another. These runes are powerful, so take them, turn them and twist them in all directions to suit your purposes. When you are at the Thing, use them to work the minds of the counselors to your ways. They will give voice to the speechless or those who would hold their tongue. False words spoken against you will be dissolved and the lies will choke in the throat of the one who utters them. They will also protect you against spellcraft and wizardry.

"These runes are powerful. Learn them and cast them well.

"Cut and learn the olrunar, the ale-runes, for they have wonderful qualities. If you want another man's wife not to betray you when you trust her, cut these runes on mead horns, and also on the backs of each hand. This procedure is also good for remedying the effects of a love-potion given in trickery. Nick the naud runes upon your nail to call forth the protection of the Norns. Use the luck of the leek as well. Cast it into your drink to keep ill luck out of your life. Keep a supply of your own ale and mead that you have blessed. In that way you will never swallow a deceitful drink of mead mingled through and through with poison. Use the cup cut with olrunar to bless your ship against the rages of the sea.

"Cut and learn the bjargrunar, the help runes, for they will help the woman struggling in childbirth with a low-laid child. They are also good for the healing of wounds won in battle. Always cut them into the hollow of the hand of the person you would heal and call upon Mardoll for help. In the case of the woman troubled in childbirth also wrap your arms about her waist as you call upon Mardoll to help you with the delivering of the child.

"Cut and learn the limrunar, the branch and limb runes. These, too, are useful for healing, and work very well when the name of Mardoll is called as they are carved. They work best when carved on the boughs that point towards the east. Cut them on the bark, the leaves and the buds. Use them also to trail those running away from you through the forest. You'll easily find them. It will be as if they had cut a clear path behind them for you to follow.

"Cut and learn the bokrunar and meginrunar, the book runes and strength runes.

"The hugrunar, the thought runes of wisdom and knowledge, will make you greater and wiser than all men and women. They will turn foes into friends since they lessen hatred. The hugrunar are the strongest of all runes and were the first cut in ages past by Hroptr. They were born of the Precious Mead that leaked from Heiddraupnir's Skull and Hoddrofnir's Horn, when it was stolen by Midvitnir and guarded over by Sokkmimir. In times past they were carved on the shield Svalin that is hung in front of the sun, on Arvarkr's ear, Alsvin's hoof, the wheel beneath Rognir's chariot, eight-legged Sleipnir's jawteeth, a sleigh's traces and runners, the bear's forepaws, Bragi's tongue, the wolf's claws, the eagle's beak, on bloody wings, on the bridge's end, on the midwife's palm and feet, the trail of tears, glass, gold, silver amulets, Gungnir's point, Grani's chest, the jotun's breast, the Norns' nail, and the night owl's neb. The runes can also be found in wine, port, and the throne of the Volva. The runes mixed with the Precious Mead live with the Æsir, Vanir, and Alfs, and some with men and women. Those who use them in good faith and not for trickery or evil will be rewarded with success and happiness. Learn all these runes and use them, and good luck will follow you through your life. You will never flee from a fight, nor fear death."

Sigurdr longed for more knowledge. "I was never born to be a coward and run from a battle. I was born without fear. I will keep your counsel, treasure it and follow it throughout my life and for as long as the Æsir shall prevail. Your words are the wisest I've ever heard. Are there other things I might learn from you?"

Brynhildr answered. "There is much I can teach you. Listen and learn my wisdom.

"When you have a friend treat him or her always with kindness and as you would be treated. If they make a mistake forgive them and help them as you would also be helped.

"Hold your anger and think before you take vengeance. However, if you must take vengeance do it as soon as possible and kill your foe no later than the next day, lest he be able to raise an army against you. Bide your time well and choose the right moment for your vengeance. If you are one and your foe is a hundred do not attack. Wait until the odds are in your favor when he is one and you are a hundred.

"Swear no untrue oaths at the Thing.

"Don't waste your time arguing with ignorant fools, for such a dispute you can never win no matter how right you are. But if lies are yelled out among others don't be afraid to dispute them. Your silence will only yell out your agreement with the charges and show you to be a coward.

"Be careful of a young woman's love and another man's wife. Don't be lured by the thought of a large dowry into a false marriage. Nothing good can come of it.

"If you are journeying and night comes and the only lodging available is with a witchwife, then avoid it. It's better by far to sleep in the prickliest of thickets than to sleep next to a witchwife. Bad luck will come of it.

"Sleep not near the edge of the road at night since spæwights and beings that will charm your mind are there.

"Beautiful women offering you drinks at a banquet are to be avoided. The drink is tainted with draughts of forgetfulness and love. Once enchanted you will no longer care for your true love.

"Pay no attention to the ravings of a drunken man. Often witless words are spoken and taken the wrong way. Then feuds start and senseless killings result.

"Battles are best fought in the field, rather than in your home. It is one of the greatest dishonors to have your Hall burned out from under you. Be serious about all the oaths you swear, and break none of them. If you are uncertain about an oath then do not take it. Broken pledges against friends, and vows of love are the worst to break. Ill luck will follow you.

"Honor the dead and bury them properly and respectfully, no matter if they have died of illness or wounds. Bury your enemies lest they revenge themselves upon you with their spoiled bodies. Wash and comb their hair, cut their nails, and raise a barrow for them. Prey for their safe journey after death. No matter if you do this for a foe, do not tarry long with their kin if you have slain the departed. Do not trust the kin of one you've slain, no matter how friendly they seem to you. They are honorbound to slay you. Leave as soon as possible, even though you've paid weregild and feel safe in their company.

"Be wary of your friends and their advice. Sometimes it's not true. Although I'm not skilled in seeing the future, I can see that your wife's friends will be your friends. That is all I have to say."

Sigurdr spoke, "In all my travels I've never come across anyone with your knowledge. Nor is there any woman I've seen who is fairer than you. My heart is lost to you. If you will agree, I would be your husband and you my wife."

Brynhildr answered, "I swore to Odin I would only marry the one who was without fear. Of all those in this world, that person is you. Gladly will we be joined."

They pledged their love and Sigurdr stayed the night. After they became lovers Brynhildr could no longer claim any rights as a Valkyrie being no longer pure of body.

The next morning Sigurdr asked Brynhildr to leave with him. She pointed out her home, "Look and see the land in the distance. I live at Hlymdale in Hunland. We will meet next at King Heimir's Hall. I have things to do here before I can leave. I'll see you sometime in the future. Remember our pledges to each other. I'll remain faithful and true until we meet again."

Sigurdr took the ring Andvaranautr from his finger and placed it on hers. "Remember me with this ring. Return it when we pledge our love to each other again." He left and rode off towards Hunland.

Brynhildr remained there many months and eventually gave birth to a daughter whom she named Aslaugr. The child had inherited the burning eyes of the Volsungrs. Her story soon will be told.

CHAPTER 15
SIGURDR AND BRYNHILDR MEET AT HLYMDALE

After leaving Brynhildr, Sigurdr rode until he came to King Heimir's Hall in Hlymdale. King Heimir was married to Bekkhildr, Brynhildr's sister. He was also her foster-father. Bekkhildr was unlike her sister Brynhildr in every way. Instead of riding to battles as one of Odin's Valkyries, clad in a byrny and gathering up dead warriors, she had stayed home and learned sewing and household crafts. She had been wooed by King Heimir and had gone to live in his Hall as his wife. They had a son named Alsvidr, who was generous and well mannered.

Many men were standing outside the gates of the Hall joking about. They looked up and saw Sigurdr approaching and went to get a closer look. They had never seen his like before. Alsvidr was the first to speak to him, "You're welcome to stay here a while if you come in peace. Many Halls are beset by marauders and we can always use a stouthearted warrior."

Sigurdr answered, "I thank you for your friendly welcome. I come in peace and have been sent here by Brynhildr."

Sigurdr dismounted and gave Grani's reins to one of the stableboys. Four men carried Andvari's Hoard into a treasure chamber. Once they began removing the gold from the chests it expanded to fill up and overflow the entire treasure chamber.

A fifth man stood guard over it. The men looked through it and were awed at what they saw. There were golden rings, glistening warrior gear, and goblets. Many of the weapons had precious jewels pressed into them. Never had the men seen such a treasure.

At the feast that night Sigurdr told them the story of his victories in battle and over Fafnir. He told the stories well and became very popular in the Hall.

o   o   o   o

As the months passed Sigurdr's stories were embellished and changed to such an extent that he could hardly recognize them when he heard them told by those in the streets. Skalds sang stories of heroic deeds he had never performed.

He and Alsvidr became true friends. They often practiced weaponry and swordplay against each other and developed their warrior skills together. With Sigurdr as his teacher Alsvidr's skills improved. The two could often be seen in the woods with their falcons and goshawks hunting for small game.

o   o   o   o

In the meantime Brynhildr had returned to Hlymdale. Her daughter Aslaugr was temporarily in the care of foster-parents. She had not yet sought out Sigurdr, and instead, spent her hours sitting in her bower with her serving maids, embroidering a golden tapestry that told the tale of Sigurdr's victories and his triumphs over Fafnir and Regin. Such was her skill that few could have done better.

o   o   o   o

On one morning Sigurdr and Alsvidr had ventured into the woods with their falcons and a company of men. Their hunt was successful and when they returned that afternoon they were in a good mood. Sigurdr's falcon flew up to the tower keep and alit at the window there. Everyone urged Sigurdr to climb up after his hawk. He scrambled up the side of the Hall and reached out for the falcon. As it jumped onto the leather bindings of his arms he happened to glance into the window and saw Brynhildr sitting there at her tapestry that looked to be the finest he had ever seen. He climbed back down the wall, gave his hawk and Grani's reins to the care of his attendants and went to his room. He brooded on why she had not sought him out yet.

Sigurdr sat in his room for several days eating very little. Alsvidr was worried about his friend and went to him, "What troubles you and causes lines to crease your brow? We are all worried about you. You used to be happy and join us in sports and games. Now you sit here alone. Your hawk grows so fat soon it won't be able to lift itself off the ground, no matter how hard it flaps its wings. And Grani kicks at his stall restless for adventure. Tell me how I can help you?"

Sigurdr answered, "You first offered me friendship when I arrived, so I feel I can trust you in this matter. When I climbed the tower to retrieve my falcon I happened to glance into a window. There I saw a woman sitting embroidering at a golden tapestry."

Alsvidr interrupted, "That would have been Brynhildr, King Budli's daughter, my aunt. She arrived here a short while ago."

Sigurdr continued, "Yes, that's her name. The tapestry told of my adventures, past as well as those yet to come, although the frame was at such a slant I couldn't see the future adventures too clearly."

Alsvidr spoke again, "Don't brood about a woman you can't have. There are many other fine maids around here who would be honored to have your attentions." Alsvidr was unaware Brynhildr was no longer a Valkyrie.

"I'm only interested in Brynhildr. I must go to meet her. Which way is it to her room?" Sigurdr arose and prepared to go.

Alsvidr stopped him, "I'll tell you where she is, but I don't think any good will come of it. She has never been known to let a man sit beside her or to offer him a drink. She's called as one of Odin's Valkyries, and as you well know they do not have dealings with men, other than to pick them up from the battlefield and help them on their way to Valhalla. If she had been born a man I reckon she would have been almost your equal as a warrior."

Sigurdr was impatient, "Just give me directions to her room. I think I can convince her of my good intentions."

Alsvidr led Sigurdr to Brynhildr's chamber and stood outside sharpening and feathering his arrows.

Sigurdr entered the room. Its walls were hung with beautiful tapestries. The floor was carpeted and quiet to walk on.

Brynhildr did not hear Sigurdr enter, but looked up as he spoke to her, "Greetings, Brynhildr. I've only just found out you were here. How are you?"

Brynhildr stuck her needle into the corner of the tapestry and answered, "I've been well. My family is well. But who can say how things will go with a person's life? The Norns many times add unexpected and unwanted weavings changing the hope one had for the future. No matter how hard we try we cannot change our wyrd, but must accept it, however painful."

Sigurdr took a place beside her. Brynhildr motioned for her serving maids to bring them drinks. Golden goblets filled with mead were given to each of them. Then the servants were dismissed so Sigurdr and Brynhildr could speak in private.

Sigurdr drank from the cup before speaking, "Now we are reunited as you said we would be. We can plan our lives together and return to my Kingdom as King and Queen." Brynhildr did not respond. Sigurdr continued, "This should be a time of great happiness for us, why do you seem so sad?"

Brynhildr looked away, "I've been casting runes to foretell our fates. The auguries are not good. When we met in Skata Grove you listened to the words of wisdom I spoke. If you follow those words then perhaps happiness will be ours. If you don't then we will never be fated to be together."

Sigurdr became upset at her words, "What's to become of us if we don't live together? If I do not marry you, then I will marry no one."

Brynhildr answered, "That's not true. If you forget what I said to you in Skata Grove then you will marry Gudrunr."

Sigurdr was puzzled, "Who is Gudrunr? I don't even know a Gudrunr."

Brynhildr put down her cup and motioned for Sigurdr to leave, "Gudrunr is the daughter of King Gjuki. Be on your guard once you meet her."

Sigurdr started to leave, but turned for one final word, "You wear the ring Andvaranautr on your finger. We've pledged our love with it. I'll never forget that."

Brynhildr answered, "I think maybe the Andvaranautr is not such a lucky ring to pledge one's love over."

He left. Brynhildr returned to her tapestry which showed a warrior being stabbed in his bed.

CHAPTER 16
GUDRUNR'S PROPHETIC DREAMS

King Gjuki ruled a misty Kingdom to the south of the Rhine. His wife was Grimhildr, who was skilled in the ways of sorcery and could sometimes be very cruel. She had been married to another before Gjuki and had a son named Gutthormr from that union. Additionally she had three sons and one daughter with Gjuki. Their sons were Gunnar, Hogni, and Gudmundr, who were sometimes known as Gudny. Their daughter was named Gudrunr. All of the Gjukings, as the kin of Gjuki were called, although they were sometimes known as Nibelungs, were fair of face and figure. They were strong and worthy of the fame and stories that attended their deeds. Gunnar, Hogni, and Gudmundr had all proven themselves in battle. Gudrunr was a beautiful woman and had had many Princes wooing her. But so far she had refused them, waiting for the appearance of a bold warrior to carry her away to his Kingdom.

King Budli ruled over a realm larger than Gjuki's. And larger than King Budli's Kingdom was the land his son, Atli Budlason, had won. King Atli was Brynhildr, Bekkhildr, and Oddrunr's brother. There was little resemblance between him and his sisters. They were tall and well formed, while he was deformed and extremely short almost a dvergar in appearance. He stood only three-feet-two inches high. Despite this he was a bold warrior and brilliant commander. He had an uncanny ability to position his soldiers in just the right places to have advantage over his enemies. In battle place can be more powerful than numbers of warriors. His armies were rarely bested in battle and he had conquered much of the world. He was fearsome and stern with his subjects, yet fair.

One day Gudrunr, sitting in her bower, told her attendant maids she was upset. One of the maids asked why, and Gudrunr replied, "For some nights now I've been troubled by awful dreams. They're so disturbing I don't know what to do about them. They won't leave my thoughts. They even haunt me during the day and intrude into my waking world."

One of her maids said, "Tell your dreams to us. Perhaps we can tell you what they mean. I have some skill in doing that. Many times I've found that dreams forecast nothing more sinister than the weather, and not with any particular accuracy, either."

Gudrunr answered, "No, no, they tell more than the weather. In the first dream a hunting falcon alit on my wrist. Its feathers were bright golden and shone in the sun."

The maid interpreted the dream for her. "Stories of your beauty have spread far and wide through many realms. Perhaps the golden hawk portends some great King coming to sue for your hand in marriage?"

Gudrunr continued, "Everything around the hawk was blurred. If I turned to look at the things I owned in my room, they were not clear. But it didn't matter since I would have given up all my wealth for the sake of this hawk. What does it mean?"

The serving maid thought a while and then answered, "When you wed you will prove to be the loyalist of companions. Great luck will it be to the one who has you as his wife."

"Is there no way to find out whom I am to wed? I would feel much better if I knew." Gudrunr began pacing the floor.

The serving maid watched from side-to-side as she answered, "There is one who might be able to tell you your future. Her name is Brynhildr and she is known to be skillful at the casting of runes. She is at present staying at Hlymdale since King Heimir is her foster-father and brother-in-law."

Gudrunr threw on a costly outfit and a golden cloak, and accompanied by her attendants, sought out Brynhildr. As they neared King Heimir's Hall word was sent ahead that they wished to speak with Brynhildr.

Brynhildr was informed that a company of women riding in gilt carriages approached the Hall and wished an audience with her.

Brynhildr signaled to her attendants, "It must be Gudrunr, Gjuki's daughter. I have been expecting her. Show me where she is and I'll go meet her. She is a gracious woman and welcome in this Hall."

Gudrunr was welcomed and shown into the Hall. The room they met in was wrought with silver and carpeted. While they made themselves comfortable goblets of wine were brought to them. Gudrunr remained silent, even though her attendants were beginning to enjoy themselves.

Brynhildr sat next to Gudrunr and spoke to her, "We've shown you good welcome, yet you still seem distant and sad. Let's talk of things and see if I can cheer you up."

Gudrunr reluctantly tried to keep the conversation going, "What shall we talk about?"

"Why not of Captains and Kings and the derring deeds they do?" Brynhildr took a sip of her mead.

Gudrunr made an effort, "That seems a safe conversation. Whom do you think the best Kings are? Name those who are the best thought of by all men?"

Brynhildr thought for a moment before answering, "There are many who are yet young and have not had a chance to prove themselves year after year. So, I would say the greatest Kings are the sons of Hamund, Haki, and Hagbardr. They've brought continued honor to their families."

Gudrunr disagreed, "I've heard of them, and their deeds are well known. Some of them are not very honorable. Didn't Sigar steal one of their sisters away and burn the other in their own Hall? That's enough to tarnish their reputation. But what's worse is they have yet to avenge either crime. Why didn't you name my brothers Gunnar, Hogni, and Gudmundr as the best of all warriors? Many think them such."

Brynhildr answered, trying not to hurt Gudrunr's feelings, "Although they've performed many deeds that have made their names well known, they still haven't proven themselves in battle after battle. However, as I think on the question I can think of a King who is by far better than all we have named combined. He is Sigurdr Fafnirsbani. He still had not shaven when he slew the sons of King Hunding to avenge the deaths of his father, King Sigmundr, and King Eylimi, his grandfather, his mother's father."

Gudrunr was interested, "How do you know about all of this? Why is this such an extraordinary thing? Tell me, was his mother with child when his father died?"

Brynhildr told her Sigurdr's story, "After Sigmundr had suffered his last blow, Hjordis, his wife, searched among the dead and dying on the battlefield until she found Sigmundr. She began to tend his wounds but was prevented by Sigmundr who knew them to be deathwounds. He told her about Sigurdr, a great warrior who would be born after his death. Then he died. She met King Alfr who showed her the greatest kindness in the world and raised Sigurdr as if he were his own son. Once Sigurdr reached manhood he performed at least one noble act every day. He has conquered a wide realm, owns the Treasure of the Volsungrs, and won Andvari's Hoard when he slew the dragon Fafnir, becoming known by that deed as Sigurdr Fafnirsbani. How could there be one mightier than he?"

Gudrunr had been staring at Brynhildr as she told her story. Brynhildr's manner had become softer after she mentioned Sigurdr's name. "Why is it, Brynhildr, that you speak from the heart when talking of Sigurdr? One would think you were in love with him by your words and manner. However, let's talk of other things. I've come here to talk about some troubling dreams I've been having."

Brynhildr reassured her it was all right to talk of such things. "You're among friends here. Tell me what has been troubling you? Perhaps I can help."

Gudrunr settled back, closed her eyes, and related a dream she had had the night before. "I was with a large company of my friends. We had left my bower and gone into the field. There I saw the largest hart I had ever seen. It was many times greater than any that had ever been seen in our land. It was golden and so brilliant in the sun I could hardly see past its way. Everyone tried to capture him. I succeeded in doing so without the aid of any others. I was happy and standing by the hart when you came up to us and slew him so he fell at my knees. So much grief came over me that I wanted to die, but couldn't. Then you came to me for a second time and

presented me with a wolf cub. It was covered over with the blood of my brothers that stained me as I held it. What can you make of these things?"

Brynhildr was troubled by what she heard. "This dream is easy to interpret but painful to talk about. The things you dreamed will come to pass. Sigurdr, the warrior I spoke of, will come to you instead. Although I'm pledged to him, and he to me, yet will you win him. Grimhildr will prepare a drink for him that will cause him to forget all his vows and do her will. His drinking of that mead will cause great grief. Although you'll have him as your husband, your time together will be short, but the strife caused by that wedding will last for many years and cause many deaths. After Sigurdr has died you'll wed King Atli, my brother. Your brothers will die and the deadliest of harm will come to King Atli by your hand. All of this can be prevented if you will forsake Sigurdr when he asks you to marry him."

Gudrunr was upset by what she had heard. "I don't know if you've interpreted my dreams correctly. If you have then, seeing these are all things fated to happen, there is nothing I can do to prevent them. One cannot escape one's wyrd. The fabric woven by the Norns cannot be avoided as it covers you in your final moments. I'm not the happier for having talked with you because I realize what you say is true. Yet, even knowing that, and knowing I should avoid Sigurdr, I know I will not be able to. Does not the moth fly into the flame? Things will be as they will be. Our lives have intercepted and I cannot follow the course you counsel even though I realize it is best?"

Brynhildr left knowing even though she had tried her best, things would still turn out much the same as she predicted. Returning to King Heimir's Hall she met with him and Bekkhildr to bid them goodbye. "I've decided to return to Skata Grove since my work here is finished. I'll await the return of the most renown of warriors so our vows can be made public. At his return I'll be happy. I'm certain he will come to me." She didn't sound at all convincing.

Brynhildr returned to Skata Grove and once more raised flames around it. She knew only Sigurdr riding Grani could leap over it. She waited patiently for the dogs to return to her side.

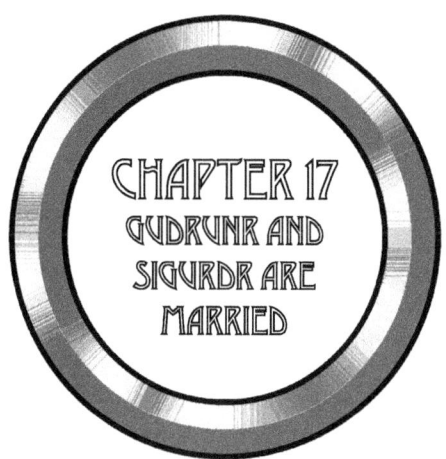

CHAPTER 17
GUDRUNR AND SIGURDR ARE MARRIED

Brynhildr did not say goodbye to Sigurdr when she left Hlymdale. Instead she sent a message to him telling him to seek adventure and win further fame. Then when his mind was clear of war and he was ready to rule his Kingdom with her at his side, he was to come to her at Skata Grove where she would be waiting for him. She also left Aslaugr behind in the Hall, her existence a secret from everyone except King Heimir and Bekkhildr. The Volsungrs had many enemies who would gladly harm or kidnap the youngest and most innocent of the Volsungr's.

After Brynhildr left, Sigurdr remained just a short while longer with King Heimir and his family. He gathered together his treasure, put on his armor, mounted Grani and rode off promising to return soon.

o o o o

Sigurdr rode until he came to the land of the Gjukings, who were also known as the Nibelungs. One of Gjuki's watchmen reported Sigurd's arrival to his superior "I think I've seen one of the gods. He's clad in silver and rides the largest horse I've ever seen. He looks to be the most powerful warrior I've ever seen. I wouldn't want to come up against him in battle, yet I'm the King's best swordsman."

News of the stranger's arrival reached the King. He went to the courtyard to meet him. "Is your business in our country peaceful? If so, then you may stay here as our guest. None have ever entered here without the permission of my sons."

Sigurdr replied, "I come in peace. My name is Sigurdr Fafnirsbani."

Sigurdr gave Grani to a stableboy who led the horse away. His treasure was unloaded and put in a guarded room. Once more the size of the chests had been deceiving. When the treasure had been removed from the chests it filled the room to overflowing.

Sigurdr followed Gjuki to his Hall where he was shown to a room he could use during his stay. He was introduced all around as a great warrior and honored guest. All hospitality was given to him.

Two of the King's sons, Gunnar and Hogni, became his friends. Sigurdr taught them many things. The three were looked upon as the greatest warriors in the land, with Sigurdr being thought the best of the three.

Grimhildr, Gjuki's wife, thought Sigurdr would make a fine husband for her daughter Gudrunr. She often engaged in conversation with Sigurdr and tried to turn his thoughts to Gudrunr. But the only woman he'd talk about was Brynhildr and how much he loved her and longed to be with her.

Grimhildr realized it would take a little special urging to make Sigurdr forget Brynhildr. She discussed the matter with Gjuki, "He's very strong and would be a wise ruler should something happen to you. He'd be able to keep your lands together after your death. His wealth is greater than yours and would be a blessing to the people of this land. Although our sons are brave they don't seem to be rulers. They love Sigurdr as if he were their brother and would accept him as King. If he were wedded to Gudrunr he would have a right to claim the throne."

Gjuki agreed, "I've had these thoughts myself. It's unusual for a King to offer his daughter to one who has not asked for her hand. But I would rather ask him to take her hand than listen to noble beseechments from other, less worthy, suitors. Unfortunately he seems enamored of another. His thoughts are of Brynhildr and the life he'll have with her. There's nothing we can do about that."

Grimhildr disagreed, "I think I can make him forget Brynhildr. Leave things to me. Treat him as your son and tell our sons to continue looking on him as their brother. Gudrunr needs no prompting. Her heart has fallen to him, although she seems to be a little worried about it. I think it has something to do with those dreams she's been having."

That night at dinner Sigurdr told them he would be leaving so he could return to Brynhildr. Grimhildr smiled and brought Sigurdr a special drink, "You've honored us with your visit and asked nothing from us in return. We want you to know how much we love you and look on you as if you were one of our own. Take this drink and drink to the love we give you and the happiness we hope for you. Remember us when you leave. However, if you should decide not to go, be assured you're welcome to stay here as long as you like."

Sigurdr took the horn, paused a moment. There was something he was forgetting. Some warning in the back of his mind he just couldn't remember. He downed the contents of the horn in one gulp. Immediately all thoughts he had of leaving left him. The drink was delicious and he asked for more which he drank again, even deeper. Grimhildr continued refilling the cup and stood behind him chanting into his ear. After a few drinks he sat as one in a trance, for the drink was a special potion of forgetfulness that allowed Grimhildr to manipulate his thoughts. She whispered into his ear many things to change his mind about what he wanted to do, "From now on you'll honor Gjuki and Grimhildr as if they were you own parents. Gunnar, Hogni, Gudmundr, and Gutthormr will be your brothers. And oaths of fealty will be sworn between your new brothers and you." Sigurdr drank some more from the cup. Grimhildr continued, "Forget about Brynhildr. Instead look upon Gudrunr and notice her beauty. She loves you and would be the happiest person alive if you would return her affection.

Sigurdr remained at King Gjuki's Hall. Within a few days he swore blood brotherhood with Gunnar, Hogni, and Gudmundr. Gutthormr was thought too young for such a noble thing. Also, he was only a half-brother and treated poorly by the other three.

The brotherhood ceremony was arranged. A doom circle was cut out of the ground. This consisted of a bare spot left when the dirt and grass was lifted up. The dirt and grass was placed on a shield that was held over the three brothers and Sigurdr. The three brothers and Sigurdr pulled back the sleeves on their right arms and each nicked a cut in their arm. They held their arms down so the blood dropped onto the bare patch of earth. Then the patch of dirt and grass was placed back on it, and they swore eternal friendship to each other by the Baugeidr, the sacred arm ring of Ullr, as well as by Var and the river Leiptr. Their blood had been mingled and now they were as true to each other as if they had been born of the same mother.

The months and years passed until Sigurdr had lived among them for two-and-a-half years. Finally Grimhildr felt it was time to arrange things even further. That night at dinner Grimhildr gave Gudrunr a drink to pour out for Sigurdr. He looked up at her as he took it. He couldn't remember ever having seen anyone so beautiful or so courteous as she. Gjuki spoke as Sigurdr drank from the horn. "Lucky was the day you rode into my Kingdom. We've been made stronger by your presence."

Gunnar continued the homage, "If there's anything we can ever do for you we will, as long as you promise to stay here with us. I relinquish my claim to the throne in your favor and will always be your liegeman in service."

Hogni spoke next, "We offer you the love of our sister. You've ever been honorable to her and made no untoward advances. There have been many who have sued for her hand, but these warriors we have refused so she could be yours."

The drink had taken its effect and Sigurdr spoke, his speech slightly slurred, "Great honor have you given me here tonight. I accept and would be happy to become Gudrunr's husband. She's the fairest in the land."

Still something nagged at the back of his mind. What was it? He spent the rest of the evening by himself trying to think what it was. He knew one thing, he wasn't as happy as he had been before he entered this land, even though things had gone quite well for him.

The wedding feast was quickly arranged and took place within days. He drank to Gudrunr's honor, as did all others. Then toasts were drunk to him, and then to both of them. Their happiness was wished by all. The feast continued for many days with the mead flowing generously. Everyone was happy. At one point Sigurdr gave Gudrunr the piece of Fafnir's heart he had carried in his pocket ever since slaying the vile worm. By eating it she became wiser and also understood the language of birds. Also, it had one other effect on her. She grew cold and distant to all but Sigurdr. Only to him could she pour out the thoughts of her heart.

o   o   o   o

Sigurdr and the three brothers raised an army and went to war so they all could gain further glory. Their battles were sung of and the names of all the King's sons they had slain were handed down from one person to another. After their campaign Sigurdr and the Gjukings returned home with even greater wealth.

Shortly after Sigurdr returned Gudrunr bore him his first son. They named him Sigmundr, hoping he'd follow in the noble footsteps of his grandfather and be as brave and well thought of by others. Next a daughter was born to them and she was called Svanhildr.

Then came the sad day when King Gjuki died. Sigurdr was offered the throne, but refused it, "I already have a Kingdom. By rights the throne is yours Gunnar. Take it and I'll be pleased. You can always depend on me to help you any way I can."

At first Gunnar refused the throne, since it had been his father's dying wish the throne pass to Sigurdr. Reluctantly Gunnar became King instead of Sigurdr.

Grimhildr spoke to Gunnar, "Now that you're King you must have a Queen so you can have children and true heirs. Your honor is great. The battles you've fought with Sigurdr and your brothers have brought you fame enough that you can have any Princess you desire. I've thought on the matter and know of one who is worthy of you. Her name is Brynhildr. She lives in Skata Grove protected by a wall of flames awaiting her true love to gee his horse over the flames and come to her.

Although Gunnar had never met Brynhildr, he had heard of her and of her beauty and wisdom. The idea grew in his head until he would have no other but her as his wife. He drank a potion from Grimhildr to give him strength. He asked Sigurdr to ride with him to Skata Grove and give him whatever help he needed. Sigurdr agreed, though for some reason he felt uneasy about riding to Skata Grove. There was some thought at the back of his mind that wouldn't come forth. Try as he might he could not pull the thought out into the open. Was it some kind of memory he was forgetting? Soon he forgot even that there was something nagging at the back of his mind.

CHAPTER 18
SIGURDR WOOS AND WINS BRYNHILDR FOR GUNNAR

Sigurdr, Gunnar, Gudmundr, and Hogni, accompanied by a few warriors, rode to King Budli's Hall. There Gunnar asked King Budli for Brynhildr's hand in marriage.

King Budli listened to Gunnar and then said, "You'd make a worthy son-in-law, however, it's Brynhildr whom you should be asking. Ever since riding as a Valkyrie she has kept her own counsel on such matters. It doesn't matter that I accept you as a husband for her, she has to accept you herself."

From King Budli's Hall they rode to King Heimir's Hall where he welcomed them. Gunnar told King Heimir of his wish to wed Brynhildr and he had come to ask permission to do so of her foster-father, who also happened to be her brother-in-law since he was married to Bekkhildr, Brynhildr's sister. King Heimir gave him the same reply King Budli had, "That decision is not for me to make. If you would have her as your wife then you must ask her permission before any marriage ceremony can take place." He pointed to a mountain rising in the distance. A light could be seen shining from its top. "There is Brynhildr's dwelling in Skata Grove at the top of that mountain. She'll only give her love to the one brave enough to ride through the flickering flames that guard her shieldbound shelter."

They didn't tarry with King Heimir. Instead they rode immediately for Skata Grove. Gunnar was riding his horse Goti, Hogni was riding Helkvi, while Sigurdr sat astride Grani. As soon as they came up to the meadow Gunnar's horse turned away from the fire. Gunnar dug his heels into his horse's sides trying to force Goti to run against the flames, but his horse steadfastly turned its back away from the flames.

Sigurdr looked back over his shoulder and asked why the others had not followed him to the flames, "Why don't you gee your horses over the flames?"

Gunnar answered, "Goti is afraid of the fire. Perhaps I could try your horse, Hogni?"

He dismounted and exchanged horses with Hogni. But Helkvi also refused to run towards the flames, although he edged a few steps forward before balking.

Sigurdr dismounted and handed Grani's reins to Gunnar, "Try Grani. He's not afraid of the fire and can easily clear the flames and shields." Then it seemed to Sigurdr as if he remembered jumping over the flames on Grani once before. But how could that be?

Gunnar mounted Grani but found the horse too wild to control. It was all he could do to get off the horse's back without being thrown. "Here, I think you're the only one valiant enough to ride Grani through the flames."

Sigurdr protested that it wouldn't be right, "I'm only recently wedded. I can't woo another woman?"

Gunnar had an idea, "Grimhildr gave me a potion which we must each drink. Then we'll be able to exchange semblances. Although you'll think as Sigurdr you'll look like me. And I, in return, will look like Sigurdr and think like Gunnar. Thus you'll be able to break through the flames on Grani, woo Brynhildr, and later change forms with me again so Brynhildr will never know of your adventure. I'll be a happy man for having gotten the most beautiful of Queens."

Sigurdr couldn't deny his friend this. They both drank the potion and their forms changed. Sigurdr in Gunnar's form girded the sword Gramr about him, and put Fafnir's Helmet of Terror on his head. He mounted Grani, who, seeing that it was Gunnar, tried to buck him off. Instead the horse was surprised and puzzled to feel Sigurdr's familiar gold spurs dig into his sides. Thus spurred on he obeyed the body that sat on him and leapt through the flames with barely an effort.

Once again the flames died down so just a fine ash remained surrounding the shields. But this ash was enchanted so neither Gunnar nor the others could cross over it. However, that wouldn't have mattered since they discovered as they inspected the barriers the shields were fastened together all round with neither entrance nor exit. The only way into Skata Grove was over the shields, and their horses weren't strong enough to make such a leap even without the flames that had surrounded the shields. All they could do was await Sigurdr's return before they could find out whether or not the wooing had been successful.

Sigurdr/Gunnar dismounted and walked towards the Hall. Every step seemed a repetition to him. Hadn't he done this before?

He came upon Brynhildr who stared at him, surprised, and said, "Who are you? When I heard the horse leap over the flames, I looked and saw it was Grani. But I expected another rider to have guided him."

Sigurdr/Gunnar answered, "I am Gunnar Gjukason. You have vowed to marry the warrior who crossed over your flames and claimed you as his wife. Here I am. I have formally asked for your hand from King Budli, your father, and King Heimir, your foster-father and brother-in-law, and they have both agreed. To you I promise to be a worthy husband and doting father to our children."

"But how can you be my husband, you're not whom I expected?" Brynhildr backed away from him.

He walked towards her, "Nevertheless, you vowed to marry the warrior who rode through the flames to be at your side, and I am that warrior. Will you keep your plighted word and have me as your husband, or bring dishonor to your name by refusing me that which I have fairly won?"

"I'm confused. When I made that vow I thought there was only one who could cross those flames. Little did I dream there would be another. However, I'll keep my word. Give me your hand and I'll give you mine that we might exchange rings." She took his hand and placed the ring Andvaranautr on it.

He placed another costly ring that had been part of Andvari's Hoard on her finger and stood leaning on the hilt of his sword, "This ring is but a small portion of what I will give you as your dowry. Gold and precious jewels will be heaped before you, such is the happiness brought to Gunnar by your acceptance of his hand."

Brynhildr sat silently in her seat for a moment overcome with sadness. She was still wearing the garb of a Valkyrie, a rich golden byrny, a helm upon her head and a fine long sword lay across her lap, "Don't talk to me of these things unless you can pledge before me you're the greatest of warriors and first among men. I leave the life of glory reluctantly. How can the rattling of pots and pans compare with the clashing of swords? I've stood on the battlefield when the King of Mirkagard fought. My sword was stained with blood, while bodies fell everywhere screaming in agony. That's the life I yearn for. How can it compare with having friends sitting in a Hall drinking wine? If you're a warrior, then perhaps there will be battles enough ahead to satisfy me."

Sigurdr didn't know quite what to say, since he knew Gunnar meant to retire from wars and tend to ruling his Kingdom, for he knew Kings off fighting wars seldom returned to happy realms. He could do one or the other, but not both. He had chosen to stay at home. "I know the deeds you've done have been great. Few women have made their way into song as have you. Many reckon you as great a warrior as many men. If you had only had an army following you, you might have ruled half the world by now, and ruled the rest by the end of your days. However, such was not fated to be. I don't know if the life you have with me will be as exciting. But I do know you vowed marriage under certain conditions and I have met those conditions."

Brynhildr arose, walked over to him, and kissed him. She offered him her hand once more, "I've given you a pledge of my intent. I've never sworn an oath falsely nor broken my word. Nor do I intend to start now. The success of our relationship depends on the truthfulness we bring into it. I will work hard to be happy with you."

Sigurdr/Gunnar remained that evening and they talked. Brynhildr invited him to stay the night. He saw there was only one bed and took the sword Gramr and laid it between them. This aroused Brynhildr's curiosity, "What is this strange thing you do? We are to be wed, so there is nothing wrong with us sleeping side-by-side."

Sigurdr answered, "This is the custom of the country where I come from. I would that you would honor it. After our marriage feast we will be allowed to truly sleep side-by-side. For now this sword will act as bundling and separate us."

Sigurdr/Gunnar remained there three nights. On the morning of the fourth day he made preparations to leave, "When shall we meet again? You'll have to have some time to arrange your departure from here, and I'll need some time to arrange our marriage feast?"

She answered while helping to saddle Grani, "In ten days' time I'll arrive at the Hall of the Nibelungs. We'll be married and I'll take on my role as your Queen at that time."

Sigurdr/Gunnar seemed disappointed, "Must it be so long? The court of the Nibelungs requires only a couple of days riding to reach."

"But there are many things I must arrange. I'll have to stop along the way at my foster-father's, King Heimir's, in order to arrange some private matters. The soonest I can reach your court will be in ten days." She was adamant.

"Very well then, I'll see you there." He mounted Grani who once more leapt over the shields.

Gunnar/Sigurdr had been dozing with his head on a rock waiting on the other side of the shields. He woke with a start when he heard Grani land, and ran up to Sigurdr/Gunnar and began bombarding him with questions, not even giving him a chance to dismount, "Have you met with her? Has she agreed to be my wife? Oh, don't give me bad news. I would rather you slew me instead. Is she as lovely as everyone has said? Did you give her the ring I gave you? Tell me what happened?"

"If you'll give me a chance I'll relay her messages to you. But first let's change our guises once more so we're comfortable in our own bodies."

Sigurdr drank the potion Gunnar gave him. The transformation took place as quickly as before. Now Sigurdr was a bit more comfortable. He told Gunnar the whole story during their ride back to Hlymdale, where they were to spend a few nights before returning to Gunnar's Hall.

When they arrived at Gunnar's Hall Sigurdr was met by Gudrunr. That evening he told her the story of the true wooing of Brynhildr. She was happy to know she was married to the greatest warrior and only Sigurdr was brave and strong enough to ride Grani through the flames and win Brynhildr for Gunnar.

In the meantime Brynhildr went to King Heimir's, much troubled. She asked him to raise Aslaugr for her in secret, "Sigurdr must never learn Aslaugr is his daughter. It would complicate all our lives too much."

King Heimir, admonished her for not telling Sigurdr he had a child. "Aslaugr has a right to her inheritance and to know the love of a father. It is Sigurdr's right as her father to know of her existence so he might spend time with her. He also has a right to know another Volsungr has been born. She may be the last of the Volsungr's and for that reason she and Sigurdr have a right to know each other."

Brynhildr refused his advice, "I know, yet somehow things are very wrong here. I thought he would ride through the flames a second time and claim me as his wife. Instead it was Gunnar who rode through the flames. Even though I was puzzled by this, what puzzled me more was that Gunnar seemed so like Sigurdr in manner."

"Do you mean that the two looked alike enough to be brothers?"

She shook her head, "No, not at all. In fact they look quite different. Sigurdr is tall with red-golden hair and is very handsome and strongly built. Though Gunnar is strong, he is not quite so tall. He is as fair complexioned, but has very dark hair which with his fair skin, makes him look a little ill. He has a face that needs a little color in it. It was the way he moved that reminded me of Sigurdr, not his looks. One of the mornings Gunnar was staying with me I saw him walking across the Hall. I only saw him from the back and could have sworn it was Sigurdr, for the gait was the same. I ran to him but saw it was only Gunnar."

King Heimir spoke, "I'm still confused why should all this prevent you from telling Sigurdr about his daughter?"

Brynhildr sat down covering her eyes. King Heimir thought she was crying. "Sigurdr will always be first in my heart. I love him more than you could imagine. Gunnar is kind, I just don't love him. I am honorbound, though, to keep my word to him. However, Sigurdr will always be my first husband and the father of my first child. We've sworn oaths that can never be broken. Sigurdr must not know he has a daughter, nor should his enemies know he has a daughter. That knowledge would surely prove deadly for Aslaugr."

King Heimr started at this. He realized Brynhildr was serious about Aslaugr's safety. His mind began racing and plotting ways he might one day use to protect his granddaughter. From then on his mind dwelt to the exclusion of everything else on one thing, protecting Aslaugr. But, he couldn't tell anyone what was bothering him. This monomania worried his advisors and subjects. They didn't understand why he seemed so distant. Why was he coming up with wild schemes and asking how best to protect a little girl?

Eventually Sigurdr, Gunnar, Hogni, Gutthormr, Gudmundr, and all the warriors accompanying them returned to the Hall of the Nibelungs where they were met by Grimhildr, anxious to find out whether or not the mission had been a success. She thanked Sigurdr for his help wooing Brynhildr, "I've prepared a magnificent feast in your honor for this evening." She took both Sigurdr and her son's hands and led them into the Hall, "This will be a time of merriment and feasting. In a few days' time Brynhildr will be here and Gunnar will be married. I will be so happy on that day."

Over the next few days warriors arrived from near and far for the celebration. Brynhildr's father, King Budli, arrived with his son King Atli. Then Brynhildr arrived and the wedding feast was held. It lasted for many days. Gunnar seemed to be the happiest of men. Brynhildr smiled often at Sigurdr who frequently felt compelled to seek out her company.

During the last day of the feast Brynhildr and Gunnar were sitting opposite Sigurdr and Gudrunr. Grimhildr stood up and raised a cup to her lips to toast the couple. As she did so Sigurdr recognized the cup and all his hidden memories came bursting back into his mind. He started as if he had just come out of a dream. Looking around he realized what had happened and was very upset. Sadly, there was nothing he could do about the matter. His eyes met Brynhildr's. She could tell

his strangeness had passed and he now remembered her as his true love. Sadly it was too late.

When he had been startled and jumped, it had caused Gudrunr, Gunnar, and Brynhildr to stare at him. Grimhildr paused briefly in her toasting while he regained his composure. Then everyone raised their cups to toast the couple, except Sigurdr. Gudrunr poked him in the side until he too raised his cup. Then they all drank to Brynhildr and Gunnar's happiness. Sigurdr drank in a daze only thinking of the vows and oaths he had sworn with Brynhildr. What could he do about them now? They were now honorbound with pledges to others.

The days passed with Brynhildr becoming more and more indifferent to her husband. She blamed him for not being Sigurdr. Finally she could stand it no longer and went into the woods for a walk so she could sit in solitude and brood over the wyrd the Norns had woven for her.

Gunnar, too, had difficulty with their marriage. He truly loved her and would have given anything if she had returned that love. A thought in his head began to grow and grow. Perhaps Sigurdr had been false to him? Sigurdr had sworn Gramr had laid between him, and Brynhildr those three nights. What if that had been a lie? That would certainly explain Brynhildr's behavior.

Meanwhile, Sigurdr tried to make the best of his life. He loved Gudrunr, but certainly not as passionately as he did Brynhildr. Honor demanded he put any thoughts of Brynhildr from his head. So, of the three, he was the most content.

Gudrunr remained the happiest of the four, blissfully unaware of the emotions raging in Brynhildr and Sigurdr, or the jealously growing in Gunnar. Her thoughts were on the future and beginning a family with Sigurdr. She was happy since she knew she had the noblest warrior as her husband. Some day Brynhildr would also realize that.

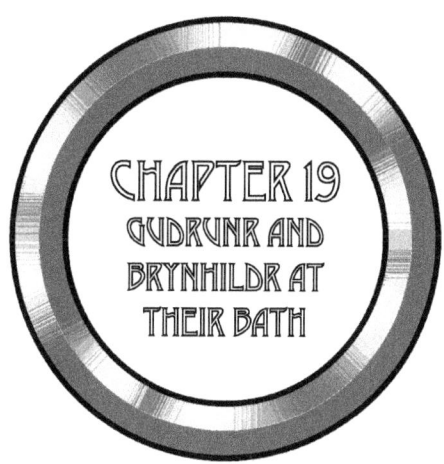

CHAPTER 19
GUDRUNR AND BRYNHILDR AT THEIR BATH

It was Laugardagr, the seventh day of the week, and Brynhildr and Gudrunr had gone to the river for their weekly baths. They both waded into the water, though Brynhildr made a point of wading further upstream before beginning to wash her hair. Gudrunr was surprised, "Why do you wade further away from me?"

Brynhildr answered, "Why should I have to use the soapy rinsings from your head since I am better than you? My father is mightier than yours, and my husband has greater fame and the larger Kingdom."

Gudrunr waded further upstream so she was now ahead of Brynhildr, "I disagree and warn you this senseless banter should stop before you learn secrets that would harm you greatly. Your husband is not the man he has always seemed. There is no man in the entire world who can compare to Sigurdr Fafnirsbani. His legend is greater, the skald's songs sung about him longer, and as for wealth and Kingdoms, the wealth of the Volsungrs plus Andvari's Hoard makes him the richest man alive. He is lord and master of many Kingdoms, while your husband has only one. You even agreed with this when you pledged your love to Sigurdr and promised to take him as your first husband."

Brynhildr had only been half-listening and didn't catch this last remark and what it meant, which was that Sigurdr had confided their secrets to Gudrunr. Instead she waded further upstream and answered, "When a Princeling Gunnar was honored as a future King, while your husband was nothing more than a stableboy for King Hjalprekr and never knew his father."

Gudrunr could hold her peace no longer concerning the story Sigurdr had told her after he returned from wooing Brynhildr for Gunnar. She waded upstream till once again she was in a superior position, and answered, "My husband sat astride Grani and leapt the protecting fire around your shield-laden Hall. While Sigurdr slept beside you, the coward Gunnar had to wait outside. Thus Sigurdr performed the man's work tending to you while Gunnar was his stableboy tending to the horses for those three days."

Brynhildr started at what Gudrunr had said and responded before moving further upstream, "That's a lie."

Gudrunr answered, "It's wise you decided to stand where you are. If we kept moving upstream we'd soon be in another Kingdom. Then, holding up her hand, Gudrunr showed Brynhildr the ring Andvaranautr that she wore on her finger. "See the ring you gave to Sigurdr as a pledge of your love. That ring he gave to me. Does that convince you? Gunnar and Sigurdr changed semblances outside your Hall since Gunnar's horse balked at the flames and Gunnar was unable to control Grani. So it was Sigurdr in Gunnar's guise who you plighted your troth to. It was Sigurdr who became your husband." There was an element of gloating in her voice as she continued waving the ring Andvaranautr at Brynhildr to keep emphasizing her point,

Brynhildr looked at Gudrunr's hand and paled as she saw the Andvaranautr. She understood all that had happened, "You'll regret what you've told me. Today you bathe in water, but one day you will swim in blood." She spoke the last words in their argument and departed for her room in the Hall.

During the evening and throughout the following days Brynhildr sat silent and downcast in her room staring out the window. Gunnar and the rest of his family implored her to tell them what was bothering her, but she remained silent and would speak to no one.

Gunnar went to Sigurdr, "We can't get Brynhildr to speak to us. Several days ago she went to bathe with Gudrunr and returned silent and unapproachable. Can you try to find out from Gudrunr what happened?"

Sigurdr agreed and went to Gudrunr, "Brynhildr is silent and upset. What happened at the river?"

Gudrunr answered insolently, "Why should Brynhildr be so sad? She has often boasted, some would say too much, she has what she desires—a Kingdom, a husband who loves her, wealth, and the praises and admiration of many. She was lucky enough to choose the husband she wished to marry. What else could she want?"

Sigurdr replied, starting to realize what might have happened between Gudrunr and Brynhildr, "Was it at the stream she praised Gunnar as the best of all men and her choice as a husband?"

Gudrunr didn't answer that question, instead she offered to help, "I'll go to Brynhildr tomorrow and talk to her about all this. Perhaps I can shake her out of her mood. We can talk of our husbands again."

Sigurdr forbade it, "I don't think that would make matters better. I feel you would be going to Brynhildr to taunt her. She's upset enough. Obey me in this or I'll be exceedingly angry with you."

The next day Gudrunr visited Brynhildr. Brynhildr remained silent and made no acknowledgement that Gudrunr was present. She continued sitting on the floor casting rune stones, trying to learn the future. "Be happy Brynhildr, forget what passed between us last Laugardagr. Perhaps something else troubles you? Tell me and I'll try to help."

Brynhildr turned to her tormenter and answered, "Ill advised is this visit of yours. Your words are not the concerned words of a friend. You came here to gloat. Your heart is black with evil. But things will change and you'll never be happy again. Sigurdr won't be at your side much longer." She turned away.

Gudrunr walked around to face Brynhildr, "You speak as if you know some dread that is to happen. Tell me what you've learned from the runes. What does the future portend? What will happen to Sigurdr? Share with me the future the rune stones foretell?" She saw the grimace on Brynhildr's face and thought perhaps Brynhildr would be asking a favor of the Norns to help Sigurdr's fate along a little. "What evil revenge are you plotting for us?"

Brynhildr answered, "Let's talk only of things which deal with you. It's easy to be happy when good luck attends your life and things go well. But how happy will you be when your love is taken from you and your future is uncertain?"

Gudrunr decided she had misinterpreted Brynhildr's talk, "At first I thought you spoke of the future. Now I see you speak out of grief and anger. Sigurdr and I will be together for a long while. We are yet young and should not brood over thoughts that make up the worries of old women. Our lives lie before us."

"Rather lies live after you," retorted Brynhildr. "Be happy with Sigurdr while you can. All the evil you've wrought will come back to you doubly. Sigurdr will die and you'll never be happy again. You won Sigurdr by trickery, his heart is still mine. I don't easily yield up what is mine. Treasure your moments with him for they won't be long now. Measure the time left in days, not years. Perhaps even hours."

Gudrunr responded, "I married Sigurdr in good faith, in public. I knew nothing of any vows or pledges you two had made in secret. My father would never have permitted such a marriage if Sigurdr's love for you had been known and the matter had remained unsettled. He would have paid you handsomely for you to relinquish your rights."

"Sigurdr was not silent about the love he held for me. He talked of nothing but me during his stay at your father's Hall, and how he longed to return to me. The night before his return was the night of Grimhildr's treachery when she gave him that vile drink. How can you believe the lies you've just spoken? I have no doubt you'll be rewarded in kind for what you've done." Brynhildr motioned for Gudrunr to leave her.

Gudrunr answered, "You've made a much better marriage than you deserve. You have pride and ambition, and I think a high price will be wrought from it. Many men will die from your anger. Be content, instead, with the wonderful husband you have. I love my brother and think him one of the greatest warriors in the land. He is a King and wealthy, and loves you dearly. Your children will be noble and strong. Be content with that. What more could you want?"

"I would have been contented with Gunnar had I not met Sigurdr beforehand. However, Sigurdr's deeds are far greater. The single act of slaying Fafnir is worth all of Gunnar's battles combined. I vowed to marry the bravest warrior. It was Sigurdr who rode through the flames—twice, not the cowardly Gunnar."

Brynhildr was becoming quite upset. Gudrunr realizing this and tried to calm her, "Gunnar failed to ride through the flames not through lack of courage, but through lack of a mount. His horse balked, Hogni's horse was brave but still failed to make the jump. Only Grani was able to leap the flames and he would do so with none but Sigurdr on his back. Don't blame Gunnar for this."

"Sigurdr, Gunnar, and you have done great wrongs to me, making me a fool before others. But the greatest harm has come from Grimhildr. She's a vile evil woman."

Gudrunr would allow no harmful words spoken about her mother, "Grimhildr has always been kind to you. She has treated you as if you were her own daughter and given you honor and much happiness."

"Grimhildr has caused all this grief. Was it for my happiness she gave a cup of forgetfulness to Sigurdr?" Brynhildr again motioned for Gudrunr to leave.

Gudrunr was unaware of the enchanted drink and defended her mother only as the innocent can defend the guilty, "That's a lie. She has always admired you. She was the one who suggested Gunnar seek you out for his wife. She wanted to have you as part of her family."

Brynhildr answered, "If I were married to Gunnar I would be safely out of Sigurdr's reach. Doesn't that make sense to you? I have only one wish for you and Sigurdr. May you both find as much joy and pleasure in your marriage as I find joy and pleasure in a life marred by your treachery and deceit."

"I assure you Sigurdr and I find more pleasure in each other than you would wish. He remembers now about his first vows to you. Yet still, he lives with me as my husband. Doesn't that tell you something?" Gudrunr walked towards the door.

Brynhildr saw there was no way out of their bitter struggles and sought to end the conversation, "Your words are evil and our talk has become circular. We are going over the same things again and again. There is no use to it. Let's talk of other things."

Gudrunr was still too caught up in the argument to let Brynhildr have the last word about it, "You started the unfriendly words between us. I came here in friendship to try and help you. Instead of love I have been met with hatred and threats. Now you've decided we should no longer argue. There must be some new trickery you've thought of?"

Brynhildr was clearly tired and just wanted to end the conversation any way she could and be left alone, "Can't we just stop all this. I didn't invite you here. I've kept to myself about the wrongs done to me, yet you've barged in and opened these wounds between us. I see it's useless to try and change things. Tell Gunnar I'll honor and love him as my true husband." She turned away.

Gudrunr was disbelieving and turned to go. As she reached the door she spoke some final words before departing, "I would like to believe you in this, but somehow I don't think I can trust your heart. Why do I think you know things you haven't spoken of?" Gudrunr left the room.

CHAPTER 20
BRYNHILDR'S DEPRESSION

Gudrunr sent word to her brother that Brynhildr had broken her silence but was still so ill she remained in bed. Gunnar went to see his wife.

"What can I do to make you happy, Brynhildr?" There was no answer so he continued, "Is it something I've done?"

Brynhildr sat up, "When you sought my hand in marriage from King Budli and King Heimir you showed up with armed troops. They had no recourse but to agree to our marriage. By force you won their consent, perhaps by trickery you won mine? I had secreted myself within Skata Grove so only the mightiest warrior could woo me. Only the bravest warrior with the noblest steed would be able to leap the flames. I knew if he passed my test I would then be blessed with a worthy husband. You won my consent at Skata Grove because you were able to leap the flames and win my hand. You surprised me, I thought only Sigurdr was able to ride Grani, since it was Grani who carried you over the flames. Because of this I thought you the most worthy of men. At that time I gave you a ring as a pledge of my love." Gunnar looked puzzled. Brynhildr continued, "Remember, it was entwined about with two serpents to represent the falsity of our love, perhaps? What did you do with it?"

Gunnar had been unaware of the ring. Why hadn't Sigurdr mentioned the ring? Nevertheless, he tried to answer the question, "Oh, that ring. I don't quite remember what I did with it. I was so excited at the time that I think I may have mislaid it. Yes, that's it. It wouldn't fit my finger so I put it away, somewhere. I've mislaid it." Then realizing he could easily get it back from Sigurdr he decided to change his story, "No, on second thought I think I gave it to my smith to have it enlarged since I found it felt tight about my finger. What has made you think of it after all this time?"

Brynhildr knew she had him in a trap now, "You liar. There never was such a ring entwined with serpents, although you're certainly deserving of such a piece of jewelry. The ring I gave you was Andvaranautr, and I know now Gudrunr spoke the truth. She told me I had given the ring to Sigurdr in your guise, for he has since given it to Gudrunr. She flaunted it in front of my face. I should have known you were too cowardly to leap the flames. Sigurdr has done many noble deeds. It was he who slew the worm Fafnir, as well as Regin, and five Kings. He has won too many battles to even count. He has even fought yours for you. What have you done Gunnar, except turn a deathly color at the thought of noble combat? The crown on your head rightly belongs to another. Your place in my bed belongs to another. Sigurdr should have taken both honors when he had the chance. Words that describe you and Sigurdr both start with a "c", champion for Sigurdr, coward for Gunnar. You've won me under false pretenses, by trickery. I promised to marry the most valiant champion and have been tricked into marrying the most cowardly. It's Sigurdr whom I love. It was he whom I first plighted my love to. It was he I second plighted my love too while he was in your guise. Did Sigurdr tell you we consummated our love in Skada Grove? Or, did he say we merely bundled as we lay those three nights? Do you think a woman could resist Sigurdr no matter his guise? Do you think I came to our wedding night pure and wholesome? How little you know of the secrets I hold."

Gunnar was having a hard time taking it all in. He knew the truth of the deceit. And then Sigurdr had deceived him by lying with Brynhildr as a husband lays? What other secrets did she hint at?

"You've caused me great dishonor by causing me to break my vow. You and your family are foul and despicable. You've given me heartache instead of love, and in such kind I will repay your family, especially that vile woman Grimhildr. She has more evil in her than any woman I've ever met. From this moment on I will plan your death Gunnar, and as many of your family shall go with you on that journey as I can manage."

Gunnar had been growing angrier as the insults from Brynhildr mounted. He had seen his brother Hogni nearby in the hallway, and several other members of his family. He lowered his voice so none save Brynhildr could hear his reply, "Your words have been unkind and disloyal. I've loved you all the while as no man has ever loved a woman. And how am I repaid? You've nothing but hatred in your heart for my family and me, and would plot all our deaths. Not only do you insult me, but you insult my mother, the best woman who ever lived. She has never spoken an ill word against you. She even suggested I marry you and urged good feelings between our families. She offered you friendship, as did Gudrunr. How have you repaid them? With insults. However, that's to be expected from the likes of you. Never has my mother tormented or caused the death of anyone. Her life has been lived so that no one can say anything bad about her." Obviously, he too defended his mother, having no knowledge of her deceits and harm against Brynhildr and Sigurdr.

Brynhildr interrupted, "That's because she's probably killed everyone who would have ill words for her."

Gunnar continued, ignoring Brynhildr's remarks, "Brynhildr, you've often done evil things, and many things are whispered behind our backs. My love is turning cold, I'm turning against you. If I had a sword with me right now I'd slay you with it."

Brynhildr answered, "It's not in my nature to do the things you've said. You've insulted me by the mockery of our marriage. It's time for my revenge."

She leapt forward and attempted to stab Gunnar with a knife. He caught her hand and struggled with her briefly. Hogni heard the noise from where he was standing in the Hall and ran to help subdue Brynhildr. He summoned guards and ordered them to cast her into chains. It upset Gunnar to see his wife bound, so he ordered the fetters be removed.

Hogni refused to allow the guards to release her. Brynhildr struck at the tapestry beside her bed, destroying it completely, and spoke, "It makes no difference how I'm bound in this house, either in fetters or by lies, the result is still the same, I'm your prisoner. And as your prisoner I vow that henceforth you'll never see me happy here. I'll never sit of an evening drinking and playing chess, nor speak with you in idle, friendly conversation. Nor will I ever embroider your deeds on tapestries so the story of any bravery by you would be recorded, although it would be a small enough task to complete, using only a few threads. However, worst of all is that you lose my counsel, which was my most valuable gift to you. Left to your own thoughts you'll soon destroy yourself and your entire family. You're none to bright, you know. At least I'll know I'll have that much revenge. I wish Sigurdr were here so I could go to him." She yelled for the doors to her chamber to be opened, "Open the doors and open the windows. I'll yell loudly so that all the Hall, all the town, all the Kingdom, will know of my grief and the wrongs that have been committed against me." Her voice was loud and all could hear the accusations she hurled at Gunnar.

o o o o

One morning several days later Gudrunr was walking through another part of the Hall and came across some of Brynhildr's bower maids sitting quite forlornly. "What's wrong that you look as if death herself were here? Why aren't you happy as you usually are?"

The maiden named Svafrlod answered, "Things aren't going right with our mistress. When she's sad, we're sad. Now she sits bound by Hogni's command, having been cheated out of her true love by Gunnar's trickery. A fine pair of brothers they are."

Gudrunr thought she might do something about the matter, "The day is wearing on and it will do Brynhildr no good to lay in bed. I'll have Hogni release her from her bonds. Go and wake her so we might embroider our tapestries together once more. Perhaps I can cheer her up. Tell her, despite it all, I still offer her my love and friendship."

Svafrlod refused, "Brynhildr has given strict orders that she is not to be disturbed. She has touched neither food nor drink since her argument with Gunnar. I don't think seeing you will make her happy. She said many unkind things about you earlier."

Gudrunr left and went to her brother, "Gunnar, you must speak to Brynhildr and tell her I'm worried about her. If she's sad, then I'm sad and will do anything to help her grief pass."

Gunnar answered, "No, I don't think I'll ever see her again. The words that have passed between us were too hurtful. Believe me, she thinks ill of our family and would do great harm to all of us if she could. Stay away from her for your own safety."

Gudrunr had made up her mind to comfort Brynhildr and nothing anyone could say would dissuade her, "If you don't see her on my behalf, then I'll see her myself."

Gunnar thought things would only be made worse by Gudrunr's visit so he promised to see Brynhildr once more.

The meeting was very uncomfortable for him. He asked her questions and asked her forgiveness. She turned her back to him without speaking a word. He left.

Later he found Hogni and asked him to see if he could talk to Brynhildr. Hogni refused. Gunnar continued asking him, with each request ever more desperate than the previous one until finally Hogni agreed to see her. He fared no better with Brynhildr than Gunnar had. She turned her back to him too, and would not speak.

Gunnar, Gudrunr, and Hogni went to Sigurdr and asked him to see Brynhildr. He refused. However, the next day, after returning from hunting, Sigurdr spoke to Gudrunr, "I've been thinking this situation over since yesterday. Things have to change. If they continue as they are I'm afraid Brynhildr will die."

Gudrunr agreed, "I don't know what to do. She won't speak to any of us. It has been a week since Hogni last tried to speak to her. Since that time she's been fast asleep. No one seems able to rouse her. I think there must be some kind of spell cast over her to cause this unnatural sleep."

Sigurdr thought of the sleepthorn she had been struck with when he first met her. Perhaps Odin had intervened with another? But he couldn't tell Gudrunr that. Instead he commented on the threats Gudrunr hadn't told him Brynhildr had made. "I don't think she's sleeping. She is deep in thought, plotting the deaths of us all. Plots that intricate require deep concentration. So much so she might appear sleeping, or as dead, to another while she dreams her plots."

Gudrunr was shocked and a little afraid, "Does she hate us all that much?" Then she began crying. "Just the thought of losing you brings tears to my eyes. You must see what you can do. Talk to her and see if there is anything we can do to cause her hatred to depart. Offer her all our gold as weregild. Perhaps her grief can be put out with gold just as fire is put out with water."

Sigurdr didn't think it would be that easy, but didn't want to dash his wife's hopes, so he agreed to see Brynhildr and offer her weregild.

When he arrived at her bower he found the door open. He entered and walked to her bed. The chains were draped across her and fastened to the legs of the bed as well as to holding rings in the wall. She looked like she was sleeping, but he knew better. He unsheathed Gramr, struck the chains, freeing Brynhildr, sheathed Gramr, pulled back the covers and shouted to her, "Awake! Rise up and greet the day—the sun is shining, the birds are singing. You've lain in bed and slept long enough to cure ten warriors of their weariness after the worst month-long battle. Forget your unhappiness and smile. It's a beautiful day."

He had hoped his positive attitude would make matters better. He was so wrong. She answered with icy words, "Why have you entered here unannounced and unwelcomed? You dare come here even though you are the chief cause of my unhappiness. You flail Gramr at me? Get out!" She stood up and pointed towards the door, motioning for him to leave.

Sigurdr forged ahead with his plan of cheerfulness, "I used Gramr only to free you from your bonds. We've missed having you at the dinner table. Things just haven't been the same." Unspoken, of course, was that things were considerably better.

"No one else to mock, I surmise," Brynhildr interrupted him.

Sigurdr continued, "Why have you stopped speaking to us? What could possibly have caused such grief in you? I hope you can give us the pleasure of your company tonight so we might entertain you."

"The best entertainment for me tonight would be your death," Brynhildr retorted. " Promise me you and Gudrunr will drink poison in your cups at dinner, and I'll gladly come."

Things weren't working out as Sigurdr had planned, "You act as if you are under a spell. Seeking wrath like this is unlike you. Vengeance is not an attractive feature. If you think I hate you, you're wrong. I've no ill feelings towards you. I love you as a sister, if you would be a true sister to my wife. You must remember things have turned out as you wanted. You're married to the man you've chosen."

The conversation was beginning to turn bitter between the two, "That's not exactly true. I vowed to wed the strongest warrior. Do you think for a moment Gunnar could beat you in combat? Maybe we should see at dinner tonight? I will gladly come to dinner if you and Gunnar fight a final battle to the death."

Brynhildr had now suggested Gudrunr, Gunnar, and Sigurdr all die at dinner tonight. It was only a matter if time before she mentioned Grimhildr, too.

Brynhildr continued, "You rode through the flames not once but twice. When you came the second time, I thought from a distance it was you. Yet up close you had the guise of Gunnar. Even though your face looked like Gunnar I thought they were your eyes when I looked into them. But I wasn't certain it was you. I couldn't believe that after the words of love we had spoken to each other, and the times we had spent together, you could play me so falsely. I believed it truly was Gunnar standing before me. I had vowed to wed the warrior before me in Skata Grove. The semblance was of Gunnar, the heart and might was of Sigurdr. So don't tell me I chose my husband and should be happy with him. I was deceived by you and Gunnar."

"The Gjukings are the noblest warriors there are. Songs are sung about the legend of Gunnar and how he and his brother slew the King of Thjod and Ty and the brother of King Budli." After he had spoken he realized the brother of King Budli was Brynhildr's uncle, which wasn't the wisest thing to have said to her.

Brynhildr backed away from Sigurdr, "For that single deed against my kin I am honorbound to seek vengeance. Why do you argue the Gjuking cause with crimes committed against my family? Your words prove what a coward Gunnar is. He betrayed me by asking you to woo me in his stead. You slew Fafnir; you rode through the flames, not Gunnar. You should be my husband, not Gunnar. You are my husband according to the vows we pledged to one another at our first meeting."

Sigurdr answered, "We are not wedded to one another. You have married a great King who has given you a rich dowry. You should be content with that."

"I've never loved Gunnar. At first I tried, but I just couldn't. I hid this from others when we were in public, but in private I could not be a wife and friend to him. How could I have him touch me when my thoughts were always on you? It is to you I gave my heart on Skata Grove for the first time three years ago, and I've never stopped loving you."

She walked towards Sigurdr, who moved away and spoke, "How can you not love a man as great as Gunnar? How can you be so angry with all of us? He loves you with such a love that you should treasure it as if it were the most precious gold." Sigurdr was only making matters worse.

"How can one love fool's gold? I have great grief from the wrongs caused by the Gjukings. Yet you have caused me more wrongs. I regret my sword is not covered with your blood." Brynhildr glared at Sigurdr daring him to dispute as untruthful anything she had said.

"Don't worry about such things. Before long your wish will be granted and a sword will be plunged through my heart. Yet you'll meet your own death even before the food at the funeral feast has been served. As sure as my death comes yours will follow after, and the time will not be long before the first event takes place." Sigurdr dropped his hands to his sides and sat down in a chair.

"I'm not impressed. Spare me your speeches. Your actions betrayed me and if the result of everything will be our deaths, then it is all your doing. Bear the blame alone. I think nothing of my life or my death."

"Try to make things right between you and Gunnar. If you can do this then I'll give you the Treasure of the Volsungrs and Andvari's Hoard."

She laughed answering, "Does that include the ring Andvaranautr which I gave to you when we pledged our love to each other? If so, you'll have to wrest it from your wife's flaunting finger. How could you ask me to love and honor Gunnar when it is you whom I pine for? You treat me with disdain and would cast me off on another man. Do you find me that hideous?"

Sigurdr's heart softened towards her, "At one time I thought better of your happiness than I did of my own life. My thoughts were always on you and the happiness we would have together. I talked of nothing else to everyone I knew. Then Grimhildr gave me that cursed, enchanted cup, which I drank. Our lives were different after that. Yet when I'm alone and think of everything that's happened, and when Gudrunr is out of my sight, for I think something in the enchantment makes me want her more when I am with her, I think of you and want only you as my wife. When Odin put the sleepthorn in your throat he promised you the bravest husband. I agree that is me. I think one day he will keep that promise and we'll be together, even if it is after death. But for now we must do what we must."

Brynhildr was touched by all he had said, especially his admitting she was right, "Why have you waited this long to tell me these things? If I had known before I could have born anything, even Gunnar's embraces."

Sigurdr answered, "Perhaps it isn't too late for us to be together. There are many couples married to others who see each other on the side. This Hall is large and there are many passageways which lead to secret rooms . . ."

Brynhildr cut him short, insulted by his suggestion, "You encourage me to dishonor my vows? There cannot be two Kings in one Hall, two husbands in one bed. Although there is little love lost between Gunnar and me, I will not betray him. I may see him murdered, but I will not be false to him with another. You have dishonored yourself by even suggesting such a thing." Then Brynhildr thought of how they had met on Skata Grove and had sworn allegiances with each other and spoke of these things to Sigurdr. "But things have not come about as we had planned and I will soon die."

Sigurdr was so overcome with grief at the thought of Brynhildr dying he heaved a great sigh. The rings of his byrny burst about him. "I cannot think of your dying. It's too impossible to conjure up in my mind. Things are wrong in this Hall. If it will save your life I'll dissolve my vows with Gudrunr and marry you instead, with all honor and ceremony."

Brynhildr, though, was too proud to listen to such entreaties, "I'll not marry you if you're doing it just to save my life, nor will I have any other as a husband. It seems there is a curse over us so things are not fated to be right between us just yet."

Sigurdr left without saying anything further.

Gudrunr came upon Sigurdr while he sat by himself thinking of his meeting with Brynhildr, "How did things go? Is she speaking again?"

Sigurdr answered, "She has certainly regained her speech. I'm not certain you'd like to hear how fluent she is. She spoke many, many words to me."

Gudrunr was encouraged, "Did you offer her gold and other precious things so the feud might be ended between us all?"

"I think things will be ended between us all, but not by gold, and not in the manner you would wish." Sigurdr looked down.

o   o   o   o

Gudrunr ran to see Brynhildr without hearing the rest of what Sigurdr had to say, "How can I help you, Brynhildr. What will make things right between us?"

Gudrunr noticed Brynhildr did not seem to be in the same happy mood as she. Brynhildr answered her, "Surely you come here all happy and fluttery to mock me. Sigurdr has betrayed my trust, and so have you. You unjustly occupy my place in his bed. The days left of my life have grown short. Perhaps your death, and perhaps Sigurdr's death can be measured in days, also. However, before I die, I would have you know that Sigurdr and I have a child. Her name is Aslaugr and she is now three-years-old. Sigurdr knows nothing of her. But I wanted to make certain you did. I don't think it would be wise for you to spread such gossip about. Sigurdr is honorable and would dissolve your marriage and marry me if he knew of Aslaugr."

Gudrunr was too shocked to speak any further and ran from the room.

CHAPTER 21
THE DEATH OF SIGURDR FAFNIRSBANI

The meetings over the last few days had been very trying for Brynhildr. To avoid the constant interruptions in the Hall she escaped to the outside and sat grieving under a tree on the far side of the Hall. There she sat bemoaning her fate, cursing to the wind that possessions and Kingdoms were abhorrent to her. Kings had a way of conquering both land and people. Because of the deceit of a family who wanted nothing but the best wife for their son she had been deprived of Sigurdr. She sat plotting how best to seek her vengeance.

Gunnar had been looking all through the Hall for her and finally had been told by one of the servants Brynhildr had gone outside. He looked around the grounds until he found her, "I'm glad to see you're up and about, Brynhildr. You had us all worried for a while."

Brynhildr didn't appreciate her husband's interruption and spoke harsh words to him, "You think things are all right now since I sit plotting under a tree rather than in my bower? Know this, Gunnar, you'll lose everything: your Kingdom and the wealth of your family, your life, your friends, your honor, and me for a wife. All this will come to pass sooner than you think. I've given orders to my bower maids to ready my things. I'm leaving this morning and returning to my father's Kingdom. I can no longer live here as long as the insults given me have not been repaid."

Gunnar became agitated, "What do you mean? Leave here? This is your home."

Brynhildr answered, "This can never be my home so long as there are two Kings in it, both desiring me." She chose her next words carefully, "Sigurdr gallantly offered me the position of his mistress in order to bring me out of my depression. He certainly is willing to make sacrifices for the good of your friendship, isn't he? When I refused Sigurdr offered to put away Gudrunr as his wife and take me instead. I wonder what he has in mind for you so that he might honorably claim me as his wife? You sent him to me to see if he could cajole me out of my black mood. Is that what you had in mind? If you would have me as your faithful wife then kill Sigurdr and his three-year-old son Sigmundr." Brynhildr knew that by including Sigmundr's death in the bargaining she would succeed in killing all of the Volsungrs, save her and Sigurdr's daughter, Aslaugr, who would then be sole heir of the Treasure of the Volsungrs and Andvari's Hoard.

Gunnar drew back from Brynhildr, upset by what she had said. Until now he had never seriously thought Sigurdr would play him falsely with his wife. Yet the meaning of her words was unmistakable. Sigurdr had violated their friendship by making advances towards his wife, the King's wife. What of his oath to Sigurdr? They were like brothers. But Sigurdr also had an oath to him and had violated it by making improper suggestions to his wife. Perhaps the sword Gramr had not lain between Brynhildr and Sigurdr in Skata Grove, even though Sigurdr had assured him it had? And what of the shame that would befall him if his wife left him? His name would be whispered about the Kingdom, with who knows what stories, all becoming more garish with each retelling. Brynhildr was the love of his life. His anger from their last meeting had long since departed, and he missed her. He thought her more beautiful than any and would have given up his life for her. But could he give up the life of his best friend for her? These thoughts ran through his head. He looked at Brynhildr and spoke, "I must think on all you've told me. I need to consult with my brother Hogni."

○　○　○　○

He left and sought out Hogni and told him what Brynhildr had said, "My heart is not in the deed. Sigurdr is the same to me as you are. We are three brothers together." He saw he was making a poor argument for slaying Sigurdr, and Hogni did not seem to be swayed. He tried another approach, "But I've given him my trust and he has betrayed it. I must regain my honor by slaying him. And don't forget, if he and his son are dead then we'll gain the Volsungr Treasure and Andvari's Hoard."

Hogni answered immediately, knowing what the honorable course of action was, "Nothing good will come of it if we break our oaths to Sigurdr. No matter he has broken his oaths and may have played you falsely. Up until that moment he had been our greatest friend. He could easily have had the crown from your head for the asking. Instead he sought a secondary role in your Kingdom. With his help our family has become the strongest in the world. Few brothers-in-law have brought so much good and glory to his wife's family. He's a valued ally and we would do great harm to ourselves to lose him. I think it would be best if you talked to him and reached some sort of agreement concerning Brynhildr. The details are yours to work out. Either share her or be paid weregild for the insult. Whatever you do, don't do something stupid that will do us more harm than good. Your head is filled with Brynhildr's counsel. Ignore it."

But Gunnar was too concerned with his honor, "I don't care what will happen as a result of our actions. Such things will happen as fated no matter what course we take. Can you think of any way the deed might be honorably worked?"

Hogni thought for a moment before answering. Perhaps it wouldn't be that awful if they did kill Sigurdr. "I have strong feelings against killing Sigurdr. There are many disadvantages. However, I can see some advantages, too. First, we will win great fame and honor for killing such a mighty warrior. That brings us to my second thought. Neither you nor I can do the actual deed, for we have sworn oaths of fealty with him. We can plot it, but our bastard brother, Gutthormr, who has uttered no such oaths, will have to carry it out. He's young and can easily be manipulated into the murder."

Gunnar hit one fist into the other hand and vowed, "Either Sigurdr will die, or I'll die."

Hogni set off to find Gutthormr, while Gunnar ran back to Brynhildr who was still sitting under the tree, "Be glad of heart, for I've made a decision which will lighten your thoughts. You're right. Sigurdr has dishonored this family and must pay for his actions. Hogni and I have plotted his death. Arise and embrace your true husband and let us retire to our chamber together."

His intentions were obvious. However, Brynhildr was having none of it, "Payment in advance is rarely a wise idea. It is hard, if not impossible, to revoke a payment already spent. I shall not come to your bed until the deed is done. Then we will celebrate as we've never celebrated before. I'll be a true wife to you then."

Gunnar hadn't felt so hopeful in months, and it had been months. He had honored his vows to her faithfully and now looked forward to the deed that must be done so he and Brynhildr could be reconciled. Sigurdr must meet his death as soon as possible so he and Brynhildr could celebrate. He ached for the celebration.

o   o   o   o

Gunnar found both Hogni and Gutthormr deep in conversation together. Hogni was now well disposed towards the deed. Nothing held them back but the doing of it. However, Gutthormr still had to be convinced. They offered him gold and a Kingdom of his own. With incentives like that it took very little time to convince him of the rightness of the action. He also had one other incentive. Sigurdr had usurped his place. After Sigurdr and his brothers had sword blood brotherhood with each other, he had been left out of everything. He was odd man out in their group, and didn't like it. Yes, he had his own grudges to settle.

Gunnar and Hogni had consulted with Grimhildr and she had revealed a formula for concocting an enchanted drink that would fill Gutthormr with blind rage against Sigurdr. Although it didn't seem to be needed they decided to prepare it anyway. Their younger brother was untried as a warrior. With Grimhildr's formula, if he proved faint of heart during the doing of the deed, they knew they could count on pure hatred to finish it for them.

They took the flesh of a dragon and the meat of a wolf, put it in a cauldron and brought the mixture to a boil, and then let the ingredients simmer together until both had become stringy and entwined about the other so they could no longer be separated. Then they threw in some sliced onions, and savory herbs. Not really necessary, but there was certainly no reason the concoction had to taste foul. All during the preparation they chanted spells and incantations Grimhildr had taught them. When it was finished they ladled it out into a soup tureen and served it

piping hot to Gutthormr along with some strong wine. He ate it heartily. With each spoonful his words towards Sigurdr became more and more hateful. By the end of the meal his brothers could hardly control him. He wanted to run and kill Sigurdr immediately. But it was still too early in the evening. They had to wait if they were to have any chance of success.

Hogni tried to explain this to him, "You're a young warrior, and certainly no match for Sigurdr in a fair fight."

Gunnar broke in, "Don't forget Sigurdr's skin is like steel. Your sword blows would only glance off him."

Hogni forcibly pushed Gutthormr back in his seat, "Great honor will be yours soon enough, however, you must follow our advice. Gudrunr has told me there is only one place on Sigurdr's body where he's vulnerable, the spot on his back between his shoulder blades that he was unable to bathe in the dragon's blood. Tonight while he's sleeping you'll have to creep upon him unawares and plunge your sword into his back and through his heart. Any other plan is certain to fail."

Gutthormr was too filled with fury to realize how dishonorable it was to stab a man in his back through to his heart while he slept.

∘ ∘ ∘ ∘

Sigurdr had gone through his day somewhat aware it was his death day, yet uncertain who would deal him his deathwound. Surely not Gunnar and Hogni, since they had sworn pledges of brotherhood together? He felt if something was fated to happen then it would no matter what his actions were. The Norns had already woven his wyrd. The matter was already settled. What would happen, would happen. He continued with his regular tasks.

Sigurdr slept somewhat uneasily through the night. The next morning before dawn while the sky was still dark he lay awake in his bed, staring at the ceiling. He was too tired to get up and wanted to try to get back to sleep. Gutthormr entered the room and looked at Sigurdr who stared back at him wide awake. Sigurdr sleepily waved him away with the sword Gramr that was laying at his side.

Gutthormr couldn't hold Sigurdr's gaze and retreated into the hallway, scared. Sigurdr hadn't seemed the least bit afraid. He ran to his brothers and told them what had happened, "How come he wasn't suspicious of me? How come he wasn't fast asleep? It was unsettling walking into his bedroom and catching his gaze full on. You didn't prepare me for that. His eyes pierced through me. And strangest and most disconcerting of all was that he did nothing. He showed no fear. He made no move against me though I was in his room for no reason, or no reason that had any good attached to it. How could he not know that? He and I rarely meet or speak. Why would I be in his room unbidden at dawn, in the dark, unless it was to do him ill? How could he not know that? And knowing that why would my life not now be in danger of his vengeance? He and I have sworn no oaths together. He can kill me without dishonor? What should I do?"

The brothers had stopped listening to most of what Gutthormr was saying. He made a lot of sense and listening to his logic might deter them from the deed. They were set on Sigurdr's destruction. They only wanted to listen on the how of doing the deed, not doubts about actually doing the deed. Hogni thought quickly and answered, "You've often entered his room in the morning seeking his company for an early hunting trip. Try again. Perhaps he has fallen back asleep."

This short answer to Gutthormr's long list of worries did not assuage his doubts. He was losing his nerve and wanted to return to his room as if nothing had happened. Gunnar and Hogni were having none of that. This time Gunnar and Hogni had to physically take Gutthormr back to Sigurdr's room. The effects of the drink were wearing off and Gutthormr was realizing he was attempting to slay a warrior who had bested hundreds in combat in a single day. A warrior who had slain a 180-foot dragon. That thought seemed paramount in his mind. He was a slight warrior in both stature and deed. He certainly wasn't on the order of a firebreathing, poison-spewing dragonslayer. Gutthormr had yet to kill anyone.

Hogni tried to address this issue, "But, Gutthormr, a dragon that large would not fit in the corridors. He would not be able to harm Sigurdr because he couldn't reach his room."

Gutthormr was not drugged so much that he could not argue against this, "Fafnir would not need to crawl and wedge his way along our corridors. He could breathe fire and poison at the walls and through any openings. He could make it so uncomfortably hot and poison the atmosphere so that Sigurdr, and all of us, would have to leave the Hall. Then, once outside, he could burn each of us individually. My form is no advantage over what Fafnir could do. And trying to convince me I have a greater advantage than a 180-foot fire breathing, poison-spewing dragon is futile. You've not convinced me to do this deed. It could mean Sigurdr's death, or mine, or both. The possible results are not attractive to me."

Hogni's poor logic was a spur of the moment thing and he realized it had been specious. They had reached the outside of Sigurdr's door. Hogni looked at Gunnar. Instead of words of persuasion and encouragement the two brothers took a more direct action. Gunnar reached over and shoved the door open. Hogni shoved Gutthormr through it. They remained safely in the hallway. Again Sigurdr was sitting up in his bed awake. It seemed to Gutthormr Sigurdr's eyes were even more fierce. Gutthormr once again fled the room and would have raced down the corridor and out into the night had he not been caught round the waist and stopped by his brothers.

This time it took the brothers an hour to urge enough courage into Gutthormr to get him to try a third time.

Eventually he did try again with better results because by this time Sigurdr was asleep, his eyes safely hidden while he lay on his stomach.

Gutthormr approached the bed and completed the action in one movement, covering his head lest Sigurdr should awaken. He watched himself in the mirror that stood opposite Sigurdr's bed and guided his deed by its reflection. It seemed unreal and his actions mirrored in a dream watching himself indirectly kill his brother-in-law in dishonor.

He thrust the sword through the place inbetween Sigurdr's shoulder blades and was surprised how easily the sword cut through the flesh. It seemed as if the hardness of Sigurdr's skin everywhere else in his body had yielded this patch into a gossamer patch, easily rended. He plunged the sword so deeply into Sigurdr that it went clear through the bed and stuck into the floor pinning Sigurdr down. Gutthormr gave a tug and pulled the sword back out. He tried to wrench it down to spilt Sigurdr asunder as he did so, but the flesh beneath the wound was too hard to cut.

Sigurdr stirred and turned on his back. The bed was rapidly becoming a pool of blood.

Though dying in his bed, Sigurdr's death had not been a straw death. Assassinations of noble warriors because of their noble deeds, or their greatness in battle, were not deaths of illness in bed. Such a death was looked on as a continuation of the battlefield, not a cowardly death away from the battlefield.

Gutthormr ran to the door as Sigurdr with all his remaining strength, picked up the sword Gramr that lay at his side, and hurled it at his murderer, avenging his own death. He assumed Sigmundr had already been killed leaving him no heir to avenge the grievous evil done him. He knew not of his elder heir, Aslaugr. Though a little girl, she would have been expected to exact vengeance on those who had murdered her father. Though sweet and innocent now, little girls grow up to be women. Sometimes vengeful ones. He had to look no further than Grimhildr or Brynhildr for examples of the determined vengeance of women. The flaw in all this was that she would not have known Sigurdr was her father, and it was unlikely she would have realized she would have been honorbound to avenge his death. Fortunately, Gramr would be Sigurdr's avenger.

Gramr whirled sideways whipping through the air and caught Gutthormr in the small of his back and split him in two parts. His legs and lower body collapsed into the hallway. His arms waving frantically fell back into the chamber. Gutthormr could see his feet twitching convulsively in the hallway before he died. His dreams of empire had not lasted long. His moment of terror seeing his body in halves would last him an eternity in Hela's realm. For that was where he was bound, to the darkest regions of Helheimr, because of his dishonorable deed. No dreams of glory awaited him in Valhalla. Poisonous drinks, hurt, pain, and despair, awaited him until the last great battle of Ragnarokr. While Hela embraced him with her bony skeleton side, and her rotten falling rancid flesh side.

Sigurdr's eternity was a braver matter. Many thought Sigurdr would be born to Valhalla by the Norn Skuldr herself, and once there embraced by Odin. A place would be set for him in great honor next to Odin. Such are the welcomes awaiting the ignoble death and the noble death. However, first he too would have to have a visit with Hela.

Gunnar and Hogni had heard Gutthormr running towards them. When they saw Gutthormr's legs exit Sigurdr's bedroom without an upper body they were both so frightened they ran in different directions. Hogni managed to have the presence of mind to run to the young Sigmundr's bed and slay him, thinking the last of the Volsungrs was dead.

All the while Gudrunr had been sleeping at Sigurdr's side. Earlier that evening at dinner she had been given a drink her brothers had stolen from Grimhildr, so she would sleep through the treachery and be able to claim innocence in any part of it. She woke up swimming in Sigurdr's blood and remembered Brynhildr's words of prophecy, that she would bathe in her husband's blood. She screamed and soon others ran into the room to see what had happened. They were surprised to see Gutthormr in two parts, both without and within the room.

As was the plight of servants, one of them automatically began cleaning up the mess as if this sort of thing happened all the time. And of course murder and revenge happened often enough that this event would be remarked on for a few days, an embellished story would make its way to the townspeople and into skalds poetry, and then into legend. Meanwhile there was a lot of blood to clean up and funerals to arrange. Servants had to be practical in order to accomplish all their tasks everyday. The body of a legend created as much mess and was just as heavy to carry as the body of a fat cook downstairs (though there was no manipulating down narrow winding stairs with the fat cook). Gutthormr was easier to deal with because each half weighed less than a whole Sigurdr with skin like iron, with a body weight to reflect that.

As a servant reached under Sigurdr to raise him from the bed, Sigurdr opened his eyes. The servant jumped back and overturned a side table as he fell. As it turned out Sigurdr was not yet dead. He pulled himself up as much as he could and tried to comfort his wife, "Don't cry. You have nothing to fear from your brothers. They love you and will not harm you. However, our son Sigmundr is in danger and may well have been killed prior to this attack on me. He is my closest kinsman and by rights should avenge my death. Protect him and see that he is safe from your brothers. Being only three he is yet too young to do this for himself. Do this even before you attend to preparations for my funeral. I pray to Odin that my son yet lives and will one day be called Sigmundr the Avenger, slayer of Hogni and Gunnar." In his mind this was the way of things. He gave no thought that telling his wife to make certain his son lived so he could kill her brothers, or make haste to prevent her brothers killing her son, might not be all that comforting for her as she was laying in a pool of blood held in the arms of her dying husband. How could anyone take that all in? Gudrunr was horrified at the circumstances confronting her, her thoughts aswirl with gathering information, decoding it, and trying to think what to do.

Gudrunr continued weeping uncontrollably. Sigurdr used all his remaining strength to speak louder to gain her attention and give her further instructions, "Your brothers haven't thought out their actions very well. My slaying will bring no happiness to your family. They will never find a brother-in-law as loyal and true to them as I was. I rode to their wars and helped defeat their enemies. I always put their interests above my own and have met with ill treatment because of it. Never will their sister have a braver and truer son than Sigmundr, the son of Sigurdr Fafnirsbani, if he is allowed to live. I've been given many warnings these events would happen, but I trusted your brothers and your family and ignored the signs. What can a man do about his wyrd anyway? Gudrunr, don't blame your brothers, or hold this against them. They're not the cause of your grief. It's Brynhildr who has prompted Gunnar and Hogni to this. Brynhildr loves me with a passion that blinds her to wisdom. She has killed her beloved since she could not have him. Love often makes us do strange incongruous things. I've always been faithful to you, Gudrunr, and have ever been a true friend to Gunnar. I've sworn many oaths to you and your family, and have held to them all. I swear by the sacred river Leiptr I have never been overly friendly with Gunnar's wife." Sigurdr gasped a bit, and continued in a much softer voice, "If I had had warning of the attack it would have taken more than a mere boy sneaking up on me to kill me. Gunnar and Hogni would have had to hire a hundred to accomplish the deed that luck has given to Gutthormr. It would have been easier to slay a mad boar in the forest, slavering and foaming in sickness, than it would have been to slay me if I had not been caught sleeping trustfully in their Hall."

Having defended his honor and explained how a barely trained lad could give such a noble warrior his deathwound, Sigurdr died. Gudrunr grew silent as the full horror of the deed came down on her.

Then her grief expanded. A servant ran into the room and told her that her son Sigmundr had also been slain. This was too much for her. She rocked her dead husband's head back and forth in her arms and uttered a low moan. She continued like this throughout the rest of the day and night.

o   o   o   o

Brynhildr lay in her bed. She had left the outer door open so she could hear all the commotion. Then there was silence as everyone went back to their rooms. Off in the distance she could hear Gudrunr's moans. She burst out laughing. This continued throughout the night.

Gunnar and Hogni came into Brynhildr's room early the next morning. She was still sitting in her bed laughing. Gunnar thought his wife looked spooky, "Do you laugh because you're happy? Are you such an evil creature as that?" Brynhildr nodded that he was right. He didn't believe her, "If that is so, then why are you as pale as death? What if your brother Atli Budlason had been slain before your eyes? Would you find humor in that too? Or, would you hold him in your arms and moan as Gudrunr does with Sigurdr. He was our friend. There is no good that will come from this death. Laugh all you want, you'll cry many tears soon enough."

Brynhildr finally answered, "No need to mock me with the deaths that are to come. After all, yours might be among them. As for my brother King Atli, I'm sure he thinks more on your death than on his own. He'll outlive you and gain more wealth and renown than both you and Hogni together. Don't be foolish enough to threaten a King who is already more powerful than you."

Gunnar looked at Brynhildr and thought of what he had done in order to win her love. Had it been worth it? She continued talking, not caring whether Gunnar or Hogni listened, "Once I was happy. The noblest warrior in the world rode to Skata Grove to fetch me as his wife and we pledged our love." Then turning and speaking to Gunnar, "Unlike you, Sigurdr was a man skilled in making a woman happy. He was your true friend, who never gave you cause to doubt him. You've an odd way of repaying your friends."

Hogni tried to remind her she was the one who urged the deed be done, "You prophesied this event, then you urged your husband to carry it through. Your hands are no less red in the blood of Sigurdr than are Gutthormr's, Gunnar's, or mine."

Gudrunr entered the room, still soaked in her bloody night clothes. She stared at all three, then spoke to her brothers, "You've slain my husband. And you have also slain the most valiant warrior you have. Soon you'll ride to war again, and when you look to your left and right and see that Sigurdr is in neither place, then you'll miss him the most. You'll realize his strength and courage led your men forward. His strategies won the battles, not your childlike maneuverings. He could move men and nations. Would that he had lived and we had had more children. Then our Kingdom would have become even greater. You had nothing to fear from Sigurdr. You have everything to fear from this moment on."

Later that day Gunnar and Hogni formally claimed the Volsungr Treasure and Andvari's Hoard as their own.

Gudrunr had returned to her room. The days passed and her grief grew. She sat quietly and with dignity in her bed mourning beside Sigurdr's body, now cleaned and covered with a funeral shroud. She had allowed the servants to tidy up and make the room presentable, but had not yet given them permission to remove his body.

The noble warrior's blood had been sopped up with many linen cloths that had subsequently been buried out in the fields. Mere water and soap could not wash away the dishonor of this deed. Neither Hogni nor Gunnar ever wanted to wonder if the bed linens they slept on at night had been the ones swaddling Sigurdr at his death. Only nightmares could come of that. And they both had enough nightmares with which to contend.

o　o　o　o

Many women wail and cry of their fate to the heavens when beset by sorrow. Not Gudrunr. She was visited by many who tried to ease her sorrow by making her cry. So far none had succeeded. She was now being visited by a group of noblemen and their brides. They were all arrayed in gold and sat before Gudrunr as if it were a party. Each bride told Gudrunr how badly off she was and how lucky Gudrunr was to have such minor troubles. Gudrunr didn't appreciate their visit, however, she bore it out of politeness.

The first bride to speak was Giaflaug, King Gjuki's sister, "I'm the least loved person on all the earth. I've seen the deaths of five husbands, two daughters, three sisters, and eight brothers. I'm extremely lonely because of this loss."

Gudrunr paid no attention to Giaflaug's sadness, so overcome with her own grief was she from the death of Sigurdr.

The next to speak was Herborg, the Queen of Hunland, "My fate has been even worse than Giaflaug's. My seven sons and husband were all poisoned down in the Southlands. I had hardly had time to recover from this tragedy before the next one happened. My father, mother, and four brothers had gone to sea. Suddenly a storm blew up out of nowhere and they were all drowned. Just think of the trouble I had keeping everything straight. These tragedies all occurred in a single season. As if that weren't bad enough, at the end of that same season I was captured in a battle and held in service by an enemy Jarl. I was forced to work as a maidservant for the Jarl's wife. She set me to work binding her shoes every morning at the break of day. She knew I was the daughter of a King and missed no opportunity to mock me and make fun of the situation I found myself in. She beat me with lashes and was the worst master or mistress I've ever heard of. It was a blessed day when I escaped from there."

Gudrunr paid no attention to what Herborgr was saying.

Next Gullrondr, the daughter of King Gjuki spoke, "Gudrunr, have you ever heard a sadder tale than the one told by Herborgr? However, I'm curious to see what Sigurdr looks like in death." She commanded a servant pull back the covers from his body. She lifted Sigurdr's body by the shoulders and laid his head in Gudrunr's lap, "Look at what has become of your husband. Press your lips against his as if he were still alive." Gudrunr looked once and only once at Sigurdr. She saw his hair all matted with blood, and his staring eyes, glazed with death but still fierce. Gudrunr could contain herself no longer and burst into tears. She sank back in her bed overcome with grief. Soon her pillow was soaked with tears. Her wailing was such that all the geese in the fields, and the fowls that Gudrunr owned started screaming along with her.

Gullrondr, satisfied with the success of their visit said, "Surely there has never been a love for another as great as the love you had for Sigurdr? Never were you glad of heart except when Sigurdr was with you to bring you happiness."

Gudrunr answered inbetween sobs, "Many years ago, in my youth, I was thought to be the fairest woman in the Kingdom, even more beautiful than any of Herjan's Disir. But what am I now? My beauty is gone, my husband is murdered at my side, I am covered in his blood, and my only son is dead. What will become of me? I miss Sigurdr and miss him being near me. My present fate has all been brought about because of the sons of Gjuki, Gunnar, Hogni, and Gutthormr, my own brothers. I curse them and wish the vilest things to happen to them. May their Kingdom be plagued by drought and bad crops so the starving people will rise up against them. They deserve no better. They've broken sworn oaths of fealty. Gunnar, if you can hear me from wherever you're hiding, know this. You'll never have happiness from the treasures you've won. It'll be your death, all because you broke your oath to Sigurdr. How could you have forgotten the friendship that was between the two of you? It was because of him you were able to wed Brynhildr. This is the thanks you give him, to have his bloody head laying dead in his wife's lap, in your sister's lap? You'll rue this day." Then as an afterthought, and an important afterthought at that, Gudrunnr added, "By rights as Sigurdr's wife I had a better claim to the Treasure of the Volsungrs and Andvari's Gold than any of my brothers. You have stolen Sigurdr from me; you have stolen my son Sigmundr from me; and you have stolen my heritage and wealth from me. I curse all of my brothers. I cures my family for bringing me to the pass."

Brynhildr had heard the wailing from her bower and had just entered Gudrunr's room. She stood leaning against a pillar, "I've heard this screeching on the other side of the Hall. Something must be done to stop her. Now I offer her my condolences and best wishes that she might never find love again, nor find herself ever sick with child. I'll be glad if she spends the rest of her days loveless and childless. If it is in my power to curse her with those thoughts, then I do so now."

Gullrondr was shocked at Brynhildr's words, "Loose not such words with your tongue. There is no one here who wishes to speak with you. You've brought scorn and dishonor to your name. There's no one in this Kingdom who does not hate you. Friendless you shall exist, because the life before you can never be called living. You've never been well liked, have you? Your foul words and evil deeds have caused you much grief, and even greater grief to others. You've been working evil so long you can't do anything else. You've caused the death of seven mighty Kings, as well as great suffering to their wives and families. Go back to Skata Grove. I promise no warrior would be foolish enough to try to cross the flames to win your poisoned love."

Brynhildr answered, "What you say is a lie. The only person who has brought trouble to this King has been my brother King Atli. And long since has my debt been paid for his crimes."

Brynhildr stood by a pillar and hugged it against her. Her eyes burned with a piercing gaze so that none could look at her. She spat out words of venom and looked at the assemblage. Then her eyes were drawn to the body of her beloved. She could see his red-golden hair now matted crimson red, and dirty. His eyes were the only ones there that could hold her gaze. They stared back at her, but there was nothing behind them. They were blank. Then looking further down Brynhildr saw the gaping wound in his chest. This wasn't how things were supposed to turn out for her and Sigurdr. They had been meant to spend an eternity in love together with their daughter Aslaugr. Oh, Aslaugr, what was to become of her? What had she done? Brynhildr sunk down to the floor in grief. What had she done?

CHAPTER 22
THE DEATH OF BRYNHILDR

Brynhildr sat in her bower, sad and weeping, consumed with grief. This puzzled everyone, for hadn't it been Brynhildr who had plotted Sigurdr's death? Hadn't she laughed when her plot had succeeded? Why the tears now when the deed was her doing, anyway?

Gunnar visited her and she related the dream she had had, "In this dream my bed was empty and cold. I was nowhere to be found. You came looking for me and then rode off to the land of your enemy knowing it would be your death. Beware and heed what this dream is telling you. Bad things are likely to occur to you since you broke the sacred oaths you had sworn with Sigurdr. Your blood was mingled with Sigurdr's. Now you have shed your brother's blood and ill luck will follow you for that deed. He repaid your brotherhood with victories against your enemies. You repaid his brotherhood with a victory against him. Somehow the payment has to be made more equal. He had good thoughts of you, and was ever true to all the oaths of fealty he had sworn. The sword Gramr separated us when he wooed me in your name. His loyalty and goodness have been repaid with cowardly treachery. You couldn't even face him in honorable combat. My happiest days were after I first met Sigurdr and then lived with King Heimir and King Budli waiting for my love's return. It never occurred to me things would one day turn out like this, and my husband would not be Sigurdr, but Sigurdr's murderer. I took refuge in Skata Grove and then you, Sigurdr, and Hogni rode into my father's land and asked King Budli and King Atli for my hand. Then you visited King Heimir with the same request. I waited for Sigurdr, knowing he was the only warrior capable of breaching the walls protecting me. Instead treachery caused him to woo me falsely for you. And now it has all come to this. Sigurdr is dead and soon I must die."

She was silent. Gunnar embraced her, putting his arms around her neck, and swore his love to her, "I've always loved you, and love you even now more than ever. You are dearer to me than life itself. Forget what has happened and be my wife

again. Live and share my Kingdom, take all my wealth. Such things mean nothing to me if you aren't there to share them with me."

"Nothing will persuade me to live a life without Sigurdr. I'll no longer share my life with you. Now I must die." She laid down in her bed and drew the sheets around her.

o   o   o   o

Gunnar sought out Hogni for his counsel, "Go to Brynhildr and convince her to live. I love her so much. My life will be ruined without her. Tell her I'll wait apart from her if it is her desire until her grief has passed and she is ready to see me again. I'll wait for years, if necessary. Just persuade her to give me some hope."

Hogni refused to intercede, "No, it's best she be allowed to die with some dignity. Her life has been spent bringing misfortune to others. We've had nothing but bad luck since she came here."

Gunnar was inconsolable.

o   o   o   o

Brynhildr ordered gold be brought to her and invited many people to her bedside, especially the poor and those who had served her. While they looked on she took a sword and thrust it under her armpit into her side and lay back in bed. The blood slowly began seeping onto the sheet in an ever-widening circle. She began distributing the gold amongst those who had come, "I'll give to each servant a gold necklace. Others can have pieces of gold and jewels as long as my supply lasts."

No one stepped forward to take the necklace she held proffered in her hand. She urged them again, "This gold is given in happiness, take it and prosper." Finally a poor beggar reached over and took the necklace.

She turned to Gunnar and spoke, "This is the future, Gunnar. Listen well and heed these words. Gudrunr will leave this Hall, given in marriage with my brother King Atli against her wishes. Soon after this an invitation will arrive for you to visit her. This trip will be urged on by Grimhildr. The wisest thing you can do in your life is return the invitation. Stay in the safety of your own Kingdom so no harm can come to you. If you're a fool you'll venture forth on a journey you know is filled with deceit and death, your death, and your brother's death. Gudrunr is now with child. The child born of the union between her and Sigurdr will be called Svanhildr, the most beautiful child in the land. King Atli and I have a sister named Oddrunr. Your grief for me will be short-lived and you'll seek Oddrunr's hand in marriage, though King Atli will forbid it. This will not deter you. You'll seek out her company privately, and both of you will be very happy in your love. But it's a hapless love and King Atli's men will soon find you out. You'll waste money on useless bribes that only buy you a little time before King Atli casts you into a pit of snakes where you'll die. Then King Atli, his sons, and many of his household will be slain. Gudrunr and Svanhildr will escape to the realm of King Jonakr. Gudrunr and Jonakr will marry and she'll give him many fine sons who will gain fame and

renown throughout the world. However, Svanhildr's fate is less fortunate. She will be betrothed to King Jormunrekkr, a vile King of strange habits. His evil counselor will be Bikki, whose words will cause Svanhildr's death. After Svanhildr's death all the Gjukings will have been slain. None will be left to seek vengeance against Jormunrekkr. However, Gudrunr will continue to live a life of sorrow."

She paused for a moment. Gunnar stepped back, disbelieving what he had heard. She continued, "I ask one last favor of you, Gunnar. Prepare a magnificent funeral pyre for Sigurdr and me and those who are slain with him. I've thought about this very carefully, and these are my instructions. Hang rich draperies, fresh flowers, shields and weaponry on the walls. Take the tapestries I've embroidered telling of Sigurdr's exploits and hang them leading into the pyre. Make certain they are safe and won't be burnt once the flames envelope us. I want Sigurdr's legend to live on. Our pyres should be raised up on supports in our chariots, both of which should stand side-by-side. Cover our bodies with cloth dyed red with the blood of the Gautir's. I'll be to the right of Sigurdr, my retainers given to me by my father, including five bondswomen and eight bondsmen, will be on the other. Place two of my thralls at his head, and two at his feet. My two falcons should be there, as well as my two hounds. Once more lay the sword Gramr between us, as it was on our wedding night. Even in death we shall lie pure in our love, yet be burned as one. I'll follow behind him so the door to Niflhel will not close behind his heel before I enter too. I'm glad I've been able to give these instructions. My wound prevents me from speaking any further. Carry out these instructions so we'll have the most magnificent funeral ever given. Invite many Kings to attend. For they should see how a great King is laid out on his pyre, and should be there to honor him." I have more to say, but my breath comes hard now, so now I'll rest.

She settled into her bloodstained sheets and died. Gunnar ordered things be prepared as she had instructed him. Sigurdr was dressed in his finest battle armor. Fafnir's Helmet of Terror was set on his head for the last time. The pyre was piled high with kindling so the flames would continue to burn strong enough to consume all the bodies, human and animal, as well as the other objects that had been placed on the funeral pyre. In addition to those warriors Brynhildr had instructed to be included in the fire, Sigurdr's three-year-old-son Sigmundr, as well as Sigurdr's slayer, Gutthormr, were burned with them.

Brynhildr lay next to Sigurdr for the final time. The fire was kindled and soon blazed high into the sky.

o o o o

After Brynhildr's death she guided her chariot on helveg on her way to Niflhel, following behind Sigurdr. Their journey would eventually take them to Valhalla, but because Sigurdr had not died in mortal combat, the road he traveled was not the warrior's road, which is an easier road with help along the way. His was the worst route to Valhalla since it led through Niflhel and on into Hela's Hall.

At the Gjallarbru Bridge Sigurdr paused briefly to speak to Modgudr, the jotun skeleton maiden and guardian of the bridge. He was allowed to pass over Gjallarbru.

Brynhildr rode up but was stopped by Modgudr who would not let her pass, "I'll not allow you to pass over this bridge and follow such a noble hero as Sigurdr. Find another route. This way is not for those whose hands are still stained with the blood of those whose death they've caused. It would have been better if your life had not been spent lusting after another's husband. Since you have committed many crimes, and have disobeyed Odin in battle, you cannot travel the easy way to Niflhel."

Brynhildr answered, "Your blame is misplaced. I've ridden as a Valkyrie, one of Herjan's Disir, and have been called to the battlefield to decide the fates of many warriors. If this had been the only thing I had ever done, then I would still have been thought better of than you, you who have lived with the Svartalfrs."

Modgudr replied, "Insults will not get you across this bridge. Brynhildr, daughter of King Budli, sister of Atli Budlason, Bekkhildr and Oddrunr, instigator of Sigurdr Fafnirbanis' murder. You are the vilest creature ever born. All of King Gjuki's children will die because of you. Their Hall will be destroyed and the Kingdom of the Gjukings will be no more. What worse deed or more cowardly action could you do than that? All ways into Niflhel are poisonous and painful. Yet over my bridge is the least painful. You don't deserve this way into Niflhel. Depart."

Brynhildr defended herself, "You blame me for the wrongs of Gudrunr and Grimhildr, and all the Gjukings? All the members of that family have thought nothing of breaking oaths, or causing others to break theirs. Sigurdr was my true love first, but was enchanted away from me by trickery. So, never have I lusted after another woman's husband. He was my husband first. Because of this everything that followed happened. The blame should be placed with Gudrunr. Have her get her feet wet in the poisonous river Slidr when she journeys this way. I hope you'll be meeting her soon."

Modgudr guided Brynhildr back to her story, "Don't worry about the path Gudrunr will take. You also have yet to be free of the river Slidr."

Brynhildr continued her story and told of how Sigurdr had wooed her in disguise, acting in Gunnar's behalf. "Sigurdr was true to his friend and placed the sword Gramr between us for those three nights. Never was there a better trundle than the sharp edges of the great sword Gramr. Though it might cleve the finest hair in two, it also separated us that night."

Modgudr interrupted, "Why didn't you see through the guise and know it was Sigurdr wooing you? As a Valkyrie you have such gifts."

Brynhildr answered, "I was not completely recovered from the sleepthorn given to me by Odin. My hamingja was fooled so that I couldn't see that it was Sigurdr in disguise. I was no longer a Valkyrie and was denied those powers." She omitted that she had lost her powers as a Valkyrie because she had previously violated her oath and slept with Sigurdr when they first met, and had even born a child, Aslaugr, by him. Reason enough for her to no longer be able to ride clad in Golden byrny and helmet as a Valkyrie.

Brynhildr finished her story. Modgudr was impressed and let her pass, "I've heard your story and know now that you've been greatly wronged. Follow after your beloved Sigurdr. Hurry and catch up with him before Hela entwines him in her embrace. She saves the best warriors for herself."

Brynhildr rode across the bridge on her way to Niflhel seeking Sigurdr. Perhaps now they could finally be together and find happiness once they reached Valhalla.

CHAPTER 23
THE MARRIAGE OF GUDRUNR TO ATLI BUDLASON

udrunr had been with child at Sigurdr's death and soon after gave birth to a daughter whom she named Svanhildr. But even her daughter could not help Gudrunr overcome the uneasiness she felt living amongst her husband's slayers.

For many days Gudrunr sat alone in her bower reflecting on all that had happened, "How sad my life has become now that Sigurdr is slain. He was better by far than other men, surely the greatest warrior who ever lived. My brothers Gunnar and Hogni were jealous of this. Through envy they had him slain, and have slain his proper avenger, his son Sigmundr, my son. My brothers have killed my son, their nephew. Now they have falsely claimed the Volsungr Treasure and Andvari's Hoard as their own, when it should belong to Svanhildr. Greed and ill luck travel hand-in-hand. They'll rue their actions and the grief they've brought to me. Sigurdr was as gold to iron; or a leek to the wild grass and herbs growing in the field; or the strength of a hart against the other creatures of the forest. How well I remember Grani drooping and falling to the ground when the body of his master still clutching the sword Gramr in his death, was carried past him. He fell into grief for Sigurdr, as if he were human. I believe he has felt the loss as keenly as I have. How can I remain here amongst my husband's murderers? I must leave this tainted Kingdom. I can't remain in the presence of those who have robbed me of the only happiness I've ever known."

So Gudrunr readied her things and left. As she traveled through the woods she heard the wolves howling and the crows cawing and felt death would be a greater blessing than life, "If I were dead, then perhaps I would be reunited with Sigurdr?" Her mind was filled with dark thoughts as she traveled along.

She journeyed through the forest for five days and eventually came to the Hall of King Alfr, where she was welcomed. King Alfr had been Sigurdr's foster-father. His wife, Hjordis, had since died and he had married Thora, the daughter of King Hakon. She and Gudrunr became close friends. Gudrunr remained there for three-and-a-half years.

Gudrunr spent most of her time embroidering tapestries telling of Sigurdr's greatest deeds. She also wove tapestries telling of King Sigmundr's sea battle against Sigar and Siggeir to the south of Fjon.

Her weaving helped lessen her grief. During the times when sadness engulfed her she sought out Thora and the two took long walks together talking about their lives. Thora tried to help Gudrunr in whatever ways she could. However, the greatest comfort to Gudrunr in her grief was Svanhildr, the daughter she and Sigurdr had together. Every day the child grew more and more like her father. Svanhildr's eyes were dark and brooding, carrying the gaze of the Volsungrs in them. No one could look at them for long.

o   o   o   o

After Gudrunr's departure Grimhildr sent messengers throughout the lands to find where her daughter had gone. Eventually they brought her word Gudrunr was staying with King Alfr and his family.

Grimhildr sent for her sons. She had other plans for Gudrunr, "It's in our best interests Gudrunr should be back with us as soon as possible. You must offer her weregild to make up for the loss of her husband and son, and bring her back to us. And don't forget you must also bring Svanhildr back. Gudrunr is of no use to us staying with King Alfr. As Sigurdr's wife the Volsungr Treasure and Andvari's Hoard are rightfully hers. At Sigurdr's death the treasures went to his son Sigmundr. You killed his son, so the treasures rightfully belong to Gudrunr, and if she dies, to Svanhildr. You might have a claim as her brothers to become her guardians if you can prove her grief has made her lose all reason. As her guardians you can force her return to us as being in her best interests. And where she goes, Svanhildr will go."

Grimhildr smiled for a moment at her devious treachery and continued, "Then she might own the Volsungr Treasure and Andvari's Hoard, but you would control it. And we could make certain she never regains any reason before her untimely death. There have been rumors many Kings will come a wooing to see Gudrunr. Fame attends the King who weds Sigurdr Fafnirsbani's widow, and he becomes Svanhildr's stepfather. If she marries a King whom we have not bargained with for her hand, then he as her husband is her guardian and has control of the Volsungr Treasure and Andvari's Hoard. If she should die, then the treasures are his completely and rightfully, beyond Svanhildr's claims. If she dies before marriage then Svanhildr inherits. And we will be Svanhildr's closest relatives and can claim her as our own, to raise as our own. We cannot let her marry, or die in a marriage to a King who has no obligation to us. Her death can only be as a widow, living here with us, under our control. You never should have let her leave this Hall."

Andvari's Hoard had worked its greed on her sons who were opposed to giving away any part of their claimed wealth to their sister. Hogni spoke, "She seems happy where she is. What use could she be to us? Why lessen our fortunes to bring a sad person back to our Kingdom? As to the Volsungr Treasure and Andvari's Hoard being hers. They are guarded in our treasure room. She has abandoned the treasures. And if she should marry again and then die, well, let any King foolish enough to come here to claim the treasures just try. We will be waiting for him with swords made from the melted treasure."

Grimhildr added, frustrated with her son's inability to see beyond gold, "Hogni, why complicate things? Offer her a bit of weregild. In her grief she seems to have no interest in the Volsungr Treasure or Andvari's Hoard. However, if she marries another King matters change. He has no grief for Sigurdr's death. He will make claims. Give her a minor bit of weregild, and in the contract write in as small a hand as you can that by accepting the weregild she gives up all claims and rights to the Volsungr Treasure and Andvari's Hoard. Better to give her a small portion and legally gain the rest, then have to battle a future greedy husband."

Hogni still was not convinced, "She's a woman, which isn't necessarily bad, they do have their uses. If she were more like Brynhildr was, then I could imagine her riding off to war with us and being of some help. Then she might be worthwhile. Remember how Brynhildr could outfight just about any man around...?" His thoughts trailed off as he remembered Brynhildr in her warrior garb.

Grimhildr lost patience with her sons, "Can't you think ahead? Look around you. Think about what's happening in the world. Gudrunr is more valuable to us than a thousand warriors. Beautiful unmarried daughters of Kings are in short supply, unwed Kings aren't. If Gudrunr returns with Svanhildr then we have two marriages we can arrange, Gudrunr's now and Svanhildr's in the near future. Our choices are limited. We have a possible threat on our borders from King Atli who has since become King of the Huns, and even now calls himself Atli the Hun. He blames his sister Brynhildr's death on us and wants vengeance of some sort. We can gather together an expensive army of many thousands, meet King Atli in combat, and if we're lucky, defeat him. Or, we can wed Gudrunr to him and gain an ally at the expense of a marriage feast. Which is better? Which is surer? Which is more cost effective? By which plan do we rightfully gain the Volsungr Treasure and Andvari's Hoard. Better she be married to King Atli after we've paid her weregild and gotten her to sign a contract ceding us all of the Volsungr Treasure and Andvari's Hoard. Think beyond your greed. Weregild is a small price to pay. "

Her sons nodded, although Hogni voiced a note of concern about marrying Gudrunr off to King Atli, "What will their children look like, if they have them? King Atli is so short and misshapen, maybe with troll-blood in his veins? Do we want trolls introduced into our family lineage? I doubt he even comes up to my knee in height.

Sometimes the depth of her son's ignorance amazed her. Why couldn't her sons realize it didn't matter how attractive King Atli was, or how pleased Gudrunr would be to have him as a husband, or what sorts of things she would bear with King Atli as the father. Grimhildr responded to her son's concerns, "Misshapen inconvenient things can always be dealt with as they have been from time immemorial. The dead do not inherit. What matters is that our borders would once again be safe, and we'd rightfully have the Volsungr Treasure and Andvari's Hoard."

Hogni seemed unconvinced.

She continued, "But your thoughts mean little, Hogni. I've already arranged this marriage. King Atli will now be our ally." She shoved her sons to the door. "Go to your sister and make peace with her. Offer her whatever it'll take to get her to sign the contract. I've already promised her to King Atli, and he grows weary of waiting for her to be at his side."

As Gunnar and Hogni were leaving Hogni made some last remarks, "Plot, plot, plot. Must we always plot? I'll bet you plot about which enclosure out back you use to relieve yourself. Tell me, was the marriage between Gudrunr and King Atli arranged before or after Sigurdr's death?"

Grimhildr turned away and did not answer. Hogni thought he knew what the answer was.

∘ ∘ ∘ ∘

Gunnar and Hogni assembled their entourage. Accompanying them on their journey were their finest warriors. Everyone wore their most expensive raiment. Their byrnies were cut short in the latest style. Over their war gear they wore red fur coats. Each horse was bedecked with a fancy covering and a bridle of gold and silver. The mail worn by both rider and horse was made of finely woven precious metals and intertwined with beautiful ribbons and fabrics. The group fairly glistened with wealth. Their coverings were unsuitable for war, but clearly suitable for making a fine impression. Five hundred noble warriors rode with Gunnar and Hogni, including Valdemar of Denmark, Eymod III, Jarisleif, the Saxons, Franks, and the Longobards who had only just recently changed their name to Lombard. At the last minute Grimhildr decided to accompany her sons. Such an important mission could hardly be left to ordinary means, or the dim wits her sons possessed. In great majesty the procession rode to the land of King Alfr.

∘ ∘ ∘ ∘

Gunnar and Hogni approached Gudrunr quietly and begged their sister's forgiveness. They presented her with many fine gifts and expressed their grief for Sigurdr's death.

Gunnar spoke first, "We've missed you at home. Please come back with us and bring your daughter Svanhildr so we can raise her in a manner befitting her station."

Gudrunr answered, "She's already being raised in a King's court with all due respect paid to her. What can you offer me that I don't already have here? Nothing. I do not want to leave my friends. I'm comfortable here and am accepted as one of the family. At last I have a home."

Hogni tried his hand at persuading her, "Many are the times I've gone to your bower to talk with you, only to find it empty. I miss the advice you used to give me and the good times we used to have together."

Gunnar replied, "You should have thought of all that before you killed my husband. There are no more good times for me at your Hall. I don't trust your words. I hear more in them than what you speak out loud. You speak but I hear Grimhildr's words. You entertain me with a voice miming act."

Grimhildr saw her sons were making a mess of it. She excused herself briefly and then returned with a drink for Gudrunr. It was the same type of drink she had once given Sigurdr to make him forget Brynhildr. Grimhildr using charms had mixed in the depth of the sea, the roots of trees, the might of the earth, as well as her son's blood. Additionally she added the blood of the wood, charred acorns, and soot from a hearth. Lastly she included the bowels of a sacrificial animal, and swine's liver that had been boiled in blood. "Drink this wonderful elixir as a token of our love. It'll clear your head and make you feel better."

She handed Gudrunr a magnificent golden goblet which was carved within and without with magic runes, and encrusted with precious jewels. It was filled to the rim with the delightful drink. Grimhildr noticed Gudrunr admiring the magnificent goblet and added, "Of course, drink and cup are a gift for you to keep. A goblet this magnificent is hardly worthy enough for one such as myself, so I gladly make a present of it to you."

Gudrunr, though looking longingly at the magnificent goblet seemed to hesitate. Grimhildr continued her entreaties, "Please accept my humble gift and its contents with the love it is given. Look as I fill my ordinary golden cup with a humble servant's wine which I drink in a toast to the memory of Sigurdr. Was there ever a braver warrior than Sigurdr Fafnirsbani? Let us drink to his glory."

She looked at her sons and then at the extra goblets. Her sons didn't get it. She looked back and forth until finally Hogni got it. He poured the lesser wine into two other goblets, one for him and one for his brother Gunnar, "To the glory of Sigurdr Fafnirsbani. May his legend live on in Sagas for the next thousand years."

He poked his brother in the ribs. Gunnar raised his goblet, "And even longer than a thousand years. Until, until, um, the stars fall from the sky, and the moon and sun are swallowed up."

Well, that was unfortunate. He had just reminded everyone of Ragnarokr, the final doom of everything when evil triumphed in the world and everything was destroyed.

Gunnar continued, "To Sigurdr Fafnirsbani, Gudrunr, and Svanhildr. May they be reunited."

Grimhildr looked in amazement at her son. He'd just given a toast in honor of Gudrunr and Svanhildr's death, making a mess of things again. She tried to put things right, "May Gudrunr and Svanhildr live long and blessed lives so they may each weave tapestries telling the glory of Sigurdr Fafnirsbani." As an afterthought she had an idea, "And once they are safely back home with us, I will be hiring the greatest skalds in the land to begin putting their legend into words, words told by Gudrunr. One skald will be her amanuensis in the morning, the other at night." The plan didn't seem to leave much time for a husband.

Gudrunr could not refuse a toast honoring her husband and drank from the cup. After just a sip Gudrunr started to put the goblet down. Realizing a sip would be ineffective Grimhildr reached over, touched the bottom of the goblet pushing it back to Gudrunr's mouth and kept it at Gudrunr's mouth, tipping it up further forcing Gudrunr to drink the entire contents. She kept pushing until the entire contents of the goblet had been emptied into Gudrunr's mouth, with a lot of it overflowing onto her clothing. She wanted to make certain Gudrunr had swallowed enough to have the desired effect. And it did.

The drink's effects were immediate. Gudrunr forgot her grief and agreed to return with Grimhildr and her brothers to their Kingdom. The drink had not only lifted her grief, it had made her downright effusive with happiness. She decided to arrange a great feast to honor Sigurdr and celebrate her departure.

o   o   o   o

That evening Grimhildr met with her sons to explain her plans.

Grimhildr, "This feast is our chance to solidify Gudrunr's marriage to King Atli.

Gunnar added, "Yes, it is always best if the bride knows about her betrothal at a feast honoring her recently murdered husband."

Hogni looked at his mother, "Sigurdr is barely cold in his barrow and you want to turn her departure feast into a wedding announcement?"

Gunnar added, "Plots, always plots."

Grimhildr shook her head. Where would her sons be without her? She knew. She was certain they'd be cleaning the slop out of pig enclosures. "And it is by plots we will have the Volsungr Treasure and Andvari's Hoard. Send messengers off immediately to King Atli."

Hogni responded, "There is not enough time. King Atli is several days ride from here. And it'll take him several days to get back. The departure feast is day after tomorrow."

Grimhildr, "And that's why it is always wise to plan ahead. King Atli and a hundred of his men are but a few hours from here. I sent invitations off to him the day we left our land and started our journey to make certain he would be nearby. Now just find some other nearby Kings to compete for Gudrunr's hand so his presence won't seem such a contrivance."

Gunnar added, "Plots, always plots."

Hogni sent riders to King Atli and several other nearby Kings with the following message, "You are invited to a feast celebrating the life and death of Sigurdr Fafnirsbani, as well as the departure of his now single beautiful wealthy widow and their beautiful daughter to live with her mother Grimhildr, and her brothers."

o   o   o   o

The day of Gudrunr's feast arrived. Even though preparations had been hasty, they looked impressive enough to honor a great warrior like Sigurdr Fafnirsbani.

King Atli, riding Glaumr, as well as two other Kings arrived in time for the feast. A few people wondered how King Atli could have been sent for and made the journey so quickly. As their goblets overflowed with wine and their trenchers never went bare everyone forgot this incongruity.

All three sought Gudrunr's hand in marriage. King Atli, however, had the self-assured manner of one who knows the contest is rigged and that the prize is already his.

At the feast Grimhildr toasted her daughter. She walked up to Gudrunr and spoke, "I give you good greeting. However, I feel that is not enough to make amends for the many wrongs done to you. Your brothers and I present you with the weregild we earlier agreed on, and other precious things and continue to give you the love we have never withheld, but which you have sometimes refused to accept. Here are rings and fine linen. We also present you with the Hall Lodver so you'll have a place of your own. These small, unworthy gifts will not bring the mighty warrior Sigurdr Fafnirsbani back, but we hope they will at least dim the memory of the tragedy of his death and serve to welcome us back to your arms as friends and kinfolk. We are glad you've decided it is time to be with your family."

Grimhildr paused and motioned for King Atli to come forward. She continued, "Even though we cannot bring back Sigurdr, we can try to erase your loneliness. Sigurdr was a great warrior, one of the mightiest. There is only one who could hope to take his place, and that is Atli Budlason. He has already agreed to become your next husband."

Atli stepped forward. Gudrunr may have been drugged from the drink, but she still had some of her senses about her. She wasn't that drugged that she'd easily accept King Atli as her husband without even having time to mourn and come to terms with her grief. And Atli? That little troll? Clearly he wasn't even half the size of the noble and great Sigurdr Fafnirsbani. She slammed her fists on the table, causing all the dinnerware to jump as she leapt to her feet, "No! I'll never marry that evil svartalfr. Never, never will I be wedded to a little troll who has to crawl back and forth in bed to perform his duties. I'll never marry the brother of Brynhildr. Nor will I bear his children and increase the family of my enemies. It would be an insult to my husband's memory for that vile little man and me to wed and have children."

Grimhildr answered, "Hold your anger. Atli Budlason is a mighty warrior, and the sons you have by him will be as great as if they were the sons of Sigmundr or Sigurdr."

Gudrunr sat back down, "I can't take him as my husband. My thoughts still return to Sigurdr and the times we spent together."

Grimhildr was firm, "None but a great warrior and King will do for you. King Atli is the only one who could hope to take Sigurdr's place."

Gudrunr was adamant as she spoke, as if she were in a trance, "Only evil will come of this union. I can see the death of my kin, and even of the sons I would have with him, if this marriage were to take place. There is not the slightest good in it. Don't you realize, Grimhildr, you are signing away your own sons' lives with this marriage?"

Grimhildr clearly was unimpressed with her daughter's performance. She edged closer to Gudrunr and stared into her eyes. She raised the cup to Gudrunr's lips and forced her to drink another sip from it. So anxious was Grimhildr that she forced the cup a little too hard and some of the drink dribbled down the corners of Gudrunr's mouth. The blood-red wine caused a heart-shaped staining on the front of her white bodice as the bitter liquid was forced down her throat. Grimhildr whispered into her daughter's ear, "Do as I say and be happy in the marriage I've arranged for you. Your brothers and I give you our friendship and love. King Atli will take care of any loneliness you may feel. Additionally, we will present you with the Halls named Vinbjorg and Valbjorg."

Thus drugged Gudrunr nodded her ascent, "I agree, though I know what I've seen will come about. Further bloodshed will cover our family until all drown in it. My mind as well as the words I speak agree to the marriage, but this is still against my will. I'll receive no pleasure from King Atli's small company and unasked for and unwanted attentions."

o   o   o   o

The next morning the various groups departed for their Kingdoms. Gudrunr and Svanhildr left with King Atli. They rode over land for seven days, and over sea for an additional seven days, after which they traveled another seven days over land until they reached King Atli's towering Hall.

Once in King Atli's realm the byways were lined with cheering crowds welcoming their new Queen. Great feasts were prepared and there was celebrating throughout the Kingdom. At the marriage feast King Atli and Gudrunr exchanged vows and rings. Gudrunr placed the Andvaranautr on King Atli's finger, dooming him to the same curse that had already taken its toll in blood on the Volsungrs.

o   o   o   o

Their life together brought great joy to King Atli, and nothing but grief to Gudrunr. She hated King Atli. All the deeds which others found brave and noble she found abhorrent and detestable. But her duty as a wife was done, however reluctantly, and as infrequently as possible. Eventually she bore him two sons, Erpr and Eitill. She loved them, a love made easier by the fact they seemed to have inherited all of the character and shape of the Volsungrs, and none of King Atli's or the Budlings. They did not resembled their father in the least.

Gudrunr spent most of her time apart from her husband and children thinking of what might have been if Sigurdr had lived. Thus she lived her life in a fanciful dream that never was, seldom roused to the concerns of the real world. She could often be found sitting under a tree, staring into the middle unfocused distance of her world in which Sigurdr lived and she was happy. Seldom did she focus on the reality of the horror of her present life.

CHAPTER 24
ATLI BUDLASON
SENDS FOR
GUDRUNR'S
BROTHERS

Gudrunr lived more and more in the past. At dinner she talked to no one in particular about the wonderful life she had had with Sigurdr, the Volsungr Treasure and Andvari's Hoard, and the luxurious things Sigurdr had given her because of that wealth. Atli overheard this litany night after night. Although he was wealthy, the wealth of the Volsungr's Treasure and Andvari's Hoard had become legendary. Greed grew in his heart. After all, the wealth had been Sigurdr's, and after his death it had passed to Gudrunr. Atli felt she had been tricked into signing it over to her two murdering brothers. And by rights, as her husband, he had some claim to the Volsungr Treasure and Andvari's Hoard. He determined to retrieve the gold for his wife and the sake of family honor, and if his wealth should happen to increase because if it, then so be it. He was willing to make the sacrifice. His thoughts now turned to how he might accomplish this.

o   o   o   o

One night Atli woke from his sleep with a start. He sat up, thankful it had only been a dream. The nightmarish vision had been all too real. Gudrunr had been awakened when he sat up and asked what was wrong. He answered, "In my dream you attacked and ran me through with my own sword."

Gudrunr thought for a moment and then told him what his dream meant, "When one dreams of iron then fire will come about in real life. It seems, also, that your dream has an element of pride to it in that you find it absurd that you could be run through with your own sword."

Atli continued, "As you were speaking, more of my dream has been coming back to me. Two reed tree saplings grew here, and I took it upon myself to protect them so they would come to no harm. Yet you pulled them so fiercely out of the ground the roots came out with them. And instead of dripping with the moisture of the earth, the roots dripped blood. You prepared a broth with these roots and sat it

before me at my table, where I was compelled to eat it. Then my dream shifted and two hawks sat on my arm. I shook my arm and they flew off. It was only after they were in flight I noticed how starved and thin they were. Both of them plummeted to the ground after only gaining a little height. They fell through the earth down to the deepest most treacherous part of Hela's Kingdom, Helheimr, where they were welcomed and seemed well fed in comparison to the others in her land. I followed them there and watched as their hearts were cut from their bodies and mixed with honey. The plate containing this gruesome dish was brought to me and I was commanded to eat of it. And finally, I once more sat in my own room, with two young dogs at my side. Then I watched in horror as they were both killed and served before me, and I ate the terrible meal, compelled to do so even though I didn't want to."

Gudrunr answered, "Your dreams represent events that will come to pass. The trees, hawks, and dogs are your two sons. Soon they will die, making your life a misery ever after. Their deaths will lay heavily upon your conscience."

"There was one other thing I dreamed," Atli continued. "I was at my bath and could hear people outside my door discussing the best way to kill me. I put on my clothing and checked, but could find no one outside the door. I went to my bed and waited. I knew my death would occur shortly thereafter."

Gudrunr interpreted the dreams as best she could.

Time passed and the dreams were forgotten. King Atli continued to think of the Volsungr Treasure and Andvari's Hoard as his and wrongly taken from him by the evil connivances of Gudrunr's brothers. He also put more effort into trying to make Gudrunr happy. Unfortunately, though not unexpectedly, their marriage did not improve.

The rightness of King Atli's claim to Gudrunr's inheritance grew in his mind. He determined to get it as his own and sought advice from his counselors on how best to do this, "What can you tell me of the Volsungr Treasure and Andvari's Hoard? Where is it kept? Is there a possibility the guards are lax or can be bribed?"

His counselors could offer him very little information. Vingi, sometimes called Knefrud, seemed the most knowledgeable of King Atli's counsellors, "As far as we know their wealth is not guarded at all. This is because Gudrunr's brothers have hidden it somewhere. Gunnar and Hogni are the only ones who know its whereabouts."

King Atli was disappointed, "Do any of you have any suggestions about what we can do?"

Vingi spoke again, "Gunnar and his brother are now your brothers-in-law. They have not seen Gudrunr in quite some time. You've every right to offer them your hospitality. If you were to invite them here, you would have them in your midst and their wealth in your grasp. They will surely come unarmed to visit their family. Under the right circumstances their wealth would make a good bargaining chip, say, in exchange for their lives?"

Atli liked this idea. The next morning at breakfast he spoke to Gudrunr, "It's been a long time since you've seen your brothers. Perhaps we should invite them here for a visit. It might lift your spirits." Grimhildr's drink still worked it's spell on Gudrunr and she had very little recollection her brothers had killed her husband.

This was certainly unusual because Gudrunr knew how much King Atli despised her kin. Her thoughts turned on possible motives behind her husband's offer before she spoke, "Perhaps it would be better if I were to visit them instead. That would be easier than having to arrange accommodations and feasts, as well as other entertainments for them if they visited here."

Atli dissuaded her, "No, we have room enough in our Hall for all your kin to visit at once. As for food, my lands have some of the finest game in the world. I'm sure we can offer them a time they'll never forget. It's settled then. I'll send an invitation off to them today."

Gudrunr felt uneasy about the matter. There was too much eagerness in her husband's voice. He only became this excited when warring and conquering other nations."

Vingi was given an invitation bidding Gudrunr's brothers to a feast to be held in their honor, and prepared to deliver it. In the meantime Gudrunr overheard some of the preparations being made for the feast. These included construction of cells and various methods of torture to make them reveal the whereabouts of the gold. Gudrunr hurried to find Vingi before he left. "I'm glad I found you. I have a few presents I'd like you to give my brothers when you see them." She handed him two packages. They contained a bar on which she had cut some runes of warning, and a gold ring on which she had twined a wolf's hair.

Vingi put the packages in the same pack with the invitation, "I'll be back with your brothers before you know it."

"Have a safe journey. Perhaps my brothers will have other engagements and not be able to return with you at this time." She turned and went back into the Hall.

Vingi and his party set out on their journey. While aboard ship during the sea leg of the journey Vingi sat looking at Gudrunr's presents to her brothers. It took little thought for him to convince himself it would be best if he opened the gifts. He read the runes and realized their message warned the brothers not to return with Vingi. He took out his knife and recarved some of the runes until the message read quite differently. It now promised them a great feast and begged them to come and see her. He casually glanced at the ring, which seemed ordinary enough with no inscription of any kind on it. He did not see the wolf's hair. He rewrapped the gifts.

Eventually Vingi and his entourage arrived at King Gunnar's Hall in Limfjord where they were welcomed with a great feast prepared in their honor. The central table bowed and groaned with plenty of wine and food. The servant Fjornir was given the sole task of making certain Vingi's cup was never empty. Vingi presented the brothers with Gudrunr's packages, as well as Atli's invitation, "I've been sent here by noble Atli to invite you to his Hall so he might honor the mighty deeds of his brothers-in-law. He wishes to give a great banquet in your honor. There will be music, fine food, and even finer wine. He intends to place before you armor, shields, battle implements including swords and lances. He offers you wide lands and sumptuous Halls to stay in during your journey there. You will be treated befitting your station and given everything you deserve. There is even talk that the lands of Gnitaheidr and the Myrkvidr Forest, which many in your Kingdom call the Black Forest, will be given to you as gifts, as well as the noble steed Danpr. What more can I say to tempt you to visit your lovely sister?"

Gunnar and Hogni stepped out of hearing range to consult with each other, whispering between themselves, "What do you think of this strange invitation, Hogni? What are we to make of his bidding? He tempts us with great wealth, land and gold, yet what is such an offer to us. We are far richer than he is, since the gold that once covered Gnitaheidr, is now ours. How fitting he should offer us that plot of land. And what of the army he offers us. Does it come fully armored? Can we trust such an army to be loyal, or is it a trick to position his warriors in our midst ahead of his invasion?"

Hogni answered, "He places before us an army, which might not be the same as offering us an army."

Gunnar continued, "Our clothes are more costly, many being woven within and without with fine strands of gold. Yet noble raiment will be ours if we visit? The steed Danpr is tempting, however, there are horses in my stable that are that fine stallion's equal. What should we make of gold, land, armies, and horses offered to us, when we have no need of them? Could it be friendly? Has Gudrunr changed him with her love?"

Hogni responded, "That would be hard to do since I don't think her thoughts dwell on Atli. Her thoughts and love are still with Sigurdr. I think we should put more weight to the army that is to be presented to us. I don't think this is a friendly offer, and would advise against us going. We must think of an excuse that will not offend King Atli."

Gunnar opened Gudrunr's gift and read the runes, "These are runes of welcome. Clearly Gudrunr wants us to come. She would have no part in any of Atli's trickery since she loves us and has always been a true sister. Look, she sends us a gold ring of welcome. Perhaps we should reconsider? We might be able to reject Atli's invitation, but we certainly can't reject our sister's."

Hogni inspected the runes closely, "There's no doubt the runes are welcoming, without threat and certainly bid us come. However, they seem to be overscratched, with some cut more deeply than others. Perhaps there has been an effacement of this bark? It's hard to tell. And look at the ring. There seems to be a wolf's hair twined around it. This bespeaks some trickery and is surely a warning from her telling us the invitation comes as a wolf does, with deceit and treachery. I feel we're fated not to return to our own Kingdom if we go on this journey. I still advise against it."

The two returned to Vingi and expressed their doubts to him.

Hogni spoke, "Although everything seems to be in order, there is a wolf's hair around the ring. Is this not a warning that we should not come?"

Gunnar added, "Why would Atli offer us so much of his realm? He has children who should be his rightful heirs?"

Vingi thought fast, "Ah, yes. I recall when your sister was wrapping the bark there was a dog at her side which she was stroking. At the last minute she thought her gifts looked rather paltry next to Atli's, so she removed this ring from her own finger and tied it in with her package, instructing me to be certain you knew it was her very own ring and she was giving it to you out of love. I'm certain the hair you mistake for a wolf's is only that of her pet dog."

This seemed a reasonable explanation and the two accepted it. Vingi continued, "As for his beneficence towards you. You are kith and kin to him, and great in your own right. He finds his sons Erpr and Eitill disappointing. They don't seem to follow warrior ways. They are gentle and unable to rule with a firm hand. So what is he to do with his Kingdom? Let it be broken by dissension at his death? He would rather you two have it. Both of you have the power and skill to ward off the greed of others who would be King. Perhaps, Hogni could be King of Atli's Hunland, while you remain as King of this realm?"

Hogni was flattered Atli thought him a worthy successor. Vingi knew the ego of second sons who thought they could rule as well as first sons, and knew Hogni would readily accept this explanation. Hogni urged Gunnar to visit Hunland, "Atli means us no harm, and indeed intends us great honor."

The feast continued through the night. Gradually everyone retired, except for Hogni's wife, Kostbera, and Gunnar's wife, Glaumvor. Kostbera reached over and picked up the bark. She looked at the runes, "These seem to be overstruck. If I ignore the deeper, fresher cuts I can easily read words of warning. Why are our husbands ignoring this?"

Glaumvor could offer no reason. Soon the wine caught up with them and they both fell asleep. Somehow, runes cut on a stick just didn't seem too important just then. Their dreams were not peaceful.

The next morning Kostbera awoke and went to her husband to warn him. She found Hogni dozing under the banquet table, woke Hogni and told him her reading of the runes, "Don't leave here. There is great danger if you do. Your first instincts were right concerning Gudrunr's warnings. You've never been able to read runes very skillfully and have misinterpreted these. Gudrunr is good at cutting runes and would never have made the mistakes these cuts contain. They have only been guilefully worked as best they could to conceal their true message which is a message warning of your deaths if you two go."

Hogni didn't like being reminded about his lack of skill in reading runes and tended to discount the warning even more so, "I think I'd feel it if my sister were warning me about something."

Kostbera reminded him he had been uneasy about the invitation. She then related her dream to him, "We were both sitting in our Hall. Suddenly there was a thunderous roar. The river running near here had welled up from its banks and sent a great torrent of water crashing through the walls, pulling them down around us. We were both killed."

Hogni took little note of the dream, "Like all women, you're suspicious and seek evil where there is none. As a man I can see Atli has sound reasons for inviting us to see him. He is our family and would never do us harm. He offers me a Kingship. Would you have me refuse?"

Kostbera was disgusted. Sometimes her husband could be so obtuse, "I suppose you are determined to see this good welcome first hand. And when you do, remember, I've warned you. There is no friendship for you in that realm. However, I also had another dream. In this one the river broke through the walls and tore down the poles holding up the throne. Perhaps it would be wise for them to be moved to our other residence along with the throne. Ill luck would certainly befall our house if these symbols of your brother's reign were destroyed. It would be a simple matter for a servant to dismantle the dais and take it and the throne to another Hall."

Hogni again ignored her dream, "Your dreams don't make sense. You dream of rivers, while we will be traveling by land and have nothing but fields and plains along the way. Fertile hay and fields of plenty will surround our legs, not rushing waters."

Kostbera tried once more, "Then my dream changed to our bedroom and you were sleeping soundly. Suddenly the covers on the bed burst into flame and the dark cloak you wore around you caught fire and you were consumed in the flames. Then the flames climbed up the tapestry on the wall and over the other hangings until soon the entire room and then the Hall was engulfed in fire. No one escaped."

Hogni seemed self-assured. Holding up his cloak he answered her triumphantly, "That dream was a harmless fable. Here is my cloak. See, it is light in color. You dreamed of a dark cloak. We are safe from your fantasies. These stories are becoming interesting. Perhaps you should tell them to the skald so he can put them into verse?"

Kostbera continued trying to warn her husband, "Do not be so dismissive of my tales. They are not fanciful, but prescient. I also dreamed a polar bear came into our Hall and grabbed the King's throne and broke it asunder. He waved the splinters at us frightening everyone in the Hall. Then he dropped the sticks and bounded towards us, gathering us into his mouth. We were horrified and didn't know what to do."

Hogni once again scoffed at her dream. She continued, "The bear disappeared. Then, after we thought we were safe a giant erne flew into the Hall. When I first saw it I mistook its face for Atli's. It flew overhead and rained down blood upon us. Everyone in the Hall was splattered in red. You and King Gunnar were nowhere about. This surely is a warning that he has evil in mind for you and your brother?"

Hogni discounted it all, "I'm tired and you waste my time with these tales. I can explain this one easily. Every day we slaughter animals for our own use. This is a messy business, and many of us are splattered with blood when this happens. This dream just foretells a great feast in our honor. Atli has promised us a feast. This dream just confirms that. The eagle you dreamed of actually represents an ox to be served at our feast. Now leave me. I'm tired of interpreting these dreams for you."

Kostbera left thinking to herself it was silly to interpret an eagle as being an ox. She knew she was right, but Hogni was determined to go. Nothing she could say, no stories portending doom, could dissuade him. Flattery certainly could make a man lose his sense.

∘ ∘ ∘ ∘

Glaumvor had also had premonitory dreams that night. She went to Gunnar and warned him. Each dream told of some forthcoming evil. However, Gunnar, as Hogni had done, interpreted them differently.

Glaumvor related the first one, "A warrior carrying a long sword dripping with blood entered the Hall and walked up to the throne where you sat and ran you through with it. There you sat, with the sword sticking through you and wolves licked both ends of the bloody instrument."

Gunnar tried to reassure her, "The worst you have to fear is that I might be bitten by a dog. I was once told that blood covered in blood often foretold of dogs."

Glaumvor scoffed at this and continued, "I've never heard such a thing. Perhaps my next dream will trouble you more. Women, bleak and sad, came into the Hall and walked up to the throne where you sat. They claimed you as their mate. I'm certain they were your guardian spirits come to take you away."

Glaumvor had more difficulty with this dream, "I don't know what to say to this one, other than what is fated to happen will happen, no matter what I do. Therefore, why dwell on these matters? Hogni and I are determined to visit our sister. Death warnings will not deter us. We leave tomorrow morning."

The next morning Hogni and Gunnar took several trusted servants, dug up the Volsungr Treasure and Andvari's Hoard and reburied it in the Rhine, unknowingly at a spot near Andvarafors. Thus was the gold returned to its source. All, that is, except for the Andvaranautr which their sister Gudrunr had given to King Atli. So they were still cursed, and would remain so until Andvaranautr was also returned to the Rhine and united with Andvari's Hoard.

While Hogni and Gunnar were out burying the Volsungr Treasure and Andvari's Hoard, the rest of the household was preparing for their departure. Upon their return Gunnar went to Fjornir and awakened him, "Fjornir, go and fetch us some of the finest wine from the tuns in the cellar. If we are to believe our wives this will be our last celebrating for a long while."

Rather than a joyous departure, at the end it turned rather solemn with many of the servants openly weeping. They, too, felt the journey was ill advised and neither Gunnar nor Hogni would return alive, if at all. Accompanying the two were Hogni and Kostbera's sons Golar, Snævarr, and Solarr, as well as the great warrior Orkningr, Kostbera's brother. Nibelungr did not accompany them on the journey.

Up until their moment of departure their advisors tried to dissuade them from the journey. Glaumvor tried one last time down at the ships as the provisions were being loaded onboard. She spoke bitterly to Vingi, "Nothing good will come of your having visited us. It's my suspicion you've over-carved the runes so they now welcome my husband and his brother to your land rather than their original intent which was to warn them away."

Vingi replied, stoutly maintaining his innocence, "Even as I speak truthfully to you now, I have not lied to you in the past. The gifts I brought Hogni and Gunnar came from their sister's hand. The welcome and kindness I bring from Atli are the same that any King of a lesser Kingdom would send to one of a greater. Curse me not for doing what has been bid of me. If I have lied within the course of these words, then let me be hung from the highest gallows, and the worst tortures be performed on me." Neither brother was smart enough to discern Vingi's convoluted words and clever phrasings meant the opposite of what he actually said. If only they had taken the time to untwist his phrases.

Glaumvor answered, "Somehow your speech has the ring of truth, but I think I perceive riddles within it." She had not been fooled. She knew though, her husband and her brother would discount her suspicions as ravings.

Kostbera came up to them, "The ship is ready to sail, you had better board it now Vingi, or be left behind in our Kingdom. I wonder what would happen to you once we receive word of our husbands' deaths?"

Vingi ran to the ship and scrambled aboard as the loading plank was being pulled aboard. Hogni and Gunnar stood at the prow waving to their wives.

Kostbera yelled out after them, "May you have good luck on your journey."

Hogni yelled back, "Don't worry. We'll return soon." He motioned for the oarsmen to pull hard on their oars. The ship shot forward so quickly the holes of the gunn'l holding the rudder in place broke, and the keel split slightly.

Thus did their journey start ill omened.

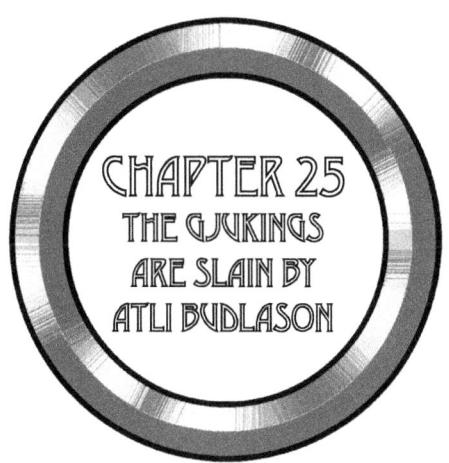

CHAPTER 25
THE GJUKINGS ARE SLAIN BY ATLI BUDLASON

They traveled only a short distance by ship before putting to shore at the edge of the Myrkvydr Forest. After their ship was anchored securely they continued on horseback through the forest for the remainder of their journey. Travel was difficult, since little light shown through the trees, even at midday. At night it was impossible to see anything.

Hogni and Gunnar huddled together listening to the terrifying sounds of the forest, occasionally seeing red animal eyes staring at them. Hogni wasn't certain he wanted this as part of the realm King Atli was offering him.

On they traveled for several days and were both relieved when early one morning they journeyed just a little ways and found themselves out of the forest at the base of a mountain.

Vingi spoke, "Just over this mountain is the valley where King Atli has his Hall. We'll be there before evening."

When they reached the top of the mountain, Hogni and Gunnar looked out over King Atli's realm and were surprised to see King Atli's army camped in the valley, fully armored and ready for battle. They could also see over the wall surrounding King Atli's Hall. Here too were armed warriors ready for battle. As they stared at this ominous sight, King Atli rode up behind them on his horse Glaumr and startled them with his greeting. He was dressed in full war gear. "How are my brothers-in-law? As you can see, I've assembled my army to honor you. I'll ride on ahead and have things readied for your arrival."

He rode off. Somehow Gunnar and Hogni had not been comforted by his greeting. Nevertheless, they rode up to the outer gate of the city that they found barred to them. The gate attendant refused to open it.

Exasperated at this delay Hogni yelled once more to be admitted, "We're the guests of King Atli Budlason. Let us in or you'll be in grave trouble. We are his brothers-in-law."

The gate attendant replied, "I have my orders to admit no one. Leave here at once or the grave trouble might be your own."

Hogni turned as if to ride away. He then geed his horse at the gate and smashed it open with a single blow from his battle-ax. The party rode into the city.

When they reached the central square they were suddenly surrounded on all sides. Vingi spoke, "You'll regret having broken the gate to our city. You've been lured here with only evil in mind. You should have paid attention to your wives. Great was the wisdom which you two tossed off as foolish womanly prattle. You'll all remain here while I search out the proper gallows trees befitting the honor we wish to present you."

Hogni yelled out at Vingi, "You have before you six mighty warriors. We'll not be so easily taken as you think. You battle us with words ordering us to submit to your gallows tree. I prefer heavier objects for my fight."

With that he suddenly raised his battle-ax and struck Vingi a blow. The King's messenger fell from his horse mortally wounded, the first casualty of the battle.

King Atli had ridden up to the square and watched as his messenger was struck down. He gave a signal and all his soldiers descended on Gunnar, Hogni, Golar, Snævar, Solarr, and Orkningr. The bravery of these six was such that it appeared for a moment they might win the battle. They drove towards King Atli who retreated to the safety of his Hall. Undeterred Gunnar and Hogni drove the battle towards King Atli's Hall until soon the fighting raged within it.

The six had barricaded themselves in the main Hall so they could handle the small number of men who could make it through at a time. Three times King Atli's warriors tried to break the barricade, and three times they were driven back. On the first assault Golar was killed; Snævar and Solarr were killed on the second; and Orkningr was killed on the third. Only Gunnar and Hogni remained of the Gjukings.

Hogni slew seven of King Atli's men during the assault and cast the eighth into the fire burning in the center of the Hall. As they entered through the door he spitted them on his spear and tossed them over his shoulder into the flames.

Gunnar and Hogni fought until evening, killing many of King Atli's men, until both sustained wounds and could fight no longer. They were captured and brought before King Atli, who had wisely, if not bravely, hung back from the battle. Gunnar and Hogni were cast down at his feet.

Hogni yelled at King Atli as he broke from his guards and lunged at him, "You vile little svartalfr. I could easily smash you if you didn't hide behind these tall warriors."

Several soldiers grabbed Hogni and threw him beside Gunnar.

King Atli nodded his approval and gave his soldiers orders, "Cast them into fetters so they are more easily controlled." He continued while looking around at the carnage in the Hall, "It's truly staggering the number of my warriors you've killed in a single day. You've more than decimated my army." He turned to the guards and gave them their orders. "Cut their hearts out in such way as they remain beating. Let them hold their still beating life force in their hands, then cast them into the flames."

Hogni showed no fear, "You think such a punishment frightens me? I'm a brave warrior and will not flinch from such a death. My heart is stout and will beat more firmly than ever, a mockery to your punishment. Many are the battles I've fought in the past. My bravery comes from the strength of having won those fights. You may command what happens to my body, but my spirit will never be yours to frighten. If you were a brave warrior yourself, perhaps I'd do you the honor of trembling. But you don't frighten me standing there behind your guard. Maybe you should stand on one of your guard's shoulders so I can see your puny little form better."

Beiti, one of King Atli's counselors spoke up, "Perhaps it would be better if we killed the thrall Hjalli instead. Servants live a lowborn life and expect punishment. Letting Hogni live is punishment for him, if we can make his life miserable enough."

Hjalli had been standing on the far side of the Hall and started when he heard his name mentioned. He had served as King Budli's cook for many years, with very little reward to show for it. In no way did he feel he deserved this treatment. He darted for the door, but King Atli's guards were too quick and barred his way. He was dragged kicking and screaming to the King and forced down beside Gunnar and Hogni. One of the guards pointed a knife towards the servant's breast. Even though the knife had not yet touched him he wailed out in agony for mercy from King Atli, "My life has been lowly and wretched. I've been abused, kicked and ill treated. Yet I've always performed my chores as best I could. Why should a battle I've had no part in be the cause of my death?"

Hogni was disgusted at the thrall's cowardliness, "If you're going to kill him, then get on with it. If not, then kill me since I find his shrieking pathetic to listen to." Then turning to the thrall he said, "At least have some dignity in your death."

King Atli motioned for the thrall to be set free. Hogni hadn't been frightened at all, and why lose a good cook for no worthwhile reason? He ordered Hogni cast into a dungeon while he spoke to Gunnar who, until now, had remained silent, "Where is the Volsungr Treasure and Andvari's Hoard? Answer this and I will spare your brother's life."

Gunnar replied, "My brother and I have sworn sacred oaths never to reveal the location. I will not break that oath, nor will Hogni. You may cut out either of our hearts and hold it before the other, yet will we remain silent. You may grasp my hand and force me to squeeze my brother's heart to stop it beating, and I will still remain silent as to the hiding place of the Volsungr Treasure and Andvari's Hoard?"

King Atli spoke privately to one of his guards and ordered him to find Hjalli and cut out his heart and bring it to him. Seems Hjalli was not to escape his wyrd that day, afterall. The guard did so and presented it to King Atli on a trencher. King Atli took the plate and held it in front of Gunnar, "I've done as you suggested. Here is Hogni's heart. Now tell me where the wealth of the Volsungrs is or I'll place your heart beside it."

Gunnar looked at the quivering heart before him, "You can't fool me. That's Hjalli's heart. Look how it still trembles in fright, trembling perhaps twice as much

as it did than when it beat in Hjalli's breast. Hogni's proud heart would lie still and noble on the plate."

King Atli gave a signal to two of his guards who then left the room and went to the dungeon where Hogni was being held. One of them drew out his knife and cut away Hogni's sark until his chest was bared. Hogni stared at the guard and began laughing without fear. The guard backed away at first but the other guard motioned for him to continue. He approached Hogni again and cut open the prisoner's chest and drew the heart forward. The other guard unfettered one of Hogni's hands and placed it upon the heart and squeezed. Then with a slice the first guard severed the heart from Hogni, who continued laughing to the end. They pried the heart from the dead man's hand, placed it on the trencher and returned to King Atli with it. Ever after they told the story of Hogni's bravery and laughter in the face of death.

King Atli took the plate and presented it to Gunnar. The heart was firm and strong and Gunnar recognized it could only be the heart of a valiant warrior. "That is my brother's heart. It doesn't tremble as the faint heart you showed me before did. Now you have made your mistake, for I alone know where the gold is and what part of the Rhine rules over it. Should some evil befall me, you'll be unable to gain the secret from Hogni. If Hogni were still alive I might have been persuaded to save his life with my knowledge. Now I have nothing to gain by revealing the secret of the hoard to you and will die before I let the Huns take it as their own."

King Atli ordered Gunnar be securely bound and cast into a worm-close, filled with all manner of serpents and poisonous snakes.

Soon news of what had happened reached Gudrunr who went to speak to King Atli, "You've dishonored your name by breaking the oaths you swore on Ullr's ring and Var and the river Leiptr. I curse your life and wish ill fortune will now be yours. My brother's death was a treachery. If you kill my other brother it'll be even worse for you. Beware of your actions against my family. May the same luck that follows me now follow you."

Gudrunr searched through Gunnar's things and found his harp. She went to the guards standing watch over the pit and asked to be allowed to play for Gunnar to ease his pain. They refused. Then one of the guards picked up the harp and cast it down into the pit with Gunnar, laughing and taunting him, "We can't let your sister ease your lot. However, see if the sweet melodies you play with bound hands can help you."

Gunnar was not deterred. He kicked off his shoes and began playing the harp with his toes. And those who heard it said they had never heard such wonderful melodies in all their lives. He played throughout the night. The songs he played were so beautiful all the serpents and snakes fell asleep at his side, save one. It continued crawling towards him. This was no ordinary snake that could be lulled to sleep with sweet music. It was King Atli's evil mother changed to her wehr-shape. She crawled up his back and over his shoulder and began gnawing at his chest. She worked her way through the flesh and then the breastbone. By dawn she had reached his heart. With a single bite she bit through his heart and began sucking out the warm blood. Gunnar's foot struck a final chord as he fell forward dead. Then the serpent crawled into the cavity of his body and bit into his liver and continued her inside out meal until all of his innards were consumed.

CHAPTER 26
THE SLAYING OF ATLI BUDLASON AND ALL HIS HOUSEHOLD

Gudrunr grieved heavily for her brothers, but received no sympathy from anyone at King Atli's Hall, including King Atli who taunted her, blaming her for their deaths, "Their deaths were your fault. If you had interceded you might have persuaded them to tell you where the Volsungr Treasure and Andvari's Hoard was. I would have spared their lives then."

Gudrunr replied, "How dare you lay my brothers' deaths at my hands, when you are the one stained with the dishonor of their blood. You swore oaths of fealty with them and broke those oaths. You'll regret having killed my brothers. While a heart beats within my breast I'll never forget the treachery you've done my family. We're enemies now and I'll work against you in any way I can." Clearly Grimhildr's forgetfullness drink had fully worn off.

King Atli sought to soften her anger, "I wish there was harmony between us once more. I've missed you by my side at night. I'll no longer taunt you with your brothers' deaths. Instead, I'll give you weregild to make up for the harm done to you and your family. Name the price needed so I might once again win your love."

Gudrunr replied, "You can't win again what you never had. If you had treated my family with honor and respect I might have eventually grown to love you. But no more."

She rose to leave. King Atli yelled out after her, "It's better to have me as a husband and lover, than as an enemy."

That evening Gudrunr sat in her chamber thinking over King Atli's last words to her. He was right. She could best seek her revenge against King Atli if she used guile.

She sought him out and told him her conditions for peace between them, "I've thought it over. I've nowhere to go, so must claim this land as my own, and you as my family. I'll accept the weregild you offered me earlier. I also would like to give my brothers funerals befitting their positions. We'll also honor the brave warriors who died in your service." King Atli was deceived by her gracious manner and agreed to her terms. She added, "To celebrate our reconciliation I'll prepare your meal personally."

King Atli was pleased at this, since Gudrunr was an excellent cook. He hadn't tasted one of her meals in weeks. He commanded the Hall be readied for a magnificent feast. A boar was spitted and hung over a great fire to roast for the rest of the guests. Gudrunr left to prepare King Atli's meal.

She went to their two sons whom she found playing on the floor. They were startled and both jumped as their mother entered the room, since they were frequently left the entire evening to play by themselves. The youngest looked at her and asked, "Have you come to play with us?"

Gudrunr looked down at her children. "Our game is a deadly one. Both of you shall die playing it."

The eldest looked at her and spoke, "We're your children and you have rule over us and can do what you will. However, shame and dishonor will follow you if you kill your own children."

She was not moved by her son's words and quickly slit both their throats. She ordered a servant to carry their bodies to the kitchen where she prepared a wonderful stew for King Atli. After she had removed the brains and cleaned the skulls she had the smith sear the outsides with gold and cover the insides with silver making them water tight so she could serve wine in them to her husband that evening. He took each child's left hand and cupped the skulls in them. Then he cut parts of each child's humorous to form a stem for the cup. Then he took each child's right hand to make stands for the goblets. Each humorous was dipped in gold and the hands dipped in silver. The skull goblets were oddly beautiful.

That evening King Atli went to the dining hall and waited expectantly to be surprised. Gudrunr entered followed by a servant who carried an ornate covered stew pot that was set on the table. Next a roast covered over with vegetables and garnishes, was placed before him. A long wide trencher on a golden tray was in front of King Atli. The hollowed bread from the trencher was set to his left for sopping up juices.

King Atli looked at the feast in front of him, his mouth watering as he complimented Gudrunr, "This looks magnificent. I'm so hungry I could eat my favorite horse."

Gudrunr smiled and replied, "Oh, your favorite horse is still stabled and eating his hay. But you have many other favorites in life to chose from."

King Atli stared at Gudrunr not quite comprehending her meaning.

Gudrunr spoke as she ladled out stew into the trencher. "The first course is a stew made of the finest young meat. It is covered over with carrots, parsley, parsnips, several varieties of chopped onions, and barley. This stew has been simmering all day to let the juices spread within, then roasted to make it juicy and tender throughout. I've also added some rare spices brought back from some Viking warriors. There is salt and pepper, and a rare bit of cinnamon in the stew. And the other day a merchant brought us a rare bulb of Egyptian garlic that I've added for taste. "

King Atli began slurping up the stew. It was delicious. Gudrunr told him about the next course, "While you eat this course, the roast will rest and reabsorb its juices to make it even more tender, juicy, and delicious."

King Atli finished the stew, and even ate the trencher. "That was delicious the meal is truly a part of me. Yet I'm still famished, it has been a busy few days."

Gudrunr thought of the deaths of her two brothers that had caused King Atli so much difficulty over the previous days. "Next is a wonderful roast. It is filled with mystery." She carved off slices of roast and layered them on a golden plate and set it in front of King Atli.

Gudrunr uncovered three more dishes to go with the roast and explained their mystery to King Atli, "Recently an expedition of Vikings returned from our settlements in the new world with a strange bit of food. These round, brown objects are interesting indeed. I have been experimenting with them. You can leave their skins on and bake them. Afterwards you can slit them open, salt, pepper, and butter them and eat them skins and all. That is the preparation on this first plate." She uncovered the plate and set it as a side dish in front of King Atli.

Gudrunr explained the next preparation, "Next I peeled away the skins and boiled them. After they softened I drained away the water and mashed them together. Again I added milk, butter, salt, pepper, and bits of garlic to taste, and then a little parsley garnish on top"

She set the plate to the right of the first side dish. King Atli had already eaten a great deal of the roast and had sampled the first side dish and eaten the brown objects, skin and all. He ate a bit more roast and then had some of the mashed version of his new favorite food, "I must say this is the best calf's meat I've ever tasted. It tastes so young and tender. Was it from one of our herds?" Gudrunr nodded yes it was. King Atli wanted to know more, "I don't think it could have been from my favorite herd, since I'm not aware of any newborns recently."

Gudrunr answered, "There are many types of herds with calf offspring. This calf was one of your favorite calves in the world. The stew was made from your other favorite calf in the world."

King Atli was puzzled by her remarks but too intent on eating to comment further.

Gudrunr set the final plate down, uncovered it, and explained it. "This is by far the most interesting and delicious preparation. I took some of the round objects, removed the skin and cut them into wedges, strips, and thin round slices. I cooked them in boiling oil, at various time lengths depending on their thickness. The wedges I first plunged in cold water before putting them in the oil. This gave them a soft inside, yet they are browned and crisp outside. The strips are far crispier. However, the thin slices are best of all. They've bubbled slightly, are fragile and break, yet bite into them and they mix with the juices in your mouth and can be chewed. I've sprinkled salt on all three."

King Atli tried each of the three versions. They were all delicious but the crispy final version was his favorite. He leaned back in his chair, completely stuffed with food. Suddenly he realized he had been eating alone, "Gudrunr, you did not join me for this glorious meal. Only I have enjoyed the fruits of your labor today."

Gudrunr agreed, "Yes, you have enjoyed the fruits of my labor. Perhaps not from today, but from previous labors."

King Atli was pleased and happy, "You see, Gudrunr, if you just tend to my needs, doing your wifely chores, then we can get along fine. And I can think of some other wifely chores, perhaps tonight? It has been a long time since that course has joined us together."

Gudrunr walked behind King Atli and placed her hands on his shoulders and began kneading them. Then her hands moved forward to his chest. King Atli leaned his head back hoping for a kiss. She moved her hands to encircle his neck. Then she pulled away. The time wasn't right yet, but soon would be.

King Atli realized he was not going to receive a kiss and focused again on the delicious meal, "This is certainly the best meat I've ever tasted. There is some still left. Where are our children? I'll share it with them."

Gudrunr answered, "Don't worry, they are close by. As you know I was very upset when you killed my brothers. However, now I've avenged their deaths."

King Atli looked puzzled. Gudrunr continued, "I've given you like for like. The goblets you've been drinking from tonight are made from the skulls of your sons dipped in gold and silver. The wine you've tasted from these gruesome cups was fine mead mingled with your children's blood. Their hearts were cut from their breasts and cooked just as you like your meat, rare and bloody." Gudrunr sunk into a chair realizing her revenge had robbed her of her two sons. She was overcome with guilt from the deed.

King Atli spoke, "How vile you are, to murder our sons and serve them to me as food and drink at your brothers' funeral feast."

Gudrunr spoke through her bitter tears, "You've brought me to this point in my life. I'll never forgive you, and will ever seek to do as much ill to you as I can."

King Atli looked at his wife in disgust, "What more can you do to satisfy your guilt? These deeds of yours will bring about your own death. Stoning is too good for you. I can see you now laying dead and burning on your funeral pyre. The time will come soon." He glared at the meal and the piece of meat still on his fork and then back at Gudrunr, "Your time grows short."

Gudrunr answered, "I think you see your own death, not mine. My punishment will be to live bereft of family and friends, crying bitter tears at what the Norns have woven for me."

Their angry banter continued through the night. Eventually each retired to their private chamber.

Gudrunr longed to kill King Atli, but saw no way to do it. He was too much on guard against her and found many excuses not to be in her company, especially alone.

Their marriage wasn't working out and she began to think of ways to change things.

○ ○ ○ ○

Life continued at King Atli's Hall, though the servants never again referred to Gudrunr and Atli's missing children. The smith had been paid handsomely.

There were many visitors and guests over the next few weeks with lots of feasts to feed and impress them. Gudrunr had her suspicions about King Atli's behavior with some of the female guests.

King Atli, too, had his suspicions about Gudrunr, having heard rumors of her infidelity with King Thjodrex who was visiting at that time. He arranged with his mistress, Herkja, who was also King Thjodrex's wife, to make an accusation against Gudrunr.

That night during a feast honoring King Thjordrex and Herkja, Herkja made the accusation public, "King Atli, my husband and I came here as your honored guests. However, I have heard rumors your wife Gudrunr has seduced my husband and has dishonored me by her actions. I ask that she be punished appropriately."

Gudrunr denied the accusation and now had to prove her innocence, "Herkja speaks vile lies. I have never been unfaithful to King Atli. Therefore, as is my right, I request to be put to the test so I might prove my innocence."

King Atli had no other choice but to accede to her request, "Let one who is skilled in sorcery and divining the truth be sent for. We will meet tomorrow at this time for the test. In the meantime Gudrunr will be confined in her room."

The one-eyed sorcerer wearing a broadbrimmed hat arrived early the next morning and began preparing for the tests. He ordered a large cauldron set on the floor in front of the dais so King Atli, Gudrunr's accuser Herkja, and King Thjodrex could look down on the test.

The cauldron was filled with water and stones, kindling and wood placed under it, and a fire lit. It took all day to come to a boil, but was ready by that evening.

Everyone gathered in the hall. Just in case the situation might become difficult King Atli ordered seven hundred of his best men stand against the walls to witness the events, and be ready with their weapons should the need arise.

The sorcerer and Gudrunr stood facing King Atli and those on the dais. The sorcerer walked around the cauldron consecrating it to Thor and Var, "I consecrate this cauldron to Thor and swear oaths by Var that the truth will become known. Let Gudrunr be put to the test. She must remove all the stones, and her hand and arms remain unscathed in order to prove her innocence. Begin."

Without any hesitation Gudrunr plunged her hand into the boiling water, time after time, removing the stones one-by-one until just a single stone remained. Then she plunged her hand in one final time and removed that stone, too. The sorcerer examined Gudrunr's hand, "Gudrunr's hand remains whole and uninjured. This proves her innocence. She has told the truth."

Then, unexpectedly, Gudrunr turned, raised her hand, dripping with the water of innocence, and pointed an accusing finger at Herkja, "Accusers should make certain they are pure and not subject to similar accusations. I accuse Herkja of being

King Atli's mistress and challenge her to prove her innocence as I have proven mine."

King Atli's plot that evening to have Gudrunr found guilty of adultery had fallen apart. Apparently Gudrunr was innocent. And now he was in jeopardy with his own mistress having to prove her innocence, or lack thereof.

The stones were thrown back into the cauldron, more wood was piled underneath, the flames stoked, and the cauldron was brought back to a boil.

The crowd, particularly the seven-hundred soldiers, looked back and forth between King Atli and Herkja. The sorcerer motioned to Herkja as he spoke, "The cauldron is once again ready to determine the fate of another; to determine her guilt or innocence. I consecrate this cauldron to Thor and swear oaths by Var that the truth will become known. Let Herkja come down here and be put to the test."

King Atli had no choice. He motioned Herkja to the cauldron. The sorcerer continued, "Herkja, it seems you have made a false accusation against Gudrunr, and she is within her rights to make an accusation against you. You must also be tested to prove or disprove the truth of her accusation. The cauldron is ready. Go to it and remove a stone to prove your innocence."

Those assembled began murmuring, "Just one stone?" "Gudrunr had to remove all the stones!" "She should remove all the stones, that's the rule."

King Atli quieted the crowd, "There are no written rules to this test of guilt or innocence. There is only tradition. And my interpretation of tradition is that the accuser should not have to prove anything. Accusing the accuser can be seen as unjust retaliation by the accused."

King Atli conveniently ignored the fact the accused had been proven innocent and had every right to bring an accusation in rebuttal. The crowd realized this also, but was overruled by King Atli, "Since you, Herkja, were the original accuser, and unsuspected of being guilty of anything (which wasn't true—many knew of her assignations with King Atli) you will only have to retrieve one stone to prove your innocence." King Atli hoped Herkja was strong enough to bear a moment's scalding to retrieve one stone.

For obvious reason, the fact she was guilty, Herkja was reluctant to take the test. Instead of walking to the cauldron and plunging her hand in, she turned to leave. Guards caught her and had to drag her back to the cauldron. She yelled out as her arm was forced into the boiling water and scalded. Her unfaithfulness was proven, her guilt proclaimed before all present. King Atli had no choice but to send his mistress to her death.

Gudrunr yelled out a final insult to King Atli that everyone in the Hall heard, "I'm surprised she would sleep with you? I wonder how she found you? I wonder if she found you? You're so small in stature, in every way and all your parts, you are so easily lost under the covers. Maybe she's been making love to a pillow or your sword scabbard?"

Herkja was dead before Gudrunr finished her remarks.

○ ○ ○ ○

The relationship between King Atli and Gudrunr was now more strained than ever. Previously at least King Atli had had Herkja's attentions to take his mind off things. Now what did he have? A cold wife who had insulted him as vilely as she could in front of the most important people in his Kingdom. And his mistress, who had brought some comfort and passion in his life, was now put to death by his order. Life was not going as well as it could have.

○ ○ ○ ○

Word soon reached Kostbera and Glaumvor of their husbands' deaths. Gunnar and Glaumvor had been childless, but Hogni and Kostbera had had three sons. Golar, Snævar, and Solarr had been killed in King Atli's Hall with their father. Only Nibelungr remained. He immediately set out for King Atli's Hall determined to avenge his father and uncle's deaths.

He arrived at the Hall in disguise offering his services to King Atli, claiming to be a powerful warrior wishing to gain honor and wealth by serving him. King Atli's troops had been greatly diminished from the battle with Gunnar, Hogni, Golar, Snævar, and Orkningr. However, many arrived at the Hall every week seeking fame and fortune as liegemen of King Atli. Even though his forces were depleted King Atli still maintained a high standard and would only accept the bravest and strongest.

Nibelungr had the look of a mighty warrior, but he still had to be put to the test. King Atli ordered his best warriors, one by one to fight Nibelungr. The young champion bested every warrior put before him, sometimes two and three against him at once. King Atli realized he was an extremely powerful warrior and welcomed him into his service. He drew the lad aside and gave him his instructions, "You are to watch Gudrunr and make certain I'm protected from her. She is wont to do me great harm."

Nibelungr went to Gudrunr's chamber and dismissed the guards outside her door, "Leave her to me. I can protect King Atli from her without any further aid."

Gudrunr heard the changing of the guard and didn't even bother to look up from the tapestries she was weaving. Both panels were in quarters telling their stories. One was titled "The False Accusation," and the other was called "The Death of the False Accuser".

She was surprised when her chamber door opened and someone entered. The visitor's shadow fell across the part of the tapestry where the arm of the embroidered version of her was being plunged into the cauldron. She looked up to order the impertinent guard to leave her presence, "I may be under guard, but that doesn't mean I have to ..."

Her voice trailed off as she recognized her jailer as her nephew Nibelungr. She leapt up and threw her arms around him, overjoyed at seeing a friendly face, "Why have you come here? There's danger from King Atli if he finds you in my chamber."

Nibelungr laughed and told her about his recent appointment, "King Atli has sent me here to protect him from you. However, I come here to seek your advice on how best I might avenge our family's sorrow."

That evening at dinner Gudrunr sat next to King Atli, encouraging him to drink more and more wine. He thought it strange, but hoped things might once again be right between them. "The chill I've lately felt from you seems to be thawing. Perhaps desire and longing will make us friends again." He reached over to take her hand.

Gudrunr looked at the short twisted man who struck fear in so many, and repulsion in her. She took his hand and smiled at him, "Leave your door unlocked tonight. Perhaps you'll be surprised by a visitor."

King Atli continued drinking until he had to have guards carry him to his bed where he almost immediately fell into a drunken slumber. Before collapsing, though, he commanded his chamber be left unlocked and for the guards to quit his presence for the evening.

Later that evening Gudrunr and Nibelungr crept up to his unguarded door, entered the room and stood over his bed. Vengeance would soon be theirs. Nibelungr raised Gramr, Sigurdr's sword, and stabbed down with it. Gudrunr grabbed the hilt and pulled it out and thrust it back into her husband's body.

King Atli yelled in agony as he awoke, "Who has given me my deathwound? I fear no amount of binding will heal the gashes in my body."

Gudrunr answered first, "These blows are the only love taps you'll receive from me tonight."

Then Nibelungr added, "You should have looked into my eyes when I arrived in your Hall. You might have recognized the eyes of a Volsungr. Now my father's uncle's, and brother's deaths are avenged. They can continue their journey to Valhalla in peace."

King Atli spoke to Gudrunr, "This was wrong for you to do. Even though you had some duty to your family you had a greater duty to me, and should have remained loyally at my side no matter what my actions. Our marriage was an honorable one sought out by your family. In return I gave them your dowry consisting of thirty men at arms, some of the loveliest maidens of our country, and many thralls and laborers. Because of that you owed me your fealty and love. Instead I think you would have rather had rule of my Kingdom yourself."

Gudrunr felt no pity for King Atli as she answered, "You've brought all this upon yourself. I would have been loyal and true to you if you had shown me you loved me. As it was I felt as if I were some prize, no more important to you than a winning horse at a fair. Sometimes animals turn on their masters, it's all in how they're treated. Many animals want their freedom and resist being told what to do and when to do it. I'm a person with a free will. That's something you forgot many times. Often you've lied to me and I've ignored it. I admit sometimes I've been difficult to live with. But this has often been with just cause. We were not fated for each other and nothing except evil could come of our union. My life was far better when Sigurdr Fafnirsbani was my husband. He's the only person I've

ever truly loved. I've never loved you at all. With Sigurdr I was his equal partner. We fought together in battle and won the wealth of many Kings. All this we did on our foes' borders. You brought the fighting into our own Hall, even into our bedrooms. Sigurdr was just and wise. If a King wished to save his Kingdom by putting himself under Sigurdr's rule and protection, then a friend was won rather than a foe defeated. That's why Sigurdr's Kingdom was far greater than yours ever was, or now ever will be. After Sigurdr was killed, I was proud to be his widow and wanted nothing further in life. However, a grief far greater than Sigurdr's death awaited me, and that was to be your wife. Before, I was a partner with the greatest warrior the world has ever known, then I was wedded to a twisted little svartalfr troll who pretended to heights of greatness. The saying that the best always win in battle was disproved by you time and time again."

Gudrunr could have continued her harangue against King Atli all night but finally he interrupted her, "I've only a short while before I die, so let me refute what you've said. My words will do little to heal the rift between us. That's all past now since the rift you've given me with the sword Gramr has rent me pretty much asunder. All I can ask of you now is that you do me one favor. You've done nothing for me in the past. Now is your chance to do me some service. In honor of the fact I was ever true to you and held your interests as my own, give me a hero's burial. Let my funeral feast be the equal of the one so recently held for your brothers."

Gudrunr answered, "I'll be happy to prepare such a feast for you. For the eating of it will bring an end to the horrible life I've had with you. I'll personally wrap the best white linen around your body, tightly so you'll never be able to stir from it. However, there will be no flaming funeral pyre sailing you into the sunset. Instead I'll make certain a deep grave is dug and you're placed in it. After it's covered over with dirt I will erect a heavy unmarked stone above it so you'll remain safely under it. You ask of me a favor I can gladly bring about, though not how you would want. No hero's funeral. You will be consigned to the dirt and buried in as much dishonor as possible." She then thrust the sword once more into his breast and King Atli died." She took the Andvaranautr ring from his finger and placed it upon her own.

Gudrunr was true to her word. His funeral feast was held and he was buried with full dishonor. He was wrapped in a woolen shroud and buried in an oak and stone coffin, covered with unconsecrated dirt, set over with a plain unmarked, undecorated stone. In a few generations his burial place would be forgotten.

After the ceremony the guests returned to the Hall and continued their drinking and merrymaking. Soon they all fell into drunken reverie. Gudrunr and Nibelungr had only pretended to drink, and had remained sober and had kept their wits about them, waiting for their moment, which was now since everyone was in their cups, passed out from their drinks. The two threw out burning brands from the center fire onto the tapestries hanging on the walls. Soon the Hall was ablaze, engulfed in the purifying flames. The guests awoke in the midst of an inferno and began to argue amongst themselves about who had caused it. Instead of attacking the flames they began attacking each other, hewing and hacking away limbs. The Hall burned quickly and soon all were consumed in the cleansing flames.

○ ○ ○ ○

The Volsungrs and Gjukings had been the mightiest warriors the world had known. They had conquered many Kingdoms and had amassed great wealth. Now they were nearly all dead, and to what purpose? What good was the Volsungr Treasure and Andvari's Hoard now?

Gudrunr escaped the flames. However, Nibelungr had been on the other side of the Hall when his way had been barred by flames. He died a noble death.

○ ○ ○ ○

After her vengeance on King Atli, Gudrunr no longer wished to live. She had one child still living, Svanhildr, who was her daughter by Sigurdr. Svanhildr resembled her father more than any of his other children. Her coloring was the same as his, and she had been born with the same deep-set piercing eyes. No one could hold her gaze. She was dark-haired and exceedingly beautiful. Even this reminder of her noble husband was not enough to deter Gudrunr from what she set out to do. Her life had been mostly filled with grief and now she could see no hope of it improving. She filled her pockets with stones and carrying a large stone in her arms, walked across the land to the water's edge and cast herself into the sea determined to drown herself.

But the Norns had not yet decreed her time was at hand. There were still spools with thread left to weave a few more yards of her story.

Gudrunr slept as if in a dream whilst great waves carried her far from the water's edge, over the sea, and continued carrying her to a distant shore, to the land ruled over by King Jonakr.

One beautiful morning several of King Jonakr's servants were walking along the shore and found Gudrunr on the beach. They looked around and saw no boat and assumed she had fallen overboard from a ship and been washed ashore, dead. Then the warming sun shone on her, and her eyes flickered slightly, and she woke up from her long sleep. The servants took her to see King Jonakr.

He was looking out a Hall window when he saw his servants returning with a young woman. She wore no jewels and only a loose shift. There was nothing about her to indicate she was a Queen and the former wife of Sigurdr Fafnirsbani. King Jonakr looked at her and she seemed to him to be the most beautiful woman he had ever seen. He fell in love with her at first sight and hurried down to meet her as she entered the Hall.

King Jonakr welcomed her and offered her the hospitality of his Hall. He had a great feast prepared that night to honor her. Over the next several weeks he got to know her better, and fell more in love with her than ever.

Gudrunr returned his affections and felt safe once more. The love she had for King Jonakr was not the same as the one she had had for Sigurdr. That love had been about passion and heroics, this one was about comfort and constancy.

Within weeks King Jonakr had asked and she had accepted his marriage proposal.

It was a happy marriage. Eventually they had three sons, Hamdir, Sorli, and Erpr. The three took after the Volsungr's more than King Jonakr's side of the family. They had raven-black hair and deep piercing eyes. Seeing them reminded Gudrunr of her daughter. She sent for Svanhildr who came and was raised by King Jonakr with great kindness. He adopted her as his own daughter and treated her as if she were of his own true blood. He never showed any favoritism to his natural children over her.

Gudrunr and Svanhildr lived there in happiness ... for a while. She still wore the ring Andvaranautr from Andvari's Hoard. And it was still cursed.

CHAPTER 27
THE WOOING AND MURDER OF SVANHILDR

Svanhildr took after Sigurdr more than had any of his other children. She was blessed with dark good looks, keen intelligence, and a firm gaze. As she grew to womanhood her beauty and graces were celebrated in songs that traveled through many Kingdoms.

King Jormunrekkr of Gautland heard of her and fell in love with the legend of the woman sung about in those songs. King Jormunrekkr was tall and noble of bearing with striking red hair. His wife had died leaving him widowed and lonely. He sued for Svanhildr's hand. His Kingdom was great so it was better to have him as an ally than as an enemy. Because of this he knew he would be worthy of Svanhildr and his suit would not be refused.

King Jormunrekkr summoned his son Hrandver to his chamber, "I've a mind to marry Svanhildr Sigurdardottir. You will travel as my emissary to King Jonakr's Hall and formally request his daughter's hand for me. I'll send many fine gifts with you as the beginning of her dowry. You are to woo and win her love for me. Be not overly cruel in your description of me, but be truthful. I'm of fine figure and have the stamina of men half my age. Tell her I have all my hair, my muscles are firm, and my eyes are still keen. I'll love and honor her as my Queen and be a true friend to her family. All this is offered to her in peace. I'm trusting you to woo and win her for me. Bikki, my counselor will go with you and be there to give you advice should you need it."

Hrandver was only too happy to help his father, "I'm honored to have this mission entrusted in my care. I'll woo and win her so she'll become part of our family."

Hrandver left the next morning carrying with him many precious gifts. He was arrayed in beautiful garments and made a striking figure standing at the prow of his ship.

The journey was swift and he and Bikki were soon welcomed at King Jonakr's enormous Hall. They met Svanhildr and saw for themselves her beauty had not been

exaggerated in the songs sung about her. Indeed, the verses had not nearly done her enough justice.

Soon after their arrival Hrandver had a private visit with King Jonakr, "My father sues for Svanhildr's hand in marriage with honorable intentions toward her. We offer you great wealth and many valuable treasures as her dowry. We also offer you an alliance with our country. Be assured this will not be an arranged, loveless marriage. My father is smitten with her, even though he has never seen her. She'll be honored and esteemed above all others in his Kingdom."

King Jonakr was impressed with the young man's presentation, "I'm sure Svanhildr will find much happiness there, especially if your father is anything like you. You have my and my wife Gudrunr's blessings."

This was not quite true. Privately Gudrunr was opposed to the marriage, "I'm of a mind that happy marriages can only come about after the couple have known each other. Jormunrekkr claims to be in love with Svanhildr, but he hasn't even met her. He's only in love with being in love with her. If Svanhildr does not live up to his dreams, then he could easily cast her aside. I can't agree with your decision."

However, Jonakr had already given his word and couldn't back out now. All of Svanhildr's things were packed and loaded onto the ship. She was reluctant to leave her homeland, however, she was an obedient child who had never given her parents any trouble. She obeyed her foster-father.

She sat at the ship's stern at the beginning of the journey. After they were safely under way Hrandver came and sat next to her. This was the first of what would prove to be many conversations with her. She was every bit as intelligent as she was beautiful. Hrandver soon fell in love with her, but did not show it since he wanted to honorably carry out his duty to his father. Svanhildr also fell in love with Hrandver.

Bikki saw the budding romance between the two. He was loyal to Jormunrekkr only so he could have a position of power at court. In truth he was ambitious and coveted the throne for himself. Here was his chance. Father pitted against son over the Queen was certainly enough to cost both Jormunrekkr and Hrandver the throne. He would be prepared to step in and take it when this happened. In the meantime he did what he could to encourage the situation. He always spoke kindly of Hrandver to Svanhildr. He need not encourage Hrandver since the King's son was already smitten with her, though it didn't hurt to remind Hrandver that his father was an old man, "What a pity such a woman will be wasted on a man of his years. One's prowess decreases as time goes on, you know. I've heard it spoken of among the chambermaids that Jormunrekkr had not been able to be a husband to your mother for many months before her death. I believe this was due to some injury he suffered in the recent war. Too bad Svanhildr will never know the joys marriage can bring. Too bad a strong young man, such as yourself, isn't marrying her and turning her into a woman."

Hrandver gave thought to this argument. Bikki thought of an even better reason for Hrandver to go against his father and woo Svanhildr himself, "Of course your life would be a lot easier if Svanhildr and your father married."

Hrandver looked puzzled, "How will my life be changed if Svanhildr and my father marry?"

Bikki measured his words carefully, "Have you and your father always agreed?"

Hrandver answered truthfully, "Not always. Until my mother's death we had been at odds. It is only recently we've been speaking. I was heartened he trusted me with the task of winning Svanhildr for him."

Bikki now knew he could manipulate Hrandver to his purposes, "But you haven't been wooing Svanhildr for him. You've fallen in love with her yourself. Don't you realize the problems that will cause you?"

Hrandver again looked puzzled. He didn't understand what Bikki was implying.

Bikki continued, "You and your father have been at odds. You're an only son. King Jormunrekkr's only heir … "

Bekki's voice trailed off. He still didn't understand what Bekki was getting at.

Bekki was even more direct, "He has one son … you. He is wooing a young, fertile woman, who comes from the noblest family in the world. She's Sigurdr Fafnirsbani's daughter. Her son will have the blood of the greatest warrior in history flowing through her veins. Do you think you can compete with such a lineage? When Jormunrekkr dies will his warriors follow you or the grandson of Sigurdr Fafnirsbani? The throne is rightfully yours as the first son. But only if you have an army and the countryside to back your claim.

Hrandver realized his inheritance was in jeopardy, "What must I do? I'm the one destined to be King."

Bekki responded, "We make our own destiny. Take yours in your hands. Take Svanhildr in your hands. Woo her. Win her. No matter who the father is, her son will be Sigurdr Fafnirsbani's grandson. However, who will be his father? The child can be your little brother of far more noble birth than you. Or he could be your son, and Jormunrekkr's grandson. The difference is when the throne comes to him, after Jormunrekkr's death as King Jormunrekkr's designated hair? Or after your death as your designated heir? He will be King some day. Will he succeed you or usurp you?

Now it all made sense to Hrandver.

Bekki continued, "You must marry Svanhildr if you have hopes of being King."

Hrandver was anxious, yet excited.

Bekki practically pushed Hrandver out the door, "Go, find Svanhildr. Woo her. Win her. Marry her. Don't let her out of your sight if you would be King."

Hrandver immediately ran on deck to find Svanhildr. It was almost as if he expected to find his father with Svanhildr, proposing to her. He mustn't waste any more time.

o   o   o   o

Hrandver sat next to Svanhildr and was very attentive towards her. She did not reject his attentions, or push him away. Hrandver began talking about his father, "My father is a very honorable man, though he has been very upset since my mother's death. He just hasn't' been the same. I don't think he'll ever be able to love anyone ever again."

This puzzled Svanhildr since Hrandver had been telling her the day before how Jormunrekkr was a changed man since falling in love with her from afar.

Hrandver decided to throw caution to the wind and whispered in Svanhildr's ear, "I love you. I've loved you since my father described you to me."

His heart leapt as she said the words back to him, "I love you, too, since I first caught sight of you.

His joy was short-lived when he realized they would soon be back in King Jormunrekkr's Kingdom. Bekki's manipulation faded the closer they got to home. Hrandver decided he didn't want to do anything to dishonor himself or Svanhildr. "Even though I love you, I'll speak no more of it once you are married to my father. I will honor the vows you make to him. We cannot be."

Svanhildr also had had second thoughts, and though she had come to believe Hrandver was her true love, she felt honorbound to fulfill her promise to marry Jormunrekkr. She held to the agreement.

Svanhildr and Hrandver might have decided not to go against Jormunrekkr, but Bekki decided to adjust his plot. His only hope was to meet with Jormunrekkr before Hrandver and Svanhildr did.

Immediately after they arrived at Jormunrekkr's Hall Bikki left Hrandver and Svanhildr and sought an audience with Jormunrekkr, "I've bad news for you. During the journey I watched the growing friendship between your son and Svanhildr. One evening I heard them speaking words of love to each other. I'm afraid you've been deceived by your son and the woman you've chosen to marry. They are lovers and you must do something to regain your honor."

Jormunrekkr could hardly believe the story. Yet Bikki was one of his oldest and most trusted counselors and he could think of no cause for him to lie. He didn't realize how many times he had been led astray in the past by Bikki's deceiving, self-serving advice. Once again he followed it and summoned Hrandver before him, "Bikki has told me you are in love with Svanhildr."

Hrandver answered truthfully, "That's true, and I've done nothing to dishonor our family. I've never forgotten Svanhildr is to be your wife, nor has she. Our friendship is chaste and Svanhildr remains pure and here to marry you."

Jormunrekkr heard nothing else once Hrandver admitted he loved Svanhildr. His son had deceived him and had to be punished. He yelled for guards, "Take my son to Thieves' Hill and hang him beside common pickpockets and thieves so he is a warning to everyone in my Kingdom."

If Jormunrekkr had stopped to think it through he would have realized he was making his son an example for a crime no one else in the Kingdom could commit.

The guards carried out their orders. Hrandver was taken to Thieves' Hill overlooking the city. While the rope was being prepared Hrandver's hunting hawk flew up to him. He grabbed it and plucked all the feathers from it and gave it to a servant with instructions to take it to the King. He hoped this symbol would act as his defense.

After receiving this parting gift from his son the King held the bird in his hands and realized what it meant. Bikki also saw the hawk and hurried to the gallows.

The King spoke to those in the Hall, "This hawk, bereft of feathers, can no longer fly. My Kingdom, bereft of my heir, will fall to chaos at my death. I'm old and may not have other children. What have I done? Guards, go to the hill and stop the murder of my son. I believe him and will ask his forgiveness. He and Svanhildr are innocent."

The King's guards arrived to rescue Hrandver, unfortunately they were too late. Bikki had already given the order and Hrandver's body swung gentle in the breeze.

The guards cut Hrandver's body down and brought it back to Jormunrekkr, who collapsed, overcome with remorse seeing the almost unrecognizable swollen features of his son. In his grief he listened to Bikki's ill-advised counsel for the final time.

Bikki knew just the right words to use to manipulate the King in his sadness, "The grief you feel must be great. Let it not be from guilt. You're not the cause of your son's death. You gave the order, but the cause was that unfaithful woman who lured your son astray during the journey here. She dressed in unseemly clothes designed to entrap your son. It's she who should bear the blame and punishment for your son's death."

Jormunrekkr was willing to listen to anything that absolved him of the guilt he felt for his son's death, "I suppose you're right. I leave her punishment to you. I wish to remain here alone with my son and mourn his passing in my own way."

Bikki left the Hall and ordered the guards to immediately bring Svanhildr to the main courtyard. He was taking no chances Jormunrekkr might change his mind. He wanted the execution carried out immediately.

The guards found Svanhildr drying her hair in the sun near the main gate, having just washed it in the river outside the courtyard. She was unaware Hrandver had been hung on Thieves' Hill.

Bikki ordered her tied to the main gate leading into the courtyard. He then ordered horses to be ridden over her so she might be trampled to death. However, her gaze was so fierce the horses averted their heads when she looked at them and would not run towards her. Bikki ordered her head covered with a sack. This was done and the horses rode over her, stomping her under foot until she was dead.

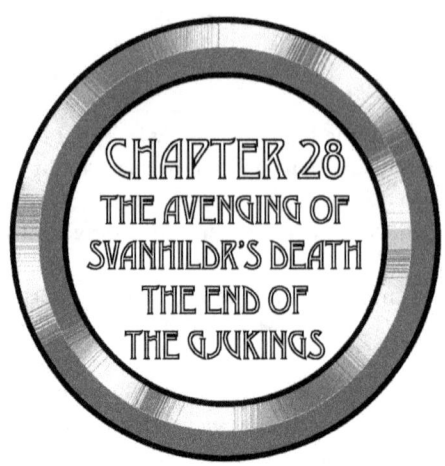

CHAPTER 28
THE AVENGING OF SVANHILDR'S DEATH
THE END OF THE GJUKINGS

ord reached Gudrunr that King Jormunrekkr had had Svanhildr trampled to death. She sent for her sons Hamdir and Sorli, and berated them for not avenging the wrong done to their sister, "Why are you still here feasting and drinking in the Great Hall every night, enjoying yourselves? Your sister has been cruelly murdered, shamefully trampled to death. It's up to you to avenge her death. Gunnar and Hogni would already have been on their way to Jormunrekkr's Hall if they had still been alive. Even now your half-brother Erpr is preparing to leave for Jormunrekkr's Hall to seek vengeance."

Hamdir and Sorli had always been jealous of Erpr, whom they considered their mother's favorite. They disliked him more than ever now. Hamdir was the first to speak to his mother, "You didn't have such fine words for Gunnar and Hogni when they slew Sigurdr and you laid beside him in his bed, your sheets red with his blood? And what honor did you bring when you slew Erpr and Eitill in order to punish King Atli? Why is there honor for us if we kill Jormunrekkr and his household? "

Sorli added, "You urge us on to a deed that might be looked upon by others as something not quite honorable. But perhaps we should go perform this deed so you'll keep quiet about it and leave us to continue our evening fun in peace."

Despite their arguments and reluctance, Gudrunr was able to pressure them to avenge Svanhildr's death.

That evening she held a special feast honoring her sons before their departure to King Jormunrekkr's Hall.

Hamdir and Sorli were enjoying themselves. Their brother, Erpr, whom everyone praised as the best and most noble of the three, had been off hunting so all the praise had been for Hamdir and Sorli. The two enjoyed the attention since they very seldom received any honor or praise from anyone. Even Gudrunr praised them. Usually her praise had been reserved for Erpr, her favorite and the most popular amongst the people. A dinner in their honor was something that never happened.

An hour or so after the celebrations started Erpr entered the Hall to great applause. Hamdir and Sorli had been dressed rather simply. Erpr had changed from his hunting clothes into a rather fancy dress outfit.

Erpr kissed his mother on the cheek. She motioned for Hamdir and Sorli to move over to make room so Erpr could sit beside her. Things were now like they usually were. As he sat beside her, Gudrunr laughed and raised her goblet to toast him. The rest in the Hall joined in. Reluctantly Hamdir and Sorli joined in and raised their goblets to toast their much-admired brother.

The dinner was magnificent and no one lacked for as many helpings of all the courses. At the end of the evening Gudrunr presented each of her sons with special armor and special war equipment which she had had forged, "These byrnies and helmets are so strong iron will not pierce them. They have been guilefully worked and are impervious to normal weapons of combat. However, they have a fatal flaw. They'll give you no protection against rocks and stones. Luckily warriors throw spears, and rarely resort to throwing stones. However, avoid battling in the open where these things might be pelted against you in desperation."

Gudrunr continued giving them instructions on how best they could accomplish Jormunrekkr's death, "Steal into his bed chamber at night while he's sleeping. Hamdir and Sorli should cut off his feet and hands, while Erpr cuts off his head."

Hamdir and Sorli didn't like the plan because it gave too much of the glory to Erpr. This was typical of their mother, thought Hamdir. Erpr was the youngest and her favorite. He always received the best slices of meat at meals, the finest woven fabrics for his clothes, or the strongest byrnies for his armor. Sorli also thought this.

The two revealed their feelings only to each other. Gudrunr and the rest in the Hall had no idea of the jealousy they harbored for Erpr. Instead Hamdir raised his goblet in a final toast, "Mother, drink to the health of your sons and their success in this venture. We leave you for the last time. I feel the next mead you drink in our honor will be at Svanhildr's funeral feast, which I believe your sons will attend as more than guests."

Sorli added to the toast, "I'll honor what you ask of me, though I feel we three leave this Hall with our doom upon us. Many tears will you weep after we've left."

o   o   o   o

The next morning Hamdir and Sorli rose before everyone else, hoping to leave before Erpr had awakened. They each shook their cloaks and put them on. Short swords hung from their sides. Their long swords were fixed to their saddles.

Erpr arose shortly after they departed. He had readied all of his gear the night before so all he had to do was say goodbye to his mother Gudrunr before leaving.

Gudrunr wished him well and gave him a departing gift. She removed the Andvaranautr from her finger and gave it to her favorite son. Erpr thanked her, kissed her on the cheek and left quickly not realizing he would never see his mother alive again. He soon caught up with his brothers.

o   o   o   o

Gudrunr retired to her chamber thinking of her past and became quite depressed, "My life has mostly been spent in misery. I've called three Halls home, and three men husband. Of them all Sigurdr Fafnirsbani was the best and I was happy, the last happiness I've known. But he was murdered. Then I was given in marriage to the repulsive Atli Budlason. He killed my brothers Gunnar and Hogni. Blinded by hatred I slew my own children and murdered King Atli. My grief took me to the sea. Yet even that attempt to end my life led to further grief. Waves carried me here where I have wedded a kind husband, yet I don't love him. I sent my only daughter, and favorite child, to a horrible death at the feet of unshod horses. Her loss I mourn almost as much as Sigurdr's. Now my sons depart to more vengeance and most likely will not return. What more can happen to me? How much more grief can I bear? I would that Sigurdr come and take me away from all this. Sigurdr you promised to keep watch over me if you died first. But look at all that has happened. Can't you help me now?"

Sigurdr's hand was upon her and she died of grief. A funeral pyre was prepared and she was delivered to the next world with a great ceremony befitting her station.

o   o   o   o

Her sons continued on their journey unaware their mother had died.

Erpr offered his assistance to Hamdir and Sorli, "I've prepared our things for the journey. I offer you my assistance, even as hand helps foot, or foot helps hand."

Hamdir scoffed at the allusion, "What a silly expression. How can the hand help the foot, and the foot the hand? I think you've been at the mead stores and drinking early this morning."

Erpr answered, "Shall I show you how one can help the other?"

Sorli began taunting his brother, "Why the help you offer us is no help at all. You mock us with your words."

Hamdir took up the theme, "I'll not be mocked by a bastard. Especially one who can't fight. While we were studying warrior skills you hung around our mother taking on her ways and learning the warrior skills of cooking in the kitchen. Your sword was a butcher knife, your shield the covering for a pot. A noose you used to keep together the innards of a roast. For Sorli and me a fork is a decision of direction in the road. For you it's something to eat with at dinner."

Sorli added, "Even though Svanhildr is dead, Gudrunr still has one other daughter left. Go home and tend to your sewing and other womanly tasks. Perhaps if we like Jormunrekkr we can offer him you in marriage. You probably would have made a better wife to him than Svanhildr, anyway."

Hamdir drew his sword, "I'll show you how my hand can help." He struck his brother, who fell to the ground.

Sorli leapt from his horse and kicked Gudrunr's fallen son, "And this is how my foot helps you."

Repeatedly they struck him until his wyrd was upon him and he died. They felt better now that Erpr wasn't tagging along. He had always been weaker and the least skilled in warrior ways of the three brothers. They moved his body to the side of the road, disposing of it dishonorably. Soon it would be picked over by ravens and wolves, the eyes plucked out first, then the tongue, and then all of him would be a feast.

Hamdir and Sorli continued on their way, a third less in strength. Unbeknownst to Sorli, Hamdir had removed Andvaranautr from Erpr's hand and had secreted it in his pocket.

They hadn't traveled far before Hamdir tripped. He grabbed against a tree branch to steady himself and exclaimed, "Erpr was right. My hand has helped my feet."

Sorli pointed at the ground, "Look you've broken the rocks beneath your feet which is certainly an evil omen."

They resumed their traveling. As they were walking along a steep road made up of loose gravel Sorli was leaning on a pole for support. It slipped from his hand, but he was able to twist around and steady himself, "Erpr was right again. My feet helped my hand. What can all this mean?"

Hamdir pointed to the ground, "You've also disturbed the rocks beneath your feet. I think we'll have mixed success on our journey."

Sorli added, "Or, maybe no success. I feel uneasy. It was wrong of us to slay Erpr. But it wasn't our fault. He taunted us on, bringing about his own death."

They both agreed to this rationalization and continued until they reached Jormunrekkr's Kingdom. The road they traveled on the way to the city wound around by the newly named Gallow's Hill which overlooked the Hall. It now honored more than just thieves. Though some said that Hrandver had been a thief in that he had stolen his father's betrothed from him. He had been a thief of the heart, the worst kind of thief.

A noble corpse twisted slowly on the gallows. Already its features were becoming unrecognizable as birds swooped down carrying away strips of flesh in their beaks. One bird was lucky enough to pluck out an unseeing eye in one try. Another pulled off the lower lip that had so recently spoken words of love to Svanhildr.

Pausing only briefly to view the sight, they rode on towards the Hall. A sentry sounded a bugle warning Jormunrekkr that strangers were approaching. A messenger rushed into the Hall to warn the King, "I think they are relatives of the woman you have slain. Be on your guard. Take them by surprise and attack before they reach here."

However, Jormunrekkr had been drinking heavily and was filled with the false courage brought on by too much wine. Sleepily he answered, "Let them just try to attack my Kingdom. I'll see them dangling from the end of a rope, too, as my son does. My son … my betrothed and true love Svanhildr." Perhaps he was experiencing a moment of regret for the deaths of his son and betrothed. It was just a moment, though, and then he yawned and belched as his head fell forward onto the table.

Hamdir and Sorli rode their horses into the Hall where they were questioned at the doorway by an old woman named Hrothglod, "How can you two hope to fight against the thousand warriors within King Jormunrekkr's Hall? I foresee you'll kill two hundred of Jormunrekkr's finest warriors, then both of you will fall before the greater number. I was Svanhildr's friend after she arrived and don't want to see harm come to her kinsmen. Leave here at once, while there's still time."

They ignored her advice and rode up to King Jormunrekkr. He was not awed by the magnificently armored heroes sitting on horses in front of him, and spoke to the two strangers, "I can see you've come from the direction of Gallow's Hill. It should set you to trembling, seeing the punishment meted out to my enemies, even my very own son. Just imagine the punishments I'll have thought up for strangers."

Hamdir replied, "Your time is near an end. Soon we'll cut your hands, feet, and head from your body and fling you piece-by-piece into the fire. A sooty fireplace is the closest you'll come to a funeral pyre."

Jormunrekkr rose to summon his guards but Sorli grabbed the King to prevent him doing so. Hamdir continued, "It'll do you little good to summon your warriors against us. Our armor is enchanted so iron and weapons will not cut it."

Jormunrekkr dropped his drinking cup and began struggling in earnest against Sorli's grip. Sorli yelled out to his brother for help. Hamdir cut off Jormunrekkr's feet while Sorli attended to his hands.

Hamdir cursed Jormunrekkr as he cut off the King's feet. The blood flowed copiously from the open stumps and mixed with the King's ale. "You mixed ale with blood, we mix blood with ale. Our deeds are now equal, our sister is revenged. We'll now sacrifice you on the fire."

While they struggled with the King's body, Jormunrekkr was able to call out for his guards. The two brothers dropped the King's body and turned to defend themselves. Sorli called out to Hamdir, "Mother was right. We did need three to succeed. If Erpr had been here he could have cut off the head. A man with neither brain nor mouth would have been unable to call his guards against us."

They fought fiercely and bravely. The floor was so slick with blood everyone was sliding against each other. Hamdir thrust his sword into a warrior. It twisted as he tried to pull it out. He kept struggling with the blade but could not pull it out because it was stuck in his foes breastplate.

Meanwhile Sorli was having his own difficulties. He cut across another warrior's body, severing him in two. His sword came to rest, embedded in a pillar. In desperation the two weaponless brothers began hurling stones at their enemies, ignoring the warning their mother had given them.

King Jormunrekkr watched his guards rushing the two brothers. The blows struck Hamdir and Sorli but glanced off their enchanted armor. The two remained unharmed.

Then a tall one-eyed man entered the Hall and spoke to the King, "What kind of warriors are in your service that they can't defeat weaponless men? They outnumber Hamdir and Sorli hundreds to one, yet they can't bring the two noble brothers down."

King Jormunrekkr replied, "The armor the two Gjukings wear is enchanted. It cannot be harmed by iron."

The old man replied simply, "If iron will not work then use something else. Stone them and send them on their way to Niflhel."

King Jormunrekkr yelled out his last command before dying, "Heave pebbles and rocks at them. Tear up the very foundations of the Hall if you must, but kill them."

Soon the Hall was a storm of rocks and pebbles. Hamdir and Sorli raised their arms to ward off the shower of pebbles and stones of all sizes raining down on them. The storm of rocks proved too much for them and they staggered down under the weight of it all and soon both died covered in funeral mounds of rocks. The guards had pulled stones from the walls to hurl against Hamdir and Sorli. This had loosened the rest of the stones so the walls of the Hall fell in crushing the entire household of King Jormunrekkr. The old one-eyed man stood unharmed in the rubble, a lone figure. He saw a hand sticking up through the rubble. He knelt down and removed Andvaranutr from Hamdir's hand. He turned and could be seen walking away in the distance towards Gallow's Hill to pick up a new warrior for Valhall.

Such was the end of the Gjukings and all the Volsungrs, save one. And she was a little girl whose name was Aslaugr safely staying with her increasingly unstable grandfather, King Heimir.

PART 2
THE SAGA
OF
RAGNAR LODBROKR

CHAPTER 29
THE PROTECTION OF ASLAUGR

King Heimir was grief struck after hearing about the deaths of his daughter Brynhildr and son-in-law Sigurdr. He sat in his Hall at Hlymdale pondering what to do. Aslaugr, the daughter of those two doomed lovers, now three-years-old, played merrily at his feet unaware of the tragic past that trailed her and the uncertain future before her. Brynhildr and Sigurdr had had many enemies who would delight in killing their daughter should her existence become widely known. She was now heir to the Volsungr Treasure and Andvari's Hoard and prey to many. Although King Heimir had never announced his relationship to Aslaugr, many in his Kingdom surmised it. Why else would he pay so much attention to an orphan?

King Heimir's mind was unsettled by grief and his thoughts were bizarre. "I must give up my Kingdom and devote myself fully to protecting Aslaugr. If we stay here they'll find us and murder us. If I move about with her they'll have to hunt for us."

Thus he determined to travel his Kingdom, moving from place to place as inconspicuously as possible. "But how shall I conceal Aslaugr?" He moved around his room thinking on the matter. He passed by the harp he played and plucked idly at its strings. Then a thought occurred to him, logical only in his unhinged mind, "I'll have a huge harp constructed and conceal Aslaugr in it along with gold, jewels, and clothing for our travels. I'll make my living as a musician."

King Heimir commanded his luthier to build a magnificent harp for him. He described the secret compartment it would contain as part of the soundbox. The harp was to be set with a normal complement of strings, and to all appearances seem a simple traveling musician's harp. However, it would have wheels attached so he could roll it along. He was no longer young and carrying Aslaugr all around the countryside might prove tiring.

In a few days his luthiers called him to their workshop and showed him the instrument. He plucked gently at the strings. The sound filled the room and made everyone smile. One of the luthiers explained its construction, "We've set the strings

so they will never need tuning, nor will they ever break or need to be replaced. The joints and hinges for the secret compartment are concealed along the side so it looks in every aspect, and from every angle, like its all carved from one piece. No one will be able to open it unless they know the secret." The luthier motion to King Heimir, "Try."

The King felt around the harp prying at the sides with his fingers. However, his efforts were unsuccessful. He could find no faults that would indicate there was a secret compartment. Then the luthier stepped forward and played several notes. "However, by playing this series of notes the vibrations will unlatch the fittings on the inside so the door springs open." The door instantly popped open revealing a cushioned seat and plenty of room for gold and jewels.

The luthier described the extremely roomy interior, "The harp is all over covered in enchantments from the ljosalfar. The interior compartment can hold both you and Princess Aslaugr, um, er, your ward Aslaugr, at night should you need protection from the cold or storms, or from summer warmth. It can both warm you or cool you off, as need be."

King Heimir seemed not to have noticed the luthier's gaff in referring to his daughter as a Princess.

Another luthier stepped forward and lifted the harp with one finger. "The wood we've used is light, yet extremely strong. It was carved by the ljosalfar and carries their enchantment on it. You won't need wheels for it, since it'll float in front of you and can easily be guided by as little as one finger. In fact if you tire, lean on it, or stand on the pedals or feet and it'll carry you along too. You'll be able to travel up the steepest hills with no effort at all."

King Heimir smiled, pleased with the harp. It was just what he wanted. He gave his luthiers many honors and great wealth for the wonderful instrument they had created for him.

It took just a few days for everything to be made ready. Then while Aslaugr slept King Heimir placed her in the harp along with a King's treasure of gold and jewels. The interior seemed to expand the more he placed inside, yet the outside dimensions of the harp never changed. He placed cushions inside for Aslaugr's comfort and realized she could even lay down inside. He had been concerned how comfortable she would be having to sit all the time in the harp. However, the interior was magically big enough for her to be extremely comfortable, and even have room enough to play.

King Heimir spent the morning outfitting the harp. Just as he was leaving his quarters he saw the sideboard and realized it might be practical to take lunch and dinner with him, too. He wrapped up some food and took a couple of containers of mead. He played the notes on the harp, the door opened, and he placed the food and drink beside the sleeping child. The door closed and the harp followed floating obediently behind him as he left the Hall.

He traveled all that night and by the morning of the next day he had reached a stream that ran on the outskirts of his land. He saw a stranger squatting by the stream dipping his broadbrimmed hat into it and gather up water to drink.

Heimir approached the stranger, "Do you know what land this is?"

The stranger did not answer that question, but another, "It is not wise to be traveling in these parts. You would do well to go back where you came from. Will you take my advice?"

Before answering Heimir bent over to scoop up some water to drink. When he turned the stranger was gone. However, on the ground where the stranger had been Heimir saw a wonderful ring. He picked it up and put it on his finger.

He thought this was a nice place to stop and rest for a while. He plucked the strings of the harp to open the door. Aslaugr was just waking up. She got out and washed in the stream. He took a leek from the package of food and gave it to her to eat. As is the nature of children of her age, she was quite particular about food, and leeks were just about the only thing she'd eat. Fortunately leeks are so nutritious she was able to subsist quite well on this diet.

After eating she turned to her grandfather and spoke, "When will we be returning to the Hall, grandfather?"

It was now King Heimir's painful duty to tell her the truth, "We will not be going back. There are evil people who would do you great harm. It's for your protection that we've left my Kingdom."

Aslaugr began to cry. All but a few of her favorite toys had been left behind, and she hadn't even had time to say goodbye to her friends. King Heimir removed the ring from his finger and gave it to Aslaugr. She liked that it was so shiny. Then King Heimir seized the harp and began to play upon it. She started to smile. At first he played soothing music until she had calmed down. Then he changed to a livelier tune until she was dancing about having forgotten her sadness.

Soon it was time to begin traveling again. He carefully placed her in the harp, closed the door and began walking. In no time at all they were in Norway. They traveled for many days until they came to Spangareid, the home of Grima and her husband, Aki. As it happened Aki was out. He didn't like visitors and probably wouldn't have welcomed King Heimir if he had been there. For this very reason Grima bid the stranger into her house. She hadn't had any visitors in the longest while and was lonesome for fresh company, and longed for new stories to entertain her.

She asked him several questions at once, not waiting for a reply, as is the habit of those left to themselves, who constantly talk to themselves and answer their own questions as they ask them. "What's your name? Why are you traveling through this land? And all by yourself? I can tell that you're a stranger here. Do you know how? You talk differently than we do. Though you are dressed as a beggar your manner gives you away as someone important."

Finally she paused and the stranger answered, "I'm now a poor beggar, though once I was rich. I've lost all my money through unwise speculation. All that remains of my past are my good manners, which will hardly buy me an evening meal. However, I can offer you a pleasant evening of music in exchange for a meal."

She put more wood on the fire so he could warm up. She also prepared some food for him. In the meantime he set up his harp and began playing and singing.

Grima sat down across from him humming and swaying along with the music. As she did so she saw some fringes of material hanging out the bottom of the harp. How could that be? Wasn't the harp made of one piece? Then she saw another strange thing. As he warmed up the stranger unhooked his cloak, although he didn't take it off. Occasionally as he moved back and forth in his playing she could catch sight of what looked like gold trimming around his shirt. Clearly this was no ordinary beggar.

Soon the food was warmed up and he stopped playing so he could eat. After he finished she asked him to play some more for her, "Your music is so beautiful, I just feel like sitting and listening to you all afternoon. My, my I do seem to be very naughty since I'm neglecting my chores. I can't seem to help myself."

He played well into the evening. Soon she saw he was beginning to nod off as he played. She got up and motioned for him to follow her. He carried the harp with him as they went outside and around to the side of the house. "When my husband returns home he's usually in a talkative mood, so it would be best if you slept out here in the grain shed so our talking won't keep you awake."

He thanked her for her hospitality, "This will be fine. I'm most grateful for the kindness you've shown us."

She looked at him inquiringly, "Us?"

He realized his slip, "I was thinking of myself and my harp. I talk to it as I travel and think of it almost as if it were a companion following me down the road."

"Oh. Well, I hope you'll both be comfortable in here. Don't worry about getting cold. The nights around here are pretty warm." She left him.

King Heimir lay down among the rye and barley, carefully placing the harp at his feet. He was tired from all the traveling he'd done in the last few days and soon fell into a deep sleep.

∘ ∘ ∘ ∘

It was quite a while before Aki returned. He yelled at Grima as he walked into the house and saw it had not been cleaned all day, "Such is my lot that I'm married to a layabout. While I'm out working all day you laze about here doing nothing. My life isn't right. Things aren't fair. I have to work all the time so you can loaf. Many are the times I've thought ..."

Grima cut him off mid-sentence, "Be quiet and listen to what's happened. Perhaps we'll gain great fortune from the work I've been doing all day."

Aki looked puzzled. While she talked he took a bowl and began to dip out some stew for his supper and saw to his dismay there was very little of it left. He interrupted her, "What's this? You aren't content to have me support you, you're intent on starving me at the same time?" Then noticing the two chairs by the fire he continued, "Or, perhaps you've had visitors during the day?"

She put out her hand to calm him, "If you'll listen for a moment I can explain what's happened. We have a visitor."

At this news he rose from the table, "You know I don't like strangers. Tell him to leave at ..."

She cut him off again, "Don't be silly. He's a wonderful musician, although I think he's more than that. And if we act carefully with him we might gain a lot."

He scoffed, "Bah, all this hope from a begging musician?"

"A begging musician wearing a tattered and worn outer cloak, but a shirt that I could see was lined with gold. How do you explain that?"

Aki jumped at this. He was clearly interested, "Tell me more about him. What does he look like?"

Grima continued, "He's now old and bent and looks as if he's carrying a great load on his shoulders. Although he's heavy, he's not fat. At one time he must have been a fine figure of a man. He looks pretty good now." She stopped and looked at Aki whose youthful muscle had already turned to old-age flab. His potbelly hung over his belt; he was dirty and grizzled looking. The exact opposite of a fine figure of a man. The stranger sleeping in their grain shed, though perhaps twenty or thirty years older, looked more fit then her husband.

Aki got up and went outside, walking towards the grain shed carrying a candle with him to light the way. Grima followed. Aki looked in and shown the candle so he could see their sleeping guest. Heimer was so deep in sleep he was not roused by the light shining on him. Seeing the sleeper had not stirred, Aki moved closer and shown the light the length of their visitor. As the light passed over King Heimir, Aki saw the harp beneath the stranger's feet. He and Grima left the grain shed.

Back in their cottage Grima plotted while Aki listened, "He's deep in sleep, having eaten and drunk his fill. Now is the time to kill him and take his treasure."

Aki hadn't suspected his wife's plans included murder, "I thought you wanted us to offer him hospitality and then perhaps he would reward us with treasure. It's bad luck to treat a guest unjustly. The Æsir frown on such behavior."

Grima was perturbed, thinking her husband's reluctance had more to do with the visitor's size than Aki's sense of propriety that, perhaps, one shouldn't murder a sleeping guest. "Are we to remain in this dark dingy cottage all our lives with hopes of nothing better? Have you no ambition beyond this? If not, then perhaps I'd better cast my lot with the stranger and take him as my husband instead." Grima saw Aki had reacted to this and continued in that vein, "Of course, I didn't tell you everything that happened tonight. True, he played and sang to me, but the songs he sang were meant to arouse me. He then spoke to me of love and how tired he was of traveling about. Wouldn't I like to have a constant admirer in attendance?"

Her story was having an effect on Aki. She continued, giggling and flouncing around coquettishly as she remembered how she had wanted the stranger to act, "Of course, I reminded the handsome gentleman I was married, but that didn't seem to bother him or stop his advances. He made other suggestions to me that were most improper. Perhaps he's so tired and deep in sleep for reasons other than journeying all day?"

Grima caught up the sides of her greasy skirt and twirled about the room. Aki's jaw dropped. Even as a young schoolgirl Aki had never seen his wife twirl. He sank into the chair by the fireplace, dumbfounded. He could think of nothing to say.

Suddenly Grima stopped twirling. She stood over him. Aki had never been afraid of his wife. It was he who had always kept her in line with a beating or two, or three, or, maybe, many more. Now she leaned on the arms of the chair, bent with her face inches from his. Her voice was stern and threatening. Aki had never seen his wife like this. For the first time in his life he was afraid of what she could do to him. Grima spoke to him in a slow, measured tone. Aki was trembling. "So make your choice. Either you kill him, and we live wealthily, or he and I will kill you and live wealthily. Either way my life is going to be a lot easier. And no matter which choice you make, I will have servants to carry out the drudgery that has made up my life. I will give you one moment for your decision. Make the wrong one and it will be your last moment."

Grima stood up, taking the fireplace poker in hand.

Aki, shaking uncontrollable, nodded.

That wasn't enough for Grima, "What? Speak you little twerp." Grima was filled with a new power that greed and lust had brought on. She didn't fear the consequences of anything, and it was certainly having an effect on Aki. Pastimes he would have by now had her beaten and curled up on the floor her hands and arms trying to protect her head. Her crooked, badly healed, broken jaw, and missing teeth reflected how ineffective that had been.

Now Aki cowered before her, "Speak! Let me hear your decision. Aki tried to say something, yet nothing came out. "You open your mouth but words don't come out. You shake like a cat's cornered mouse." She moved towards him, poker upraised. "Now you tremble frozen in place like a rabbit or deer in the field. You are disgusting. SPEAK!"

Aki, fearing the fireplace poker finally summoned up enough strength to answer his wife, "You, you, you, you…"

Grima was tiring of her husband. How had she ever been afraid of him? He was so weak. "SPEAK! Why you miserable little … I ought to murder both you and our guest. Then I'll have it all for me."

Aki finally assembled some wits about him, "No, no, that'll never do. Kill the stranger, but not me. If you kill us both and suddenly are rich, people will suspect something. No one knows about the stranger. His wealth we can pass off as the result of years of frugality."

Astonishingly, Aki made sense. Grima lowered the poker.

Aki was becoming increasingly worked up by his wife's speech, and the thought of massive amounts of gold. He looked at the ax standing by the doorway. It was newly sharpened, since he had intended to chop more wood a few weeks ago, but hadn't gotten around to it just yet. The blade glistened, reflecting the fire on its surface. He could almost see the betraying treachery of the stranger played out for him on the blade. He saw his wife and the stranger together by the fire entwined in each other's arms laying on the sooty floor in front of the fireplace, which reminded him he must clean the flue.

Suddenly Aki grabbed the ax and ran to the grain shed where he burst in through the door. King Heimir looked up and saw the ax descending. It lodged in his chest.

His arms convulsed upwards and grabbed at the handle. Aki was frightened out of his wits and ran from the shed. King Heimir look at his chest, cut open. There was nothing he could do about his deathwound. His death was upon him. He yelled out curses upon Aki and Grima. His voice boomed with the unnatural sound of the dead, or near dead. The ground trembled until the foundation of Aki and Grima's cottage shook. The crossbeams gave way and the roof and walls collapsed inward.

At his death he had had some measure of revenge upon his slayers. However, his last thoughts were not of that. They were of Aslaugr. What would become of her now? As he lay dying he reached down to pull the harp nearer so he could pluck the strings to release Aslaugr from what was now a prison, perhaps a tomb. With his last bit of strength he touched the crown of the harp and it rose up and floated a little was towards him. He stretched his fingers as far as he could, but could only reach the higher strings. The freeing tune was in the lower register. He died, his final thoughts and words for Aslaugr, "I have given up one crown, and can only touch this crown. I am so sorry, but I am unable to free you. Forgive me Aslaugr. Your life was placed in the hands of a foolish old man who did what he thought best. I love you."

The reign of King Heimir came to an end, alone, surrounded by no courtiers, an ax in his chest and the unknown heir to the throne trapped in a harp. No proclamations shouted out his death to his people. No one mourned.

o   o   o   o

At the stranger's first yell, Aki and Grima had both run into the forest. They waited there until the booming and crashing had subsided and eventually emerged from the forest into an eerie silence. The air seemed alive and crisp. The two walked up to the pile of rubble that had once been their cottage. Aki seemed to derive some pleasure from their present circumstances, "Is this what you meant by bettering our lives? Now we don't even have a place to sleep, dingy as it was. I didn't even get to finish my meal." He began searching among the rubble hoping to find a piece of bread.

Grima paid no attention to her husband's remarks. She was searching for something, too. He watched as she shoveled through the rye and barley where the grain shed had been. A bloodstained heap of barley and grain was behind her. The handle of an ax barely poked out from the top. Grima dug about like a dog searching for a bone, tossing more grain onto the bloodstained pile. Eventually her persistence met with success and she stood up smiling, having found what she was looking for. "Here's the harp. It's the key to our wealth."

Aki didn't understand, "What do you mean, key to our wealth? Neither one of us can play? Our singing would scare people away. I don't think things are going very well for us."

Grima put all her weight into raising the harp and was surprised to find it practically righted itself. The harp stood on end. She pounded at it and found the soundboard, though she didn't know that's what it was called, seemed hollow. She

pried all about its edges trying to find a chink or catch that would open a door. There was none evident. She could not pry the harp apart.

Aki noticed it was a finely constructed instrument and realized it might be the only wealth they had, providing Grima didn't destroy it. "Careful there of the harp. We might be able to sell it in town, or at the upcoming fair to some traveler. It's the only thing we have of any value. We certainly can't sell bloody grain or barley at the fair."

Grima did not stop clawing at the harp. Maddeningly frenzied by her lack of success she reached into the large pile of grain and pulled the ax out. With a fierce blow she struck the harp. Though the wood was light, it was extremely hard. The ax blow had not even so much as nicked a splinter out of the harp's side. She swung at the stings thinking maybe the sting's tautness somehow kept the harp together, and if cut the harp would fly apart. The ax just bounced off the strings.

She tired herself out flailing at the harp. Then when she was too tired to raise the ax she motioned for Aki to try. He put all his heft into his blow, but met with the same results. The harp was as good as new.

Suddenly a gust of wind blew around them. The grains of sand were stirred up and blew about in tiny whirlpools. Some of the grains were blown through the harp strings. Weird music sounded, the magic sequence of notes played, and the secret door opened.

Aki and Grima ran up and looked in, thinking to see it packed full of treasures. They both gasped in unison and backed away. A little girl lay sleeping, swaddled in costly garments, jewels, and gold.

Aki was the first to recover what was left of his wits after the excitement of the night, "Ill luck will attend the ill deed we've performed. Perhaps she's a magical child, a changeling who will torment us for the rest of our lives for killing her father."

Grima was less superstitious than her husband, "Don't be silly. She's nothing but a child. How can she ever harm us? Today is our lucky day, for now we have someone to help us with the cleaning and baking."

Aki astutely observed, "But where is there to clean? How can you bake? Our cottage is gone, along with the kitchen."

Aslaugr had now started to wake up and had raised her hands to her eyes to wipe the sleep from them. Aki jumped back and covered his head, thinking some spell was going to be hurled his way. "Watch out for the flames and fire, Grima. She's going to call monsters forth to eat us."

He collapsed into a prostrate heap, whimpering and begging for the three-year-old's mercy.

Grima kicked him in the side to try to get him to stand up. He thought a demon was at his side and cried out even louder for mercy. Grima managed to finally get his attention, "Aki be quiet. No one's hurting you, although you might hurt yourself if you continue rolling around like that. She's just a sleepy child." Then turning to Aslaugr she began questioning the child, "What's your name? How do you come to be sleeping in a harp? The man who was your champion, who was he?"

Aslaugr was confused and looked about for her grandfather. "Where's my grandfather?"

Grima broke the news to her, "Your grandfather had to leave on important business. He's left you in our care. What's your name?" Aslaugr didn't respond, so Grima continued, "We've always wanted a child, and now you'll be ours. Since you won't tell us your name I'll give you the name I was saving for my daughter, if I'd had one." She looked at Aki, blaming him for their childless condition. Oh the many arguments they'd had about that. "From now on you'll be called Kraka, the name my dear departed mother had."

Aki rolled his head upward, but was too upset by all that had happened to protest. He was confused about how they would explain things, "What will we tell our neighbors? I've never mentioned a child to them before."

Grima answered, "You've never mentioned much of anything to them before. Since I've been held a virtual prisoner here, and have no friends in the village, who can dispute that I haven't had a child all these years and been home taking care of her?"

Aki looked at the beautiful child with her heroic features and deep piercing eyes. He turned away unable to hold her gaze. "But who'll believe that a child with such a highborn appearance would have been born of us? Should our child not look like the other scruffy peasant beast children in the village? This child clearly comes of better stock."

Grima considered this, "Perhaps you're right for once. We'll have to make her uglier than she is. Get a razor so we can shave her head.

While Aki was looking through the rubble for a razor, Grima started a fire and set a pot filled with tar on it. As the tar heated up she added other items to the mixture. This was an old recipe her mother had once taught her, mostly used for the curing of fevers. Unfortunately, it made the sufferer bald.

Aki returned with the razor. Grima removed the tar from the heat and set it aside to cool just a little. She took the razor and cut off the child's beautiful golden hair. Aki watched his wife cutting and pulling at the child's hair, not certain they were doing the right thing. Grima began smearing the tar on the child's head, explaining her plans to Aki at the same time, "This mixture will prevent her hair growing. We'll dress her in old patched clothes and tie a hood around her head, and tell everyone she lost her hair through illness and that she wears a hood to conceal the ugly marks left by her illness. In that way no one will see how beautiful she really is." Aki looked dubiously at his wife. The child, even covered in tar, still looked too beautiful to be theirs.

Grima continued, "And of course who's to say she doesn't take after me. After all I was quite beautiful when I was younger. The years of hard work and suffering I've had to endure being married to you have since robbed me of my looks."

Aki had known Grima all his life and try as he might could not remember anyone ever thinking her beautiful, unless warty blemished skin and a knobby face passed for beautiful. Many less than good looking people made themselves beautiful with their personality. Here, too, Grima was woefully lacking.

This had certainly been one of the roughest nights of Aki's life, and he had no interest in prolonging it, so he didn't dispute what his wife had said about her past beauty. She accepted his staring at her as his thinking back on the beauty she had been. How little couples know the true feelings the other is thinking.

Over the next few months the two rebuilt their cottage, a little bit grander than before. Soon the wealth that had been in the harp was spent, mostly through overpayment, and they were once more subsisting as best they could. They had no concept of money, never having had any, so they had no idea how much wealth had been in the harp. When the blacksmith asked for a pound of gold to make a new ax, they paid. When the thatcher asked for a bushel of gold to thatch their roof, they paid, including another half bushel to pay for the sedge, straw and rushes. Soon townspeople were lined up selling cups and plates for nuggets of gold.

What happened in the town through overcharging the strange couple in the woods was extraordinary. Many in the nearby village now had grand estates and great wealth. The money they accepted as having been hoarded by Aki and Grima was the making of the town. Great fortunes brought in more workers to clear the land and increase farming. Soon people from all over we're moving to the booming town. Fortune after fortune was made in new manufacturing industries. News of the wealth of the town was spreading and many people were moving there.

Even great and noble warriors were hearing of the town and thinking it might be a good place to go adventuring.

Kraka was often seen around the village. She was a solemn child who spoke very little and usually kept to herself. She grew up in great hardship and frequently was in want of food never realizing the wealth of the town was actually hers, having been built from the Volsungr Hoard of gold.

Kraka's life was a hard one, and filled with sadness.

CHAPTER 30
THE STORY OF THORA BORGARHJORT

Now our story moves to Gautland, and a Jarl named Herraud who lived there. His daughter was Thora Borgarhjort, known throughout the land as Borgy. Her beauty was far greater than other women's, even as the hart is better thought of than other animals.

Herraud was very proud of his daughter and delighted in the admiration she excited in others. When she came of age he had had a magnificent bower house built for her just outside his main Hall. It was red-gold and shown in the sun and was surrounded by a sturdy wooden fence.

She had always been a dutiful daughter and had never given him any trouble. Therefore, it was quite easy to justify his habit of sending her at least one gift every day so he could show the great love he felt for her.

One day Borgy went to her father, concerned about the presents she was always receiving from him, "You must stop sending me gifts every day. There's no need for it. You've been the best father a child could have. Just knowing I have your love is enough for me. I would rather you gave more to the poor."

Jarl Herraud was overwhelmed at his daughter's generosity, and answered her, "I shall gladly increase my aid to the poor. However, I'll also continue giving you gifts as a reward for your generosity. Let's not speak any more of it. As long as I live I shall see you are sent a gift every day. It gives me great pleasure to reward such a wonderful daughter. I have friends who have children who have been nothing but a constant source of pain to them, always badgering them for things or getting into trouble. In all your years you've never given me a moment's trouble. Let me have the pleasure of honoring the love I have for you by giving you gifts."

Reluctantly she consented and upon awakening every morning was happily surprised with another present.

o   o   o   o

One morning she opened a box and found her father had sent her a small worm. She thought it looked cute, picked it up, and then hugged it. It wriggled about in her hand. She saw it was the sort of worm that would grow up to be a serpent, so she placed it on a pile of gold in a golden casket. She knew worms of this sort liked to lie on such things. She stood back watching it. To her surprise both the worm and gold began to increase in size. The casket overflowed with red gold and the worm encircled it by that evening. By the morning of the next day gold filled most of the room. The worm, now a large serpent, had crawled outside and was now encircling the bower, catching its tale in its mouth, laying there protecting its hoard. Its body was wide enough so that one side touched the house and the other side rested against the wooden fence surrounding the bower. No one could enter the house, nor could the Jarl's daughter leave it. The only person allowed to approach near the house was the servant who brought the serpent its meals. Several times a day he reluctantly approached and left off the dead carcass of an ox from the Jarl's prize herd.

But what would happen once the herd had been eaten? This worried Jarl Herraud greatly. He sent messengers throughout the land proclaiming that the noble champion who rescued his daughter from the dragon would win her hand in marriage, taking the gold within the bower as her dowry.

Even though this was a tempting offer, no warriors showed up to challenge the dragon, who now had reached full maturity and spit out fire and poison when it was angry, or just when it felt like it.

The Jarl's messengers returned and reported to him that they had traveled the length and breadth of his Kingdom without success. There were no warriors brave enough to risk their lives for Thora Borgarhjort and the gold.

Jarl Herraud commanded his messengers to travel to other Kingdoms offering the same terms. Surely there was someone brave enough to rescue his daughter?

Some of the Jarl's messengers made their way to Denmark, which was at this time ruled over by King Sigurdrhringr, who was both wise and brave. He was known far and wide in songs sung by the skalds as the King who had met King Harald Hilditann, also known as Harald Wartooth, at Bravoll and bested him in combat.

King Sigurdrhringr had a fifteen-year-old son named Ragnar who was tall and muscular, and had yet to be beaten in single combat. Unlike many great warriors he was pleasant to be around since his interests ranged beyond that of warfare. Although young in years he had already raised his own army and ships and had conquered many lands. He had heard of Jarl Herraud's offer countless times in the lands he had conquered. Now he was urged on to the task by many of his friends, yet seemingly paid no attention to their entreaties.

It was at this time he gave instructions to his tailor to make him an odd set of clothes. The outfit consisted of furry breaches, tabard, and cape. The tailor was ashamed to show the outfit to Ragnar. It was more the thing a peasant would wear.

However, Ragnar was pleased with it and gave his tailor one further command, "This outfit is exactly what I had in mind. Now boil it in pitch, wrap it up, and bring it to me."

This was done. Ragnar's advisors were curious to know what use he had for the outfit, but he didn't tell them. He put it away and notified his advisors he would be taking his army to Gautland later that summer.

o   o   o   o

The time for adventuring soon came. He left his Kingdom for Gautland.

He guided his ships into a secret inlet he had learned about from a conquered King who had revealed the secret to spare his life. As it happened the inlet was quite near Jarl Herraud's Hall.

The next morning Ragnar arose early and put on the pitch-covered outfit. He commanded his men to stay aboard while he went ashore unarmed, save for his spear. His men could see him acting very strangely on the shore. First he rolled about on the beach so the sand covered the tar. Then he removed the pinning nail from the shaft and head of his spear. He began walking inland and was soon out of sight of his ships. Many onboard wanted to follow to give him some protection, but were reminded he had commanded they all stay onboard ship.

It was still early in the morning when he arrived at Jarl Herraud's Hall. All inside were still sleeping. Cautiously he made his way to Thora Borgarhjort's bower. The dragon was sleeping peacefully, with small puffs of smoke coming contentedly from its nostrils at regular intervals. The dragon had never feared an attack while it slept, knowing that everyone was afraid to approach.

Ragnar crept up behind the dragon's head and thrust his spear deep into its neck. The dragon rose up, and turned towards Ragnar. Ragnar took this opportunity and quickly ran under the raised head before the dragon could see him. He climbed up on the tail and thrust down under the dragon's chin into the dragon's neck until he reached the worm's heart. The dragon tried to flail out with his tail but couldn't move because of the wooden fence surrounding the bower. The dragon twisted its neck to one side, while Ragnar twisted his spear in the opposite direction. The unsecured spearhead came loose from the shaft, and remained in the dragon's heart as Ragnar pulled out the shaft. The dragon howled hideously from its deathwound. The land trembled beneath Ragnar's feet as he ran from the serpent. It hissed out at Ragnar and sent a mixed stream of poison, blood, and fire at him. The serpent's aim was accurate and Ragnar was struck between the shoulders, but with no ill effects, since his pitch-covered outfit protected him.

Everyone in the Hall had been awakened by the noise from the battle and the dragon's death howl. Borgy watched from an upper room in her bower. Soon the dragon breathed its last and lay dead around the bower. She yelled out to her rescuer, "Who is it who has changed my wyrd and released me from this prison?"

He yelled back, "Though only fifteen I've rescued a beautiful maiden, and gained great honor thereby. But no matter how great the honor, it could not match the honor of knowing a beautiful maiden was once more set free."

He left without telling her his name. She watched as he walked into the forest using the broken spear as a walking stick.

Borgy returned to her bed to rest. She still couldn't leave the bower since the dragon's body blocked the front door. The Jarl and others in the Hall had heard all the commotion and had come out to see what was causing it. Jarl Herraud was happy to see the dragon had been slain and ordered its carcass be cut into pieces and carried away separately. The spearhead was cut from the dragon's heart and returned to Jarl Herraud.

Borgy rushed to her father's arms, happy once more to embrace him. "Who rescued you, my child?"

She answered, "I don't know. He seemed to be a young lad, and said he was but fifteen-years-old. His strength, though, was that of one much bigger and older. I think he might have been some sort of sorcerer. Yet he was very strong and handsome, just the same."

The Jarl smiled at his daughter, "You'll no doubt be pleased if he claims his reward, and I would be honored to have such a brave lad as a son-in-law. I wonder, though, how shall we find him?"

The Jarl's counselors, standing nearby, advised the warrior would probably return to claim his prize on his own."

Borgy suggested her father call a Thing, "And order all warriors and leaders of armies be present. If more than one claims my hand and the gold as slayer of the dragon he may prove his claim with the shaft of his spear. If it fits into the spearhead and the markings match then he will win my hand."

Jarl Herraud was proud of his daughter's wisdom in thinking up such a solution. He sent word throughout the land of the Thing that was to be held the following week. Over the next several days warriors gathered from every quarter of the Jarldom, many carrying shafts hoping to try and claim all that gold ... as well as the hand of Thora Borgarhjort. But mainly it was the gold.

Ragnar also attended in the company of his warriors. He commanded his men keep apart from the other warriors, and together so should a fight arise they would be prepared to defend themselves as a group.

The day of the Thing arrived. Jarl Herraud looked down from an upper window in his Hall into the courtyard, and saw it was packed with mighty warriors, none of whom looked even close to fifteen year's in age. Many of those with gray hair seemed to be accompanied by their fifteen-year-old grandsons.

Jarl Herraud stepped out onto the balcony and spoke, "Thank you all for answering my summons. As you know the vile dragon who held my daughter captive has been killed. And true to my word, the warrior who risked his life to free my daughter will be given her hand in marriage and her gold as a dowry. I can see there are many claiming the reward, however, only one can win it. My counselor will hold the spearhead. All those wishing to claim the treasure must file past him and insert their shaft into the spearhead. If it fits then you will be separated into a second, more select group. If your shaft is too great or too small you will pass on, unrewarded. Then a second fitting will be held, and the shaft and spearhead studied to see if the markings match. If one is found that matches precisely, then that warrior will win the reward, no matter if he is the lowest born in my land, or the highest. For it's the heart and spirit of a warrior that counts, not his accident of birth which might have placed him in an unfortunate lowly situation."

The warriors filed past. Some of the older ones sent their grandsons at the last minute. Especially those already married who wanted to prevent strife at home. Some of those whose marriages weren't working out that well convinced themselves they looked a lot younger than others thought they looked. An image reflected in gold can distort one's image and convince a man that a balding head was merely an extremely high forehead; a paunch overflowing a belt was the result of a shirt not properly tucked in; and the youthful handsome young man staring back was not a delusion, but as he saw himself every day.

A few whose shafts fit were asked to stand together. After all the shafts had been checked, those in the second group were asked to reinsert their shafts. The counselor inspected each shaft but could find none that matched exactly. The Jarl was disappointed at this and asked the shafts be checked again. The result was the same. None of the shafts had markings that precisely matched those on the spearhead, though some were close.

Jarl Herraud looked out over the assemblage and saw a group of men standing together. He yelled out at them, "Have your shafts been checked?"

Ragnar yelled back, "Not yet. I was waiting until everyone else had been checked since I know mine is the mate to the spearhead you hold, and I'm the mate to your daughter."

Ragnar walked forward, knelt before the Jarl and handed him his spear shaft, "I give you my spear shaft and ask humbly that I be granted your daughter's hand in marriage. I have loved her in legend on my journey here, and in reality when I saw her at the window stroking her hair with a golden brush."

Thora stared at the youth. He certainly looked as if he were only fifteen. Yet she recalled the young warrior who had rescued her had been considerable dirtier and dressed in lowly clothing. Yet he knew the detail of her brushing her hair, that she had not mentioned to her father, thinking it of no significance.

The Jarl personally fitted the spearhead onto the shaft. The fit was snug, and all the markings matched. Ragnar took a nail from his pocket and placed it in the pinhole making the spear whole once more. Ragnar spoke, "I would be most honored if Thora Borgarhjort would be my wife. However, I would force no woman to marry me because of a brave deed that I did as much for my own glory as for her rescue. If she finds me attractive and consents then we will be wed. Otherwise, she is free to choose whomever she desires. I make no claim upon her gold. She has suffered greatly for it, and it rightfully should remain as her possession, even if we are wed. I do not hold with those who think a woman and her property all become the husband's after the marriage. I have gold of my own to bring to the marriage."

Thora Borgarhjort reached out and took Ragnar's hand, "I've loved you since the first moment I saw you. We shall be very happy together."

The wedding feast was prepared and great celebrations were held throughout the Jarldom. Skalds traveled the countryside singing the story of Ragnar's bravery and his wooing and winning of Thora Borgarhjort. The skalds began calling him Ragnar Lodbrokr in honor of his killing of the worm.

After the wedding Thora Borgarhjort and Ragnar Lodbrokr returned to his father's Kingdom. In just a short time King Sigurdrhringr died and Ragnar Lodbrokr became King. Eventually Borgy bore Ragnar Lodbrokr two sons. The first was called Eric, and the second was called Agnar. They grew up taking after both parents, gaining stature and strength from their father and wisdom and gentleness from their mother, and were well thought of throughout the land.

However, Thora Borgarhjort and Ragnar Lodbrokr's happiness was short-lived. She died soon after the birth of her second son. Ragnar Lodbrokr was overcome by grief since he truly loved her. He vowed never to marry again.

After a while the memories of his life with Thora Borgarhjort in his Hall and Kingdom overwhelmed him so that he felt he had to get away for his own peace of mind. He set up a regency to run the country until his children were of age, gathered together an army, and once more went warring and conquering, hoping to overcome his grief with brave deeds.

CHAPTER 31
RAGNAR LODBROKR
AND KRAKA
MEET

Eventually Ragnar Lodbrokr's journeys took him to Norway. It was an early summer day when he and his crew sighted land. Ragnar Lodbrokr seemed happier than he had been in a long time at the news. His journey to this part of the world was not for war or gain, just to visit friends and relatives living there.

By evening his ships sat nestled in a small cove. Ragnar Lodbrokr and his men rested that evening without going ashore. The next morning Ragnar Lodbrokr sent his bakers ashore to bake bread for breakfast. The bakers saw a farmhouse in the distance and decided to visit it and find out more about where they were. The farmwife was in the front yard doing her laundry when they approached. As soon as she sighted them she began backing away.

One of the bakers held up his hand in a friendly gesture, "Don't be afraid fair lady, we come in peace. Could you tell us what part of Norway we have landed in? We are not warriors, we are bakers. We carry rolling pins, not spears."

The farmwife looked closely and saw it was true. They carried no weapons, other than the weapons of their trade used in attacking dough—rolling pins and mixing bowls. "You're on the farm known as Spangareid. It's owned by my husband and myself. I am called Grima, he is named Aki. Where have you come from?"

"We have landed in ships which are now harbored in the cove not far from here. We're the servants of the great warrior Ragnar Lodbrokr and have been sent ashore to bake bread for breakfast. Would you be able to help us?"

She had no desire to spend her time kneading dough for bread that someone else would eat, but decided it would be better not to offend them, "You're certainly welcome to use my kitchen. However, I'm sorry, but I'm old and suffer from a stiffness of the hands and won't be able to help you. I do have a strong young daughter named Kraka whom I could send to help you with your baking. Right now she's moving our cattle onto the high hill for their morning feeding. She should be back soon. Perhaps a little discipline in helping you will make her settle down, since she's been a bit wild of late and will not do as I say. You might not want her help though, since she is so dirty and ugly."

The chief baker answered, "Let us judge that after we've seen her. And kneading dough seldom requires good looks. In the meantime we'll take advantage of your hospitality."

The bakers set up their equipment and started a fire in Grima's oven.

○ ○ ○ ○

Kraka had seen the ships moored in the cove, and had caught sight of the fleet's leader standing at the prow giving orders to his men. She found him impressive and decided she would somehow contrive to meet him. Then she caught sight of her reflection in the stream from which the cows had been drinking. Her mother had forbidden her to ever wash, so she was covered with filth and smelled. She looked a fright.

Kraka began to cry at her wyrd, and then disobeying her mother she walked into the stream and bathed. The water washed the tar from her head to reveal long golden silken tresses reaching to the ground, that shown even more brilliantly in the sun once they were dry. It took a great deal of scrubbing, but after a while all the dirt had been washed away. Instead of being as dark and sunburnt as her parents, she was as fair and golden as her hair.

Her clothing, too, had changed. In fact her clothing had always been a wonder. It was the same clothing she had had as a child. As she had grown so had her clothing. Her parents hadn't questioned this since it meant they didn't have to spend money to outfit her. Even the cheapest rags cost something.

King Heimir had only packed a limited wardrobe for her, an outfit for each season, yet they had all grown with her. They had gotten dirty over the years because she had never been allowed to wash them. Yet as soon as she had walked into the stream the years of dirt fell from her clothing to reveal an expensive dress all entwined with gold filament that reflected in the sun. Kraka was beautiful, and beautifully dressed. Indeed, many would have remarked she was the fairest maiden in the land.

○ ○ ○ ○

Kraka returned home. Grima glared at her as she walked through the door at first not recognizing the beautiful fair-haired, fair-skinned, exquisitely dressed woman who stood before her.

The bakers stared at her in admiration. This is what the mother considered to be her unattractive, filthy daughter?

The chief baker spoke, "Is this the maiden you spoke of?" Grima nodded that it was. The baker continued, "If she is dirty and ugly, then I should like to see the maidens of the village whom you consider to be clean and beautiful. In all my travels I've never seen anyone so fair. Oddly, though, as I look back and forth between the two of you I see little resemblance. Your skin is pockmarked, while hers is clear. Your nose is bulbous and red with black hairs growing out of it, while hers is delicate and tilted. Her ..."

Grima interrupted the talkative baker, "Let's not talk of comparisons."

The baker couldn't help asking a question, "How is it that one with your looks should have such a beautiful daughter?"

Grima was somewhat offended, but answered, "Because of the hard work of raising her I have not aged very well. Once I was beautiful too. Looking at me you can see what she will look like twenty years from now."

The baker was still overcome by Kraka's beauty and answered, "Not in a hundred years could she ever look like you. Nay, not even in a thousand. Perhaps from here to Ragnarokr." He couldn't think of any longer timeframe.

Kraka saw the situation was getting out of hand and spoke up, "Is there anything I can do to help you kind gentlemen?"

The bakers surrounded her, "We would be most honored if you'd help us bake bread for the others on our ship so they can have their morning meal."

She smiled at them, and they all set to work with each baker trying to impress her with his baking skills, trying to outdo the baker next to him. Some even did fancy flips with their rolling pins. One even grabbed a couple of rolling pins and began juggling them. One flipped the dough up into the air spinning it into a circle with his hand as he flung it up and caught it, sometimes behind his back. However, many weren't so skillful and their dough wasn't caught and fell to the dirty floor. They quickly picked it up and kneaded in the dust and small bugs that had been crawling on the floor. Perhaps no one would notice?

One baker went so far as to say, "Great armies have great bakers. An army travels on its stomach." Somehow that didn't come out right as he envisioned whole armies crawling down the road or attacking fortresses by crawling up to the sides of the stone walls and hitting the walls with rolling pins. But, undeterred, the baker shook these thoughts from his head and continued, "If the food is bad and they ache and have to dig holes to squat in all day from poorly cooked food, then even the mightiest warrior might find himself suddenly fighting with his leggings down about his ankles." The baker realized this thought somehow had seemed more noble and romantic in his head rather than spoken aloud. He knew he was in for a future of teasing from his fellow bakers. This was the kind of story that was going to follow him from ship to ship. He could see pranksters pulling down his leggings and telling him to go fight great battles. He bowed his head and went back to kneading his dough. He pounded at the dough as if he were fighting the dragon Fafnir barehanded. That's what he did best, knead. That's what his mother had always told him he did best. He should just keep quiet and knead, knead, knead. Always got into trouble when he opened his mouth.

Kraka politely smiled at him and gave him a light kiss on the cheek. The other bakers began pounding their dough harder than ever.

They were going to need a lot of loaves, so they took the stone wall around the house and rebuilt it into a huge kiln and began firing it up to have it ready when the dough and been shaped into loaves and was finally prepared for baking.

Several of the bakers kept mixing ingredients and gave her some dough to knead. Then they began forming the dough into loaves. They used up all of their flour and ingredients. Grima watched but could not complain as they moved on to all of her flour and ingredients, using up in one morning her entire year's worth of ingredients.

By the time they had used up all the ingredients and were ready to bake the bread the kiln was hot enough. All of the loaves were shoved inside and they waited.

The bakers continued to stare at Kraka and talk with her. They were so interested in her they neglected to keep watch over the bread and managed to burn all the loaves, and it was too late to make more, and besides they had no more ingredients, so they gathered up the blackened loaves and carried them back to the ship, scrapping off as much of the charred parts as they could along the way.

Onboard the ships the bakers sliced the loaves and passed out pieces. The slices did not look very burnt, but the smoke had worked its way through the dough so they tasted burnt. The army complained loudly about their breakfast, shouting that the bakers should be punished.

Ragnar Lodbrokr called the bakers before him and questioned them, "Why is it you are serving burnt bread to my men? Surely you're capable of so simple a task as baking bread?"

The chief baker stepped forward, "Under ordinary circumstances it's an easy task. However, we had the distraction of the most beautiful woman I've ever seen helping us and none of us could take our eyes off her to properly watch the baking bread."

Ragnar Lodbrokr answered, "She couldn't possibly have been as fair as my late wife Thora Borgarhjort?"

The chief baker, realizing some tact was called for, answered, "No certainly not. But she was as least as fair as our late beloved Queen. And I would venture to say that she is the most beautiful living maiden I have seen." He felt safe referring to her as the most beautiful living maiden until he realized it reminded Ragnar Lodbrokr that his beloved wife was dead and everyone was supposed to be in mourning and not looking at living beautiful women. The chief baker decided it would be best if he could just shut up. Maybe he should sneak out and go back to the kitchen and knead something and be quiet.

Ragnar Lodbrokr motioned for some warriors to approach, "I'll send some of my warriors known to have keen eyes for beauty to look her over. If they report the maiden is as beautiful as you say, then you will suffer no punishment for serving us burnt bread. However, if they determine she is not so fair, then we will have to think of some appropriate punishment."

Ragnar Lodbrokr sent his warriors on their mission with these words, "If she is as lovely as is reported then ask her to come to me so that I might meet her. Use no force to bring her back. I don't want her frightened of me. Although beauty is an asset, I prize intelligence more. So tell her she shall come to me neither naked nor clad, being neither starved nor fed, and neither alone nor in the company of men. If she can meet these requirements then I would desire her for my wife."

The warriors were puzzled by his conditions which made no sense to them meaning they were in no danger of solving the riddle and marrying Ragnar Lodbrokr. Fortunately it was not up to them to puzzle out the riddle. They set off to deliver his message to Kraka.

Grima was the first to see the warriors and feared they had come for meat for dinner and that her herds would be gone by the time they left.

One of the warriors saw Grima and whispered to the warrior next to him, "If that thing is the fairest woman in the land, then this is a land of trolls and our chief baker had best be concerned for his head."

The Captain approached Grima, "Were you helping our bakers bake bread this morning?"

Grima answered, "Yes, I was in the kitchen with them. Have you returned to pay me for the flour and ingredients you used this morning?"

This certainly didn't seem right. The Captain asked, "We were told to look for someone who was fair-haired. Was there another woman in the kitchen with you? Younger, perhaps?"

Grima was relieved the warriors weren't looking for her. She had heard what conquering armies sometimes did to the women. It would be good to put some blame on Kraka, "I apologize for misinforming you. You speak of my daughter Kraka. I'm afraid she was more hindrance than help this morning and I was protecting her. She has taken the cattle to the high field for feeding (and to protect them from thieving bakers, though she did not voice that last part)." She pointed behind their cottage to the high field in the distance.

Captains of armies are frequently given wrong directions by local folk to deceive and tire an army searching for something. He was too smart to be fooled this way again and motioned for Grima to lead them, "It'll be faster if you take us to her. High meadows can be large and we don't have time to hunt for your daughter."

The Captain had been right. Grima had actually pointed to the wrong high field, hoping the warriors would not be able to find her cattle … or her daughter, and after tiring of looking, would return to their ship.

She began leading them off to another meadow to the right of the cottage. "I thought you pointed to the high field behind your cottage? Now we are turning to the right."

Grima didn't want her deceit to cause her harm, "I'm sorry, you must have mistook the direction. My arm is stiff with age and I held it up and pointed it as best I could. I certainly thought I was pointing to the meadow over there to the right." For good effect she held up her arm again and once more pointed to the high field behind the cottage, not to the meadow to the left. "Yes, I can see how you might have been mistaken. I feel as if I'm pointing to my right, yet my arm aims straight forward behind the cottage. It's an easy mistake."

None of this fooled the Captain, but the day was wearing on, "Come on, just lead us to your daughter."

○   ○   ○   ○

A short while later the warriors found Kraka and realized she certainly was as beautiful as the bakers had reported.

The Captain told her the legend of Ragnar Lodbrokr, and that he was interested in having her to wife, but only if she was smart and could solve his riddles.

Grima groaned, all was lost. No telling what the soldiers would do to her and Kraka in the meadow once Kraka answered incorrectly. Her fate was in the hands of her stupid daughter.

Grima noticed Kraka seemed oddly confident as she spoke to the Captain, "I have a fair head for riddles and puzzles and can be quite clever. Therefore I can frequently figure out the cleverness in others. Tell me Ragnar Lodbrokr's riddles."

Kraka's life was hard and anyone who could take her away from her present life would be welcomed. She had no future with Grima or Aki, just a lifetime of drudgery. Grima and Aki had not taught her anything, because they didn't know much. She had not been allowed to go to the village to learn anything, nor had she been apprenticed to learn a trade. They wanted to keep her dumb and ugly so she would have no other options in life but staying with them, doing all the work for them, and taking care of them in their old age. Perfect for Grima and Aki, not so perfect for Kraka.

Kraka, however, was very bright and had figured out a great many things for herself. And she had one great secret she had kept to herself. It was the sort of thing that would have frightened Grima and Aki enough to beat her. She seemed to be able to understand the language of birds, and they seemed to understand her when she spoke, and wanted to help her.

If she was trying to teach herself something and came to an impasse and couldn't figure it out, all she had to do was speak the question out loud, and her words were carried on the winds into forest trees where the question was heard by the birds. The birds flew and sat at gatherings; listened near tradesmen; were schooled at places where lessons were being taught; learned the command and strategies of warriors being trained or in battle; learned from ladies how to act; and most importantly overheard the thoughts of Kings at dinner, and learned how nobility acted, though this final knowledge came to her naturally from her breeding. The birds remembered the overheard knowledge and brought back what they heard to Kraka. Her initial question would always be answered, plus she would learn all the other knowledge the birds brought back and taught her. Thus she was taught knowledge in her youth far greater than she would have learned in the village or as an apprentice.

The Captain repeated Ragnar Lodbrokr's puzzling message, "The maiden I would wed must come to me neither naked nor clad, being neither starved nor fed, and neither alone nor in the company of men. The one who can meet these requirements I will love and accept as my wife, but only if she will have me. I will force no woman to share my life. I want someone wise, who consents, and who loves me as my partner. If she comes to me fulfilling the requirements of my riddle,

but finds she has no desire for me, then I will give her gold and treasure enough to last her the rest of her life, without me. I will only marry out of love and respect."

The message Ragnar Lodbrokr sent had won her over. And she knew how to fulfill the parts of the riddle.

Before Kraka could answer, Grima answered, "How can what you say be done? Everything is contradictory. If she stays here Ragnar Lodbrokr will feel disobeyed and probably have her beautiful head for it (and mine too, and goodness knows what else, she whispered under her breath). If she goes to him without meeting the conditions then he will also be upset. What is she to do? Ragnar Lodbrokr must be mad."

The warriors overlooked the comment about their King's sanity, since many thought the same thing, though more towards his attitude about his future Queen than anything else. If he wanted Kraka then he should just take her. None of this nonsense about being equal partners or figuring out silly riddles. How could that profit a future husband? Men should not marry women who are clever enough to figure out riddles.

The soldiers shrugged their shoulders. They didn't know what the riddle meant or what to do fulfill it, either.

Kraka then spoke, "I've been thinking about the conditions and agree to them. I'll come to Ragnar Lodbrokr's ship tomorrow morning under the conditions he requested."

Everyone was surprised, and none of them could think of anything that could fulfill any part of the riddle, let alone all of it.

Kraka went off by herself. Grima went back to their cottage grateful the warriors had spared her body and her herd, because she was still convinced she knew exactly what warriors really wanted.

The warriors returned to the ship with Kraka's message. Ragnar Lodbrokr seemed pleased to hear it.

o   o   o   o

Kraka arose early the next morning and went outside to her father who was preparing for his morning fishing excursion which was more for the peace of sitting in a boat far away from his wife Grima, than the actual number of fish he managed to catch, which wasn't all that great. She asked for the use of his net. He gave it to her, glad of an excuse to go back to bed for a little bit more sleep and then go out fishing. The extra rest and late start meant he could stay out longer, perhaps all day. Grima had been asleep when he left, perhaps she'd still be asleep and not notice he had returned. Everytime he climbed into bed she seemed to have other things in mind.

Grima had not been roused by Aki leaving that morning or returning to bed. However, upon awakening Grima had other plans for her now sleeping husband who had oddly returned back to bed after saying he was going fishing. He hadn't even bothered to change back into his night clothes. He had just climbed back into bed still wearing his muddy boots. Grima poked at Aki to wake him up, "Get up

you lazy oaf. I'm going to save your life today, though I don't know why I even bother."

Aki sat up. He tried to get up but sat back down drooping over the side of the bed. He was still mostly asleep. He wiped at his eyes. He still had his clothes on from this morning. Maybe he could just rush out to his boat and quickly row away to the middle of the waters and fish and find some peace and calm this morning. It had been entirely too busy for him.

Grima was in no mind to deal with his slowness. "Here's your morning wash and drink all in one." She threw a panful of cold water from the cattle trough on him."

"Wha ...?"

She pulled Aki up and pushed him out the door. "We're going to the village. The crowds of the village are the safest place to be if Kraka disappoints Ragnar Lodbrokr. He can't take his rage out on us if he can't find us."

All Aki could manage as he was pushed along was, "But from what you've said about Kraka having a choice makes him seem a nice enough lad."

Grima answered, "Angry Kings are never nice enough lads. Hurry along."

Being very practical Aki asked, "Did you bring money with you for breakfast or lunch, I'm not really certain what time it is."

This was what she was saddled with for life. She kept pushing Aki along, "Bah ..."

∘ ∘ ∘ ∘

Meanwhile Kraka had begun her preparations. She went back to her room, undressed and wrapped herself in her father's fishing net. Her long golden hair fell about her so that, although naked, she was modestly covered.

Next she chewed on a leek and swallowed the juices so that her hunger was satisfied and she had eaten, yet she had not eaten since she had not swallowed the leek.

Finally, she set off towards the ship, followed by Aki's hunting hound, so that she approached without the company of men, yet not alone.

Ragnar Lodbrokr stood at the prow of the ship and watched as she neared. She was indeed as beautiful as the reports had said. He called out to her, "Who are you and why have you come here?"

She answered, "I have come at a brave King's command, and in the circumstances he has described. Though unclothed, I am not naked; though not fed, I am without hunger; though not in the company of men, yet I do not come alone."

Ragnar Lodbrokr motioned for her to be brought aboard. Yet first she sought assurances from him that she and her dog would be safe and treated honorably, and that she could freely leave whenever she wanted. And she asked to be allowed to step behind some bushes and change into more suitable clothing fearing that just wearing a net in front of sailors long at sea might send the wrong message to them. She could not be certain how protected she would be by Ragnar Lodbrokr. He had been long at sea, too.

Ragnar Lodbrokr agreed, "I give you my word of honor that no harm shall come to you. You shall be treated royally, and with respect, as if you were my own wife, which I wish you will become if you agree after talking with me and learning how I am. After you have changed to more suitable garments my men will help you aboard."

It did not take long for Kraka to change and soon she was standing before Ragnar Lodbrokr. He looked even more handsome in person. He put out his hand to welcome her, but the hound leapt at it and bit him. Immediately two guards pushed Kraka out of the way and set upon the dog, killing it, thereby breaking their promise not to harm her or her dog.

Despite the unpleasantness of this incident, Ragnar Lodbrokr continued to woo Kraka, "I apologize for my men. Theirs was the reaction of warriors protecting their King. It was instinct that did the deed, not an order. Please forgive their actions and give me the honor of your company. You are the fairest maiden I've ever seen. I love you."

Kraka wanted to leave, since part of his promise to her had already been broken, "I wish to leave this ship and return to my parents."

However, Ragnar Lodbrokr persisted, "I offer you my Kingdom and hope you will leave with me."

Kraka refused, "I'll not leave with you this time. And perhaps when you return to these shores you'll no longer want me."

Ragnar Lodbrokr knew what he wanted, but would not use force to get it. He signaled for his treasurer to bring him the chest he kept in his cabin. When this was done he opened it and showed Kraka a beautiful gown woven throughout with strands of fine gold. It had belonged to Borgy. He now offered it to Kraka. "This is my dearest possession. My beloved wife made it with her own hands, and wore it during some of our happiest moments together. I would that you should have it."

Kraka answered, "I cannot accept such a gift. It would not fit in with the way I live. My clothes are old and much torn from chasing lost sheep through thickets, and smell from cleaning out stalls and pig sties. The garment you offer me would not be useful for that. As long as I live with Aki and Grima I'll continue to wear the clothes fitting and useful for that station and be called by the name Kraka. Now let me leave. If on your return to this harbor you still desire to see me, then call again."

Ragnar was puzzled because the dress she wore was almost the equal of the garment he offered her. Perhaps she had borrowed a dress in the village and had forgotten she was not wearing rags.

Ragnar Lodbrokr continued questioning her, "I can see you are of noble birth, and not the true daughter of Aki and Grima. Your piercing eyes give you away. None but a King could have given such eyes to his daughter."

Kraka answered, "I do not have the time to tell you my story now. I'll see you if ever you return."

Ragnar Lodbrokr was impressed with her wisdom and sent for another chest of gold that he gave her. Reluctantly he let her leave the ship and return to her home. He sent an escort to carry the chest of gold back for her.

When the escort returned he ordered his ships to sea and they continued on their way.

○   ○   ○   ○

It was a year before they once more put to port at Spangareid. Kraka's image had grown in Ragnar Lodbrokr's mind. Though he had seen many women during the year, none of them interested him. None came close to Kraka's beauty or intelligence. Ragnar Lodbrokr was more in love with Kraka than ever since his thoughts had only been of her for the last year.

Once moored in port he sent messengers to find her and tell her he still wanted her as his wife. They returned to the ship with the message that she could not come to him before the next morning. Ragnar Lodbrokr spent a restless night waiting for the sun to rise and the light of his life to arrive.

Kraka rose at dawn. She took the only remembrance she had of Heimir, the ring Andvaranautr and put it in her pocket. Then she went to Aki and Grim'as room and knocked softly at their door, asking if she could come in. Grima opened the door. Kraka entered and sat at the foot of their bed. "What is it you want?" asked Grima who tried to smile at Kraka, but, as usual, it looked more like a snarl, which was the best Grima could do. She had not had much practice smiling in her life.

Both Aki and Grima had been kinder to Kraka in the last year, the result of the chest of gold she had returned with from her visit with Ragnar Lodbrokr. They had taken it from Kraka, though she had not seemed interested in it. They had never questioned what she had had to do that pleased Ragnar Lodbrokr so much that he had given her enough gold to make them the wealthiest family in Spangareid, though they had hoarded the gold rather than spend it. They just knew she had somehow figured out the riddle and gone off to marry Ragnar Lodbrokr, but had returned unmarried with a chest of gold instead. And Aki's dog had disappeared.

Kraka answered Grima in a manner she had never used with them before, "I'll be leaving this morning to go with Ragnar Lodbrokr. I can no longer live here. Although I was only three when it happened, I can remember the murder of my dear grandfather Heimir quite well. I would be within my rights to demand Ragnar Lodbrokr seek vengeance against you on my behalf…"

Grima reached for Aki, terrified. Her hand landed on his pillow. Aki was now under the covers seeking that threadbare protection.

Kraka continued, "…but I won't. Instead I'll leave you with the hopes that as each day my happiness with Ragnar Lodbrokr increases, the ill luck attendant on you two will worsen. This day is the best your life will ever be. Henceforth things will begin going badly for you."

She left Grima and Aki clutching at each other, trembling. And she took the chest of gold from under the bed with her.

Aki blamed his wife, "If only you hadn't let that stranger in so many years ago. Look at the trouble that visitor has brought us. I warned you against being friendly. And I told you instead of hoarding the gold and sleeping over it, we should have bought things with it—land, houses, property, cattle, businesses. Now we are worse off than before because we have no daughter to take care of us."

For once Grima was silent.

And so it continued that their lives were cursed ever after in punishment for the foul dishonorable deed they had wrought so many years before. The Norns have ways of evening up lives and righting wrongs eventually; good always brings good, and evil always brings evil. Be careful how you live your life.

○   ○   ○   ○

Kraka proceeded to Ragnar Lodbrokr's ship where she was welcomed with great honor. She returned the chest of gold to him in the same amount he had given her. This had not been necessary, but impressed him nonetheless.

Once she was safely onboard Ragnar Lodbrokr ordered his ships to set sail immediately, lest Kraka change her mind and leave, although he did not offer this as a reason.

The wind was strong and had pushed them far from Spangareid by the evening. They weighed anchor in open sea until the morning. Ragnar Lodbrokr approached Kraka and offered to share a bed with her, "We'll soon be husband and wife, would it be so wrong for you to stay with me now?"

Kraka refused, "I've kept my virtue out of honor to my heritage all these years. We must wait until we are properly married, especially for the sake of any children we might have."

Ragnar Lodbrokr was pleased to hear this and honored her request. They slept chastely apart during the voyage.

When they neared his Kingdom, Ragnar Lodbrokr sent a smaller, faster boat ahead to organize their return welcome and see that all the preparations for their wedding feast were done. That same night they put to shore. Everything had been prepared. The feast was held and the two were married. They exchanged rings and thus the Andvaranautr found its way to Ragnar Lodbrokr. There was much rejoicing throughout the Kingdom.

That night they retired to one bed and Ragnar Lodbrokr began caressing and kissing his wife. She gently pushed him away saying, "For the sake of the son we will have, be patient. I sometimes have the gift of prophecy and see that great harm will follow our son all the days of his life if he is conceived tonight. Wait but three days and he will lead a wondrous life."

Ragnar Lodbrokr had always tried to be gentle with the women in his life, but this was asking too much. His wife had died more than a year ago, and he had been faithful to her memory, even privately faithful by himself. Meeting Kraka had aroused strong desires in him. He had honored Kraka's wishes throughout their sea journey, however, now she was his wife and he could wait no longer, "I know you are new to this sort of thing, but there is nothing to be frightened of. No more excuses. I love you very much and will be gentle with you." He had his way with her, and their son was conceived three days too early for his wyrd.

The Norns looked down on the couple and began weaving the threads that would make up the tapestry telling the story of their son's difficult life. They shook their heads as they began the task. Had Ragnar Lodbrokr only been able to control himself for three days. Skuldr put away the golden silken thread she had set aside for Kraka and Ragnar Lodbrokr's son's tapestry, and pulled out the few she had started on in advance. She reached for the black knobby thread made from coarse spinning. Such was the thread that would spin his life's story.

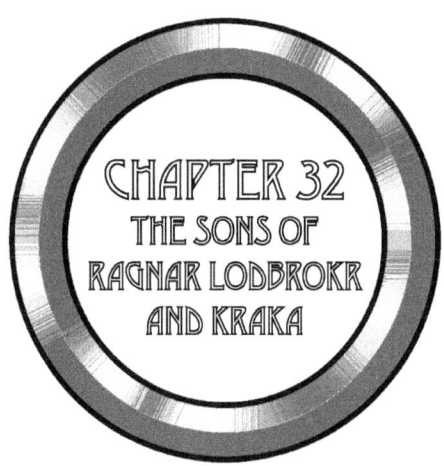

CHAPTER 32
THE SONS OF RAGNAR LODBROKR AND KRAKA

Ragnar Lodbrokr and Kraka lived together quite happily, and their love deepened over time. Yet Ragnar Lodbrokr never had the all-consuming passionate love for Kraka that he had had for Thora Borgarhjort and frequently brooded on this. It should have been enough that he had found passion twice, but it wasn't.

Soon it came about that Kraka was with child. Kraka knew the child would not be born whole because Ragnar Lodbrokr had ignored her warnings on their wedding night. And in time her premonition proved true. The midwife attending Kraka stepped back as she delivered the child. His body bent and flopped every which way in her hands. Babies in general are very supple. Their legs and arms bow, their heads loll backwards. This was true on Ragnar Lodbrokr and Kraka's newborn son, only more so for he had been born with no bones, just cartilage and gristle where bones should have been. Thus he was named Ivar Lackbones. No one expected him to survive, but he did. Kraka loved him, while Ragnar Lodbrokr was known to shun him.

Despite his handicap he grew strong and healthy over the years, and was very handsome. He compensated for his lack of locomotion by becoming very shrewd. Except for the fact he had to be carried about, it was impossible to tell by looking at him that he was incomplete because his muscles had given him a powerful-looking build.

Eventually Kraka bore Ragnar Lodbrokr three more sons. Their second son had been born strong and healthy and had been named Bjorn Jarnsida, which meant Bjorn Ironside. He was so strong it was as if he had also been given his elder brother's strength in addition to his own. Their third and fourth sons were called Hvitsarkr, which meant white sark, and Rognvaldr, which meant King's Counselor. These three sons grew up bold and strong. Yet they weren't as cunning as Ivar Lackbones whom they looked to for advice. They carried him about with them and followed his counsel in all things.

During this time Eric and Agnar, Ragnar Lodbrokr's two sons by his marriage to Thora Borgarhjort, had grown strong and skilled in warrior ways. They had already gathered their own army and gone warring and had defeated many other Princes, gaining much renown in the world.

Ragnar Lodbrokr's second set of sons felt somewhat jealous of Eric and Agnar's accomplishments. Ivar Lackbones was soon urging his brothers to gather an army together so they might win even greater fame than their half-brothers. He met with them in counsel, "It's not right that our older brothers gain all the glory for themselves. We are four in number, and far better than they. It's time we raise an army and begin claiming lands of our own."

Hvitsarkr answered, "We await your counsel. Tell us what to do and we shall do it."

Ivar Lackbones had been making plans for a long time now, and directed them with specific orders, "Very well. Here are the plans I've drawn up for three ships. See they are built exactly to my specifications. They'll be the strongest, fastest ships ever built. All three will hold several armies of men, yet ride so high in the water they will skim across the top with very little effort. Go to our father and ask his help in building them. His are the best shipwrights in the land. Also use his help in purchasing our provisions and conscripting several armies of men for our service. Make no mention of my name to remind him of the shame he carries for having an eldest son such as I. When the time comes to leave I will ride with one of you."

So the three brothers went to their father and made their requests that he gladly granted, "I'm happy to see you're taking up warrior ways. I've seen you so often in the company of Ivar Lackbones that I was beginning to think you were becoming womanly and bookish like him. That's not right for a man. You must be strong and take what you want. Ivar Lackbones always talks too much."

Bjorn Jarnsida answered, since he was Ragnar Lodbrokr's favorite, "You're right, father. We want to go out in the world and claim more glory for our family. Perhaps some day we'll be as well thought of as the Volsungrs themselves." Bjorn Jarnsida spoke these words not realizing he was a Volsungr, the grandson of Sigurdr and Brynhildr. He continued, "Here are the plans we've had drawn up for the ships."

Ragnar Lodbrokr took the sheets, looked them over and was impressed. When and where had his sons gained the knowledge to design ships?

After going over the plans with his shipwrights he sent for Bjorn Jarnsida, "My shipwrights have told me these are the strangest ship's plans they've ever seen. Each ship has its own unique features. If the projections on them are accurate they'll be the greatest ships ever built. I'm surprised my shipwrights haven't been this inventive before."

Ragnar Lodbrokr was as good as his word and soon his sons were captaining the three best ships ever built. Unbeknownst to their father, Ivar Lackbones traveled with them and directed all their moves and planned the strategies for their battles.

It was not long before Ragnar Lodbrokr's sons had won great fame and wealth in their own names. Greater renown attached to them than their older brothers,

Eric and Agnar, and even their own father. Many feared to stand against them and surrendered at their approach.

○ ○ ○ ○

Ivar Lackbones was becoming bored with the ease of their victories and longed for more excitement. He called his brothers together and told them his plan, "I long to see more fighting. Right now I would derive more pleasure watching a shepherd herd his sheep down a mountainside than the battles we've been fighting. I've heard of one King who'll stand against us and give us a real battle again."

His three brothers had grown somewhat lazy with easy victories, but had vowed always to follow Ivar Lackbones' advice, since it was his advice that had made them.

Rognvaldr questioned Ivar Lackbones, "Who is this King? Where shall we find someone brave enough to stand up against us? Our reputation has grown greater than our acts and far outshines our deeds. Where is there such a one who is not frightened to stand before us in battle array?"

Ivar Lackbones answered, "He rules in the land called Whitby."

Hvitsarkr interrupted, "I've heard of that land. It's a country left to itself. It is said the people there worship the old gods and make sacrifices of their own kin, lacking strangers to cut apart."

Ivar Lackbones continued, "You're right. It's a vile land that is shunned by others for fear of the uncivilized fate that might await them. Those brave enough to set out against them have never been victorious. Of the few who have lived to tell their story, they've lost their senses so their reports are barely credible. If their accounts are true it's no wonder they are mad having seen mad deeds."

Rognvaldr seemed upset at the prospect of fighting against the people of Whitby, "There are powers greater than what we know. Perhaps these people will use sorcery and necromancy against us?

Bjorn Jarnsida was more practical, "Only moments ago, Rognvaldr, you were saying how others were afraid to go against us because of our reputation. Is that not your attitude against Whitby? They are only men, and men can be run through with knife, sword, or spear." He thrust his arm downward to emphasize his point. The gesture did not impress Rognvaldr who still seemed dubious.

Rognvaldr answered, "What good will swords do when confronted with the dark arts? How can a knife, sword, or spear cut through a curse?"

Bjorn Jarnsida and Rognvaldr had no answer to Rognvaldr's questions, so they ignored it.

Ivar Lackbones continued, "Bjorn Jarnsida is right. I discount the magical aspects of their reputation and rely on the reports I have of their armaments. The King has a large, well trained army. However, their techniques of fighting are old-fashioned. They won't be a match for our army, though they outnumber us five men to one. Our main problem will be gaining entry to their land. It is set upon a mountain so they have the advantage of terrain for their protection. As the saying goes the victory of a bear over a shark, or a shark over a bear, depends entirely on the terrain. We'll be going against a greater force in number, and attacking them

from below. Without the strategy I've worked out this would seem to be a hopeless, foolish task."

Bjorn Jarnsida supported Ivar Lackbones' vision, "The prize that awaits us in the magnificent temple atop the mountain will be worth the fight. I've heard the temple is filled with gold enough to be the equal of the Volsungr Treasure and Andvari's Hoard combined."

Rognvaldr interjected, "Why should we risk our forces when your reports are based on the ravings of madmen. I'm against this venture."

Hvitsarkr taunted his brother, "Are you afraid of the carved statues they worship? I can tell you here and now I will double their deities when my sword cleaves in two any gods they might have."

Rognvaldr responded, "Then you only double their religious fervor by insulting their gods. Statues may be destroyed, but ideas linger. Insults to gods linger. They are never forgotten. A conquered people may not mention their gods out loud, but they are never forgotten and their names and ideas are passed down to the next generation and the generation after that. And when your rule is weakened those gods will rise up and destroy you. In short order the people will be worshipping those gods with a fervor that will surprise you. You'll wonder how it could be they all of a sudden remember their old gods. The thing is, they never forgot. They just didn't mention them around you. People don't forget their gods or their religion. If necessary they keep them behind closed doors waiting for an opportunity to worship openingly. And that opportunity always comes at the usurper's expense. Support your enemy's religion in the open, plot against it in private."

So it was decided by majority vote they would go up against the land of Whitby.

o   o   o   o

It took a few weeks to re-outfit their ships for the lands and environs of Whitby after which they and set sail once more. They had had no trouble conscripting men to fill out their army. Men fought for the glory of going to battle with the sons of Ragnar Lodbrokr. It was a sure way to wealth and honor, if you lived through the battles and returned home safe and in one piece, rather than pieces.

It took them less than a week to reach Whitby. After landing at Gnipefjord. Ivar Lackbones gave Rognvaldr the duty of guarding the ships with a small contingent of the army while the rest of them went ashore. He knew his younger brother had no liking for the place and didn't want to engage in battle. A man in that mind is sure to be plucked up by the Valkyries. He watched as Rognvaldr went below deck.

Ivar Lackbones was placed at the rail of the ship so all the men on shore in front of him could see and hear his words before they set off to battle. Ivar Lackbones warned the army, "This is a land of some enchantment. We don't yet know how much. The folk here worship cows and depend on them for protection. I've heard tell the King has in his command two troll cows. They moo with a low rumbling sound that sets many men running in fright and madness. Be forewarned and forearmed of this and stuff something in your ears so the sound is muffled, though you may still feel the rumblings in your bodies. You'll find it far less frightening.

The sound is too great to be entirely blocked out. Stand firm and strong and we'll be victorious. Right is on our side." Unfortunately Rognvaldr being below deck in the ship never heard his brother's so, so important livesaving advice.

o   o   o   o

Ivar Lackbones was borne aloft on a shield at the forefront of the army, leading his men. As soon as they approached the town they were surprised to see the gates guarding the outer perimeter were being opened.

One of the soldiers yelled out, "Perhaps we've been misinformed and the people of Whitby are as frightened of us as everyone else is?"

Another one yelled, "Look the town is opening its doors and surrendering to us without even loosing an arrow."

Another soldier yelled, "They welcome us in our victory."

Ivar Lackbones was suspicious and yelled to his army, "Do not claim victory until you've won it. Do not act victorious until your enemy's weapons are in a pile before you, and your enemies are kneeling down, heads bowing, pledging allegiance to you and awaiting your instructions."

His men thought Ivar Lackbones was being overly cautious. Then something happened to convince them Ivar Lackbones was right.

What was loosed at them was even worse than they imagined. By now the huge gates to the town were fully drawn back. At first they heard a faint lowing that soon grew to a great noise. Coming towards them were the two troll cows that towered over them. The army stood frightened, unable to move. Ivar Lackbones shouted for someone to hand him his bow. Ivar had the eye to aim more accurately than any of his men, but lacked the strength to send the arrow along its path. Another warrior stood behind him holding one of Ivar Lackbones' hands to the bow, and the other to an arrow notched against the oxen sinew that made up the string. The arrow was loosed and he felled each cow with a single silver-tipped arrow, hitting them each between their eyes.

The Whitby army came streaming out of the town towards them. Soon both sides were engaged in a fierce hand-to-hand battle. However, Ivar Lackbones' men were the better fighters. Gradually they made their way towards the town, until the fighting was within the fortified gates of the city. The townspeople had been so confident of the two troll cows that they hadn't closed the city gates.

Back onboard ship Rognvaldr heard the mooing of the cows and was ashamed he had been too frightened to go into battle. He and most of the men guarding the ships ran to the battle and were soon in the thick of things. Unfortunately, the fear in him had dulled Rognvaldr's warrior skills. He knew his time had come and he fell heroically in battle outside the city.

Inside the city the brothers' army was gaining the victory. Soon the people of Whitby fled, leaving the city to its conquerors.

Ivar Lackbones yelled instructions to the army over the tumult of victory, "Carry whatever treasures there are back to our ships, then burn the town and break

down these walls. We'll have nothing to fear from Whitby again. Dig barrows for our dead and bury them with honor."

While this was taking place he met in counsel with Bjorn Jarnsida and Hvitsarkr. The meeting lasted long into the night. While it was going on word was brought to them that Rognvaldr's body had been found on the battlefield. The three remaining brothers went to it and prepared it with great honor. They had a large barrow constructed and placed their brother's body inside. Then they covered the barrow with stones to show everyone a noble warrior rested there.

A warrior who had been a stonemason set about carving a rune stone to set at Rognvaldr's barrow. It told of Rognvaldr's glorious life and victories in battle. It ended with an account of his valorous fight against the warriors of Whitby and their strange gods.

The brothers and their army left the land of Whitby and returned home having gained great honor and wealth beyond all imagining, but also having lost their youngest brother.

CHAPTER 33
RAGNAR LODBROKR
GOES
ADVENTURING
AGAIN

At this time King Eystein was the King of Sweden. He ruled from his great Eusteing Hall in Uppsala. Many found him cold and hard. Nonetheless, he was just and ruled wisely. His daughter Ingeborg was thought to be one of the most beautiful women in all the known lands. She was barely twenty and not yet betrothed. Many Kings and Princes paid suit to her, but she did not look with favor on any of them.

King Eystein was a devout worshipper of the old gods, eagerly offering sacrifices to propitiate them. The people under his rule followed his example and altars flowed redder in his Kingdom than in any other.

The object of all this worship was a sacred cow named Sibilja. It was her nature to bellow loudly until she was sated with a sacrifice made in her honor. Her mooing could shake mountains, and was certainly loudly uncomfortable to hear. So the people were always offering sacrifices in order to have some peace and quiet.

King Eystein also used Sibilja with good effect against opposing armies. He'd set her against them, mooing and charging at his enemies. As with the two troll cows of Whitby, the dark magic of Sibilja's mooing caused warriors to lose their senses and fight against each other in a confused frenzy. This reputation spread throughout all the lands so Sweden was very rarely attacked from outside.

Other Kings and Princes knew they could travel in safety to King Eystein's Hall using only a small escort. There they were treated with respect and hospitality. Their plates were never empty; their horns were always brimming to the top with strongly brewed mead; and afterwards when retiring to their rooms they seldom found empty beds. King Eystein found many ways to entertain his visiting guests.

King Eystein was a popular host and made friends with any visiting warriors, so he had little need of Sibilja's services. She roamed her pasture, attending to the sacrifices given her, licking at a salt block, and growing fat with inactivity. She much preferred this than to harrying about on a battlefield where people were throwing rocks and propelling sharp things at her, or hewing at her with long swords. These weapons did no harm to her. As a nuisance they were distracting, much like a flea biting at a bear.

King Eystein's best friend over the years had become King Ragnar Lodbrokr. They spent alternate summers in each other's Kingdoms. This year it was Ragnar Lodbrokr's turn to visit King Eystein.

Before leaving Ragnar Lodbrokr went to Kraka and gave her the Andvaranautr, "I think you should keep this ring in safekeeping. I'm going on a long journey and want to make certain I don't lose it."

Kraka accepted the ring but was puzzled why he wanted to give it back. He had often gone on long journeys without returning Andvaranautr to her. Maybe he didn't want people at King Eystein's to see the ring.

o o o o

Ragnar Lodbrokr and his men arrived at Eusteing Hall where King Eystein welcomed them, "Rest this morning and afternoon. You and your men should eat only a little because I'm having a huge feast and celebration in your honor this evening in the great Hall. It will honor our long and enduring friendship as well as celebrate the battles our armies have won."

Ragnar Lodbrokr's men cheered this news. They had only had hard tack to eat on their journey and were ready for a real feast.

o o o o

That evening with their armies intermingled in the great Hall, King Eystein looked at Ragnar Lodbrokr, and raised his goblet to toast his friend, "Though we've fought each other's friends and enemies, we've never fought each other. A King has never had a truer friend than you. I proclaim to everyone here, Ragnar Lodbrokr is as a son to me."

Ragnar Lodbrokr, seated in a place of honor to the right of the King, answered the toast, "And you are as a father to me. I would lay down my life in your service if need be."

The evening wore on with the mead never ceasing to flow. Ingeborg attended only her father and Ragnar Lodbrokr. It was whispered at the tables that Ingeborg seemed to be paying particular attention to Ragnar Lodbrokr, and he seemed to be paying particular attention to her. Wasn't he married? But of course such things could be arranged. Distance often puts marriage out of mind, or makes men forget it entirely as something merely inconvenient.

The talk at King Eystein's table was along the same lines. Ragnar Lodbrokr looked at Ingeborg, now seated to the left of the King and spoke quietly to the King, "I'm much taken with your daughter and would wish to marry her."

Ragnar Lodbrokr's liegeman, seated to his right overheard and whispered in Ragnar Lodbrokr's ear, "Sir, don't forget you are already wedded to Kraka in a good marriage. She is a fine woman and the mother of your sons. You were lucky to find her."

King Eystein heard the soldier and nodded, disappointed.

Ragnar Lodbrokr found this reminder upsetting. He once again spoke to King Eystein, "I would be willing to put away Kraka as my wife if I had the promise of Ingeborg's hand. It's true I love Kraka and she has born me Ivar Lackbones and three strong sons, Bjorn Jarnsida, Hvitsarkr, and Rognvaldr. Though our youngest, Rognvaldr, has recently found glory and legend in his final battle. He died a brave and honorable death at the Battle of Whitby.

However, Kraka was born of a lowly station. I rescued her from her life of misery, and no doubt she is grateful for that deed and will gladly step aside when I tell her I love Ingeborg. I'm a King and great warrior. It's only fitting I am wedded to another King's daughter, not the daughter of peasants. I want to have truly royal children to pass my lands on to."

King Eystein wanted nothing better than to have Ragnar Lodbrokr as his son-in-law, "It would be an honor to have you really be a part of my family. I agree to your proposition. And, as you can see, Ingeborg also agrees. I think she has loved you secretly for a long time."

The feasting continued more merrily than ever throughout the night. The final arrangements were made. The couple would be betrothed immediately, however, the wedding would not take place until Ragnar Lodbrokr had settled things with Kraka.

○   ○   ○   ○

The journey home was uneventful. The wind was not so friendly as it had been on the outward journey, instead blowing against them as often as it blew with them. Ragnar Lodbrokr took this as a sign he should return to King Eystein and marry Ingeborg immediately. His counselors disagreed, pointing out he could not do this with any honor until he had made some sort of settlement with Kraka. That is if Kraka would agree to a settlement. She didn't have to because he was the party in the wrong. She was the wronged party.

His ships finally reached safe harbor and were anchored securely. The rest of the journey lay through the forest. When they came to the first clearing where he and his men would part, Ragnar Lodbrokr warned his men to hold his secret engagement to Ingeborg amongst themselves, "Kraka must not know what has happened at King Eystein's. I'll put her away first. Soon we'll be sailing once more to Eusteing Hall, this time for a wedding celebration, so that I might meet and wed my beloved Ingeborg. You've seen and helped yourself to all the foods, mead, and pleasures of his regular celebrations. You can only imagine what a wedding feast will be like for you. If you tell of my engagement you will not see such a feast in your life, or any other feast thereafter. If Kraka finds out word of this before I've had a chance to tell her, I'll have all your lives. We are the only ones who know and she can only learn it from one of us. Guard this secret well. Guard your lives well. Idle chatter could be your undoing. Confide not in your loved ones, mistresses, or wife, and you'll have nothing to worry about."

Ragnar Lodbrokr did not see the three birds that flew off from a nearby tree branch. They understood human speech and had overheard everything. Kraka had often fed them in the winter and given them warmth in her room from the fierce winter, and had even mended a broken wing on one of the birds. Now it was their turn to help her. They flew to her window and cheeped and pecked at it until she opened the window and let them in. She had some licorice handy and fed it to them. They fluttered about delighted in the treat, all but forgetting their message. Then one of them remembered why they had come. Kraka was surprised to hear one of the birds speaking to her in a strong, though high-pitched, clear voice, "Beware Kraka. Ragnar Lodbrokr has agreed to marry Ingeborg and put you away." The three grabbed greedily at the last of the licorice, clutched the strands in their claws and flew out the window.

Kraka sat down trying to think what to do.

In the meantime Ragnar Lodbrokr and his men had parted company. They each went their separate ways, returning to their own homes. Many feasts were held that night throughout the Kingdom in honor of the returning warriors.

o   o   o   o

Ragnar Lodbrokr had not immediately gone to Kraka's chamber after his return. Instead he sat upon the throne in his throneroom thinking of ways to deal with the situation. He didn't hear Kraka approaching and was startled when she spoke, "How has your journey been? I hope King Eystein is as well as ever?" She embraced and kissed him and continued, "I have come to return the Andvaranatur to you. I have kept it safe while you were away and slept with it on a chain around my neck to remind me of you. Why do you seem so distant?"

Ragnar Lodbrokr did not answer. He took the ring and left the throneroom and went to his own chamber. Kraka followed after him and again asked him about his trip, "I'm interested to know how things went? Was there much feasting? What did you do?"

Ragnar Lodbrokr finally answered, "I'm weary and tired from traveling. I'd like to get some sleep now. Perhaps we could talk tomorrow? Although, there isn't really much to say. My visits to King Eystein are much like his visits here. There were delicious dinners to eat and excellent conversation."

Kraka was clearly becoming infuriated, "Then perhaps I could tell you some things I've heard lately. I've heard of a great King who is married and has several children, yet the strangest thing is he has become engaged to another King's daughter? How would you explain a man doing such an odd thing?"

Ragnar Lodbrokr whirled around and grabbed Kraka by the shoulders and shook her, "Who told you such things? I'll kill him."

Kraka answered, pulling out of Ragnar Lodbrokr's grip, "Don't blame your men. No one has betrayed you. You should have greater care when discussing private matters in the forest. You never can be certain who's listening. Earlier in our forest when you talked of these things with your men you didn't pay attention to the three birds roosting in a tree branch overhead. They flew here and warned me of your intentions."

Ragnar Lodbrokr remembered Kraka's childhood stories how she could understand and communicate with birds, and it was birds that had educated her. He made note to keep his counsel, or at least whisper when he plotted and there were birds around. Maybe best to shoo the birds away, or shoot them full of arrows and also gain a meal.

Kraka continued, "I had hoped it wasn't true and perhaps they had misunderstood your speech. But I can see by your reaction it is true."

Ragnar Lodbrokr backed away and sat down on the bed. Kraka continued, "You're disappointed in my lineage. It's now time I tell you the truth. Remember when you said you thought I was more nobly born than my father and mother? You were right. I was a young child come into their care by sad circumstances. They are only my foster-parents. I'm sure you've heard of my real mother and father. They were none other than Sigurdr Fafnirsbani and Brynhildr. My real name is Aslaugr."

Ragnar Lodbrokr scoffed at this, smiling as he answered, "You haven't been out enough lately, Kraka. The lonely life you lead has caused you to invent a great parentage for yourself so you might feel worthy of the position you presently hold. If you were truly the daughter of Sigurdr Fafnirsbani and Brynhildr, why were you left with two such ignorant peasants? Why are you called Kraka, such an inelegant name for one of such glorious ancestors. I think you've become addled by jealousy."

Kraka continued, "I can't prove what I've said, other than to tell you I shall bear you a son, Sigurdr and Brynhildr's grandson, as are all our other children. He will be a great warrior, such as his grandfather was. For proof I tell you he will be born with the sign of a serpent curled around his eye, proving he is truly Sigurdr Fafnirsbani's grandson."

Ragnar Lodbrokr found this unbelievable, "How would you know such a thing?"

Turning to leave the chamber, she added one final remark, "If what I've said comes to pass then you must promise me you will not take King Eystein's daughter as your wife. If we are daughtered, or our son is free of the serpent blemish, then I will peacefully agree to a dissolution of our marriage. However, if these things are true, I ask only one thing, that our child be named in honor of his grandfather." She left Ragnar Lodbrokr to think on all she had said. The next morning he sent word to her that he agreed to her proposition.

∘ ∘ ∘ ∘

Her time soon came and she was delivered of a healthy baby boy. After looking at her son she ordered a serving woman to take the child to Ragnar Lodbrokr, who was waiting anxiously in the throneroom, attended by many of the most important men and women of the Kingdom.

The serving woman approached the King and laid the child, swaddled in blankets, in his lap. Ragnar Lodbrokr pulled back the blanket, lifting it from his son's face. He gasped, and then spoke, now referring to his wife by her real name, "The words Aslaugr, formerly known as Kraka, and the daughter of Sigurdr Fafnirsbani and Brynhildr, spoke to me were true. Here is my son, the grandson of Sigurdr

Fafnirsbani and Brynhildr." There was a murmuring in the Hall as Aslaugr's true identity was revealed. Ragnar Lodbrokr continued his speech, "My son bears the mark of a serpent coiled around his eye, and because of this he will be called Sigurdr Snake-in-the-Eye. He will be a great warrior." Then speaking to his son, he added, "As your name gift I give you this ring from my finger." He put the Andvaranautr ring on his son's finger..

Sigurdr Snake-in-the-Eye was merely a baby and did not understand the importance of what his father was doing and began squirming and wriggling in his father's arms. He managed to twist onto his stomach as the ring was offered to him. Ragnar Lodbrokr took this as an insult, but continued speaking, "Keen of vision and of a selfless nature is the grandson of Brynhildr and great-grandson of King Budli. Brave and bold is the grandson of Sigurdr Fafnirsbani, and great-grandson of Sigmundr. The blood of the Volsungrs and Odin flows through his veins more than the blood of my own family. He will bring honor to the name he bears. He is proof that the serpent Fafnir has been bested by his family and that a hero's lot is his.

Ragnar Lodbrokr finally managed to slip the Andvaranautr from Andvari's Hoard onto his son's finger. As usually the ring contracted to a size appropriate to Sigurdr Snake-in-the-Eye's finger, "I give him this ring for he is the proper heir to the Volsungr Treasure and Andvari's Hoard.

His other sons watched as he gave away their rights to the throne to a newborn baby.

o o o o

Later while changing his diaper, Aslaugr slipped the Andvarautr ring from Sigurdr Snake-in-the-Eye's finger. Such rings were not meant for babies. Ragnar Lodbrokr seldom had anything domestic to do with his children, so he never noticed his son no longer wore the Andvaranautr ring. But for Sigurdr Snake-in-the-Eye it was the best thing that could have happened to him.

CHAPTER 34
PREPARATIONS FOR THE BATTLE AGAINST KING EYSTEIN

Ragnar Lodbrokr was true to his oath with Aslaugr and decided not to divorce her or return to Sweden for Ingeborg's hand in marriage. He hesitated telling King Eystein. Yet, something had to be done. The date on which he and King Eystein had agreed he would return and claim Ingeborg's hand in marriage was fast approaching. Trying to pretend calendars didn't exist was futile.

Ragnar Lodbrokr was less than honorable. He sent word to King Eystein of his reconciliation with Aslaugr, explaining because of this he would be unable to marry his daughter, Ingeborg, but hoped King Eystein would understand what a predicament he had put himself in. Ragnar Lodbrokr truly thought this was the honorable thing to do and King Eystein would understand based on their long friendship. He didn't even comprehend how cold his message was and how insulting it was to Ingeborg.

King Eystein took the news very badly. He did not understand. All he knew was publicly he had accepted Ragnar Lodbrokr as his future son-in-law and his daughter was hurt and spending all her time in her room crying. His family had been given a great insult. He sent word back to Ragnar Lodbrokr they were no longer friends and he could never expect safe passage in Sweden again.

Eric, Ragnar Lodbrokr's eldest son, and Agnar, his youngest from his marriage to Thora Borgarhjort, learned of King Eystein's message and took it as a personal insult and a challenge to them. They met in council.

Eric, as the eldest, spoke first, "We've always been free to roam throughout Sweden. We've never harmed the people there, nor given them any cause to fear us. Why should we be banned? If King Eystein decides to put restrictions on our freedom to travel the world and go adventuring, then it's up to us to teach him he has no authority over the Princes of another land." Eric, of course ignored the fact the other land was King Eystein's and the restrictions only extended to his borders. Their father, Ragnar Lodbrokr, put similar restrictions on several foreign warriors who were not allowed to travel through his Kingdom.

Agnar agreed with his brother, "Between the two of us we have many followers who are as yet unproven in battle and long for the sight of blood and the glory and wealth victories can bring."

The two brothers dispatched messengers throughout their father's Kingdom for warriors who might want to gain glory and honor in brave combat to join their army. Many heeded the call and came to Ragnar Lodbrokr's Hall. While the warriors were being outfitted and drilled in warrior ways, Eric and Agnar commissioned the building of two warships, one for each of them.

○ ○ ○ ○

At last all the preparations were made and everyone had assembled at the port's edge for the two ship's launchings from parallel platforms. Eric's ship was launched first. It rolled majestically down the rollers and into the sea, listed side to side, and finally gained its balance and floated off.

Then Agnar's ship was prepared for launch. A man standing at the bow, working unseen by those on the launching platform was unfastening some ropes holding the ship fast on the railings. The guiding ropes at the stern of the ship were released. Nothing held the ship back so it began rolling forward, first pinning the sailor in front of the rollers, and then crushing him beneath it as it rolled over him. His screams had been drowned out by the sound of the ship's movement down the rollers. Everyone assembled was shocked to see the launching rollers red with blood as the ship made its way to the sea.

A seeress ran up to the brothers giving them fair warning with her prophecy, "The reddened rollers are an ill omen. Nothing good will come of your journey. Don't leave the safety of this land at this time since the moment is not right for you to win victories in battle."

There was a murmuring in the crowd as her warning was repeated, rolling back through the crowd. Many voices were in agreement with her and began yelling for Eric and Agnar to postpone their journey.

A voice sounded faintly from the back, "Why must you start your journey today? Wait a week, or until the omens are better."

A second voice yelled out, "You are our bravest warriors. Wait a week so we will not lose you."

Another voice added, "Why the haste? Revenge loses nothing by simmering a bit. It even improves with the waiting. Wait until the seeress says it is safe."

Voice after voice yelled for them to delay their journey. None of the voices urged them to start the journey that day, except for one. It was from a stranger wearing a spotted, hooded cloak, the cowl of which he pulled back to reveal a broad-brimmed hat pulled low over his forehead to hide his missing right eye. The stranger was barefoot, but wore skintight knit leggings laced at the knee. "You can only gain glory by doing valiant deeds. Delay is for cowards. Stay if you are afraid to go. However, if you seek glory, make haste and begin your journey."

The seeress spoke once more, "Heed the omens. Ill portends this journey if you begin it today. Wait just a week more. Do not listen to a lone voice yelling in the crowd. He might have his own reasons to spur you to leave. Even Odin has been known to give victory to the lesser combatants so he can gain more mighty warriors for Valhalla. Even Odin has urged battles on his favorites that were woven against by the Norns. Wait one week more and your names and your warrior's names will be sung of by the greatest skalds. You will be legends."

Eric pushed the seeress aside and yelled out to the crowd, "I'll pay no heed to the ramblings of an old woman who has never even seen the glory of battle. I'm as strong as I ever was, my reflexes just as quick. My men are well trained and strong. I'll not put off our adventuring because one man was careless and neglected to get out of the way of a ship. The only one here giving me advice to start this journey is the only one of you who looks as if he's a mighty warrior and has flung a spear in battle. His is the advice I will take. His encouragement is all I need."

Agnar agreed, "My brother is right. We've never been bested in battle, and are stronger now than ever before. Those of you who are too afraid to come with us can stay home and listen to this old woman. Those of you who lust after killing, have a desire for gold, and the other pleasures of war, can follow us."

Eric looked in the direction of the mighty warrior, "You, sir, join us and I will make you First Mate to me and our brother and give you great honors for daring to oppose this crowd."

Eric and Agnar looked on air for the mighty stranger was gone, though none could remember seeing him leave. His words and that he had been there at all was rapidly fading from everyone's memory, including Eric and Agnar's.

Eric whispered to Agnar, "It is sad no one agreed with us or urged us on, though I feel someone in the crowd was on our side. Do you feel that?"

Agnar agreed, "The words I hear in my head urging us on this journey seem real enough. But no matching wraith do I see out in our audience, though I feel I can describe him."

Eric responded, "Me, also. I can see him in my mind's eye as if he had been standing over there." He pointed to the spot where the stranger had stood.

The stranger had influenced Eric and Agnar's followers. The momentary doubts left their followers minds. The two finished their final preparations for the journey. That evening Aslaugr went to her stepson Eric and gave him a gift, "Take this ring for luck. My grandfather gave it to me when he hid me in the harp. I've kept it always, and now want you to have it so you can think of me."

Eric placed the Andvaranautr, the prize of Andvari's Hoard, on his finger, "I don't need a ring to remind me of you. It would be hard to forget how beautiful and wonderful you are. I love you as dearly as if you were my real mother. Even though you've forgiven our father, Agnar and I have not. We intend to reclaim your honor at the points of our swords. Have no fear for us. Our army is strong and brave. We'll return home before the end of the harvest." He kissed his stepmother goodnight.

The next day Eric, Agnar, and their followers, left and steered a course straight for Sweden. Once there they began ravaging the countryside, up and down the coast. They met with little resistance. King Eystein's people had known peace for so long they no longer had a standing army and were unable to defend themselves.

Word was sent to King Eystein in Uppsala that the sons of Ragnar Lodbrokr were attacking villages all along the coast.

King Eystein sent word throughout Sweden for all men who would fight beside him against the intruders to gather in Uppsala. Thus, he raised a great army, trained them in warrior skills, and armed them with the finest weapons that had ever been made.

He led his men to the coast in search of Eric and Agnar. He had also thought to bring along the cow Sibilja, who had only budged from the comforts of her pasture after many bloody sacrifices had been made in her honor, along with the promises of more bloody meals on the battlefield.

King Eystein spoke to his men, "We've camped in this wood because our scouts have told me Eric and Agnar are camped on the other side of this wood in a large field. We are three times theirs in number, and have nothing to fear from them. The strategy for the battle will be this. A third portion of our army will attack as if they were the full force. Eric and Agnar's men will fight with their full fury hoping to quickly end the battle. Half of our remaining army will circle around behind Eric and Agnar's army. The rest of us will break into two parts and position each half to the left and right of Eric and Agnar's army. They are out in the open in a meadow. We will wait on these three sides in the forest. Then, just when they think things are nearly over, the rest of us will charge from the rear and both sides. Sibilja will charge on her own from the front to help those who are already in the battle. Her bellowing and the size of our numbers will send what's left of our enemy scattering to the winds each hoping to make it back to his home in one piece. But we'll not let that happen. We'll pursue them in all directions and cut them down, showing them the same mercy they've shown the villagers they've attacked and killed in our country. They and others who might have thoughts of coming after them will learn it's a very bad idea to attack King Eystein's Kingdom and his people. We are might. The Æsir are on our side. We will win."

∘ ∘ ∘ ∘

Before sun-up the next morning, Eric and Agnar awoke to a strange silence, and knew it to be the silence that precedes a battle. Their men solemnly gathered on their war cloaks and made certain their weapons were sharp and ready.

All was calm.

Then they caught sight of their enemy and were relieved to see their work yesterday had killed many and they had an army of equal numbers opposing them.

Eric yelled to his men, "Let's have at them and finish this quickly so we can get back to our breakfasts. We've easily bested twice our number in a short time. This small host should be no problem to deal with. The Æsir are on our side. We shall win."

The armies charged towards each other and were soon engaged in hand-to-hand combat on the open field. The battle continued for several hours that morning until the battlefield was covered with blood. Eventually the tide had turned and it was clear Eric and Agnar's armies would be victorious. Those who were left of King Eystein's army began running back towards the woods.

Agnar ordered his warriors to follow, breaking a basic strategy in battle to never disperse your warriors into small groups, "After them. We want no survivors who can sneak up on us in the night."

The men ran in pursuit of their enemy. As they neared the forest they heard a rumbling noise. The soldiers in the front ranks stopped in their tracks, dropping their weapons and clutching at their ears trying to block out the deafening sound. Then she appeared. Sibilja ambled towards them, mooing. She was in no hurry. Closing in from their rear and both sides were the other two-thirds of King Eystein's army, their ears stuffed so they were deaf to Sibilja's lowings.

The mooing became louder. Eric and Agnar's men clasped their hands over their ears which worked for only a moment. Then the mooing caused their very insides to hurt. Eric and Agnar's men lost their senses. The two sons of Ragnar Lodbrokr watched in horror as their men began fighting and slaying each other. Sibilja walked among the bodies crushing some of them as she stepping on them, bending her head down to chew on others. Many were not dead as she began her meal, pulling an arm off here, a leg off there. Occasionally she stopped to lick at their wounds so she could taste their nice salty blood. The sacrifices offered her that day were greater than even King Eystein had supposed they would be.

Eric and Agnar were the only two of their army unaffected by Sibilja's mooing. They charged again and again at King Eystein's men, and slew a great many. Unfortunately, even they could not battle alone against an army and the magic of Sibilja and hope to win.

Eric looked to his left on their final charge against King Eystein. He saw Agnar fall from a fatal blow. Eric fought, overcome with the madness of his grief, whirling around and slaying one and all who came near him. Finally, exhausted, his strength waned; he sunk to the ground and was captured.

King Eystein had been impressed with the might of this warrior. He rode over to him and offered him his forgiveness and peace, "If you'll join forces with me I'll give you command of my armies. I've never seen anyone fight as bravely as you have today. If our numbers had not been as great, and if we had not had the aid of Sibilja's witchcraft, you would have easily overpowered us. To prove to you how much I desire your friendship I also offer you the hand of my daughter, Ingeborg. Our families will be united through this marriage, and all the old insults forgiven and forgotten. What do you say to my offer?"

The men who heard it mumbled King Eystein was certainly the most generous King there ever was. However, Eric took a different view of things, "You've slain my brother and my army, then you offer me your castoff daughter and peace? What am I to think of such an offer? Should I sleep with a woman who under other circumstances would have been my stepmother? You do me a great dishonor with this gesture. Better you should raise up your spears and spit me upon them so I might die an honorable death. That certainly would be preferable to sleeping with

Ingeborg. The only thing I ask is you let those of my men who writhe on the battlefield and might yet survive, whether injured or whole, leave this land."

King Eystein replied, "That's not the answer I had hoped for. However, it will be as you wish." He turned to several of his soldiers and commanded them, "Raise up several spears. Dig holes and stick them midway in the earth so they stand up straight and strong and able to hold Eric's weight. His body shall be tossed upon that uncomfortable bed, giving him eternal rest."

While preparations were made for Eric's death, soldiers searched the battlefield for those of Eric's men who still lived. They were all injured, many missing limbs, none were unaffected by the battle. They stood or were laid next to the bed of spears.

Eric spoke his last words to his brave warriors, "Bravely I meet this death as a King's son should. Let the wolves on the battlefield tear at my flesh, let the ravens pluck out my eyes, I'll die with greater honor than any other Kings' son before me." He walked over to the spears which were now gleaming in the newly risen sun. He took off the Andvaranautr ring that Aslaugr had given him before their journey and gave it to one of his men to be returned to her, "Tell my stepmother my last thoughts were of her. Tell Aslaugr the battle is finished and my brother Agnar, most of our brave warriors, and I have lost. Both of her stepsons have fought bravely and have died honorably defending her. I leave all of my possessions, such as they are, to her, along with all my love. I wish things had turned out differently."

He signaled to King Eystein he was ready. King Eystein motioned to four of his guards. They lifted Eric over their heads. At that moment a raven flying overhead landed on Eric's chest. Eric shouted at it, "Wait just a moment more and you'll be able to eat hardy."

The four soldiers heaved Eric into the air. He arched upward and landed on top of the spear points, many of which pierced completely through his body. Yet he did not cry out. The blood didn't spurt from his body. Instead it flowed down the spearshafts and stained the ground beneath.

o   o   o   o

The remnants of Eric and Agnar's army left Sweden immediately and made their way back to Ragnar Lodbrokr's Hall. They decided to rest for three days before returning the Andvaranautr ring to Aslaugr.

o   o   o   o

Unfortunately, at the time Ragnar Lodbrokr had gone to a Thing of Kings. King Eystein had sent word to all the Kings he would not be attending because of trouble in his Kingdom. Ragnar Lodbrokr did not let on he had any extra knowledge of what that trouble might be, despite everyone around him speculating on who would be foolish enough to attack King Eystein.

○ ○ ○ ○

After three days Eric and Agnar's warriors ask some servants where they might find Aslaugr, and were given directions. They came upon her in very informal circumstances. She was sitting at her dressing table with a cloth covering her knees. Her hair was down. She picked up her brush and began to brush it. She saw the men reflected in her mirror and turned around, shocked they would come into her private chamber, "Who are you that you think you can barge into my private chamber unannounced? What business do you have with me?"

Their leader spoke, "Of late we were fighters in Eric and Agnar's armies. Now it is clear their wyrd has been woven by the Norns and their tapestries are finished. There are just a few of us who have survived the magic King Eystein set against us."

Aslaugr stood and welcomed them, "Then I should give you better greetings. Please, tell me what has happened to Eric and Agnar? You speak as if they are dead. They are both strong warriors and had a great number of followers to fight at their sides. How could anyone have prevailed against them?"

The leader spoke again, "All you say is true. But even the bravest warriors cannot fight against witchcraft and numbers that overwhelm them. As I said before, the sons of Thora Borgarhjort and Ragnar Lodbrokr are dead. Agnar fell in battle, while Eric bravely sacrificed his life so his remaining men would be allowed to leave Sweden unharmed. He has sent this ring back with me to give to you along with instructions that you are to become the sole inheritor of his possessions."

Aslaugr took the Andvaranautr and began weeping blood-red tears that fell hard as stones to the floor. This was the first time anyone had ever seen her cry. After a few moments she regained her composure and was never again known to grieve in front of others. She spoke, "Return to your homes for now, and stray no further. When my husband returns home I'll urge him on to avenge these deaths. You and your men have already fought bravely and need not be there when Ragnar Lodbrokr offers King Eystein the same reward he offered Eric and Agnar, whom I loved as dearly as if they had been my own sons."

○ ○ ○ ○

At the time Ragnar Lodbrokr was enjoying himself at the Thing of Kings and was in no hurry to return to Aslaugr. His sons, Ivar Lackbones and his brothers, were bored by the thrice-told tales of old warriors. To them battles were not for the telling, but for the winning.

Hvitsarkr and Bjorn Jarnsida carrying their brother Ivar Lackbones on a shield, found Ragnar Lodbrokr in a dining Hall regaling others with his story of the wooing and winning of Thora Borgarhjort, and the slaying of the worm that encircled her bower. This was a story the brothers knew by heart, having heard it so often. They waited until there was a good part they could interrupt, because they did not want to listen to the full story again.

The brothers bumped the shield edge against Ragnar Lodbrokr so Ivar Lackbones could interrupt the story, "Forgive the interruption father, but I and my

brothers are leaving to return home. Lands are unsettled as King Eystein's problems show. It is wise that Aslaugr not be left alone. The Volsungr have many enemies, and there are those who would make a name for themselves by killing her."

Ragnar Lodbrokr didn't want to see his sons go since it meant he must leave too, and he was having too much fun being the center of attention, "Then I must needs leave, also."

Ivar Lackbones responded, "No, it is not necessary. We are enough protection for Aslaugr. Stay here, finish your stories—all of you—" he turned to address the other Kings who had yet to tell their stories, such we're the numerous and long stories Ragnar Lodbrokr had been relating.

Ivar Lackbones turned back to his father, yet spoke loudly enough so the others would hear, "No, father, stay here and build up alliances and friendships amongst the other Kings. One day we may need the united might of all assembled here. This is the more important work for you to do."

Though Ragnar Lodbrokr knew his sons were departing no matter what he said, he spoke loudly, "Then I give you and your brothers, and any of my warriors you wish to take with you, my permission and blessings to return to my Kingdom to protect Aslaugr and any other of my subjects who might be in danger." He immediately turned back to the other Kings, "There was I stealthily creeping up on the sleeping worm. Step-by-step I crept closer to my destiny and glory. A glory that has brought me to these Halls today to relate this amazing, legendary, story."

Ivar Lackbones' brothers held the shield up high. Ivar Lackbones thought he might have seen a few nodding off amongst the crowd, only to be started awake by a poke from another King.

With that they departed.

o   o   o   o

Their journey home was quick and uneventful They made it back in a few days. They had not yet heard of their half-brothers' deaths.

Aslaugr heard her sons had returned and immediately went to see them. They had just finished changing from their dirty traveling clothes and were heading to Aslaugr's chamber.

Aslaugr met them in the hallway outside their rooms. Accompanying her was Sigurdr Snake-in-the-Eye, who was just barely three-years-old. The three brothers were glad to see their mother.

Hvitsarkr was the first to speak, "Tell us what news we've missed since we've been gone. You look worried. Is it still our Kingdom? No one has usurped father yet, have they?"

Aslaugr ignored his jokes and told them the story of their half-brothers' Eric and Agnar's deaths.

Hvitsarkr became serious, for he also had bad news, "It is my sad duty to inform you that you've lost another son, Rognvaldr." He told her the story of the Battle of Whitby in which Rognvaldr had fallen. Aslaugr paid no attention to it. She was too set in her grief for Eric and Agnar that she didn't realize one of her natural sons was also to be mourned.

She spoke of Rognvaldr's death with great honor, "His was a noble death in a fair fight. Odin saw his bravery and skill at swordplay and decided to call him to Valhalla. His is a death I can understand. However, I cannot understand the treachery of Eric and Agnar's deaths. They must be avenged. It is your duty to avenge the deaths of your half-brothers. I'll give you whatever you need to do this."

Ivar Lackbones spoke, "I've heard your story and sympathize with it. But what good would it do if we went to Sweden and were bested by King Eystein in the same way. He uses witchcraft, which no warrior can stand against."

Aslaugr was surprised and disappointed. She continued asking them, even begging them, and each time her sons refused.

Disappointed she tried to shame her sons, "So this is the respect you give your older half-brothers? Do you think they would even have to be asked to avenge your deaths if any of you had been killed? They would have sought justice immediately. I wouldn't even have had to put the ideas in their heads. Even though they were only my stepchildren, after hearing of your cowardness in this matter, I would they had been my real sons rather than you. I fear the blood of Sigurdr Fafnirsbani and Brynhildr flows very shallow through your veins, if at all. Is fear of witchcraft your only reason?"

Ivar Lackbones answered, "Isn't that enough? King Eystein has many followers who have no care for their own safety during their fighting, thinking they are protected by the magic of Sibilja. And what we've heard of Sibilja is scary. You must have heard she sent Eric and Agnar's men into such a frenzy they began fighting amongst themselves, slaying each other. How can we hope to best such an enemy?"

Aslaugr turned from her sons and started to leave, saying to them, "How can you hope to win fame and honor if you do nothing to deserve it? Think of strategy. Did King Eystein's men begin battling each other?"

The brothers realized that only their men had been affected. Why was that, they wondered. Aslaugr answered their thoughts, "Of course not. They stuffed their ears with cloth and fought on to victory. Great warriors come up with plans. All battles can be won. All battles can be lost. The winning or losing depends on the warrior, the field, the strategy."

While she was impassionately imploring her sons to seek revenge Sigurdr Snake-in-the-Eye pulled at her skirt to gain her attention, "I ask your permission to speak, mother." Aslaugr nodded indicating he could continue, "I'll seek vengeance against King Eystein on your behalf. If I leave now I can be at King Eystein's in Uppsala in three days. Before the week is finished he will rule no longer. I'll seek nothing less than his death. The weregild he might offer will not tempt me."

Aslaugr smiled at her brave son. She knew no matter how brave he was, and no matter how noble his words, he was still too young for the task, "You speak brave words, but I think you'd need the help of your brothers to carry out such a deed. One day you will be a mighty warrior on your own and carry the name of Sigurdr

to greater glory. There is no doubt that you are Sigurdr Fafnirsbani and Brynhildr's grandson."

Bjorn Jarnsida, who had until now remained silent, spoke, "Even though I have been quiet, it doesn't mean I agree with my brothers. Though my eye carries no mark on it, and my name is Bjorn, not Sigurdr, I can seek vengeance just as easily. Eric and Agnar were my brothers, and I can avenge their deaths without my other brothers, if I wish. Tell me what I must do."

Hvitsarkr broke in, resigned to the fact they were going to have to do battle against King Eystein, "Very well, if we are to avenge these deaths then we must do it together and do everything we can to insure our chances are successful. When Agnar and Eric left for their doom, the seas were still open since winter was just then upon us. Now the seas are rough and our ships lay trapped in the harbor, frozen in the ice. We'll have no success in our adventure until we've freed our ships."

Ivar Lackbones, hoping everyone would forget his recent opposition to the plan joined in with great fervor, "Death to King Eystein. Our journey must begin as soon as possible. I'll send orders for our sailors to begin working to free our ships, and they are not to stop until they've succeeded. I'll see our ships are properly provisioned and armed. Victory will be ours. Vengeance will be ours."

Aslaugr placed the Andvaranautr ring on Hvitsarkr's finger, "Wear this to remind you of the horrible death Eric suffered at the hands of King Eystein." She left the four brothers to continue their planning.

o   o   o   o

As it happened Sigurdr Snake-in-the-Eye had a foster-father who helped him gather together ships of his own. It took him only three days to gather together five ships filled with men eager to win glory fighting for the grandson of Sigurdr Fafnirsbani.

It took Hvitsarkr and Bjorn Jarnsida a couple of more days after this to complete their preparations. Between them they had fourteen ships. Ivar Lackbones had outfitted ten ships, while Aslaugr added ten more of her own to the fleet. Each ship carried between three hundred and five hundred men.

o   o   o   o

A week after their last meeting the brothers met one final time to plan their strategy. Unfortunately, this meeting turned out to consist of more boasting as to who had gathered the better crew and faster ships. Ivar Lackbones topped them all with his announcement, "In addition to the fine ships I've outfitted, and the men I've trained, I've already sent a party of warriors ahead by land."

Aslaugr started, upset she had not thought to send her own men off by land, "If I'd have known such a thing were possible I would have sent mine out last week."

Ivar Lackbones brushed her remarks aside, "No matter. At least some men are already on their way. It's better we now concern ourselves with what we do next, and plan our strategy."

Aslaugr broke in, "It's my intention to journey with you so I can see the death of King Eystein. Then I'll know the deaths of Eric and Agnar have been truly avenged."

Ivar Lackbones was against her traveling by sea, "The sea journey will be too brutal for you. It's better you catch up with the men I've sent by land. You'll lead them." Aslaugr nodded in agreement. Ivar Lackbones continued, "In honor of your new position we will change your name. Henceforth you will be called Randalin. You will be the leader of great men. We are your servants."

The rest of the meeting was taken up with deciding their destination and the best strategies for the upcoming battles.

They departed the next morning, sailing or marching by different routes. Each raided along the coast of Sweden as they made their way to the meeting point. Death and destruction followed in their wake. They were more vicious than ever in their vengeance, battling not only the men of the village, but killing the women and children as well as laying waste to everything in their path.

Again word was sent to King Eystein that the coast had been attacked, this time by the other sons of Ragnar Lodbrokr.

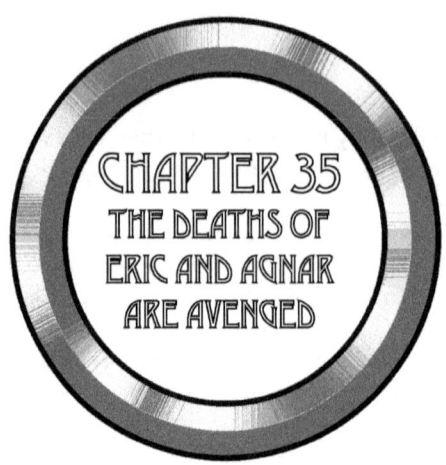

CHAPTER 35
THE DEATHS OF ERIC AND AGNAR ARE AVENGED

After hearing his Kingdom had once again been invaded by sons of Ragnar Lodbrokr, King Eystein summoned men from throughout his Kingdom and gathered together an army even mightier than the one that had beaten Eric and Agnar. He led them to the coast and addressed them on the morning of the battle, "This may all seem familiar to some of you. It seems the sons of Ragnar Lodbrokr just won't give up no matter how outnumbered they are, or how certain the defeat is. To protect my forces I'm loosing Sibilja first so she can do most of the work for us. Then we'll go in and clean up after her. Have a nice breakfast while she takes care of the fighting for you."

Sibilja was loosed and went off towards the enemy encampment. At first she mooed lowly as she ambled along. However, as she heard the sound of the other army the thought of bloody sacrifices worked her into a frenzy. Soon she was running towards the camp bellowing as loudly as she could. Then she backed off. Why not have some fun with them, she thought. So all day she pretended to attack and then didn't. This had the desired effect and the enemy army became very nervous.

Ivar Lackbones had been the first to hear Sibilja. Ordering his men to their positions and gave them their instructions, "Beat your shields and weapons together so our noise will overshadow that awful cow." Then he gave two of his men special orders, "There's a sapling on the far side of the camp that's almost grown, yet still retains its flexibility. Cut it down and fashion a bow from it. Use its branches to make me a set of strong arrows. When Sibilja appears keep up your cacophony while I attack her." Many of the men wondered how Ivar Lackbones could possibly attack Sibilja, when he couldn't even walk.

Then Ivar Lackbones cupped his hands together and yelled at the top of his voice, "ALL WHO CAN HEAR THIS KNEEL DOWN."

Almost everyone kneeled. Ivar Lackbones looked out and saw scattered here and there a few men yet standing. He gestured for them to approach. And first when

he spoke the men looked puzzled. He yelled as loudly as he could, "Why didn't you kneel when I commanded it?"

The first man spoke, "I'm sorry, as a child I suffered a spotted illness and have been hard of hearing ever since." The other three men nodded that such was the case with them also.

Ivar Lackbones spoke, "You four will be my personal attendants. I'll need you to carry me to the battle while I lay on your backs and draw the bow against Sibilja."

○ ○ ○ ○

Everything was in readiness. Ivar Lackbones' men were lined up along the battlefield hitting their shields, swords, and spears together as they advanced. Ivar Lackbones was carried aloft by his four personal attendants.

Ivar Lackbones had exercised over the years and though his muscles seemingly had no bones to attach to, they had become hard as bone and he could now draw a bow, whereas in previous battles a warrior had to stand behind him and hold his hands and draw for him.

Ivar Lackbones lay on his back drawing the bowstring with both hands and pushing at the bow with his feet. Soon Sibilja appeared and was bellowing so loudly she still was able to drown out the war noise of Ivar Lackbones' army. The racket they made gave them as much protection as if they had approached in silence. Many of the men began fighting each other. The men carrying Ivar Lackbones did not yet hear Sibilja's bellowing and continued advancing.

Ivar Lackbones pulled back the arrow until the tip touched the bow. He aimed and let it loose. Before it had found its mark he had drawn another arrow and let it loose. He did this until his supply was exhausted. His aim was true and one by one the arrows found their marks. Each landed on top of the others in Sibilja's eye. She momentarily stumbled, but soon regained her footing. Bellowing more loudly than ever from the pain, she began advancing again. The men carrying Ivar Lackbones were beginning to be affected by her yells. Ivar Lackbones was being jostled about as his bearers were trying to hit and kick at each other. Ivar Lackbones yelled one final command at them, "Throw me at Sibilja and I'll finish her off."

The men were trying as hard as they could to follow his orders. Fortunately he was very light and they were able to toss him towards Sibilja before they fell to fighting each other. Ivar Lackbones twisted and turned in the air so that he landed upright on Sibilja's back. Immediately his weight increased until he weighed as much as a boulder, crushing Sibilja to death under him.

As soon as the last of her bellowings had echoed off into the distance Ivar Lackbones' men ceased fighting each other. His attendants ran up to him and boosted him once more onto their shoulders. Ivar Lackbones yelled out at his men in a voice that was so great even in the distance they could hear everything he said as if he were standing next to them, "The hardest part of out battle is finished with the killing of Sibilja. We only have to fight against men such as ourselves. Forgive your comrades who were so recently attacking you because of Sibilja's unnatural bellowings, and let's join together and attack our real enemy, King Eystein and his army."

    o   o   o   o

Back at King Eystein's encampment King Eystein stopped and noticed something. There was quiet. He could no longer hear Sibilja bellowing. He misinterpreted this as meaning only one thing, she was enjoying the sacrifices offered to her on the battlefield. He could imagine no other cause, so he commanded his men to assemble and follow him so they could kill any of Ivar Lackbones' men who might still be alive.

King Eystein and his men came to an abrupt halt at the edge of the battlefield. Before them they saw Sibilja's carcass being torn apart by wolves and ravens. Looking beyond her they saw Ivar Lackbones and his men assembled, their weapons sharp and gleaming in the sun.

It was time for Ivar Lackbones to try King Eystein' former victory strategy against him.

Hvitsarkr and Bjorn Jarnsida led charges against King Eystein from each side. Randalin had circled around through the forest and brought her men up behind King Eystein's army, while Ivar Lackbones and Sigurdr Snake-in-the-Eye commanded their men to attack straight on.

Even though King Eystein was encircled and outnumbered his men fought bravely that day, but Ivar Lackbones' force was the mightier and the advantage was his. Today King Eystein was to meet the wyrd the Norns had just completed weaving for him.

The slaughter continued for only a short time more. Then King Eystein was slain and those of his men who were left surrendered. Ivar Lackbones gave them peace and a safe passage back to their homes. Then he spoke to his men, "We've done all we set out to do in this land. Let's leave. I'll not fight landless Kings or Kingless lands. We have no further glory to win here and risk dishonor by conquering a land without a ruler. There are other lands and Kings to the south for us to fight. Let's proceed to them. Randalin, you're welcome to come with us. You've proven yourself to be the equal of any as a leader."

She answered, "My son, I think it would be wise if I returned to our Kingdom. I doubt Ragnar Lodbrokr has returned, so the throne is at present left unattended."

Ivar Lackbones agreed and she and her men went on their way the next day. Sigurdr Snake-in-the-Eye stayed with his brothers, hoping to win further glory fighting at their side.

They journeyed south laying siege to many burgs with great success. Songs were written and sung by skalds in many lands telling stories of their mighty deeds.

    o   o   o   o

One day as Ivar Lackbones, Hvitsarkr, Bjorn Jarnsida, and Sigurdr Snake-in-the-Eye and their men were riding along they saw a great Hall in the distance. As they neared it they could see it had the best fortifications of any they had yet come against. It would certainly be a challenge.

Ivar Lackbones asked their guide about the Hall. He answered, "It's the burg of a great Prince named Vifil, and as such, is called Vifilsburg. He has never been defeated in battle. Distances are deceiving around here. I believe we are still many days from reaching Vifilsburg."

Ivar Lackbones answered, "Very well, then we'll have some adventures on the way. Perhaps word of our deeds will reach him and he'll be ready to honor us when we meet."

Ivar Lackbones' men ravaged throughout the countryside. Some of the villagers escaped and made their way to Prince Vifil so as to ask for his protection against the marauders attacking the land and people. Unfortunately Prince Vifil and most of his army were away at the Thing of Kings Ragnar Lodbrokr was attending. It was still going on and so filled with food and good times none of the Kings wanted to leave. This was bad for their Kingdoms,

Ivar Lackbones arrived at the Hall unaware Prince Vifil wasn't in residence. He spoke to the guard at the gate, "I command your Prince come down and meet us so he might show us the honor we deserve."

The guard answered carefully, hoping not to anger Ivar Lackbones, "I'm afraid my liege lord has not yet returned from the Thing of Kings. You are welcome to wait." He quickly backed away, shutting, and securing the heavy gate behind him.

Ivar Lackbones ordered his men to set up camp around the Hall. They would wait for Prince Vifil's return.

As day-after-day passed Ivar Lackbones could see his men were becoming more and more restless. He ordered his attendants carry him to the Hall wall. There he yelled up to those guarding the outer perimeter, "I'm tired of waiting for your Prince. Perhaps he's been inside all the while? Hiding? No matter. I offer this settlement with you. If you'll give up the Hall and all its wealth we'll let you live. If not, then we'll fight you, showing you no mercy, and gain all the wealth and the Hall anyway. The choice is yours."

The guard answered back, "Those are certainly fierce words for one who is locked without. Fight if you will. Batter at our walls until your knuckles are bare. Perhaps you can have man after man stand on each other's shoulders until you are raised high enough to be tossed over the wall. Maybe as you're flying through the air you'll see we've made a bed for you to land on like the one we made for your brother Eric. " There was laughter from the other guards. The guard continued, "We can last in here through the rest of the season and into winter. What will your men do when there's snow on the ground and they have nothing to eat?"

That night Ivar Lackbones gathered together Hvitsarkr, Bjorn Jarnsida, and Sigurdr Snake-in-the-Eye so they could work out a strategy for capturing the Hall. The next morning they made their assault only to find the guard had been right. They were no more than ants pushing at a tree. No matter how many ants there are, a tree is still a tree, with roots deep in the ground. It will not fall over. Better for the ants to gnaw at the leaves and the tree lose its cover so the sun will beat down on it and destroy it.

Every day of the next fortnight was spent attacking the Hall by some stratagem or other, all with the same result. Finally they could think of no assaults that had not been tried and failed. They prepared to depart. Why waste their time futilely battling for an uncertain treasure?

It was now that the overconfident people in the Hall made their mistake and forgot the main thing about victory. If you've won the battle be quiet and stop fighting. However, they were so overjoyed they had won the siege they decided to gloat over their victory. Costly gold-woven tapestries were hung from the ramparts. Treasures of gold and silver, as well as emeralds, rubies, diamonds, and other jewels, were laid along the wall, glittering temptingly in the sun.

One of the folk in the Hall yelled down to the departing army, which had stopped dead in its tracks at the sight of the costly items piled on the Hall walls, "See what you could have had, had you been strong enough to defeat us. Many have tried to win our treasures, but none have succeeded. When we heard the sons of Ragnar Lodbrokr had laid siege to us we were worried for your reputation is indeed fierce. I guess our experience dealing with you has shown us the skalds have a way of enlarging the exploits of their subjects. You gave us no difficulty at all. I even think King Eystein made a better try than you did."

Ivar Lackbones felt insulted. He also was depressed by what had happened. He ordered his army to encamp around the Hall again. He didn't feel well enough to leave.

Ivar Lackbones' condition deteriorated over the next few days. His brothers were concerned. Word was sent to them that Ivar Lackbones wished them to attend him, bringing along their most trusted advisors.

They immediately went to Ivar Lackbones' bedside. Hvitsarkr spoke first, "How are you feeling, brother? What can we do to help you?"

Ivar Lackbones wasn't interested in talking about himself, "My condition is of no account. What's important is how we are to assault the Hall. What plans have you come up with over the last few days?"

Bjorn answered, "We've been so worried about you we haven't given any thought to that. Anyway you're the one with the ideas."

Ivar Lackbones spoke, "There's one thing I know that we haven't tried. Tonight we'll leave our encampment and go to the forest near us and each man will gather up as much wood as he can carry. Our enemy will think we're sleeping in our beds. Instead we'll creep up around the Hall, laying the wood on all sides as we do so, followed by those who cover over the firewood with leaves, kindling, pitch, oils, and wax. After we've encircled the Hall we set fire to it. The heat will cause the lime between the Hall stones to loosen, and then we can pound at their walls with our catapults and rams. The treasures in the Hall will soon be ours."

The battle plan instructions had been exhausting for Ivar Lackbones to give. He sank back down on his bed to rest.

His orders were carried out, and worked as he had thought they would. The sons of Ragnar Lodbrokr and their army broke through the walls of Vifilsburg. They were met on the other side by the guards whom Prince Vifil had left behind. Everyone else in the Hall had been asleep, but soon awoke to the smell of smoke. They stumbled to the courtyard, surprised to see a gaping opening in the Hall wall and the guards engaged in fighting against their enemy. Some of them went to their aid, while others fled the Hall. Those who fled were the lucky ones, since Ivar Lackbones had ordered that no one inside was to be spared. He said nothing about those who fled into the night. The fighting didn't last long. After the army looted the Hall of its treasures they set fire to the inside.

When they departed the next morning they left behind them just the smoking rubble of what had been Vifilsburg Hall.

The next burg they came to was Lunaburg, where they were welcomed as heroes by the townspeople and given many gifts. The story of Vifilsburg and the other Halls they had conquered on their way had reached those in Lunaburg. Even their young children were chanting rhymes telling of the bravery of Ivar Lackbones and his brothers. It had been decided welcoming the invaders was far safer than opposing them. Their Hall was not nearly as well fortified as Vifilsburg had been.

Ivar Lackbones was feeling much better now that they had defeated Vifilsburg Hall. He and his brothers met to decide what glories to seek next.

Ivar Lackbones spoke first, "I've heard of a city called Rome that has a history of great Kings and rulers. It has seldom been conquered. I think if we should lay siege to it and be victorious our fame will be complete."

Hvitsarkr added what he knew, "I, too, have heard of this fabled city. It's filled with objects of wealth. Golden temples abound where their strange gods are worshipped. How far away is it? Do you have any idea? Do you know what dangers we'll meet on the way?"

Bjorn Jarnsida was a bit more practical, "We've a large army following us, and more and more men are joining each day. How will we ever feed them as we wander around looking for this city? A city that may at best be an exaggeration, and at worse a myth." Before his brothers could answer him, he noticed an old man in the distance, "Who is that?"

The three turned and saw an old man approaching dressed in beggars' clothes, "I couldn't help but overhear what you've been talking about."

Hvitsarkr interrupted, "You certainly have keen ears for an old man."

The beggar replied, "Keen ears can come in handy when you sleep outside all the time and have to beware of thieves. However, there are more interesting subjects to discuss than my hearing. For instance, I have just recently returned from Rome."

The brothers jumped and began speaking at once, "What's it like?" "How far away is it?" "Are the streets really made of gold bricks?" "What of the gods they worship?" "How much power do they have over our gods, if any?" "Are human sacrifices offered to them?"

The old man held up his hand to calm them, "What a lot of questions you have. I'll only answer one. Decide among you what it will be."

The brothers looked to Ivar Lackbones who asked the question, "How far away is Rome?" Can we lead our army there and be assured of enough provisions on the way?"

The beggar answered, "You asked two questions. I'll answer the first and then perhaps you may discern the answer to the second. It's hard to describe the distance to Rome and back. Maybe I can give you an idea. Have a look at the iron shoes on my feet and the ones slung over my shoulder. When I left on my journey both pairs were new, and I was wearing the ones that now hang limp and useless over my shoulder. The ones dangling on my feet, held together only by leather thongs, are broken apart so badly it's long past the time they should have been replaced. Excuse me I must now leave."

As he turned to go Ivar Lackbones tossed a coin at him, "Here's money enough for you to buy yourself several new pairs of shoes. You've given us good advice. It would be foolish for us to journey to Rome. The treasures we might win, depending on how strong the Romans guard their city, just might be enough to buy new shoes for our army for the return march."

It was agreed amongst the brothers they would stay near to the lands they had conquered. At no point would they go farther than a month's journey from the throne that Randalin was now protecting for them. There was glory enough to be won in these lands. Glory and death in a far-off land with songs carried back to their own lands of their valor and bravery didn't seem to be all that attractive. Local glory was glory enough. Especially since no one in their Kingdom had any idea this land called Rome even existed, despite what the stranger had said. Perhaps it was a phantasm? And victory over a phantasm was like holding smoke in your hands. You could see the smoke and make it swirl around if you moved your hands in circles. But ultimately you had nothing in your grasp. Only rings of smoke dissipating in the wind.

CHAPTER 36
RAGNAR LODBROKR GOES ADVENTURING FOR THE FINAL TIME

Ragnar Lodbrokr returned to his home, leaving behind him many successful battles and conquered lands he had added to his Kingdom. He had suffered few defeats. However, upon his return he learned his wife and sons had also gone adventuring, seemingly with greater success. Soon songs praising the bravery of his sons and wife could be heard being sung in the streets. It was through these songs he learned Kraka/Aslaugr was now called Randalin. Some of the songs praised them even more than the songs praising Ragnar Lodbrokr. He became jealous and decided to go out adventuring and win even greater fame for himself through more conquering and killing. Then there would be no doubt whom the skalds sang about more gloriously.

He ordered his shipwrights to design and build two ships using the best trees in the Kingdom. These ships were to be the largest, swiftest, and strongest in all the lands. "Make them large enough to carry my entire army in two lots. They should be able to keep upright even in the fiercest seas beset by the worst storms. Disguise them as ships of trade so we may come upon our enemy unawares. I've a mind to venture to lands where we've seldom conquered."

He also sent out a summons promising wealth and fame for all men in the Kingdom who would join his army. Unfortunately the best warriors were still off in distant lands with his sons and wife. When Randalin finally returned few of her men joined his cause, thinking she had now become the better commander. Ragnar Lodbrokr had strong weapons and armor forged for those who did join. He didn't reveal what lands he expected to conquer but the name England was whispered about.

The news of his war preparations reached other Kings who set up guards along their shores hoping to sight his ships as soon as possible so they could offer their best defense, which might include surrendering under favorable terms.

While all this was in progress Randalin told Ragnar Lodbrokr the adventures she had had with her sons, as well as the successes she had had on her journey home, including adding several new lands to their Kingdom.

He confided his plans to her, hoping also to impress her with the ambitiousness of them, "I've set my sights on England. The waters guarding that island are treacherous, I know, so I've ordered only two strong ships thinking they'll be easier to command and sturdier on the voyage. And why would the English send a great army to oppose only two ships? They won't know they contain my entire army."

Randalin cautioned against the adventure, "But think how great your losses will be if only one of the ships capsized in the water. You'd loose half your army. And if both ships met with trouble, you'd be in a sorry state indeed. I think it would be better to venture forth with the same numbers of warriors, few in a ship, and with more ships. You spread your risk out so the loss of one ship isn't so disastrous and the men from that ship can be easily welcomed on the other ships."

Ragnar Lodbrokr wasn't used to his wife advising him on matters of war and reacted accordingly, "It seems your recent adventures have made you an expert in battle planning. May I remind you I've been conquering lands far longer than you and know what I'm doing."

Randalin retorted, "But my recent adventures have been somewhat more successful than yours."

Ragnar Lodbrokr ignored her remarks and continued, "What songs will they sing about me if I journey to England with fleets of ships and conquer the English? Anyone can do that. But oh what a glorious feat it would be if I were able to conquer that land with just two ships. And if I were to lose, then my losses would not be as great. I would only lose two ships, not an expensive fleet."

Randalin tried to argue with him, "But your losses would be as great. Your army would be destroyed. Conquering England, no matter how many ships you used, would be reckoned a mighty feat. You seem to think it a point of honor not to go prepared to the best of you ability. If it's so easy to conquer England then why didn't Sigurdr or Sigmundr do it? If you want to try to conquer England, then make plans that will be successful."

Ragnar Lodbrokr refused to see her side of the argument. "I'll have more glory conquering England with two ships, and certainly less defeat if I don't succeed."

She continued her argument, "The loss in lives would be the same and the expense in design and special construction for these two massive ships would certainly pay for an entire fleet of regular-sized ships. What sort of honor will you gain by sneaking into a Kingdom disguised as something you're not? If you're a commander of an army approach your enemy as one. As it is you'll win praises as the powerful dry goods merchant who conquered England. And what if you're unsuccessful? Won't your enemy show you and your men more mercy if you've come to battle honorably rather than by trickery?"

Ragnar Lodbrokr laughed, "You're still inexperienced in war. I'll prove to you who the better commander is."

Randalin decided not to go on the adventure, not that Ragnar Lodbrokr had invited her.

The preparations proceeded as Ragnar Lodbrokr had commanded. Soon everything and everyone was ready. All that was needed was fair weather so they could depart with a fine wind behind them. That day arrived and everyone gathered at the two ships.

Randalin and Ragnar Lodbrokr had once more become used to each other and weren't quarreling as much. She went to the ships to see him off and gave him a parting gift, "When we first met you were kind to me and gave me something to wear, the beautiful dress that had belonged to Thora Borgarhjort. I now wish to repay you for that kindness. I've had this shirt made by a woman gifted in the magical arts. It's made from hair and knitted in such a way that there are no seams or breaks in its construction. It'll protect you from all wounds. Wear it always, to battle and when you rest. We've had problems with our marriage, yet I still love you and hope you win more fame and honor than ever before. Return home safely to me. We have found a comfort together and are once again comfortable with each other having overcome our past problems. And many times that's a fine substitute for a grand passion."

She handed him the grey-colored shirt. He was touched by her words and embraced and kissed her, "I'll wear this shirt always, not for the protection it might give me, but for the memory of you. I'll return soon so we might be together and get to know one another once more.

A strong wind guided the ships safely out of the harbor onto the open seas. This wind following them on their journey growing ever more fierce as they approached England. Soon a storm began pounding down on them. High seas slapped at the sides of the ships throwing the prow of the ship high into the air and pulling it back down again. Eventually both ships ran aground, breaking apart on the coast of England. However, some luck remained with Ragnar Lodbrokr since none of his men had been lost or injured, and they had lost none of their weapons.

Ragnar Lodbrokr commanded his men as they began their raids up and down the coast. This was a chancy thing to do since they had no means of retreat if they should meet up with a more powerful army.

Like other Kings, King Ella, who then ruled in England, had set up guards along his coast to inform him of any invaders. They soon brought him news that a mighty warrior named Ragnar Lodbrokr had landed and was attacking the coastal cities. King Ella gathered together his army and made preparations to go against this Ragnar Lodbrokr. They made their way to the coast, set up camp, and planned their strategy for the upcoming battle.

King Ella gave his men their instructions, "I think we have little to fear from Ragnar Lodbrokr. However, he has sons who have better soldiers under their command, and a wife who has become a great commander in her own right. If we kill their father and Randalin's husband, they'll be honorbound to avenge that death. They might not be so easy to defeat. It's my order Ragnar Lodbrokr is to be

spared in the fighting. Do not raise your weapons against him, even if it means your own injury or death."

Word that King Ella's army had set up camp nearby was brought to Ragnar Lodbrokr. He gathered his men together and spoke to them, "King Ella has brought his army against us. They're made up of shepherds and farmers, so we have little to fear." He had forgotten his army also consisted of men who until recently had been shepherds and farmers, rather than professional soldiers. He continued, "Tomorrow there will be a great battle. If we win, England will be ours. More wealth than you could ever imagine will be given to each and everyone of you. Make your preparations tonight and get a good sleep. Eat a hearty early breakfast before the battle. We'll meet on the battlefield at dawn. By our regular breakfast time England will be ours, and I'll be its new King—it's first Danish King."

That evening Ragnar Lodbrokr sharpened his sword. He took the spear that so long ago had slain the dragon guarding Thora Borgarhjort and had brought him his first fame, sharpened and re-pointed it. After finishing his preparations he slept.

The next morning after eating, he and his army assembled on the battlefield. For protection he wore only a helmet, the grey hair shirt Randalin had given him, leggings, and regular shoes. Having faith that that was all the protection he needed he had given his byrny to a young soldier who had had his damaged in an earlier encounter.

Many of Ragnar Lodbrokr's men began trembling when they saw the size of King Ella's force, which greatly outnumbered them. Ragnar Lodbrokr yelled words of encouragement to his men, with little effect, "Forget their number, fight and slay each one in turn. Numbers don't matter, it's strategy and fierceness that win battles. We shall soon whittle down their numbers until they are more manageable."

Ragnar Lodbrokr was a great commander that day. He rode in and out of the ranks urging his men on. Many times he rode ahead and charged at the enemy slaying scores of soldiers at a time to give his men courage. His men watched as the enemy attacked Ragnar Lodbrokr, hacking at him with swords, stabbing at him with spears and knives, and firing arrows at him, all with the same result. The blows glanced off him; the arrows struck him and fell harmlessly to the ground. However, his army was still inexperienced and doubted their own strength. Their armor could be pierced by the enemy, and his men began falling in greater numbers.

Soon all had been slaughtered, save for Ragnar Lodbrokr who was captured and put in bonds. He was brought before King Ella who questioned him, "What's your name? Why have you attacked England? Are you Ragnar Lodbrokr whom we have heard so much about?" Ragnar Lodbrokr stood mute and did not answer. King Ella continued, "I've asked you simple questions which I hope you'll have the courtesy to answer. What is your name?"

Ragnar Lodbrokr remained mute. King Ella turned to his men and gave them orders, "He plays us for fools. Soon he shall beg us to listen to him speak. Throw him into the snake pit so we can be finished with him. Have guards stationed nearby so if he yells out his name is Ragnar Lodbrokr he can be quickly rescued."

This was done. Ragnar Lodbrokr sat in the pit in silence. The snakes kept their distance and did not come near him. News of this was brought to King Ella. "He is a man protected by magic. The weapons at the battle today would not bite through his shirt, and now the snakes hold their distance. Have the grey shirt stripped from his back. I think this is the cause of his good luck."

One of the guards was carefully lowered into the pit and pulled Ragnar Lodbrokr's shirt from him and then quickly scrambled out of the pit, thankful he had not been bitten doing the bidding of his King.

As soon as the shirt was off Ragnar Lodbrokr, the snakes lashed out at his body. They bit into him, hanging on and sucking at the wounds.

Ragnar Lodbrokr called out in pain, "There would surely be a grunting among the young pigs if they knew how the old one was being treated."

Men ran to King Ella and told him the prisoner had been bitten and was speaking at last. King Ella hurried to the pit and yelled down at the prisoner, "Are you Ragnar Lodbrokr? If you are, then no harm will come to you and I'll honor you as one King to another."

Still Ragnar Lodbrokr did not answer. Instead he began singing songs of his adventures, "In my life I've fought fifty-one battles, and thought the end of my life would come on the battlefield. Little did I know that worms would strike at me and poison my body. Oh how my sons will avenge this death."

He turned slightly in the pit, looked straight up to King Ella, and continued, yelling out the history of his battles, "Many are the men I have killed. I still had my youth when in the east my army and I fought Eyrasund. The victory that day went to me. We waded waist deep in the blood that covered the fields. Hawk and wolf were well fed after that battle.

"I grew strong and brave from my conquests. By the time I was twenty I was known and feared far and wide. At Dvina's Mouth I fought and bested eight Jarls who had united in company together against me. Well did they rue the pack that had brought them together. It cost them their lives. And with those eight the Valkyries also carried the Helsings to Valhalla.

"For my next battle we journeyed by sea and put to shore by Ife. We won that one, too, and handily. Then at sea again we engaged Herraud in battle. He fell before my blows. My fame grew. Armies cast aside their weapons and fled before us in terror. This did happen at Skarpa-Skerry before Rafn Fell.

"The hawks and wolves followed after us assured of a full meal. They gorged themselves in the Enderdis Isles. At Bornholm we fought during a fierce storm. It was hard to tell whether the clashing noise and flashing lights were from our swords or the thunder and lightening in the sky. King Vulnir met his wyrd that day. Our battle on the Flemish plain claimed Freyr and many other brave warriors. Our battles have broken many a woman's heart.

"Again by sea we went to battle and met a most fearsome foe by Angelness. Their ships numbered in the hundreds. It took us six days of brave fighting before they were slain. We sent Valthjof to Valhalla in that battle.

"At Bardfirth we fought on land once more; hand-to-hand, sword-by-sword, battleax against battleax. I was lucky. My battleax, forged long ago by Svelnir was the strongest on the field. It hewed off many full helmets that day.

"And at Hedninga Bay we again felt the firm earth beneath our feet. We won a great victory there. Once more in the rain we fought in Northumberland. The blood mingled with the rain and flowed in torrents from the battlefield. The next morning my men had no one else to fight. The battlefield was a carpet of bodies they walked on.

"But not every battle was glorious. One of the saddest was in the Southern Isles where we fought Herthjof. There Rognvaldr, my son, fell. I shall never forget that day. But other days brought other battles and other glories. King Marstein of Ireland came against us by Vederfjord. He rues that day. The ravens and wolves rejoiced.

"Then in battle my son was slain by Egil. Spears flashed against each other and sparked as they sharpened each other throughout the day.

"We battled on Vickskeid in ships. The men had a hard time holding their footing on deck. The sea was calm but our decks were red and slippery from the fight.

Then there was the time we fought bravely against the three Irish Kings just as the sun was coming up by Lindisore. Not many survived that one.

"But other battles followed. Many warriors just out for their first battle fell the same day King Orn fell. Yet ever more battles came our way. Who could forget the Princes in battle by Angelsey, and the red-pointed arrows by the banks of the river Ore?

"We fought on through many more battles. The fates of many were woven, and finished. King Ella beckoned me to his shores. On I sailed leading my ships into the Scottish seas.

"Many battles have I fought, outnumbered as greatly as fifty-to-one, and still had the victory. Never did I think I would fall at the hands of another King. Odin calls to me, ready to welcome me to his table. I can hear the thundering hooves of his battle-maids, come to carry me off to even greater glory. Tonight I sup in Valhalla. It's a joke on you King Ella, to send your enemy to far more glory than you will ever know. I thank you. You now have to fear the sons of Ragnar Lodbrokr."

Ragnar Lodbrokr died laughing at his enemies. And it was as he had said. Odin was there to greet him. Valhalla had need of warriors such as he.

King Ella heard Ragnar Lodbrokr yell out his name and rushed to the pit, leaned over and pulled Ragnar Lodbrokr's body up, hoping to rescue him. Sadly, it was too late. A noble warrior had met his wyrd. The Norns put away his tapestry, now woven with images of all his great battles. The Gods in Valhalla awaited his arrival.

After Ragnar Lodbrokr was buried with full honor, King Ella met with his counselors. One gave him good counsel, "Ragnar Lodbrokr's sons will eventually hear of this deed. It's better you send messengers to inform them and tell them their father Ragnar Lodbrokr died with honor and was buried as befitting a King. Try to put the best light on the situation. After all, his expedition was foolhardy and his sons probably realize this. Offer them some weregild for the unfortunate death of their father. Tell them it was not your wish Ragnar Lodbrokr be killed. Have your messengers observe the reactions of his sons when they hear the news of their father's death. You'll then be able to gauge what their actions towards you might be. Make certain your messengers emphasize the weregild."

King Ella thought the advice good and followed it. He asked for volunteers to journey to Denmark as his personal messengers to take news of Ragnar Lodbrokr's death to the noble warrior's sons. At first no one volunteered. Who would want to be the bearer of bad tidings, unprotected in a foreign land? King Ella offered great estates and wealth to those who volunteered. Finally several messengers offered their services and departed with their instructions at the first favorable wind.

At the time Ragnar Lodbrokr's sons were still conquering lands on their southern journey. They destroyed all the villages they came across. People fled before their advance. Their victories proved too successful. The fields had been abandoned and few crops had been planted. Those who had been in the ground died from lack of care or the trampling feet of their army marching over them. It was becoming harder and harder for the brothers to find provisions for their army.

One morning Bjorn Jarnsida awoke and spoke to his brothers of a dream he had had the night before, "I saw ravens flying southward overhead leading us to our next battle. But they were so weak from hunger that one-by-one they fell to the ground. Thin, scraggly wolves came out of the forest and began eating the ravens. But they too were weak from hunger and fell to the ground."

Ivar Lackbones interpreted the dream for them, "I think it's time we rode northward and returned to Denmark. We've nothing more to accomplish by further adventuring at this time. Let's go home and find out how Randalin has fared in her journeys. Perhaps our father will have returned with stories of his adventures to tell at dinner?"

Such are the thoughts of warriors that they entertain no notion that their fellow warriors in far off lands were meeting with the same degree of success. The thought their father lay dead and buried never occurred to the brothers.

So they turned their armies northward and headed for Denmark.

CHAPTER 37
RAGNAR LODBROKR'S DEATH IS AVENGED

fter their return to Denmark the brothers met with Randalin who told them of their father's expedition to England. They gaped in disbelief that he should attempt such an ill-advised campaign and with only two untested ships. It was a foolhardy adventure.

Several days later the brothers were resting and eating a late afternoon meal. Word was brought to their chamber that several messengers wished to have a word with them. They signaled the messengers should be allowed to enter.

Ivar Lackbones had been placed on the high seat. He was enjoying the meal set on a table before him. Hvitsarkr and Sigurdr Snake-in-the-Eye were seated at the center table in the Hall playing chess. Bjorn Jarnsida sat off by himself on the floor, near the entranceway. He had a whetstone and was sharpening his spear.

The messengers bowed as they entered, but did not speak first, waiting instead to see which of the brothers was given the honor of speaking before the others. Ivar Lackbones addressed the messengers, "Welcome to our Hall. In whose service are you? What message do you have for us?"

The chief messenger replied, "We have been sent here by King Ella of England with news of your father."

The other brothers looked at the stranger. Ivar Lackbones spoke, "I've never been to England but trust you'll find the accommodations we provide for you and the others satisfactory. What news have you of our father? We knew nothing of his expedition and probably would have advised against the manner in which it was undertaken."

The chief messenger backed away a little, knowing messengers were frequently held accountable for the messages they carried, and said, "I'm afraid your father is dead. He died bravely and with great honor. King Ella gave him a funeral befitting that of a great King. Our entire land mourned the passing of so great a warrior."

He carefully studied the brothers' reactions to the news. Bjorn Jarnsida knocked over the King on his side of the chess table as he grabbed hold of the table.

Hvitsarkr's hand tightened around the pawn he was holding. Its edges ground into his hand until blood dripped onto the chessboard. Bjorn Jarnsida had stood up at the first mention of his father's name and had been leaning on his spearshaft. He pressed down so hard on it that it split in two. He picked up both pieces and held them in his hands.

Ivar Lackbones seemed to be the only one who had remained calm at the news. "What can you tell us of the details of how he met his fate?"

The chief messenger cleared his throat and began to speak, addressing his comments mainly to Ivar Lackbones, feeling him to be the more sympathetic of the three brothers. He related all he knew of Ragnar Lodbrokr's journey from the time he left Denmark until he met his death in England. He became so carried away with the telling of the story he neglected to put King Ella's side in the best light. Finally he came to the part where Ragnar Lodbrokr had been cast into the pit and the messenger yelled out at the top of his lungs, "There would surely be a grunting among the young pigs if they knew how the old one was being treated."

The messenger suddenly realized what he had said and stopped. He stood there trembling in front of the brothers, looking at each one in turn. He saw Bjorn Jarnsida's hands curled around his broken spear so tightly when he finally dropped it, the imprints of his hands could be seen on the broken pieces. Hvitsarkr who was still holding the pawn in his hands, gripped it even tighter until it crumbled under the pressure. Sigurdr Snake-in-the-Eye sat paring at his fingernails, but was so affected by the messenger's yelling out of his father's words he didn't even notice he had cut through his finger to the bone.

Ivar Lackbones began asking the chief messenger questions, probing until he found out the whole story of his father's treatment at the hands of King Ella. While he listened his countenance changed, first red with anger and finally he paled at the awful treatment his father had received. His entire body became swollen with the anger in him.

Hvitsarkr then spoke, "Let's begin avenging our father's death by killing these representatives of King Ella whom we have before us."

Bjorn Jarnsida approached, pointing the end of his broken shaft at the messenger. However, Ivar Lackbones held up his hand to stop his brothers since things seemed to be getting out of hand, "No. They travel in our country with the same safe passage our messengers would expect if they were traveling in King Ella's country." He turned to the chief messenger, who seemed greatly relieved at Ivar Lackbones words, and addressed his comments to him, "You may leave here with our protection, and if there is anything you need to make your journey home more pleasant, please let us know and it will be provided. You may stay in our country as long as you wish, and in complete safety."

The chief messenger answered, "There is nothing we need. Thank you for your kindness and the honorable way you are treating us. I think it would be best if we returned to England immediately."

The messengers fairly ran out of the Hall and back to their ships, anxious to get away before Ivar Lackbones changed his mind. They sailed immediately, even

though the breeze was not as favorable as it might have been. Upon their return to England they went to King Ella and told him all that had happened.

King Ella listened attentively and then gave orders to everyone in the Hall, "This is not good news. Ivar Lackbones knows his father's last words were of revenge on us. I believe the son will try to do what the father failed to do. I command sentries are to be set up along the coast so we might be on our guard against any attack from Ivar Lackbones and his brothers. I fear we are in for an uneasy time of it."

In the meantime Bjorn Jarnsida, Hvitsarkr, and Sigurdr Snake-in-the-Eye had approached Ivar Lackbones about what action they should take to avenge the death of their father. To their surprise Ivar Lackbones refused to seek revenge. He answered, "If we had been here we would have counseled against such a foolhardy venture. It was doomed from the start and our father died the death he deserved for having undertaken such a risky venture. He attacked King Ella for the sheer glory of it. There had been no ill words between the two beforehand, and there was no justification for what our father did. Likewise we have no just quarrel with King Ella. He had asked our father's identity, but our father remained mute. I believe it was King Ella's intentions to give him great hospitaity if he knew he was dealing with a King. However, our father remained mute until near the end of his punishment. Once King Ella knew his true identity he tried to rescue him. Our father is as much a reason for his death as the worms that turned him into wormfood. Had he revealed his identity immediately upon being brought to King Ella he would have been spared, and I have no doubt, given safe passage about to our land. King Ella did nothing that we would not have done in his stead. I'll send word to him that we will take a payment of weregild for our father's death and then hope to live in peace with him."

The other brothers couldn't believe what Ivar Lackbones was saying. Bjorn Jarnsida was the first to speak, "How can you mean this? Our father has died a dishonorable death at the hands of a vile King who dares send messengers to us to gloat over it."

Ivar Lackbones responded, "That's not how I see it. King Ella showed us a courtesy in sending his messengers to report our father's death. They were brave messengers for bringing us the message. After all had we not been honorable men we could have killed them. We will accept weregild for this death, not a blood payment."

Hvitsarkr spoke next, "Our reputation will suffer if we let our father's death go unavenged. People will say we sit idly wasting our time while our father's death goes unavenged."

Sigurdr Snake-in-the-Eye continued, "Your reasons for not avenging our father's death aren't sound. Many are the innocent Kingdoms we've set upon and conquered. Have we had a just quarrel with our enemies before every battle?" Sigurdr Snake-in-the-Eye failed to see that he had just admitted that many of his battles and conquerings had been dishonorable.

Bjorn Jarnsida spoke again, "Let's send word throughout Denmark so that every man who would wish to avenge the killing of their King should meet here.

We'll have ships readied so they will all have a place. Then let's sail to England and teach King Ella a lesson."

Ivar Lackbones saw his brothers were set upon waging war and there was nothing else he could do but join them, "Then let it be as you wish. I see the sons can be as foolish as the father. I'll journey to England with only one of my ships. The others will remain in port."

o　o　o　o

Ivar Lackbones' brothers sent word throughout Denmark for all able-bodied men to join them. This call had been send out many times in the preceding months, so they were surprised there were still men who responded to the call. A great many held back because so many had been killed following Ragnar Lodbrokr to England. They had been offered no reasons why another invasion so soon after the defeat of the most recent army would be successful. It had been whispered about that even Ivar Lackbones only reluctantly joined in the recruitment of men. If Ivar Lackbones was not of a mind for the journey, then there must be something wrong with it.]

However, there will always be young men who rally to the call of the glory of battle, even an unjust battle fought against a larger enemy. No young man thinks he will be killed in battle. At that age he is invincible. All he can thing of is the glory of battle and the bounty to be won. For the young it is an easy way to wealth and fame. The brothers had quite an impressive army at their back."

o　o　o　o

The preparations took but a few weeks. King Ella's messengers had barely enough time to return to King Ella's Hall and report what they had seen. England's coastal cities had set up watches so when the sons of Ragnar Lodbrokr landed, word would be immediately sent to King Ella.

Soon King Ella received word of that the sons of Ragnar Lodbrokr's ships had been sighted. He summoned his army and they marched off towards the coast so they would be there to meet the invaders.

His army was huge. It stretched on for miles and miles from either side of him and behind him. So far did it reach, in fact, that standing at its head it was impossible to see the tail of it as it snaked along the road and fields beside the roads. The warriors in it were the best trained in the land. Already filled with the glory of having defeated Denmark's famous King Ragnar Lodbrokr, they now approached his sons equally confident of victory.

Soon they met up with the armies of Bjorn Jarnsida, Hvitsarkr, and Sigurdr Snake-in-the-Eye. Ivar Lackbones was nowhere to be seen, having kept to his ideas that the brothers should seek weregild instead of blood for their father's death.

King Ella's army proved to be the better. Soon the sons of Ragnar Lodbrokr and what remained of their army were fleeing for their lives. The victory belonged to King Ella that day.

o   o   o   o

Bjorn Jarnsida, Hvitsarkr, and Sigurdr Snake-in-the-Eye made their way to the shore and their ships. There they were met by Ivar Lackbones who was being carried ashore. Hvitsarkr was the first to speak, "The glory belongs to King Ella, for the moment. But this land should be forewarned, we'll return someday to give proper justice to the memory of our father."

Bjorn Jarnsida added, "Let's all return to Denmark and set our thoughts on how we might defeat this King."

However, Ivar Lackbones signaled for his men to continue disembarking, "I'm still of a mind to meet King Ella in peace and settle the matter between us. I'll accept weregild for our father's death so our countries may remain at peace."

Sigurdr Snake-in-the-Eye spoke, "Beware the hospitality of King Ella. It may be that he will offer you spears and arrows in greeting rather than a firm grasp of the hand."

Ivar Lackbones answered, "When I come in peace I do not fear the other. Depart and return to Denmark where you three shall rule in my stead. But be ready to send me whatever I ask for. I may in the future have need of gold and some of our wealth to accomplish what I set out to do."

Bjorn Jarnsida was the last to speak to his brother, "If you go in peace and expect weregild, then what need will you have of our gold? Remember, our father is worth more than just a few copper coins. Why will you need to spend our money in England? I don't understand why you wish to befriend our father's killers?"

The brothers left each other on an uneasy note.

o   o   o   o

Ivar Lackbones and his army proceeded until they came upon King Ella. The Danes carried a flag of peace as their standard which King Ella honored. He went forward to meet the son of his enemy.

Ivar Lackbones greeted King Ella, "I come to you seeking peace and hope that we can put the recent unpleasantness between our two countries behind us. My army is smaller than the armies of my brothers that you so recently fought and defeated, so you can be assured my intent is not warlike. I am not foolhardy, nor do I seek the deaths of my followers. Rather, I will let you deal with me as you wish, hoping you will give me the respect due the son of a King."

King Ella was much impressed with the young man who sat tied to a horse in front of him so he would not fall off. He had heard of Ivar Lackbones' strange physique, but could not help staring when he saw him. He was also relieved there wouldn't be another fight. He answered him, "I've been warned about you and your brothers. I was surprised at the small army your brothers brought to attack me, and now I am puzzled by the offer you make me. What form of trickery is it? Are you trying to catch me off guard and then have your brothers attack full force with a large army you may have hidden? I'm not certain what to think of you."

Ivar Lackbones responded, "My brothers and I are not one with this venture. They have sought to defeat you with might and have failed. I offer you peace and hope thereby to win. It all depends on you. True, if something were to happen to me my brothers would be able to raise a vast army in Denmark that could overrun your island quite easily. However, that's not my wish. There are times to conquer through battles and times to conquer through peace. At the moment the choice of method is yours. I come to you in peace. If you send one of your soldiers to the inlet where our ships are moored you'll see that only one remains. My brothers have already departed for Denmark, under my orders."

King Ella considered what Ivar Lackbones had said and then responded, "What do you want? You speak of weregild. That seems a simple enough thing to arrange. Is it gold you would want?"

Ivar Lackbones responded, "If you grant my offer of weregild then I would swear to be as a brother to you. Your enemies would be my enemies, your friends my friends. And all I ask is that I be given all the land that can be covered with an ox hide, and that you build a fortifying wall around it. Do this and we will live in peace."

This seemed a simple enough request to King Ella, "That seems a mild request in order to atone for the death of such a mighty warrior as Ragnar Lodbrokr. However, it will be so. Make the following oath, that you Ivar Lackbones, representing the Kingdom of Denmark, swear never to raise an army to make war against the realm of England, nor will you ever advise others to do so. We will live as friends and brothers so both our countries can aid each other against any common enemies. And with peace and friendship both our countries will thrive.'"

Ivar Lackbones swore the oath.

King Ella continued, "Very well, we are as brothers. Find the largest ox hide you can and spread it out as large as possible. My surveyors will accompany you. Whatever land is blanketed by the ox hide will be deeded to you and your heirs forever. You have the word of King Ella and England for it."

Ivar Lackbones and his men set up camp near King Ella's army. Ivar Lackbones sent men to retrieve a special packet he had onboard his ship. Later when he unwrapped it in front of his counselors they were surprised to see it was an ox hide. Ivar Lackbones commanded some of his men to prepare it for him, "This is the hide of the largest ox my father had in his prize herd. It has only been tended to once since it was stripped from that animal's back. I order that it be prepared and softened three times, and that each time it should be stretched as wide as is possible. Then let the skin be separated from the hide and stretched out so it is made twice as long. Finally cut it into one narrow strip that can be used to mark out a wide expanse of land. This will be our weregild for the killing of Ragnar Lodbrokr. I think King Ella has agreed to something he thought would be considerably less expensive."

Ivar Lackbones' instructions were carried out precisely. The hide was even larger than Ivar Lackbones had supposed it would be. It covered an area of land wide enough to give him one of the largest estates in all of England. King Ella's surveyors marked off the boundaries, then King Ella sent builders to build the fortifications around the land. Within the walls ordinary dwellings were built as well as a large Hall where Ivar Lackbones would live. He named his estate Lundunaberg, although the English called it Londonburg, and eventually just London.

Ivar Lackbones spent his money freely in his adopted country. He helped all those around him and over the years he lived there won the respect and trust of many of the English nobles. King Ella relied upon him for counsel in many matters. He was called upon to resolve seemingly impossible disputes, and soon gained a reputation for being very clever. After a while many of the nobles in England actually preferred him to King Ella and were soon openly saying he should be King instead, since most of what King Ella did was the result of Ivar Lackbones' counsel. Why have an intermediary? But Ivar Lackbones in no way openly sought the throne of England.

Ivar Lackbones saw his plan was working well. Unfortunately, he had spent all his ready cash. So, he sent a messenger to Denmark to his brothers asking for his share of their hoard of gold and silver. At first his brothers were reluctant to part with such wealth, especially to a brother whom they now considered their enemy. However, after questioning Ivar Lackbones' messengers they realized the strategy their brother was employing and sent him all the silver and gold he asked for."

Ivar Lackbones continued lending money and helping all the powerful men in the country, including King Ella's closest counselors. In exchange he exacted promises of fealty should he and the King ever war against each other.

Soon the time came when Ivar Lackbones thought his position was such that he could conquer England. He sent messengers to his brothers instructing them to gather together the greatest army they could and sail to England. The brothers responded quickly. They send word throughout Denmark that all able-bodied men were henceforth conscripted to serve in their army. They then took the unprecedented step of conscripting soldiers from Gautland for their army, as well as men from other lands they had conquered. The army they assembled was magnificent. They set sail for England, trusting Ivar Lackbones would have only sent for them if he thought victory was assured.

They sailed without rest hoping to arrive before word of their departure reached King Ella. However, King Ella did hear of the invasion force and summoned his army once more to his side. As he looked about he saw its ranks were greatly depleted. He asked why and found that many of his most trusted officers had sworn loyalty oaths with Ivar Lackbones. King Ella sent for Ivar Lackbones who came as quickly as he could. He and King Ella held counsel together.

King Ella was the first to speak, "Ivar Lackbones, you have sworn fealty to me. You have sworn you would never bear arms against me. You have sworn that my enemies are your enemies. I trust you are honorable enough to uphold those oaths?"

Ivar Lackbones nodded, agreeing all King Ella had spoken was true, "As you know I have enjoyed the life I've made for myself at Lundunaberg and have no wish to leave this country, my adopted country. I will meet with my brothers and see what I can do to persuade them to the right course concerning this matter."

King Ella was satisfied Ivar Lackbones could handle the matter and ordered his men to relax their guard somewhat.

   o o o o

Ivar Lackbones met with his brothers and the counsel he gave them would have shocked King Ella had he heard it. "I'm glad you've answered my call in such a bold manner and with such a great army. Proceed against King Ella. His forces are not what you came up against before. Many of his best warriors are now honorbound to fight at my side, which will be against King Ella."

Bjorn Jarnsida was still a little angry with his brother when he spoke, "We don't need your encouragement to fight against King Ella. It matters little whether you advise us to caution or to war. We are intent upon what we've set out to do and have been planning this revenge for a long time, without your help. You've lived an easy life in Lundunaberg, and only recently taken any interest in avenging our father. Have someone carry you over to the sofa so you can sleep while we do the work men are supposed to do."

After the meeting with his brothers, Ivar Lackbones returned to King Ella to report what had transpired, "I'm afraid my brothers are filled with the battle fury and will not be contained by my words. I've spoken of the good will between you and me and that we should all live in peace. But they would hear none of it. I'm afraid I've done all I can do. I'll honor my oath and refrain from engaging in battle on either side. For it would be just as wrong for me to raise arms against my brothers. I do them a great injustice as it is by standing aside while they fight. So, now it's up to Odin and the Valkyries to decide the outcome of the battle."

Ivar Lackbones was as good as his word. He retired to his Hall and awaited the outcome of the battle. Often during the day's preparations King Ella sent messengers requesting that the warriors who had sworn fealty to Ivar Lackbones be released from their oaths and allowed to fight at King Ella's side. Ivar Lackbones refused each time.

   o o o o

The two armies approached each other early the next morning just as the sun was coming up. King Ella stared at the legions before him that vastly outnumbered his army. He was concerned. His men saw that concern and were fearful.

The sons of Ragnar Lodbrokr made the first attack. A group of their best warriors charged into King Ella's ranks, hacking and hewing with their swords. Many of King Ella's greatest warriors were killed during that first encounter.

The two sides fought each other throughout the morning and afternoon and well into the evening. There was no doubt as to the eventual victor. King Ella's men had fought so bravely they had prolonged the battle far longer than it should have gone on considering how much they had been outnumbered.

It is always unwise to fight in the dark, so that evening King Ella gave the command for retreat and he and his men began running for safety. Hvitsarkr yelled

out to his men, "Forget about King Ella's men. Don't let King Ella escape, he's our real prey in this matter."

King Ella was soon captured and brought before the brothers. Ivar Lackbones was now with them, and appeared to be in charge. He spoke to King Ella, "I've kept my word and stayed out of the fight. Since you have been defeated I see no reason why I cannot now join my brothers. The sons of the man you so barbarously killed will devise your death. However, have no fear it will not last long. My brothers and I have decided what it will be."

Hvitsarkr signaled for one of the soldiers to come forward. He was carrying a very sharp knife. Hvitsarkr ordered the punishment, "Blodorn rista shall be his punishment. Let the blood eagle be carved on King Ella's back. Draw it slowly so King Ella can be treated to the sight of his own innards."

The soldier did as he was commanded. King Ella's clothes were striped from him. He was held down as the soldier first cut a vertical line down King Ella's back and then carved around under his rib cage to the front. After King Ella's chest was cut open his ribs were parted and his lungs were carefully lifted out and put into the King's hands. Up until this moment King Ella had remained conscious. Then the shock and pain of seeing and holding his own pulsing lungs mercifully caused him to pass out. With King Ella unconscious there was no more sport to the game, so his lungs and heart were severed and King Ella died. The sons of Ragnar Lodbrokr had finally avenged their father's death.

Ivar Lackbones told his brothers his intentions, "I've come to love England and now claim this land and the throne as my own. I resign my claims to the throne of Denmark, all the lands of our father and mother, as well as all the lands we have conquered together. Let's now live in peace and as brothers. Let our Kingdoms live in peace and as allies."

Bjorn Jarnsida, Hvitsarkr, and Sigurdr Snake-in-the-Eye thought this was a very fair arrangement and agreed to it. They returned to Denmark while Ivar Lackbones returned to Lundunaberg, which he made the capital of England. He ruled there for many years in great glory until his death, of illness, not of war.

CHAPTER 38
THE DEATHS OF THE SONS OF RAGNAR LODBROKR

The three brothers returned to Denmark and told Randalin that Ragnar Lodbrokr's death had finally been avenged. She was pleased. Soon after, Hvitsarkr and Sigurdr Snake-in-the-Eye took their armies and went out conquering in different lands of the world. Bjorn Jarnsida remained in Denmark to rule.

Such was the way things passed for many years. Randalin grew old but remembered the past glories of Sigmundr, Volsungr, Sigurdr Fafnirsbani, and Brynhildr, and the present glories her sons still won. Her life had been good and glorious.

o   o   o   o

Her son Hvitsarkr was in the Baltic warring against the Russians, trying to conquer them. He chased them all the way to Hunland before the tide of battle turned against him. Hvitsarkr met with his first and only defeat and was captured. Nobly he requested he be allowed to choose the manner and place of his death. "I have lived upon this earth and would die by the fire of my enemies, and find my final rest in water. During our battles I saw a pleasant inlet with a waterfall. That is the peaceful spot where I would like to rest."

His instructions were carried out and the skulls of the men he had killed in battle against the Russians were piled up to form a pyre and seeded through with kindling and dry logs. He took his place on these heads, unafraid. The pyre was lit and so he met his death.

After the fire had burned down to ashes and bones, and was cool to the touch, his bones were gathered into a bag The Anvaranautr ring had reshaped itself onto Hvitsarkr's bony finger. No one noticed the ring when the boney finger was scooped up and tossed into the bag. The bag was weighted with stones and tied up and tossed into the Danube at the inlet near the waterfall. Unknowingly Andvaranautr had been flung into the Andvarafors from whence it had come. The ring was returned to its home, Andvari's Curse was no more.

When Randalin heard news of Hvitsarkr's death she sang songs praising the bravery of her son and the death he had chosen. She never thought of the ring.

o   o   o   o

Her other son, Bjorn Jarnsida, gave up the throne of Denmark to Sigurdr Snake-in-the-Eye and went to rule in Sweden. His sons all became great warriors. One of his most famous descendants was Thord who lived in Hofdi on Hofdastrand.

o   o   o   o

Sigurdr Snake-in-the-Eye took over as King of Denmark and lived a long life there. He had many children, all of whom were noble in bearing. His eldest was a daughter named Ragnhildr who was the mother of Harald Fair-hair. Harald Fair-Hair eventually won the Kingdom of Norway as his alone, the first King to unite that contentious land.

o   o   o   o

It was at this time Ivar Lackbones died in England. Upon his deathbed he commanded his bed be taken to the coast and set where the land was least protected. He died there guarding his Kingdom to the last. A funeral cairn was erected at that spot, and Ivar Lackbones was laid to rest inside.

After hearing of his uncle's death Harald Fair-Hair of Norway journeyed to England intending to claim England as his own since Ivar Lackbones had died childless. He landed at the spot where Ivar Lackbones' burial cairn had been built. He was defeated in battle. The throne of England for Harald Fair-Hair had not been the wish of Ivar Lackbones.

Later William the Bastard landed in that same spot. He commanded the burial cairn be burst open. He and his men stepped back after looking inside. Ivar Lackbones stared back at them whole and unrotted, guarding the Kingdom he loved so well. The would-be King commanded his two bravest soldiers to enter the tomb and bring forth the body, whereupon it was placed on a funeral pyre and burnt until nothing save ashes remained of it. These William cast into the sea so no trace of Ivar Lackbones would be on English soil protecting the country, after which William easily conquered the island and gained the name change from William the Bastard to William the Conqueror.

CHAPTER 39
TWO SOLDIER'S STORIES

After a time it came to pass all the sons of Ragnar Lodbrokr had met their deaths. The men who had served them were now scattered throughout many realms, fighting in many armies. And all of those men thought they had never fought under better leaders than the sons of Ragnar Lodbrokr.

Two of these soldiers traveled the world separately trying to find Princes or Kings to serve under who were as brave as Randalin, Ivar Lackbones, Bjorn Jarnsida, Hvitsarkr, Rognvaldr, or Sigurdr Snake-in-the-Eye. But without success.

One of the soldiers was traveling in Norway when he heard of a great funeral feast being held for a King who had died. The King's two sons had sent word any and all warriors who heard of their summons for the next three winters should meet for a banquet honoring their father during the summer following the third winter. In the meantime the sons prepared their land for the feast. Great Halls were constructed to house the warriors. Cattle was fatted especially for the feast. Strong mead was brewed so none would lack for what they usually drank, and more.

A former soldier of the sons of Ragnar Lodbrokr made his way to the feast. He was surprised to see how many warriors had assembled to honor the dead King. He made his way to the main Hall and addressed the two Princes. He was by far the largest man of any there. "Pray, where would you have me sit? Motion to the spot and I will sit there, even if it be among the kitchen help, such is the honor I feel being at this funeral feast to honor such a great King."

The two Princes were impressed with this soldier. The eldest son said, "Sit up at the main table with us. I'm sure we can make room for you."

After quite a bit of squeezing this was accomplished even though he took up the places of two men. A large serving platter was set before him along with the largest tankard of mead the servants could find. He lifted the plate and consumed the meat in one swallow. Then he washed it down with the mead, which he also swallowed in one gulp. He looked disdainfully at the others around him who had much smaller portions. More food and drink was brought to him.

Then a second man appeared at the feast. He was much larger than the first. Their clothing appeared similar. Both wore wide hats and fur coverings made of the same type of animal. This soldier addressed the Princes courteously, "Where is it you would have me sit? I will not be offended even if you place me in the stables among the hay and horses, such is the honor of being at the funeral of so great a King as your father."

This time the youngest Prince spoke, "We are honored by your presence. If we squeeze together a little more we can make room for you at this table."

However, this didn't prove to be the case. Try as they might, they couldn't make room enough for the stranger until three of the men left the table and went to a lower bench, which though not as honored was at least more roomy.

The second warrior proved to be a greater eater and drinker than the first. Unfortunately he couldn't hold his liquor. He turned his back to the others and would only talk to the first soldier. The two began yelling out stories of their battlefield triumphs.

The first soldier spoke, "I've often been on the battlefield which was covered with the blood of my enemies. But I gather from the looks of you that your greatest wars were at the food table, and you seem to have lost those."

The second warrior countered, "I have journeyed far and wide into strange lands of even stranger customs, while you sat near your mother's side afraid of the dark. The wolves and ravens have become fat on the meals I've given them on the battlefield."

The first, not to be outdone, elaborated on his victories, "I've sailed far and wide traveling under the command of the most noble brothers. I've fed the wolf, the raven, and the eagle, while you sat at table eating and telling other's stories of glory as your own."

The second one continued, "Funny, when I sailed in the ship under the three brothers I didn't see you there. Nor were you on shore to greet us when we landed, fresh from our victories over a mighty King."

They suddenly realized they had both been boasting of the sons of Ragnar Lodbrokr, and that they had once been kindred in arms. The first soldier continued his boasting, "I think we've sailed together, you by the mast, while I stood at the prow. We sailed with the sons of Ragnar Lodbrokr and took part in their glory together."

The second warrior agreed, "You're right. Now I remember you. We both fought side-by-side at Bulgarland, but I fell wounded in the side. You killed the enemy who had attacked me, and for that I owe you my life."

The two continued on throughout the night, yelling of the noble deeds of the other as well as praising the glory of the Volsungrs, Niblungs, Sigmundr, Sigurdr Fafnirsbani, Brynhildr, Randalin, Ragnar Lodbrokr, Ivar Lackbones, Bjorn Jarnsida, Hvitsarkr, Rognvaldr, and Sigurdr Snake-in-the-Eye.

The two Princes, as well as the others at the feast, were glad their boasting had changed to shouts of camaraderie and praise one for the other, thus avoiding a very unpleasant evening. As it was, it was proving to be rather loud.

CHAPTER 40
FINAL PRAISES OF RAGNAR LODBROKR AND HIS KIN

Ogmundr the Dane was a great warrior. On one expedition he commanded five ships that had set out from Denmark to go conquering in the name of Denmark's Kings both past and present.

One evening he ordered his ships to anchor by Samsey in Munarvag Harbor. There they rested for the night. The next morning Ogmundr the Dane sent his cooks ashore to see if they could find anyone to help them prepare breakfasts for the crews of the five ships. They were willing to pay any volunteers in silver.

While they were gone several of Ogmundr the Dane's soldiers went ashore to explore the woods and see if there was anything there of interest. They reported back to Ogmundr the Dane an amazing discovery.

The first soldier began the story, "We were walking in the forest until we came to a clearing. Set in the middle of that meadow was the giant figure of a man carved in wood."

The second soldier took over the story, "It must have been forty ells high if it was anything."

The first soldier took over again, "We walked up to it and saw that it still had its countenance. It had not been worn away in the slightest by the weather, which was most unusual, since it was in the middle of a meadow with nothing to protect it from any fierce winds that might blow in from the sea. We could see it was very ancient, yet the wood, in a way, looked fresh and new. It gleamed in the sun as if it had been newly oiled."

A third soldier continued the story, "We walked up to touch it. Then we jumped back because after our hands touched it, it immediately began speaking as if it were alive. It spoke of long ago when Ragnar Lodbrokr's sons had first gone adventuring by sea. 'The sons of Ragnar Lodbrokr raised me up by the shore and gave sacrifices to me that I might grant them victory in battle. Then they set me up here by a thorn bush so I could look out over the world and see the mighty deeds they wrought, the wars they fought, the Kingdoms they won. So I've stood here all

these years and watched the sons of Ragnar Lodbrokr meet their deaths, as well as their sons' sons, and their sons' sons' sons. The moss has grown at my feet, while the rain in summer and the cold snow in winter has fallen on me. But I've been proud of what I've seen and can now once more shout out the praises of Ragnar Lodbrokr and his noble sons.'"

The first soldier concluded the story, "The wooden statue commanded us to leave him and travel throughout the land singing the praises of Ragnar Lodbrokr and his sons. And this we have done to you and will do to everyone we meet. Such was the force of the command."

o   o   o   o

So ends the stories of the Volsungrs and their descendants. Think of their stories and tell them to those you meet so their legend will never die.

GLOSSARY

GLOSSARY

Ægir (Ægir, Æger, Æge, Œgir, Eagor) [destruction]: Sometimes known as Hler. Ruled the sea with his wife Ran, who was also his sister. They had two other brothers, Loki and Kari. Their father was Fornjot. They had nine wavemaiden daughters (Himinglæva, Dufa, Blodughadda, Hefring, Udr, Hronn, Bylgja, Drofn, Kolga). Both were frequent visitors to Asgardr. He had a long flowing white beard, green hair, and was tall and gaunt. Ægir and Ran's Hall was on an island in the Kattigut also known as Hlessey. He owned a giant kettle for brewing mead that had been fetched from the jotun Hymir for him by Thor and Tyr.

Æsir (Æsir, Asar, Anses, Asas, Asa-folk): The name for the group of gods known for their power rather than fecundity.

Agnar (Aganar): Audi's brother. He stole the swan guises belonging to Brynhildr and the other Valkyries with her and would only return them if she disobeyed Odin and gave victory to him that day over Hjalmgunnar, Odin's favorite. She did, thus angering Odin by what she had done.

Agnar: Ragnar Lodbrokr's youngest son by Thora Borgarhjort. His elder brother was Eric. He died in battle fighting King Eystein.

Aki (Haki, Aiki): Married to Grima. They killed King Heimir and raised Aslaugr as their own after renaming her Kraka.

Alfr (Álf, Helfrat, Hálf, Helferich): King Hjalprekr of Denmark's son. Hjordis' second husband, therefore Sigurdr's stepfather. Alf's second wife was Thora. They befriended Gudrunr after Sigurdr's death.

Alfheimr (Álfheimr, Álfheim, Álfheimar, Alfheim, Alvheim, Elfheim) [elf land, elf home]: Home of the ljosalfar (light elves). Situated midway between Asgardr and Midgardr. Given to the Æsir Freyr as a tooth gift.

Alfhildr (Alfhild) [elf warrior]: Daughter of King Gandalf of Raumarike. Married King Hringr.

Alf Hundingsson (Álf Hundingsson): Lived in Thjod. Hunding's son and Helgi's enemy. His brothers were Eyjolf, Hervardr, and Hagbardr. He and his brothers fought Helgi and Sinfjotli's army on Logafjollum and were defeated and slain beneath the area known as Eagle Rock.

Alfs [elves]: Another name for the elves. Also known as Alfen and Elfen.

Alf the Elder: Sent for Hoddbrodr to battle against Helgi and Sinfjotli.

Alsvidr (Álsvidr, Álsvid, Alsvid, Alswid) [all swift]: King Heimir and Bekkhildr's son.

Alsvin (Alsvinn) [the swift one]: One of two horses pulling Sol's chariot. The other was Arvakr.

Andvarafors (Andvare-force, Andvari's Force, Andvari's Fall): The force or waterfall in which Andvari kept himself hidden in the form of a pike. His golden hoard was hidden there.

Andvaranautr (Andvarenaut, Andvaranaut, Andvarinaut, Andvari's Doom, Andvari's Gift) [Andvari's gemstone]: Andvari's ring cursed by him when Loki stole it. It is that curse that brings on the tragedy to whomever wears the ring. The curse will be lifted only after the ring is returned to the Andvarafors.

Andvaranautr, People who wore the Ring: 1. Chapter 11: Norn, 2. Chapter 11: Andvari (Andvaranautr, 3. Chapter 11: Odin, 4. Chapter 11: Hreidmar, 5. Chapter 11: Fafnir, 6. Chapter 13: Sigurdr, 7. Chapter 14: Brynhildr, 8. Chapter 18: Gunnar, 9. Chapter 19: Gudrunr, 10: Chapter 23: Atli Budlason, 11: Chapter 26: Gudrunr, 12. Chapter 28: Erpr, 13. Chapter 28: Hamdir, 14. Chapter 28: Odin, 15. Chapter 29: Heimir, 16. Chapter 29: Aslaugr/Kraka, 17. Chapter 31: Ragnar Lodbrokr, 18. Chapter 33: Kraka, 19. Chapter 33: Ragnar Lodbrokr, 20. Chapter 33: Sigurdr-Snake-in-the-Eye, 21. Chapter 33: Aslaugr, 22. Chapter 34: Eric, 23. Chapter 34: Soldier (to return to Aslaugr), 24. Chapter 34: Aslaugr, 25: Chapter 34: Hvitsarkr, 26. Chapter 38: Danube at Andvarafors.

Andvari (Andvare) [wary, cautious spirit]: The dvergar son of Oinn, cursed by a Norn to guard his hoard of gold. This hoard was stolen from him by Loki so it could be used as weregild to pay for Otr's death. Andvari laid a curse upon the owners of the hoard. The various owners would have tragedy brought to them and their families until the hoard was returned to Andvari. He owned the ring Andvaranautr that he cursed. Ill luck would follow all who owned the ring until it was returned to the Andvarafors. He lived in the water in the form of a pike, swimming around guarding his hoard.

Andvari's Hoard (Andvare's Hoard): The hoard of gold that covered Otr's skin. The Andvaranautr ring was part of the hoard. The hoard and ring were cursed until they were returned to their right owner, Andvari.

Angel-ness: A six day sea battle Ragnar Lodbrokr won against King Valthjof, who was slain during the encounter.

Angelsey: A battle in which many Princes were defeated by Ragnar Lodbrokr.

Arvakr (Árvakr, Aarvak, Árvak, Arwakr) [early waker]: One of the two horses pulling Sol's chariot. Runes were carved on his ear. The other horse pulling the chariot was Alsvin.

Asgardr (Ásgardr, Ásgarth, Ásgard, Asgard): The city in Asaheimr atop Mt. Idavollr that was the home of the Æsir.

Aslaugr (Áslaugr, Áslaug, Aslaug, Asla): The daughter of Sigurdr and Brynhildr. She was orphaned at the age of three when King Heimir, her foster-father, was killed by Aki and Grima (Sigurdr and Brynhildr were already dead). Aki and Grima changed her named to Kraka and raised her as their own. She married Ragnar Lodbrokr. Her children were Ivar Lackbones, Bjorn Jarnsida, Hvitsarkr, Rognvaldr, and Sigurdr Snake-in-the-eye. Her name was changed to Randalin after she went to battle with her sons.

Atheling: A term referring to a Prince.

Atli Budlason (Atle, Atli Budlason, Atli Budlison): His foster-father and brother-in-law was King Heimir. His real father was King Budli. His sisters were Brynhildr, Bekkhildr, and Oddrunr. He married Gudrunr (her second husband) and was murdered by her. Hodbrodr sent for him to battle against Helgi and Sinfjotli on Logafjollum. His horse was named Glaumr.

Audi (Aud, Autha): Agnar's brother.

Baltic: Hvitsarkr met his death and defeat here against the Russians.

Bardfirth: A land battle fought by Ragnar Lodbrokr.

Baugeidr: The name for eternal friendship such as that sworn by Sigurdr Fafnirsbani, Gutthormr, Hogni, and Gunnar.

Beit (Beiti): One of King Atli's evil counselors.

Bekkhildr (Bekkhild)[small river warrior]: Daughter of King Budli, sister of Brynhildr, Atli Budlason, and Oddrunr. She married King Heimir of Hlymdale, who was also her foster-father. They had a son named Alsvidr.

Berghildr (Berghild): She was married to Helgi Haddingskadi and gave birth to their son Braalund.

Berserkrs (Berserkirs, Berserkers, Berserks) [bear shirt, bare sarks, bare shirts — without armor]: Warriors so filled with the ecstasy of battle they wore neither armor nor any other form of protection. They fought in a frenzy usually with the strength of a madman brought on by a lack of fear and caution. They didn't care if they were hacked up or killed in the process. Their mood was so euphoric they felt no pain when they were injured. They were known as ulfhednar (wolf-skinned) when in their frenzy they howled like wolves to frighten their opponents. Also dressed in bear skins.

Bifrost (Bifröst, Bifrest, Bfraust, Bivrost, Bilrúst, Bilóst, Bilöst, Bilrest, Birfr, Birfrost) [trembling way]: Also called Asbru and the Rainbow Bridge. It connected Midgardr to Asgardr. The colors in the bridge came from the different elements—red from fire, blue from air, and green from the sea. Heimdallr guarded Bifrost. The golden gate at the top had a diamond lock. The only key to open the lock was held by Heimdallr. The sound it made when it opened was both sad and happy, like the dripping of leaves after it rains. Thor was too heavy to cross it and had to wade through the rivers under it.

Bikki (Bekki): Jormunrekkr's evil counselor who accompanied Hrandver, Jormunrekkr's son, to woo and win Svanhildr for him. He betrayed Hrandver and Svanhildr to Jormunrekkr after they had fallen in love. Also known as Sibich in some versions.

Bjargrunar (Bjargrúnar, Biarg-runes) [help runes]: Runes good for women in childbirth, or healing those wounds suffered in battle. They were cut in the hollow of the hand and it was best to call on Mardoll for their use.

Bjorn Jarnsida (Bjorn Járnsída, Bjorn Jarnside) [Bear Ironside]: Ragnar Lodbrokr and Kraka's second son. His brothers were Ivar Lackbones, Hvitsarkr, Rognvaldr, and Sigurdr Snake-in-the-Eye. He was Ragnar Lodbrokr's favorite and the strongest of he and Kraka's children. He eventually became King of Denmark after Ivar Lackbones renounced the throne to assume the throne of England. He later gave the throne to Sigurdr Snake-in-the-Eye so he would then be free to accept the throne of Sweden.

Blodorn rista (Blódorn rísta) [blood eagle]: The form of punishment in which an incision was made in the back, the ribs were separated and the lungs were drawn out of the body, usually while the person was still alive. This practice was known as cutting the blood eagle.

Blood Payment: Instead of accepting weregild for a death sometimes the family would only accept blood payment, a life for a life.

Bokrunar (Bôk-Runes) [book runes]: Runes of learning.

Borghildr of Bralundi (Borghildr, Borghild) [the hild or battle-maiden, dwelling in the castle]: Usually called Borgy. She was Sigmundr's first wife. Their two twin children were Helgi and Hamund. Her brother was betrothed to the woman Sinfjotli fell in love with. She poisoned Sinfjotli which caused Sigmundr to leave her. She later died under suspicious circumstances.

Borgy: The contracted version of Borghildr of Bralundi. The name she was eventually known by.

Bornholm: The place where Ragnar Lodbrokr easily won a victory during a fierce storm. King Vulnir led the opposing army.

Braalund: The son of Helgi Haddingskadi and Berghildr.

Bragi: God of poetry. Runes were carved on his tongue.

Bragi: One of Hogni's sons. His sister was Sigrunr, his brother was Dagr. He was slain in battle against Hoddbrodr.

Bralundi (Bralund, Brálund, Braalund) [brow land]: The land where Borghild bore Helgi. Part of Sigmundr's Kingdom.

Brand Isle: See Hedinsey. Some of Helgi's men traveled from here before battling Hoddbrodr.

Branik: A city in Osterhotland province in Sweden near Bravoll Field.

Branstokk (Branstock, Barnstock, Barnstokk) [stem of the children, sword-trunk]: The tree standing in the midst of Volsungr's Hall in which Odin thrust the sword Gramr. Sigmundr was the only one able to pull the sword from out of Branstokk's trunk.

Bravoll Field (Brávoll Field, Bravell Field, Bravells Field): Located in the eastern part of Sweden, near Branik in Osterhotland. It was a plain where the mythical battle between King Sigurdrhringr and his uncle Harald Hilditonn (Harald Hilditann) took place around 750 A.D. The outcome supposedly led to the breaking apart of Denmark and Sweden as separate Kingdoms. Sinfjotli was accused by King Granmar of having been a mare to Grani here.

Bredi: Skadi's servant who was slain by Sigi.

Bredi's Drift: The term for a large snowbank, given in honor of Bredi who was slain by Sigi and hidden in a large snowdrift.

Brim Runar (Brimrúnar, Brim-runes) [sea runes]: These runes were carved on the stern of a ship and its rudder blade and oars.

Brynhildr (Brynhilda, Brynhilde, Brynhild, Brunhildr, Brunhild) [maiden in byrny]: Her father was King Budli. Her foster-father and brother-in-law was King Heimir of Hlymdale, who was married to her sister Bekkhildr. Her other sister was Oddrunr. Her brother was Atli Budlason. She owned a swan-guise that she could change into when she rode as a Valkyrie. The horse she rode as a Valkyrie was named Vingskornir. She had a daughter, Aslaugr, by Sigurdr Fafnirsbani. They had vowed to wed, but Sigurdr was tricked into forgetting his vows and married Gudrunr. Instead, she later married Gunnar, Gudrunr's brother. In some versions of the legend she was known as Sigrdrifa.

Budli (Buthlu, Buthli, Budli): He was a King and father of Brynhildr, Bekkhildr, Oddrunr, and Atli Budlason.

Budlings (Budlungs, Buthlungs): The relatives of King Budli. The Norns proclaimed at Helgi's birth he would be the best of the Budlings.

Busiltarn (Busiltjörn): The swiftly flowing river that ran through Alf's land. Grani swam it and was picked by Sigurdr as his horse, with Odin's help, because of his strength in crossing the river and not being pulled under by its strong current.

Crow-Guise: The guise assumed by Gna flying overhead to drop the fertilizing apple in Rerir's lap.

Dagr (Dag): King Hogni's son. The brother of Sigrunr and Bragi. The three had been honorbound to fight on Hoddbroddr's side in the battle against Helgi. Hogni, Bragi and Helgi. In order for his life to be spared Dagr vowed fealty to Helgi, a promise he broke when he slew Helgi at Fjotur Grove. Odin lent him Gungnir to do the deed.

Danpr (Danpi): A horse owned by King Atli which Vingi hinted might be given to Gunnar and Hogni, along with the lands of Gnitaheidr and Myrkvydr, when he tried to tempt them to visit King Atli.

Daughters of Dvalin: Another name for the Disir, the guardian norns who accompany a hero.

Dis (Dís, Dîs): Plural of Disir. They were attendant spirits or guardian angels. This term could also be used to signify any female deity.

Disir (Dísir, Dîsir): The plural of Dis.

Dvergar (Dvergr): Another name for the svartalfars/dwarves. The first svartalfar was Modsognir. He and the others were created from the maggots crawling in Ymir's decomposing body. They collected gold, other precious metals and gems and hid them away in the ground. Their hoards were used to fashion magical weapons and jewelry. They were masters of runes and magic songs. Other names for them included brownies, trolls, goblins, pucks, gremlins, Huldra folk, and kobolds.

The svartalfar from Svartalfheimr were particularly mischievous. Many wore red caps called tarnkappes, which made the wearer invisible to those on Midgardr, including the sun, so they wouldn't be turned to stone in the daylight, giving them more time to do their mischief.

Dvergues [dwarves]: Plural of dvergar.

Dvina's Mouth: A river where Ragnar Lodbrokr fought and bested eight Jarls when he was about twenty.

Dwarf: See dvergar.

Dwarves: See dvergues.

Eagle Rock: The place in Logafjollum where Alf, Eyjolf, Hervardr, and Harald (Hunding's sons) were slain by Helgi and Sinfjotli.

Egil [sword's edge]: The name of a King who slew Ragnar Lodbrokr's son.

Einherjar: The name given to the heroes in Valhalla.

Eitill (Eitil): The name of King Atli's eldest son. His brother was named Erpr. Gudrunr murdered the two and served them to King Atli for diner using their blood for wine.

Ell: A measure of length equivalent to 45 inches (114 cm).

Ella [entire]: A King who ruled England when Ragnar Lodbrokr tried to conquer it. Instead Ragnar Lodbrokr was killed by King Ella, who in turn was killed by Ivar Lackbones who then assumed the throne. Ivar Lackbones had the blood eagle carved on King Ella's back.

Enderdis Isles: A battle where Ragnar Lodbrokr easily won victory.

England: The land Ragnar Lodbrokr tried and failed to conquer. His son Ivar Lackbones succeeded and became King there.

Eric (Erik) [complete ruler]: Ragnar Lodbrokr's eldest son by Thora Borgarhjort. His younger brother was Agnar. They battled King Eystein and were defeated. However, King Eystein was so impressed with him he offered him command of his armies and his daughter Ingeborg's hand in marriage. Eric refused and instead chose to be cast onto raised spears and spitted to death.

Erpr (Erp): The name of King Atli's youngest son. His brother was Eitill. Gudrunr murdered them and served them to King Atli for dinner, using their blood for wine.

Erpr (Erp): The son of Gudrunr and Jonakr. His brothers were Sorli and Hamdir. He had raven-black hair. He was the favorite of Gudrunr and was murdered by his brothers because of this. His sister was Svanhildr.

Eusteing: King Eystein's Hall in Uppsala, Sweden.

Eyjolf (Eyolf): Hunding's son. His brothers were Alf Hundingsson, Hagbardr, and Hervardr. They were slain by Helgi and Sinfjotli.

Eylimi (Eglymi, Eglimi): King of the islands. His daughter was Hjordis who married Sigmundr. His other child was Grifir.

Eymod: A famous warrior from Denmark. King Eymod III.

Eyra-Sund: Ragnar Lodbrokr fought him in his youth.

Eystein [everlasting stone]: A King of Sweden when Ragnar Lodbrokr ruled in Denmark. His Hall was called Eusteing. He worshipped the old gods, including

the cow Sibilja. Ingeborg was his daughter. He was Ragnar Lodbrokr's best friend until Ragnar Lodbrokr jilted his daughter. Defeated and slain by Ivar Lackbones, Bjorn Jarnsida, Hvitsarkr, Randalin, and Sigurdr Snake-in-the-Eye.

Fafnir (Fáfnir, Fadnir, Fâfnir, Fafner) [the embracing one, he who surrounds with his arms]: A dragon guarding the hoard of gold that originally belonged to Andvari the dvergar. His father was Hreidmar. His younger sisters were Lyngheidr and Lofnheidr. His younger brothers were Otr and Regin. He plotted with his brothers to kill Hreidmar. He actually wielded the sword that slew their father.

Fengr (Feng): An ekename for Odin. See Hnikar.

Firth: An inlet along the coast, usually at the mouth of a waterway. Similar to a fjord, but with less steep banks.

Fjolnir (Fiölnir, Fjolner, Fiolnir): See Hnikar.

Fjon (Fion): The Danish island off Funen. Sigar and Siggeir fought Sigmundr south of Fjon.

Fjornir (Fjönir, Fiernir, Fiornir): An ekename for Odin.

Fjornir (Fjönir, Fiernir, Fiornir): King Gunnar's servant who was given the duty of attending Vingi during his visit.

Fjotur Grove (Fjoturland, Fjoture Grove, Fetter Grove): The name of the grove where Dagr slew Helgi.

Flemish Plain: The battle where Freyr was slain by Ragnar Lodbrokr.

Foglhildr (bird-hild): In some versions of the Nibelungenlied Saga, Svanhildr is referred to as Foglhildr.

Frankland: The land south of Denmark where Sigmundr moved after Borghildr poisoned Sinfjotli.

Frekastein (Frekastone) [wolf stone]: A place in Solfjoll where Helgi and Sinfjotli battled and defeated King Granmar's sons. This action left the way clear for Helgi to marry Sigrunr. Granmar accused Helgi of having been given the land unlawfully by Sigmundr at his birth.

Freyr (Frey): A warrior defeated by Ragnar Lodbrokr on Flemish Plain.

Frigg: Odin's wife. He asked her to intercede for Rerir whose wife was having difficulty becoming pregnant. Frigg sent her servant Gna to him with an apple that helped matters along.

Gallows' Hill: The hill where King Jormunrekkr ordered his son Hrandver to be taken and hung for falling in love with Svanhildr. He regretted his action but was too late to save his son. His evil counselor Bikki had already given the order for Hrandver's hanging. It had originally been named Thieves' Hill but was renamed since Hrandver had not been a thief. Though some thought he had been a thief, stealing Svanhildr away from his father.

Gandalf: King of Raumarike. His daughter was Alfhildr, who was married to King Hringr.

Gautland (Gothland, Land of the Goths, Götaland, Gothia, Gothenland, Geatland): The land in the southern part of Sweden ruled over by Siggeir and Signy. Hunland was united with Gautland by their marriage. The inhabitants were called Gautar (Geatas) or Goths. It was generally thought to be located between lakes Vennern and Vättern in the old province of Götarike, Sweden.

Gautar (Getas, Goths): The people of Gautland. Siggeir was their King.

Geitir [goat-herd]: The guard Sigurdr confronted in front of his uncle Grifir's door.

Giaflaug: Gjuki's sister. She saw the death of five husbands, two daughters, three sisters, and eight brothers. She tried to outdo Gudrunr in her grief after Sigurdr's death by telling Gudrunr of her sad life.

Gjuki (Gjúki, Gjuke, Giuki, Giúki): The name of the King who was married to Grimhildr. Their sons were Gudmundr, Gunnar, and Hogni. Their daughter was Gudrunr. His stepson was Gutthormr. His sister was Giaflaug. His grandsons were Golar, Nibelungr, Snævarr, and Solarr.

Gjukings (Gjúkungs, Gjukungs, Giukings, Gjúkungar, Niflungar, Nibelungs (Niblungs, Niflungs, Nibelungs, Nibelungen, Burgundians): The descendants of King Gjuki, also known as the Gjukungs.

Glaumr: King Atli's horse.

Glaumvor (Glaumvör, Glaumvor): Gunnar's second wife. She and Kostbera had premonitory dreams of death and warned their husbands not to visit King Atli. Their advice was ignored with tragic results.

Gna: The daughter of the jotun Hrimnir who brought an apple to Rerir to give to his wife so she would become pregnant. She was also known as Hljod when she ceased living in Asgardr and married Volsungr. Her children included the twins Sigmundr and Signy as well as nine other sons. She was known sometimes as Frigg's casket-bearing maid.

Gnipalund (Gnipa Grove): The place where Helgi anchored his ships at Una Bay before battling Hoddbrodr at Frekastein in Solfjoll. See Thorsness.

Gnipefjord: A port Ivar Lackbones, Bjorn Jarnsida, Hvitsarkr, and Rognvaldr used on their way to Whitby.

Gnitaheidr (Gnitahead, Gnipaheath, Gnita-heath, Gnítaheidr, Gnîtaheid, Gnipa Grove, Gnitaheidr, Gnitaheidar, Gnitaheath) [glittering heath]: The place where Fafnir lived in the form of a dragon guarding his hoard.

Godmund (Godmundr): Lived 500 years.

Go fukt dyr (go fukt dyr) [noble beast]: An ekename for Sigurdr.

Golar: Hogni and Kostbera's son. Gjuki's grandson. His brothers were Snævarr, Solarr, and Nibelungr. His uncles were Orkningr (Kostbera's brother) and Gunnar, (Hogni's brother). They were honorbound to fight against Helgi and Sinfjotli. All except Nibelungr traveled to King Atli's Hall and were all ordered slain by King Atli. Golar was slain first. Nibelungr and Gudrunr later avenged their deaths by killing King Atli.

Golnir: King Granmar accused Golnir, a jotun, of being King Granmar's goatherd.

Goths: The people of Gautland. Also known as Gautar. Siggeir was their King.

Goti: Gunnar's horse.

Gramr (Gram) [wrath]: The sword Odin thrust into Branstokk. Sigmundr was the only one able to pull it out. It was split asunder at Sigmundr's death and reforged by Regin so Sigurdr could use it to slay the dragon Fafnir.

Grani (Grane, Grání) [Greyfell]: Sigurdr's horse, which he picked out with Odin's help. It was a descendant of Sleipnir's, and had runes carved on its breast. Granmar accused Sinfjotli of being Grani's mare on Bravoll Field.

Granmar (Granmer): King Granmar of Svarinshaug. Hoddbrodr's father. Fought with Hunding against Helgi as well as Gudmundr and Starkadr. All his sons were slain by Helgi and Sinfjotli at Frekastein in Solfjoll.

Grifir: (Grîfir): Son of King Eylimi. His was Hjordis' brother, and therefore, Sigurdr's uncle. He had the gift of prophecy and told Sigurdr how his future would come to be. The guard outside his door was named Geitir.

Grima: Married to Aki. They killed King Heimir and raised Aslaugr as their own daughter after renaming her Kraka.

Grimhildr (Grimhild, Grimhildd, Grimhilr, Grímhildr, Grimhildr, Grimhíld) [helmet maiden, maiden in helmet, vizar]: Gjuki's wife. Their sons were Gunnar, Gudmundr (Gudny), and Hogni. Their daughter was Gudrunr. She also had another son, Gjuki's stepson, who was named Gutthormr.

Grindur (Grind): More than 15,000 of Helgi's men waited here before the battle against Hoddbrodr.

Gripir (Grîpir, Greipir, Grípir): Alf's stud-keeper. He told Sigurdr where the horses were grazing.

Gudmundr (Gudmund, Guthmund, Gudmund): Gjuki and Grimhildr's son. He was called Gudny in some versions of the saga. His brothers were Hogni and Gunnar. His sister was Gudrunr. His stepbrother was Gutthormr. He had raven-black hair, as did most of the Gjukings.

Gudmundr (Gudmund, Guthmund, Gudmund): Granmar's son. His brothers were Hoddbrodr and Starkadr. His horse was Sveipudr.

Gudny: Another name for Gudmundr, the son of Gjuki and Grimhildr.

Gudrunr (Gudrún, Guthrún, Gudrune) [battle comrade]: Daughter of Gjuki. Wife of Sigurdr Fafnirsbani, Atli Budlason and Jonakr. Her brothers were Gudmundr, Gunnar, and Hogni. Her stepbrother was Gutthormr. She had raven-black hair. She had three sons by her third husband, Jonakr. They were Hamdir, Sorli, and Erpr.

Gullrondr (Gullrond): King Gjuki's daughter. Her brothers were Gudmundr, Gunnar, and Hogni. Her sister was Gudrunr. Her stepbrother was Gutthormr.

Gungnir: Odin's spear. Once thrown it supposedly never missed its mark. Odin lent it to Dagr to use to kill Helgi.

Gunnar Gjukason (Gunnarr, Gunnar Gjúkason) [leader in battle, strife]: Gjuki and Grimhildr's son. His brothers were Hogni and Gudmundr. His sister was Gudrunr. His stepbrother was Gutthormr. His Hall was in Limfjord. He was married first to Brynhildr and after her death to Glaumvor. He married Brynhildr's sister Oddrunr after Brynhildr's death. He was one of Sigurdr's best friends. He had raven-black hair. His horse was named Goti. Went with Orkningr and Hogni, and his nephews Golar, Snævarr, and Solarr, to King Atli's where King Atli ordered all of them slain. Golar was slain first. Nibelungr and Gudrunr later avenged their deaths by killing King Atli.

Gutthormr (Guttorm, Gudhorm, Gotthormr, Gutthormr): Gjuki's stepson. His mother was Grimhildr. His stepbrothers were Gudmundr, Gunnar, and Hogni. His stepsister was Gudrunr. He slew Sigurdr, but was cleaved in two and slain by the sword Gramr in the process.

Hagal [skillful]: Helgi's foster-father.

Hagbardr Hundingsson: Hunding's son. See Alf. Brynhildr cites his sons as being great Kings. He was slain by Helgi and Sinfjotli, along with his brothers Alf, Eyjolf and Hervardr on Eagle Rock in Logafjollum.

Haki: One of Hamund's sons. His sons were cited by Brynhildr as being great Kings.

Hakon [chosen son]: Worked for King Alfr of Denmark. He was the father of Thora who was married to King Alf. She was a friend of Gudrunr's.

Halfdan: King. Sigrunr came back to life as his daughter and was a Valkyrie again. Her name was Kara. Helgi came back to life as Helgi Haddingjaskati.

Hamal: Hagal's son and playmate of Helgi. Helgi used this name when in service at King Hunding's.

Hamdir: The son of Jonakr and Gudrunr. His sister was Svanhildr. His brothers were Sorli and Erpr. He and Sorli murdered Erpr. He had raven-black hair.

Hamund (Hamond): Son of Sigmundr and Borghildr. His older twin brother was Helgi. They were born in Bralundi. His son was named Haki.

Harald Fair-Hair [Harald = army commander]: His mother was Ragnhildr, the eldest daughter of Sigurdr Snake-in-the-Eye. He was the first King of a united Norway.

Harald Hilditann (Harald Hilditönn, Harald Hilditonn, Harald Wartooth, Harald Battletooth) [Harald = army commander]: He fought and was defeated by his nephew, King Sigurdrhringr, on Bravoll Field around 750 A.D. The result of that battle eventually led to the separation of the Kingdoms of Sweden and Denmark. Perhaps a mythical story.

Hatan: One of the lands given Helgi at his natal feast by Sigmundr. The others were Solfjoll, Sinjofjoll, Himinvanga, Sigarsvoll, Hringstadir and Hringsjod the harbor in that land.

Hatun Sound (Hátún Sound): Sogn was here. This was where some of Helgi's ships waited before the battle against Hoddbrodr.

Hedinsey Isle (Hedinsey Isle, Hedensey, Heidensey, Hethin's Isle, Island of Hiddensey): Most likely the island known as Hiddense located north of Rugen (Rügen). Some of Helgi's men traveled from there and met him in Raudabjarg before battling Hoddbrodr.

Hedninga Bay: The place of one of Ragnar Lodbrokr's victories.

Heiddraupnir's Skull (Héidraupnir's Skull, Heiddraupner's Skull) [clear dripper's skull]: The name of one of the containers in which Midvitner kept the Precious Mead after he had stolen it from the Æsir. It was also known as Hoddropnir's Horn.

Heimir of Hlymdale (Heimer of Hlymdale): The King of Hlymdale, foster-father and brother-in-law of Brynhildr, Atli Budlason, and Oddrunr. He married their sister, Bekkhildr, who was also his foster-daughter. Their son was Alsvidr.

After Sigurdr and Brynhildr's deaths he rescued Aslaugr and took her into the woods. He stayed at Aki and Grima's cottage and was slain by them. They were surprised to find Aslaugr hidden in a harp. They adopted her, changed her name to Kraka and raised her as their own.

Hel: One of the worst regions in Niflheimr. The river Vandgelmir was here. It was the poisonous river liars must wade through.

Hela (Hel): She was the half-dead, half-living daughter Loki bore after eating Angroboda's heart. Her brothers were Fenriswulf and Midgardrsormr. After she was cast down to the depths of Niflheimr she became ruler of the dead there. Her Hall was called Elidnir.

Helgi: Son of Sigmundr and Borghildr. His younger twin brother was Hamund. They were born in Bralundi. Helgi married Sigrunr the daughter of Hogni.

Helgi Grekasteine (wolf-stone): Married to Sigrunr, King Hogni's daughter. Slain by Dagr. Sigrunr's brother, at Fjortur Grove. He had an army with Sinfjotli that defeated Hunding. Thus the two claimed Hunland as their own. Helgi slew Hunding with his sword. The Norns blessed Helgi's birth. His father gave him the lands known as Solfjoll, Snjofjoll, Hatan, Himinvanga, Sigarsvoll, Hringstadir and Hringsjod, the harbor in that land. He went to work in King Hunding's court in disguise. Later he killed Hunding. Took the name of Hagal's son, Hamal, when in service.

Helgi (Helge): Son of Hjorvarth and Sigrlinn. Helgi Hiörvarsson, Hiörvardr, Helgi Hundingsbani.

Helgi Haddingjaskati (Helgi Haddînskadi, Helgi the Scathe of Hadding, Helgi Hundingsbani, Helgi Hundîngsbani): He was married to Berghildr who gave birth to Braalund.

Helkvi: Hogni's horse.

Helmet of Terror: The helmet worn by Fafnir to frighten away would be thieves. Sigurdr took possession of it after slaying Fafnir.

Helsings: A family fighting with eight Jarls at Dvina's Mouth against Ragnar Lodbrokr. They all lost and were slain.

Helveg [Hel way]: The Helway Road lead to Niflhel. Brynhildr traveled it after her death.

Heming: One of King Hunding's sons.

Herborg: A Queen of Hunland. Her father, mother, and four brothers drowned at sea. Her seven sons and husband were all poisoned. Tried to outdo Gudrunr in her grief over Sigurdr's death.

Herkja: King Atli's mistress who falsely accused Gudrunr of having an affair with Thjorex. After this was found out King Atli reluctantly ordered Herkja put to death.

Herraud (Herrod): Jarl (earl) of Gautland. A King defeated by Ragnar Lodbrokr. A Jarl who lived in Gautland. His daughter was Thora Borgarhjort.

Herthjof: A warrior Ragnar Lodbrokr fought in the Southern Isles.

Hervardr (Hervard, Herward, Hervarth, Hávarth): Hunding's son. See Alf.

Herjan's Disir: An ekename for the Valkyries, since Herjan was an ekename for Odin and he commanded the disir.

Himinvanga: One of the lands Sigmundr gave Helgi at his natal feast. The others were Solfjoll, Snjofjoll, Hatan, Sigarsvoll, Hringstadir and Hringsjod the harbor in that land.

Hindarfjall (Hindarfiall, Hindarfjall, Hindfell, Hind Mountain, Hindarfell, Hindarfell, Hinda-fell, Hindarfiall, Hindarfjoll): The mountain in Frankland where Brynhildr lay sleeping with the sleep thorn caught in her throat.

Hjalli (Hialli): One of Gunnar and Hogni's thralls. King Atli had him killed and showed his heart to Gunnar telling him it was Hogni's. However, the heart was cowardly and still trembling so Gunnar knew King Atli was playing her falsely.

Hjalprekr (Hjalprekkr, Hjálprek of Ty, Hjálprekr, Hialprek of Ty): King of Thjod (Denmark) and Ty (Jutland). Alf was his son.

Hjalmgunnar (Hjalm-Gunnar, Hjálmgunnar, Hialmgunar) [helmgunnar]: Odin's favorite whom he promised victory to in his battle against Agnar, Audi's brother. However, Agnar stole Brynhildr and the other Valkyrie's swan guises and would only return them if she would award victory to him. She disobeyed Odin and gave the victory to Agnar, thereby angering Odin who subsequently put her to sleep with a sleepthorn.

Hjordis (Hjördís, Hjerdis, Hiordis): The daughter of King Eylimi. Her brother is Grifir. She is the second wife of Sigmundr. Their son is Sigurdr Fafnirsbani. Her second husband is Alfr.

Hjorleif (Hjerleifr, Leif, Hjorleif): Captained the ships from Norvasund which carried Sinfjotli to meet Helgi at Raudabjarg before battling Hoddbrodr, King Granmar's son.

Hjorvarth (Hjorward, Hjörvard, Hagbard, Hjörvard): Hunding's son who was slain by Sigurdr with Gramr.

Hle Fells (Hlé Fells): The place on Frekastein where Hrollaug's sons were slain.

Hljod (Ljod, Liod): The named used by Gna after she left Asgardr and returned to her father, the jotun Hrimnir. She married Volsungr. They had nine sons besides Sigmundr and his twin sister Signy.

Hlymdale (Lymdale) [Dales of Lym]: The land in Hunland where King Heimir lived. This was also where Brynhildr lived.

Hnefetafl (Hnefatafl) [fist table, board game of the fist]: A Norse board came dating from the 4th century. It is similar to Latrunculi (a Roman board game) and Petteia (a Greek board game). The object of the game is for the aggressor to attack and capture the defender's King. The sides are uneven in strength. The game is played on an 11x11 game baord. The aggressor usually has 24 warrior pieces, and the defender has the King and 12 defender pieces. The King's goal is to escape. He does this by reaching the outer edges of the board.

Hnikar (Hniker, Nikar) [wave-stiller]: One of the warriors riding with Sigurdr. It was an ekename used by Odin when he visited Sigurdr on his ship the Sea Dragons Keel. Hnikar also used the ekenames Karl from the Mountains, Fengr, and Fjolnir.

Hoddbrodr (Hothbrod, Hothbrodd, Hoddbrod, Hoddbrodd, Hodbrod): King Granmar of Svarinshaug. Granmar's son who was betrothed to Sigrunr. Hoddbrodr slew Isung dishonorably. His horse was Svelgjud. His brothers were Gudmundr and Starkadr. He and his brothers were slain by Helgi and Sinfjotli in a battle at Raudabjarg.

Hoddrofnir's Horn (Hoddropner's Horn, Hodd-dropnir) [treasure opener's horn]: Another name for Heiddraupnir's Skull.

Hœnir (Hönir, Hœner, Høne, Hænir, Hahnir, Honir): The member of the Æsir sent to the Vanir with Mimir as a hostage in exchange for Njordr, Freyr, and Freyja, at the conclusion of the War Between the Æsir and Vanir. He was also known as the Aurkonungr (the marsh King). In Vanaheimr he was made their leader because of his noble bearing. Unfortunately he wasn't very intelligent. When his stupidity was discovered he was sent back to the Æsir carrying Mimir's decapitated head. He survived Ragnarokr and was known for his silence after the Rebirth. He was a frequent traveling companion of Odin and Loki's, at one point traveling with them to Hreidmar's.

Hofdastrand: The land in which Hofdi was located. This was where the warrior Thord lived. He was a descendent of Bjorn Jarnsida.

Hofdi: The place on Hofdastrand where the warrior Thord lived. He was a descendent of Bjorn Jarnsida.

Hogni (Högni, Hegni): Gjuki and Grimhildr's son. He had raven-black hair. His brothers were Gudmundr and Gunnar. His sister was Gudrunr. His stepbrother was Gutthormr. He was a friend of Sigurdr's. His wife was Kostbera. Their sons were Golar, Snævarr, Solarr, and Nibelungr. They were honorbound to fight against Helgi and Sinfjotli. All except Nibelungr traveled to King Atli's Hall and were all ordered slain by King Atli. Golar was slain first. Nibelungr and Gudrunr later avenged their deaths by killing King Atli.

Hogni: Sigrunr's father. His sons were Dagr and Bragi. Helgi's father-in-law. His father was supposedly a dvergar that was why he was stooped and pale.

Holkvi (Helkvi, Hölkvi): The horse ridden by Hogni the Gjuking.

Hrandver (Randver, Randvér, Randwer): Jormunrekkr's son. He fell in love with Svanhildr, who was betrothed to his father. He let her know he was in love with her. She was also in love with him, but they did not dishonor themselves and decided to remain just friends. His father hanged him after Bikki, Jormunrekkr's evil counselor, falsely accused him of seducing Svanhildr. Svanhildr was also murdered, trampled to death by horses.

Hreidmar (Hreidmarr, Hreithmar, Reidmar, Rodmar): The father of Fafnir, Otr, and Regin. His daughters were Lyngheidr and Lofnheidr. His sons plotted his death. Fafnir did the actual slaying.

Hrimgerth (Hrímgerth): From the Saga of Helgi Hjorvathsson. He keeps her until daylight when she was turned to stone.

Hrimnir: The jotun father of Gna. His son-in-law is Volsungr.

Hringr (Hring, Ring): King of Denmark and Sweden. Married to Alfhildr the daughter of King Gandalf of Raumarike. Hoddbrodr sent to him for help in battling Helgi.

Hringstadir (Ringstead, Ringstad, Hringstead, Hringstade, Hringstadir, Hringsted, Ringsted, Hringstod) [Ringstead, Land of Rings]: One of the lands given to Helgi by Sigmundr as a name gift. Stolen from King Hringr who fought with Hoddbrodr against Helgi and Sinfjotli trying to reclaim the land. The harbor in the land is called Hringstod.

Hringstod (Hringsted): The harbor in Hringstadir.

Hrollaug's Sons: Fought with Hoddbrodr against Helgi and Sinfjotli. They were slain at Hle Fells on Frekastein.

Hroptr: An ekename for Odin.

Hrothglod: An old woman soothsayer in King Jormunrekkr's Hall who spoke with Hamdir and Sorli and told them of their destiny and warned them to leave so the prophecy wouldn't come true.

Hrotti (Hrotte, Rotti): A sword in Fafnir's treasure. He threatened his brother with it.

Huginn (Hugin, Hunin) [mind]: One of the two ravens who sat on Odin's shoulders (the other was Muninn). They flew throughout the worlds during the day searching for knowledge and then sat on Odin's shoulders during dinner at Valhalla and whisper all they had seen and heard into his ears. They were a gift to Odin from Hulda.

Hugrunar (Hugrúnar, Hug-runes) [thought runes]: Runes for wisdom and knowledge. The strongest of all runes. They were cut by Hroptr, carved on the shield Svalin, Arvarkr's ear, Alsvin's hoof, wheels beneath Rognir's chariot, Sleipnir's jaw teeth, a sleigh's traces and runners, bear's forepaws, Bragi's tongue, wolf claw, eagle's beak, bloody wings, bridge's end, mid-wife's palm and feet, trail of tears, glass, gold, silver amulets, Gungnir's point, Grani's chest, a female jotun's breast, Norn's nail, night owl's neb, wine, port, throne of the Volva. These runes mixed with the Precious Mead were kept with the Æsir, Vanir and Alfs.

Hunding: King of Hunland. Sigmundr was in a dispute with him. Lyngi's father. Father of Eyjolf, Hervardr, and Hjorvardr. Helgi defeated him thus giving Helgi the name Helgi Hundingsbane.

Hunland (Hunaland): The Kingdom Sigi conquered and became ruler of. United with Gautland by Siggeir's wedding to Signy.

Hundland: A different land from Hunland.

Hvitsarkr (Hvitsark, Hvitserk) [white sark, shirt]: Third son of Ragnar Lodbrokr and Kraka. His brothers were Ivar Lackbones, Bjorn Jarnsida, Rognvaldr, and Sigurdr Snake-in-the-Eyes. Defeated and slain by the Russians in the Baltic. He chose his own death, which was to be burnt on a pyre of skulls of the men he had slain in battle.

Ingeborg [Ing's protection, Ing is another name for Freyr, a fertility god of the Vanir]: King Eystein of Sweden's daughter. Betrothed to Ragnar

Lodbrokr, who promised to divorce his wife Kraka and marry her. He didn't and subsequently her father fought Ragnar Lodbrokr over the matter.

Ireland: King Marstein was King of Ireland when he fought Ragnar Lodbrokr by Vederfjord.

Isung (Ísung): A warrior apparently dishonorably slain by Hoddbrodr.

Ivar Lackbones: The first child of Ragnar Lodbrokr and Kraka. He had no bones and had to be carried everywhere. However, he was smarter than his brothers. Eventually became King of England. His brothers were Hvitsarkr, Bjorn Jarnsida, Rognvaldr, and Sigurdr Snake-in-the-Eye. He killed Sibilja, King Eystein's sacred cow. Ivar Lackbones' birth defect was possibly a description of a child born with polio.

Jarisleif: He was a warrior who journeyed with the Gjukings to visit Gudrunr in Denmark.

Jonakr (Iónakr, Jonakur, Jónakr, Jonak, Jonker, Jónak): Gudrunr's third husband. Their sons were Sorli, Hamdir, and Erpr.

Jormunrekkr (Jörmunrekkr, Jörmunrekr, Jörmunrekk, Iörmunrekr, Iormunrekk, Jormunrek, Jormunrekkr, Jörmunrek, Iormunrekkr, Jormunrekkr): King of Gautland. Betrothed of Svanhildr. His evil counselor lied to him and told him his son, Hrandver and Svanhildr were lovers. He had his son hung and Svanhildr trampled to death by horses. He later regretted these actions.

Jutland [Ty]: Hjalprekr was King of this land, as well as in Thjod.

Kara (Kára): She was the Valkyrie daughter of King Halfdan and the reincarnation of Sigrunr.

Karl From the Mountains [Karl = freeholder]: A name Odin referred to himself as when he was visiting Sigurdr aboard his ship in the guise of Hnikar.

Knefrud (Knefurd, Knefroed): King Atli's duplicitous counselor and messenger. In some versions he was called Vingi (Wingi). He tricked Gudrunr's brothers into visiting her. When they found out about his trickery they killed him. They then fought against King Atli and were slain by him.

Kostbera (Bera): Wife of Hogni. Mother of Golar, Snævarr, Solarr, and Nibelungr. Her brother is Orkningr. Her brother, husband (and his brother Gunnar), and sons were honorbound to fight against Helgi and Sinfjotli. They traveled to King Atli's Hall and were all ordered slain by King Atli. Golar was slain first. Her son Nibelungr and Gudrunr later avenged their deaths by killing King Atli.

Kraka (Kráka): The name of Grima's mother. Aslaugr was named after her.

Kraka (Kráka): The name Aslaugr was known by when Grima and Aki were raising her. Ragnar Lodbrokr knew her by this name. She was named after Grima's mother. She later was given the name Randalin.

Kuben (Küben): Straits of Gibralter. Norvasund was south of Kuben. See also Norvasund, Straits of Gibralter.

Laganess: The place where Sinfjotli boasts of having begat nine wolf whelps on King Granmar.

Laugardagr [bathday]: The name for present day Saturday. It was the day usually reserved for bathing. It is the only day of the week not named after one of the Æsir.

Leek: Eaten for protection and luck. It was the main source of Aslaugr's diet when she was in the harp.

Leif [heir]: Helgi's helmsman.

Leiptr (Leipter, Leipt, Leift) [quick as lightning]: One of the eleven rivers of Elivagar. It was in Niflheimr near the river Gjoll. Solemn oaths were sworn by it.

Limfjord: The place where King Gunnar's Hall was.

Limrunar (Limrúnar, Lim-runes): Branch and limb runes. Used for healing. Mardoll was also called on. Carved on boughs that point toward the east.

Lindisore: Morning battle when Ragnar Lodbrokr fought against three Irish Kings.

Lingworm: Another name for a dragon.

Logafjollum (Logafjellum, Loga Fells, Laganess, Saganess, Lowness) [flame fells]: The place where Helgi and Sinfjotli's army battled and slew Alf, Eyjolf, Hervardr and Hagbardr, the sons of King Hunding.

Loki Laufeyjarsonr (Loke, Lok, Lokki, Loki Laufeyjarson, Loki Laufeyarson) [fire]: His brothers were Byleistr and Helblindi. Their parents were Farbauti and Laufey. He was Odin's cousin, and in times past they had sworn blood brotherhood together. He was first married to Glut. They had two daughters, Eisa and Einmyria. He changed himself into a mare and had the eight-legged horse Sleipnir by Svadilfari. After swallowing Angroboda's heart he also had three more children, Fenriswulf, Midgardrsormr (also known as Jormungandr), and Hela. He was always getting into mischief and causing trouble for the Æsir. He stole the Brisingamen Necklace from Freyja and fought and lost to Heimdallr in the forms of fire, a polar bear, and a seal by the rocks Vagasker and Singasteinn for possession of it. Loki had a magic sword called Lævateinn that he had carved with runes beneath Nagrindr gate. He used this sword at Ragnarokr to slay the cock Vidofnir. He also had shoes that gave him the ability to run on air and sea to get away from those chasing him (who were many). His eldest two sons were Vali and Narfi. Their mother was Sigyn, his loyal second wife. Eventually the Æsir became fed up with him and bound him with Vali and Narfi's intestines near a bottomless pit in Niflheimr. There was a poisonous serpent hung overhead that caused poison to drip down on him. Sigyn caught as much of it as she could in a conch. When she turned to empty it the poison would hit Loki causing him pain. His writhing in agony caused earthquakes on Midgardr. He broke free at Ragnarokr and slew Heimdallr at the last great battle. In the Volsungr Saga while traveling with Odin and Hoenir he killed Otr, Hreidmar's son. After the three were caught and bound by Hreidmar he was let go so he could obtain a ransom of gold to pay weregild for Otr's death. To pay the weregild he stole the dvergar Andvari's Hoard, which the dvergar cursed as it was being taken from him. This cursed hoard of gold brought tragedy to all who possessed it.

Longobards: The name adopted by the Vinnilers after Frigg helped them gain a victory over the Vandals. The name eventually evolved to Lombards.

Lyngheidr (Lynheid, Lyngheith): One of Hreidmar's daughters. Her sister was Lofnheidr. Her brothers were Fafnir, Otr, and Regin.

Lofnheidr (Lofnheid, Lofnheith): One of Hreidmar's daughters. Her sister was Lyngheidr. Her brothers were Fafnir, Otr, and Regin.

Lunaburg: A city that welcomed the sons of Ragnar Lodbrokr as heroes in the hopes that, perhaps only their treasure would be looted and the city would be left standing.

Lundunaberg (Londonburg, Lundunaborg, London): The estate in England given as weregild to Ivar Lackbones for Ragnar Lodbrokr's death. It consisted of the area of land over which Ivar Lackbones could have an ox-hide stretched. He had the hide treated and stretched thin so it covered a vast area.

Lyngvi (Lynge): King Hunding's son. Wooed Hjordis unsuccessfully. Fought and slew Sigmundr who had won Hjordis' hand. Fought against Helgi at Frekastein. Fought and was slain by Sigurdr with Gramr in battle. The blood-eagle was cut on him.

Malrunar (Mál-Runes, Málrúnar) [speech runes]: Speech runes.

Mardoll (Mardöll, Mardal, Marpöll, Marpollr, Mardoll, Mardallar, Mardel, Marthaul): The name assumed by Freyja when she traveled in Midgardr in search of Odr.

Marstein: King of Ireland. Ragnar Lodbrokr fought and defeated him by Vederfjord.

Meginrunar (Megin-Runes) [power runes]: Power runes, strength runes.

Melnir (Mélnir) [the steed with the bit]: One of two horses (the other was Mylnir) that carried messengers to Myrkvydr summoning troops to fight with Hoddbrodr against Helgi and Sinfjotli.

Midgardr (Midgard, Midgaard, Midgh, Mithgarth) [middle land, middle enclosure]: The earth.

Midgardrsormr (Midgardsormr, Midgardsorm, Mithgarthsorm, Mithgarth-worm) [earth serpent]: Also known as Jormungandr. A giant sea serpent child born by Loki after eating the evil Angroboda's heart. His siblings were Fenriswulf and Hela. He was thrown into the sea where he grew and grew until he encircled the land and could catch hold of his tale with his mouth. He would spit out poison when angered, and was a long time enemy of Thor's. Thor went fishing along with the jotun Hymir, and almost captured Midgardrsormr using one of Hymir's prize oxen, Himinbjorg, as bait. Thor and Midgardrsormr destroy each other at Ragnarokr.

Midvitnir (Mithvitnir) [mead wolf]: A jotun who lived in Muspelheimr. He once stole the Precious Mead that was recovered by Odin. Odin slew his son Sokkmimir during the recovery.

Mimis Cup [Cup of Memory]: The drink given to Sigurdr by Brynhildr when they first met. It was ironic since he was later given a drink that made him forget this meeting, and his love for Brynhildr.

Mirkagard: Greece. Brynhildr was on the battlefield when this country's King was in battle.

Modgudr (Modgardr, Mödgudur, Mœdgud, Modgud, Módgudr, Mödgud, Modgudur, Modgudhr) [soul in misery]: The skeleton maiden who guards Gjallarbru in Gnipahellir cave. Her brother was Imr. Their father was Vafthrudnir.

Moinsheim (Möinsheim): A Danish Island also known as Moen (Möen). The place where King Granmar's sons won a great victory.

Munarvag Harbar: The name of the harbor in Samsey where Ogmundr the Dane's men found the wooden statue that told them of the glory of Ragnar Lodbrokr and his sons.

Muninn (Munin, Munnin, Mummin) [memory]: One of Odin's ravens that flew throughout the world during the day gathering information, and then at dinnertime sat on Odin's shoulder whispering in his ear what he had found out. The other raven was Huninn. Both were gifts to Odin from Huldr.

Mylnir (Mýlnir) [the steed with the halter]: One of two horses (the other was Melnir) that carried messengers to Myrkvydr summoning troops to fight with Hoddbrodr against Helgi and Sinfjotli.

Myrkvydr Forest (Myrkvidar, Mýrkvidar, Myrkvith, Myrkwood, Murkwood, Myrkwood Forest, Mirkwood, Mirkvid, Myrkvidr) [The Black Forest]: The Black Forest. Also a forest in Jotunheimr. Its trees had leaves made of black iron. Angroboda lived there. Hermodr passed through here on his way to Niflheimr.

Naud [need]: Standing for Norns. Naud Runes cut on fingernails to call forth protection of the Norns.

Neir's Sister: One of the Norn's attending Helgi's birth.

Nibelungenlied: The Saga of the Niblungs.

Nibelungr (Nibelung, Niblung, Hniflungr, Niflungar, Niflung, Niflungr, Hniflung) [sons of the mist]: Hogni and Kostbera's son. Gjuki's grandson. His brothers were Golar, Snævarr, and Solarr. His uncles were Orkningr (Kostbera's brother) and Gunnar, (Hogni's brother). They were honorbound to fight against Helgi and Sinfjotli. All except Nibelungr traveled to King Atli's Hall and were all ordered slain by King Atli. Golar was slain first. Nibelungr and Gudrunr later avenged their deaths by killing King Atli.

Nibelungs (Niblungs, Niflungs, Nibelungs, Nibelungen, Burgundians): The descendants of King Gjuki, also known as the Gjukungs.

Nine Worlds of the Tree: Where Andvari had collected his gold from the nine worlds. They were Midgardr, Niflheimr, Jotunheimr, Muspelheimr, Asgardr, Vanaheimr, Alfheimr, Svartalfheimr, and Helheimr.

Norns (Nornas, Nornies, Nornir) (singular: Norny, Nornie, Norni) [fates]: The three jotun women from the east whose coming heralded the end of the Golden Age. They were Urdr, Verdandi, and Skuldr. They wove a tapestry of the history of the world showing things as they were fated to happen. They finished their weaving at Ragnarokr.

Norvasund (Norvi Sound): Also known as Stave Ness and Tronu Sound. It was north of Kuben (Küben), which was also known as the Straits of Gibralter. See

Hedinsey. Some of Helgi's men traveled from here. Sinfjotli commanded this group. Captain of the ship was Hjorleifr.

Oddrunr (Oddrun): King Atli, Brynhildr and Bekkhildr's sister. Daughter of King Budli.

Odin: His son was Sigi. He made several appearances in the saga guiding the action.

Odin's Fourteen Appearances in the Saga: 1. Chapter 2: Throwing the sword Gramr into Branstokk. **2. Chapter 5:** Raven gives leaf to Sigmundr to heal Sinfjotli's throat. **3. Chapter 7:** Dagr prayed to Odin for help avenging his kinsmen's deaths by slaying Helgi. Odin lent him his spear Gungnir to use to slay Helgi. It never missed it's mark. **4. Chapter 8:** The ferryman who carried Sinfjotli's body to Valhalla. **5. Chapter 9:** Odin appeared at the battle between Sigmundr and Eylimi. Broke the sword Gramr and caused Sigmundr's death. Awarded victory to Lyngvi. **6. Chapter 10:** Sigurdr meets Odin while walking in the woods to the high meadow to choose Grani as his horse. **7. Chapter 11:** With Hoenir and Loki when Otter was killed. Visited Hreidmar and his sons and stole their gold. **8. Chapter 12:** Appeared to Sigurdr aboard his ship the Sea Dragons Keel. Called himself Hnikar. **9. Chapter 13:** Old man who gave Sigurdr advice on digging the pit to slay Fafnir. **10. Chapter 26:** The sorcerer who prepares the cauldron to test Gudrunr's innocence when she is accused of adultery. **11. Chapter 28:** Gave Jormunrekkr counsel on how Hamdir and Sorli could be killed. **12. Chapter 29:** Odin give the ring to King Heimir. **13. Chapter 34:** The stranger urging Eric and Agnar, sons of Ragnar Lodbrokr, to go on their journey to Sweden. **14. Chapter 35:** As beggar talking to Ivar Lackbones, Bjorn Jarnsidr, and Hvitsarkr about distance to Rome and discouraging them from going there.

Odin's Chariot: The constellation Ursa Major.

Ogmundr the Dane (Ogmund the Dane): A warrior of Denmark whose men found a giant wooden statue that told them of Ragnar Lodbrokr and his son's victories.

Oinn (Óínn, Óín, Oin): Andvari's father.

Olrunar (Ölrúnar, Öl-runes, Ale-runes) [ale runes]: Cut on mead horns, backs of each hand. Good to use against a love potion.

Ore: A river where Ragnar Lodbrokr fought a battle.

Orkningr (Orkning): Kostbera's brother. A mighty warrior who traveled with the Gjukings. Killed Thir. Went with Gunnar and Hogni, and his nephews Golar, Snævarr, and Solarr, to King Atli's. They were all ordered slain by King Atli. Golar was slain first. Nibelungr and Gudrunr later avenged their deaths by killing King Atli.

Orn: A King defeated by Ragnar Lodbrokr.

Orvasund (Orva Sound, Óresund, Órvasund) [sound of arrows]: Oresund off Sealand.

Oskopnir (Öskopnir on Vígríth Plain, Oskopnir on Vigridr Plain, Oskopnir on Vigrid Plain): The island where Vigridr Plain was located. The site of the last battle at Ragnarokr.

Osterhotland (Österhôtland, Österehötland): The province in Sweden where Bravoll Field was located. The city of Branik is located here.

Otr (Ottr, Otter, Oter): Hreidmar's second son. His brothers were Fafnir and Regin. He went about in the shape of an otter and was slain by Loki for food while in that form. Loki stole Andvari's Hoard to pay weregild for Otr's death.

Ottergild: An ekename for gold because of the weregild ransom of gold paid to Hreidmar for his son Otr's death. Also known as Otter's Ransom.

Pike: The fish shape Andvari changed into to guard his gold.

Rafn Fell: The place of a battle where Ragnar Lodbrokr easily won victory.

Ragnar Lodbrokr (Ragnar Lodbrók, Ragnar Roughen-Breeks, Ragnar Lodbrog) [Ragnar = judgement warrior, Hairy-breeches]: Son of Sigurdrhringr, King of Denmark. His first wife was Thora Borgarhjort. He became King after his father's death. They had two sons, Eric and Agnar. Later he married Kraka and had several sons by her, Ivar Lackbones, Bjorn Jarnsida, Rognvaldr, and Sigurdr Snake-in-the-Eye.

Ragnarokr (Ragnarök, Ragnarökr, Ragnarøkr, Ragnarokkr, Ragnarøkkr, Ragna rok, Ragnarek, Ragnarokur, Ragnarock) [Ragnarokr = Doom of the gods, Ragnarok = Twilight of the Gods]: The doom of the gods. The period started after Baldr's death and included the Fimbulventr, the swallowing of the sun and moon, and finally culminated into the battle on Vigridr Plain and the conflagration of all the Worlds of the Tree.

Ragnhildr: Eldest daughter of Sigurdr Snake-in-the-Eye. She was the mother of Harald Fair-Hair.

Ran (Rán, Rân, Rana, Rœna) [rob, concealer, shelterer]: She ruled the sea with her husband Ægir. They were also brother and sister. Their other brothers included Logi and Kari. They were frequent visitors to Asgardr. Their Hall was on the island Hlessey in the Kattigat, also known as Hlessey. They had nine wavemaiden daughters. They owned a giant kettle for brewing mead taken from the jotun Hymir by Tyr and Thor.

Randalin: The name given to Aslaugr/Kraka when she journeyed to battle with her sons. Ivar Lackbones gave her the name.

Ran's Net: Loki borrowed it from Ran to use to catch Andvari who was hiding in the form of a pike. Later used by the Æsir to catch Loki.

Raudabjarg (red-berg): The place where Helgi met his army before battling Hoddbrodr, King Granmar's son.

Raumarike: The land where Gandalf was King.

Regin (Reginn) [counselor]: The King's smith who became Sigurdr's foster-father. He was the youngest son of Hreidmar. His brothers were Otr and Fafnir. He reforged the sword Gramr for Sigurdr, and was slain with that same sword by Sigurdr.

Rerir: The son of Sigi. He was a King of Hunland and Volsungr's father. He died before his son was born.

Ridil (Ridel, Ridill, Refill, Rithil, Refil): The name of Regin's sword.

Rognir's Chariot (Rogner's Chariot): Brynhildr telling Sigurdr that hugrunar (thought runes) were carved on Rognir's Chariot.

Rognvaldr (Rögnvaldr, Rognwald, Ragnvald, Rognvald) [Ruler's Counselor]: One of Ragnar Lodbrokr's sons. The first of the brothers to die. He died at the battle against the city of Whitby. His brothers were Ivar Lackbones, Bjorn Jarnsida, Hvitsarkr, and Sigurdr Snake-in-the-Eye.

Rome: A city the sons of Ragnar Lodbrokr thought of conquering, but it was too far away and too mythical. They decided it was too long a journey for a city they weren't certain actually existed.

Rosts: A measure of distance equivalent to 4-5 miles.

Salgofnir: One of the cocks that crows in Valhalla to awaken the Einherjar.

Samsey: The place where Ogmundr the Dane had anchored when his men found the wooden statue which told them of the noble deeds of Ragnar Lodbrokr and his sons.

Saxons: Warriors who rode with Gunnar and Hogni and 500 others to King Alfr to bring back Gudrunr. Others who rode with them were Eymod III, Jarisleif, Valdemar of Denmark, the Franks, and the Longobards who had recently changed their name to Lombard.

Sea Dragons Keel (See Drake Keel, Dragon Keel): Sigurdr Fafnirsbani's ship.

Sefafjollum (Sefafjellum): The place where Sigrunr lived.

Sevafells (Seva Fells): The place where Sigrunr was staying before her intended marriage to Helgi.

She-wolf: The wehr-shape Siggeir's mother assumed when she one-by-one ate nine of Signy's brothers who were bound in the forest.

Sibilja (Sibilia): The sacred cow worshipped by King Eystein and his subjects. Her mooing caused enemy armies to fight against themselves. Ivar Lackbones killed her.

Sigar: Brynhildr relates the story to Gudrunr of how Sigar stole away the sister of his enemy and burned the other sister in their own Hall. Sigmundr fought in a sea battle against Sigar and Siggeir south of Fjon.

Sigar: A legendary warrior mentioned by Gudrunr in his argument with Brynhildr. A swan maiden. The sister whom Hagal says Helgi, disguised as a bondwoman, was sister to.

Sigarsvollu (Sigarsvellu, Sigarsvoll) [plain of heaven, plain of leaves]: One of the lands given to Helgi by Sigmundr as a name gift. The others were Solfjoll, Snjofjoll, Hatan, Himinvanga, Sigarsvoll, Hringstadir and Hringstjod the harbor in that land.

Siggeir: King of Gautland. He was of the Siklingar. He married Signy. Invited Volsungr to visit him and Signy after the wedding feast and then slew Volsungr as well as all Signy's brothers save Sigmundr. Her brothers had been bound in the forest and eaten by a she-wolf who was actually Siggeir's mother who liked to

travel in this wehr-shape. These deaths were avenged when all of Siggeir's sons were slain by Sigmundr.

Sigi (Siggi): A son of Odin's who killed Bredi and was exiled from his country. He conquered Hunland. His son was Rerir.

Sigmundr (Sigmund): Volsungr and Hljod's son. He had nine other brothers. Signy was his twin sister. His first wife was Borghildr. Their twin sons were Helgi and Hamund. His second wife was Hjordis. His sons were Sinfjotli, Helgi, and Sigurdr. His skin could not be harmed by poison, nor was he affected if he drank poison. He owned the sword Gramr. He settled in Denmark after marrying Borghildr, but left her and moved south to Frankland after she poisoned Sinfjotli, his son by Signy, who had helped him achieve vengeance against Siggeir. He and Sinfjotli had once taken on the forms of wehr-wolves and wandered in the forest. Reclaimed the throne of Hunland as his own.

Sigmundr (Sigmund): Sigurdr's son by Gudrunr. His sister was Svanhildr.

Signy (Signý, Signe) [new victory]: Volsungr and Hljod's only daughter. She had nine brothers and a twin brother, Sigmundr. She had four sons by King Siggeir. Two were killed in the woods by Sigmundr, while the other two were killed on her porch by Sigmundr and Sinfjotli. Sinfjotli was her son by Sigmundr. She had exchanged forms with a witch wife and seduced Sigmundr. She chose to be burned with Siggeir in the fire set by Sigmundr and Sinfjotli that burned down Siggeir and Signy's entire household.

Sigrdrifa (Sigrdrífa, Sigdrífa, Sigrdrîfa) [victory giver]: The name by which Brynhildr was known in some version of this legend.

Sigrunr (Sigrûn, Sigrún) [one who has victory runes, secret lore of victory]: Hogni's daughter. She was a Valkyrie. She had been given in marriage to Hoddbrodr, however, Helgi fought and slew him so he could have her. Her brothers were Dagr and Bragi. She lived in Sefajollum.

Sig Runes [victory runes]: Carved on hilt of sword edge and blade.

Sigurdr Fafnirsbani (Sigurdr, Sigurth, Sigirfánisvani, Sigurth Fánisbani, Sigurdr Fafnir's bane, Sigurd Sigmundrson, Sigmund Völsungsson, Sigurth, Siggardr, Sigurd Fafnir's-Bane, Sigurd Fafnisbane) [warder of victory, victory's guardian]: The posthumous son of Sigmundr and Hjordis. He had golden hair and bright blue eyes. He slew Fafnir with the sword Gramr to win his first great fame. He had a child, Aslaugr, by Brynhildr. He made vows promising to marry Brynhildr, but violated them when he married Gudrunr, even though he was suffering from a drink of forgetfulness. His children by Gudrunr were Sigmundr and Svanhildr.

Sigurdrhringr (Sigurdhring, Sigurthring, Sigurd Hring): He was King of Denmark, and became King of Sweden once Denmark and Sweden were separated. His uncle was Harald Hilditann. His son was Ragnar Lodbrokr. He was a principle in the Battle of Bravoll Field that separated Denmark and Sweden.

Sigurdr Snake-in-the-Eye (Sigurdr Snake-in-the-Eye, Sigurd Snakeeye): The youngest son of Kraka and Ragnar Lodbrokr. His brothers were Ivar Lackbones, Bjorn Jarnsida, Hvitsarkr, and Rognvaldr (who was already dead by the time

Sigurdr Snake-in-the-Eye was born). He was born with the figure of a serpent around his eye, hence the name. His eldest daughter was Ragnhildr. He eventually became King of Denmark.

Siklingar: The race to which Siggeir belonged.

Sinfjotli (Sinfiotli, Sinfjotle, Sinfjetli, Sinfjötli, Sinfjotli) [yellow spotted]: The son of Sigmundr and Signy (in the guise of a witch wife). He was sent to Sigmundr at age ten in the woods and trained by him. He and Sigmundr took the forms of wehr-wolves and roamed the forest in these guises for a while. He helped Sigmundr avenge Volsungr's death by killing two of Siggeir's sons and burning Siggeir and his household. Signy, his mother, chose to burn to death in this fire. Poison would not hurt his skin. Sigurdr and Helgi were half-brothers. His stepuncle, Borghildr's brother, was betrothed to a woman Sinfjotli fell in love with. While arguing with his stepuncle about the matter he slew him. Borghildr avenged her brother's death by poisoning Sinfjotli.

Skadi: A powerful friend of Sigi's. His servant, Bredi, was slain by Sigi.

Skald: A poet/bard/minstrel who created verses, usually extemporaneously, about the glory of warriors and battles. These verses were joined together to form family Sagas.

Skarpa-Skerry: A battle where Ragnar Lodbrokr easily won a victory.

Skatalund (Skata Grove): The grove on Mt. Hindarfjall where Brynhildr lay sleeping with the sleep thorn in her.

Skuldr (Skuld, Skulda) [future, shall be]: One of the Norns. Also a Valkyrie. She lived at Urdarbrunnr Well with her sisters, Verdandi and Urdr, the other two Norns. They controlled the fates of everything by weaving a tapestry of destiny. They also tended to the upkeep of Yggdrasyll.

Sleipnir (Sleipner, Sleipne) [tie slipper]: Odin's swift eight-legged steed. His father was Svadilfari. His mother was Loki who had taken the form of a white mare in order to lure Svadilfari away from her work. Grani, Sigurdr's horse, was his descendent.

Slidr (Slídr, Slíd, Slid, Slith) [fearful]: One of the eleven rivers of Elivagar flowing out of the east, near Gjoll and Leiptr. Its waters were filled with swords, knives and other instruments. The dead on their way to Niflheimr had to wade through it.

Snævarr (Snævar, Snevar): Hogni and Kostbera's son. Gjuki's grandson. His brothers were Golar, Solarr, and Nibelungr. His uncles were Orkningr (Kostbera's brother) and Gunnar, (Hogni's brother). They were honorbound to fight against Helgi and Sinfjotli. All except Nibelungr traveled to King Atli's Hall and were all ordered slain by King Atli. Golar was slain first. Nibelungr and Gudrunr later avenged their deaths by killing King Atli.

Snjofjoll (Snjofjöll, Snæfjoll, Snæfjoll) [snow fells]: One of the lands given to Helgi by Sigmundr as a name gift.

Sogn (Sok) [sunk]: A place on Hatun Sound where some of Helgi's ships waited before the battle with Hoddbrodr.

Sokkmimir (Sökkmimir, Sökin, Sækin, Sœkin, Sekin): A river flowing from Hvergelmir.

Sol (Sól, Söl, Sœl, Sôl) [sun]: The daughter of Mundilfari. Her brother was Maane. They were snatched away from him by the Æsir to help guide Dagr. She was married to Glenr. Her two horses were Arvakr and Alsvin.

Solarr (Sólarr, Solar): Hogni and Kostbera's son. Gjuki's grandson. His brothers were Golar, Snævarr, and Nibelungr. His uncles were Orkningr (Kostbera's brother) and Gunnar, (Hogni's brother). They were honorbound to fight against Helgi and Sinfjotli. All except Nibelungr traveled to King Atli's Hall and were all ordered slain by King Atli. Golar was slain first. Nibelungr and Gudrunr later avenged their deaths by killing King Atli.

Solfjoll (Sólfjell, Sunfells, Solfjall, Solfjöll, Solfell, Sólfjoll) [sunfells, sun-lit hill, sun-hill]: One of the lands given to Helgi by Sigmundr as a name gift. It was south of Denmark. Frekastein was located there.

Solheimr Castle (Sólheimr Castle, Sólheimar Castle, Sólheim) [sun land]: The Hall where Granmar and Hoddbrodr met before fighting Helgi.

Sorli (Sörli, Serli): One of the sons of Jonakr and Gudrunr. His brothers were Hamdir and Erpr. He had raven-black hair. He and Hamdir murdered Erpr. His sister was Svanhildr.

Southern Isles: The place where Herthjof fought and lost a battle against Ragnar Lodbrodr.

Spæwights: Guardian spirits.

Spangereid (Spangarheith): The farm in Norway owned by Grima and Aki. Kraka lived there as their foster-daughter after they killed her foster-father King Heimir.

Sparinsheidi (Sparin's Heath) [the heath sparsely settled]: One of the places where the horse Sporvitnir carried a messenger who was recruiting men to fight on Hoddbrodr's side against Helgi and Sinfjotli.

Sporvitnir (Sportvitnir) [the animal which is spurred]: A horse who carried one of several messengers throughout King Granmar's land at Hoddbrodr's orders to recruit men for the battle against Helgi and Sinfjotli. Sporvitnir rode to the land known as Sparinsheidi.

Starkadr (Starkath): One of King Granmar's sons. His brothers were Gudmundr and Hoddbrodr. He was slain in battle against Helgi and Sinfjotli. His body was found near the Styr Cliffs on Frekastein.

Straits of Gibralter: Another name for Kuben. Norvasund was south of Kuben. See also Kuben, Norvasund.

Styr Cliffs: The place on Frekastein where Starkadr's body was found in the battle against Helgi and Sinfjotli.

Surtr (Surt, Surti, Surtur, Surter) [blackened by fire]: The Liege of Muspelheimr. He was the owner of a fiery sword called med sviga lævi. His son was Glenr who was married to Sol. At the final battle on Vigridr Plain he slew Freyr and then flung his sword so that everything was engulfed in flames.

Svafrlod (Swaflod): One of Gudrunr's handmaidens.

Svafriod: One of Brynhildr's bower maids.

Svalin (Svalinn, Valin) [cooler]: The shield hung at the back of Arvakr and Alsvin to protect Sol and her horses from Skinfaxi and Gladr and the sun's brilliance. It also protected everything in Midgardr from being burned to a crisp.

Svanhildr Sigurdardottir (Swanhild, Sigurdardottir): Sigurdr's daughter by Gudrunr. She had golden hair and bright blue eyes. Her brother was Sigmundr. She was betrothed to King Jormunrekkr, but fell in love with Hrandver, Jormunrekkr's son, on the journey to meet Jormunrekkr. Bikki, the King's evil counselor reported this to Jormunrekkr and thereby brought about Svanhildr and Hrandver's deaths. Hrandver was hung, while Svanhildr was trampled to death by horses. Her brothers were Hamdir, Sorli, and Erpr.

Svarinshaug (Svarin's Hill, Swarin's Cairn, Svaringshaug, Svarenshaug): The Kingdom Granmar ruled.

Svartalfrs (dark elves, black elves): The dvergues who live in Svartalfheimr.

Svartalfheimr (Svartalfheim, Svartálfaheimr, Svartálfaheim, Svarttalfheimr, Svart-alfa-heim, Svaatheim) [dusk alf land, black alf land]: The land of the dark alfs.

Svava (Sváfa): Daughter of King Budli. A Valkyrie.

Svefnthorn (Svefnþorn) [sleep thorn]: The sleepthorn used on Brynhildr by Odin after she disobeyed him.

Sveggjud (Sveggjuth): Hoddbrodr's horse. He rode it in the battle against Helgi.

Sveipud (Sviputh, Sveipúd): Gudmundr's horse. He rode it in the battle against Helgi.

Svelnir: The name of the smith who forged Ragnar Lodbrokr's battle-axe.

Thieves' Hill: The hill where King Jormunrekkr ordered his son Hrandver to be taken and hung for falling in love with Svanhildr. He regretted his action but was too late to save his son. His evil counselor Bikki had already given the order for Hrandver's hanging. It was renamed Gallow's Hill, since Hrandver had not been a thief. Though some thought he had been a thief, stealing Svanhildr away from his father.

Thing (Þing): A council or meeting to try and come up with a group solution to a problem affecting the group. Also known as the Doomstead.

Thjodrex: A King whom Gudrunr supposedly had an affair with after she was married to King Atli. Accused by Herkja, King Atli's mistress. Gudrunr was put to a test and passed it. Herkja failed the test and was reluctantly ordered put to death by King Atli.

Thjod (Thjode, Thjöd) [Denmark]: Hjalprekr was King there as well as in Ty (Jutland). The land where Alfr lived.

Thora [thunder]: The daughter of Hakon who worked for King Alf. She became King Alf's second wife after Hjordis' death. Friend of Gudrunr who visited her after Sigurdr's death. She and King Alfr befriended Gudrunr after Sigurdr's death.

Thora Borgarhjort (Thora Borhart, Thora Borghart, Thora Borghild, Thóra, Tora) [Thora = thunder]: Daughter of Jarl Herraud of Gautland. First wife and beloved of Ragnar Lodbrokr. Usually called Borgy, a contraction of her

surname, Borgarhjort. Her two sons were Eric and Agnar. She died shortly after Agnar's birth.

Thord: A warrior descendent of Bjorn Jarnsida in Sweden. He lived in Hofdi on Hofdastrand.

Thorsness (Thrasness, Thor's Ness): A place near Gnipa Grove. Granmar accused Sinfjotli of having been gelded there by a jotun's daughter.

Tiwaz [see Tyrrune, Tyr's Rune]: It is an arrow pointing upward. It is a rune of victory.

Tronu Strand: Some of Helgi's ships sailed from here to Norvasund for the battle against Hoddbrodr.

Ty (Tý) [Jutland]: Hjalprekr was King there as well as in Thjod.

Tyrrune [see Tyr's Rune, Tiwaz]: It is an arrow pointing upward. It is a rune of victory.

Tyr's Rune [see Tyrrune, Tiwaz]: It is an arrow pointing upward. It is a rune of victory.

Ullr's Arm Ring: Ullr was the god of skiis. Oaths sworn on his ring were sacred. Such was the oath sworn by Sigmundr and Signy to avenge their father and brother's deaths by eventually killing King Siggeir.

Una Bay: The place in Gnipalund where Helgi anchored his ships after the storm and before meeting Hoddbrodr in battle at Frekastein in Solfjoll.

Unn: One of Ægir and Ran's wavemaiden daughters.

Unn's Altar: Another sacred place by which sacred oaths were sworn.

Uppland: Another name for Denmark.

Uppsala: A large city in Sweden where King Eystein had his Hall that was called Eusteing.

Urdr (Urd, Ürd, Urdr, Urdar, Urdur, Urth, Urda, Hudr) [past]: One of the three Norns. The other two were her sisters Verdandi and Skuldr. They lived near Urdarbrunnr Well and wove a tapestry of destiny foretelling the fates of all things. They tended to the upkeep of Yggdrasyll, the World Tree.

Vadgelmir (Vathgelmir, Valdarr, Valdemar, Waldemar): A poisonous river in Hel. Liars must wade through it on their way to their eternal punishments.

Værings (Verings): These were a band of Norse mercenaries hired by the emperor Byzantium. It is also a term used generally to represent Scandinavians.

Valbjorg (Valbjörg): A Hall given to Gudrunr by Grimhildr for agreeing to marry King Atli.

Valdemar, King of Denmark (Waldemar) [famous ruler]: A warrior who rode with Gunnar and Hogni and 500 others to King Alfr to bring back Gudrunr. Others who rode with them were Eymod III, Jarisleif, the Saxons and Franks, as well as the Longobards who had recently changed their name to Lombard.

Valhalla (Valhöll, Valhol, Valhell, Valhal, Valhall, Valholl, Walhalla) [hall of the slain]: The last Hall built in Asgardr. It was located near Gladsheimr and was equal in size to Bilskirnir, Thor's 540 room Hall. The roof slates were tiled with shields, while the walls were made of shafts of spears. Each door was wide enough to allow 800 warriors through at a time. An eagle hovered over the western door.

There was a bear's head above the main gate. Yggdrasyll's branch with the Satin eagle on it hung over it. The pine tree Læradr grew in the center of the main Hall. The hart Eikthrynir stood on the roof eating at Læradr. The Einherjar stayed in this Hall waiting for the last great battle.

Valkyries (valkyrja, valkyrs, valkyrjur, valkyrior, valkyriar, valkyrier) [choosers of the slain]: The warrior maidens sent by Odin to influence battles. They also served mead in Valhalla. Some were Odin's daughters. One of Odin's ekenames is Herjan, so the Valkyries were sometimes known as Herjan's Disir. All were virgins. Some of the Valkyries were Gudr, Rota, Skuldr, Hrist, Mist, Skeggjold, Skogul, Hildr, Hjor, Hjorthrimul, Thrudr, Hlokk, Gollr, Herfjotur, Geironul, Randgridr, Rostgridr, Reginleif, Gondul, Gunnr, Geirskogul, Thrimul, Sangridr, and Svipul. They frequently flew to Midgardr as swan maidens wearing swan coats. If their swan cloaks were taken while they were bathing, then the holder of the coats could order the Valkyries to do his or her bidding. They are also known as valmeyar.

Valthjof: King Valthjof fought and was slain by Ragnar Lodbrokr in a six-day long sea battle at Angel-ness.

Vandil (Vandeil): A land Dagr offered Sigrunr, along with another land named Vigdale, as weregild for Helgi's death.

Vanir (Vaner, Vanr, Van): The other faction of gods. They were generally fertility gods rather than warrior gods. They were also known as the Vans. They used witchcraft and a magic called vigspa when they fought.

Var (Vár): An Æsir goddess. Signy and Sigmundr swore oaths of vengeance by her.

Varinsey: The place where Sinfjotli accused Granmar of living with a witch wife.

Varinsfjord (Varinsfjörd, Varinsfirth, Varinsey, Varins' Isle): The place where Helgi sailed out of Norvasund to do battle against Hoddbrodr.

Vederfjord: The place where King Marstein of Ireland fought and was defeated by Ragnar Lodbrokr.

Verdandi (Verdándi, Verlandi, Verthandi, Verdande) [present]: A jotun. One of the norns. The other two were her sisters, Urdr and Skuldr. The three lived near Urdarbrunnr Well and wove a tapestry of destiny that foretold the destiny of all things. They also tended to the upkeep of Yggdrasyll.

Vickseid: A sea battle fought by Ragnar Lodbrokr.

Vifil (Vivil): A mighty Prince who lived in a magnificent Hall called Vifilsburg.

Vifilsburg (Vifilsborg, Vivilsborg, Vivilsburg): The Hall of Prince Vifil. Laid siege to by Ragnar Lodbrokr's sons. They were successful and looted it of its treasures.

Vigdale: A land Dagr offered Sigrunr, along with another land named Vandil, as weregild for Helgi's death.

Vigridr Plain (Vigrid Plain, Vígrídr Plain, Vígríth Plain, Vigrith Plain, Vigard Plain) [battle place]: The battlefield on the island of Oskopnir where the last great battle was fought during Ragnarokr. It was 100 rosts on either side.

Vinbjorg (Vinbjörg): A Hall given to Gudrunr by Grimhildr for agreeing to marry King Atli.

Vingi (Wingi): King Atli's duplicitous counselor and messenger. In some versions he was called Knefrud (Knefurd, Knefroed). He tricked Gudrunr's brothers into visiting her. When they found out about his trickery they killed him. They then fought against King Atli and were slain by him.

Vingskornir (Vinskornir): The name of the horse Brynhildr rode to battle on as a Valkyrie.

Volsi: The name for the sacred phallus of a horse. Would you have us worship you through the hindquarters of a horse?

Volsungr (Völsûngr, Volsung, Vösung, Vösungr, Vösungr, Volsunga): Rerir's son. His mother was pregnant with him for six years. While unborn he made vows not to retreat from fire or sword because of fear. He married Hljod and they had nine sons as well as Sigmundr and his twin sister Signy. Siggeir, Signy's husband killed him in battle. Inherited his father's Kingdom and became King of Hunland.

Volsungr's Hoard: The Treasure of the Volsungrs.

Volva (Völva, Velva, Vúlva, volve): The prophetess in Niflhel whom Odin, in the guise of Vegtamr Valtamssonr, sought out and raised from the dead in order to gain information concerning Ragnarokr. She had once been Angroboda. Her name is also used to represent seeresses in general.

Vulnir: He fought a battle in a fierce storm against Ragnar Lodbrokr at Bornholm.

Wehr-shape: The name given to the animal forms assumed by humans.

Weregild: Payment, usually of gold, to expiate a crime, generally the killing of one of the other party's relative. Blood payment was when the atonement was with battle, a life for a life.

Whitby: The people of the land of Whitby worshipped the old gods. They fought against the sons of Ragnar Lodbrokr, but lost and their treasures were stolen and the walls of the town knocked down and the rest of the city was burned to the ground. Rognvaldr met his death during that battle.

William the Bastard: William the Conqueror.

William the Conqueror: William the Bastard.

Witch Wife: Signy changed forms with her and seduced Sigmundr in this form and subsequently bore their son, Sinfjotli.

Wolf in Holy Places: A term for an outlaw. It was applied to Sigi after his ignoble murder of Bredi.

Wyrd [fate]: A person's fate/destiny was woven by the Norns into a tapestry of their life. One can try, but one cannot escape one's wyrd.

Yngvi: Hoddbrodr sent for him to battle against Helgi and Sinfjotli.

GENEALOGY

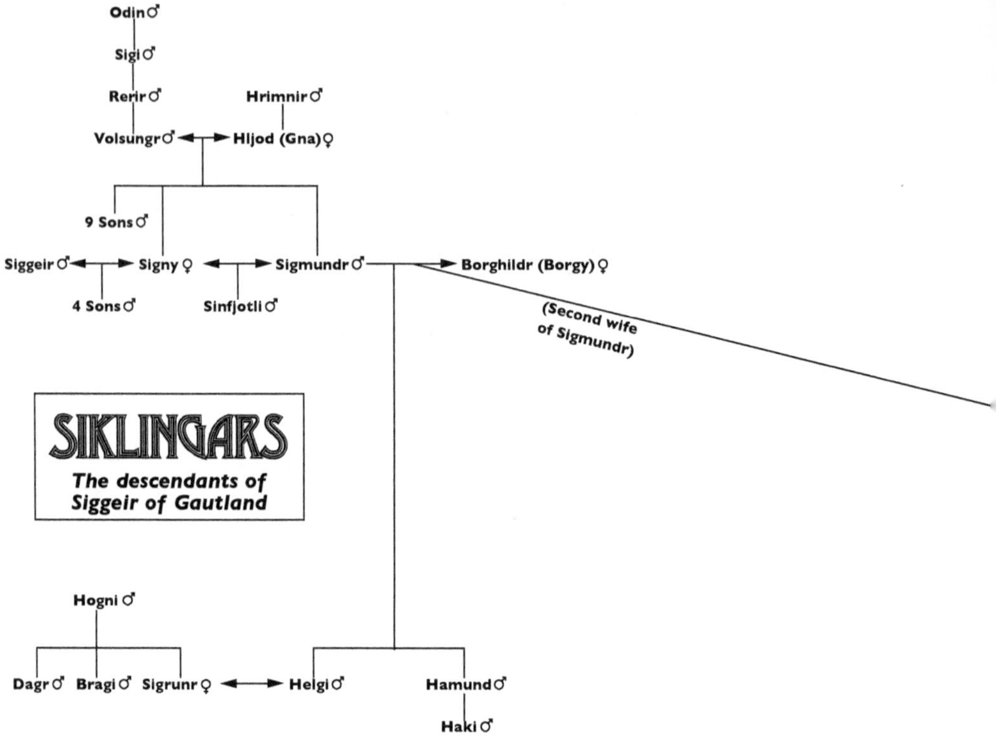

Odin ♂

Sigi ♂

Rerir ♂   Hrimnir ♂

Volsungr ♂ ◄──► Hljod (Gna) ♀

9 Sons ♂

Siggeir ♂ ◄──► Signy ♀ ◄──► Sigmundr ♂ ──────► Borghildr (Borgy) ♀

4 Sons ♂   Sinfjotli ♂   (Second wife of Sigmundr)

SIKLINGARS

**The descendants of
Siggeir of Gautland**

Hogni ♂

Dagr ♂   Bragi ♂   Sigrunr ♀ ◄──► Helgi ♂   Hamund ♂

Haki ♂

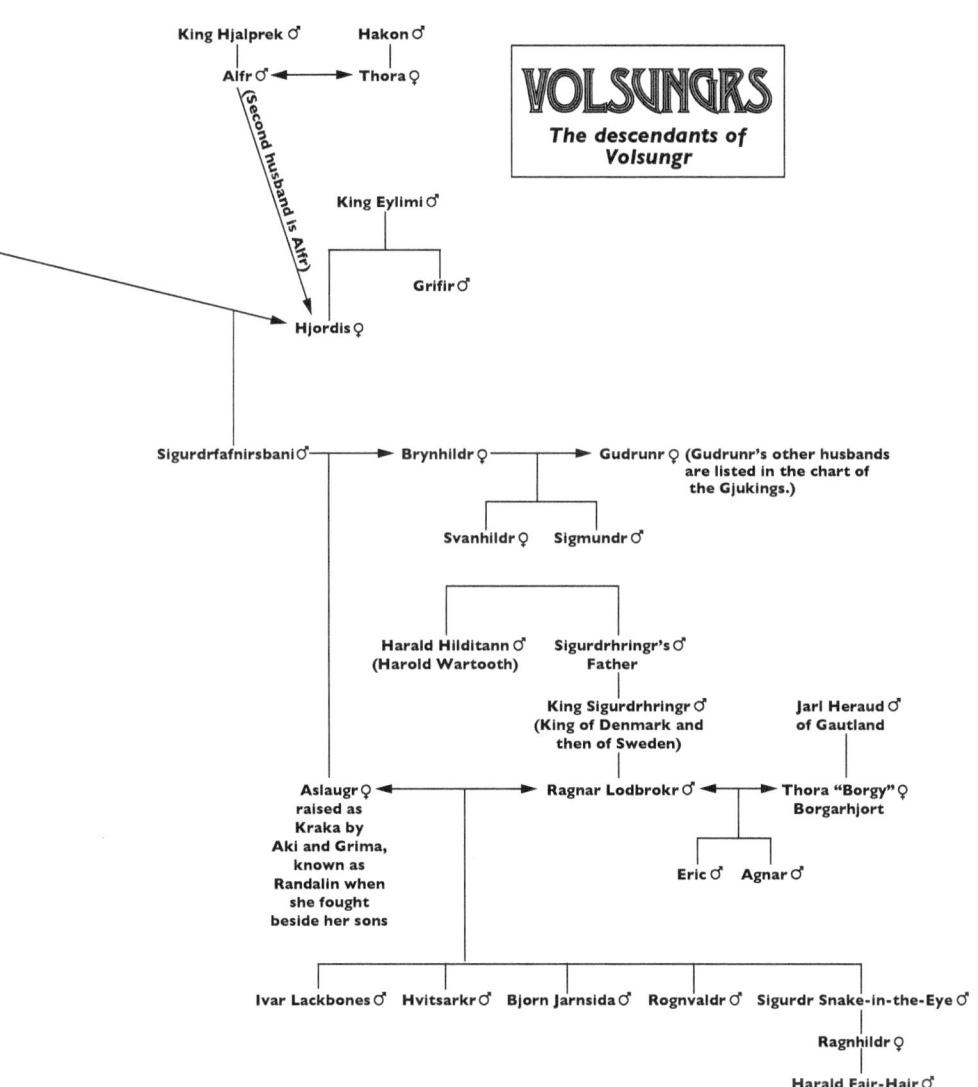

VOLSUNGRS

The descendants of Volsungr

King Hjalprek ♂   Hakon ♂

Alfr ♂ ◄────► Thora ♀

(Second husband is Alfr)

King Eylimi ♂

Grifir ♂

Hjordis ♀

Sigurdrfafnirsbani ♂ ───► Brynhildr ♀ ───► Gudrunr ♀ (Gudrunr's other husbands are listed in the chart of the Gjukings.)

Svanhildr ♀   Sigmundr ♂

Harald Hilditann ♂ (Harold Wartooth)   Sigurdrhringr's ♂ Father

King Sigurdrhringr ♂ (King of Denmark and then of Sweden)   Jarl Heraud ♂ of Gautland

Aslaugr ♀ ◄──── raised as Kraka by Aki and Grima, known as Randalin when she fought beside her sons   Ragnar Lodbrokr ♂ ◄──► Thora "Borgy" ♀ Borgarhjort

Eric ♂   Agnar ♂

Ivar Lackbones ♂   Hvitsarkr ♂   Bjorn Jarnsida ♂   Rognvaldr ♂   Sigurdr Snake-in-the-Eye ♂

Ragnhildr ♀

Harald Fair-Hair ♂ first king of Norway

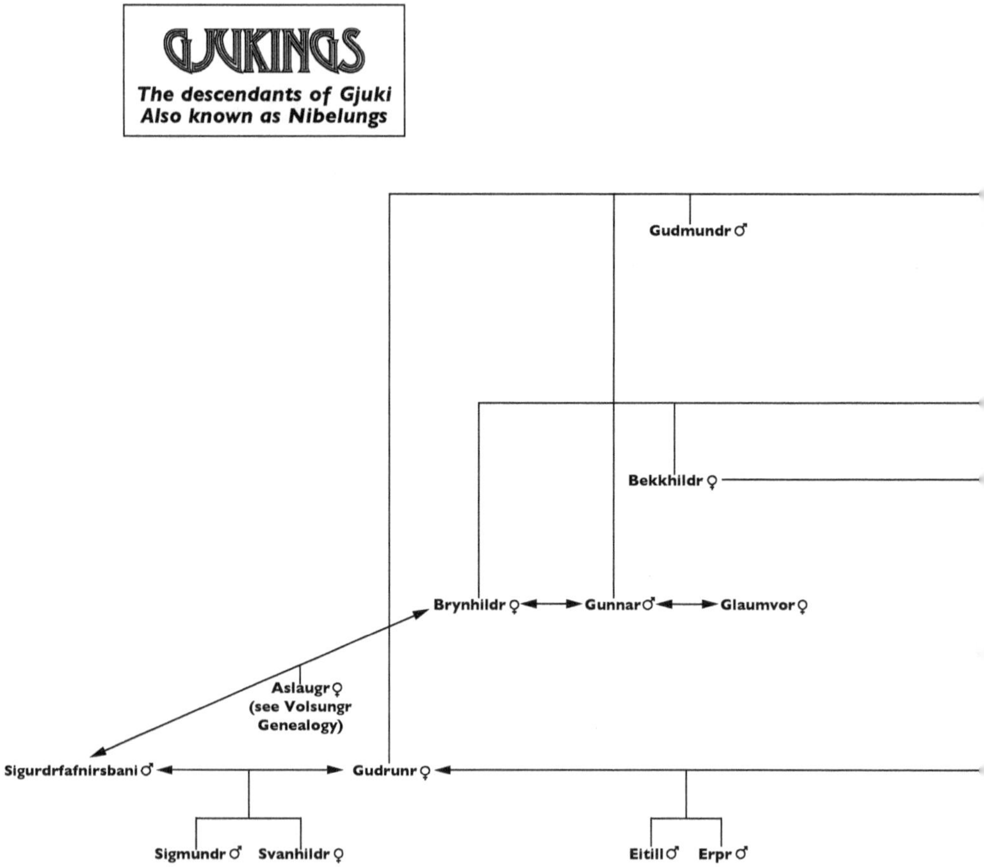

310

**The descendants of Gjuki
Also known as Nibelungs**

Gudmundr ♂

Bekkhildr ♀ ⎯⎯⎯⎯⎯

Brynhildr ♀ ◄⎯► Gunnar ♂ ◄⎯► Glaumvor ♀

Aslaugr ♀
(see Volsungr
Genealogy)

Sigurdrfafnirsbani ♂ ◄⎯⎯⎯⎯⎯⎯⎯► Gudrunr ♀ ◄⎯⎯

Sigmundr ♂   Svanhildr ♀   Eitill ♂   Erpr ♂

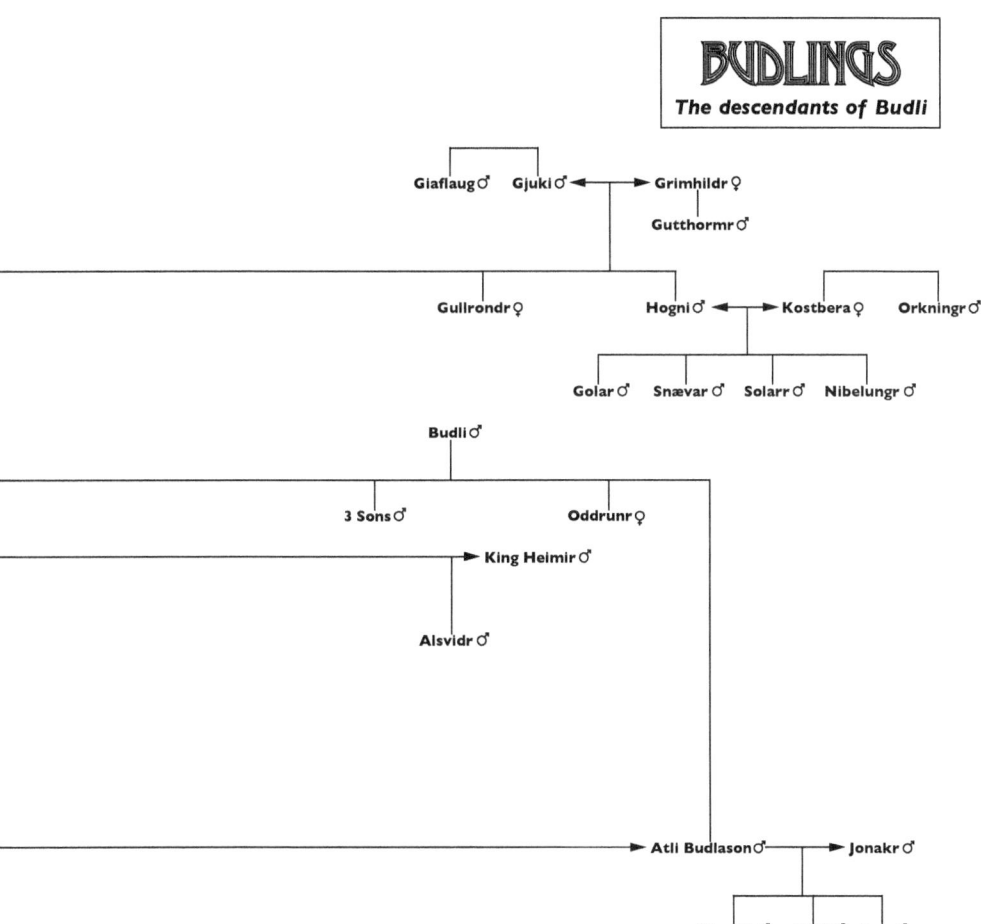

BVDLINGS

The descendants of Budli

More Books From Hollow Earth Publishing

Hollow Earth Publishing will be publishing a series of books retelling all the Scandinavian Sagas in English. We are striving to make certain they are the best retellings available. We will also be reprinting out-of-print books dealing with Scandinavian Sagas as well as publishing books on other topics.

The Norse Myths

by Heilan Yvette Grimes

The most complete version of the Norse Myths in the English language. Includes a Glossary and Genealogy Chart.

The Ring – The Legend of the Niebelungenlied: *The Volsungr Saga and The Saga of Ragnar Lodbrokr*

by Heilan Yvette Grimes

This book is a retelling of the ring saga from the Norse perspective. It makes a lot more sense than the Germanic version, and is a lot gorier. Pay attention to whomever has the ring. Nothing good will come to that person. Includes a Glossary and Genealogy Chart.

H. – The Story of Heathcliff's Journey Back to Wuthering Heights

by Lin Haire-Sargeant

This is the story of Heathcliff's lost years after he runs away from Cathy and returns three years later a gentleman with money. What happened? Who was his mentor? Haire-Sargeant masterfully combines Wuthering Heights and Jane Eyre to tell Heathecliff's story.

The Book of Twitter: *How to Get 100,000+ Followers and What to Do With Them After You've Got Them*

by Heilan Yvette Grimes

The best book available for how to use twitter. Detailed information on how to setup your twitter account, how and what to tweet, how to get followers, and how to manage your twitter account. thebookoftwitter.com

Coming Soon

The Laxdaela Saga

by Heilan Yvette Grimes

This the only medieval epic with a woman as the protagonist. Includes a Glossary and Genealogy Chart.

The Book of Runes

by Heilan Yvette Grimes

Here is everything you need to know about runes including history, kinds of runes, their properties, and how to use them.

The Viking Age, Vols. I and II

by Paul b. Du Chaillu

This a complete redesign of the 1889 legendary work about the Vikings, their customs, clothing, housing, life, weapons, and legends. In short, everything you ever wanted to know about the Vikings. Originally 1160+ pages and 1366 illustrations. Because of printing costs, this book will only be available digitally. But it will be fully searchable.

www.hollowearthpublishing

HOLLOW EARTH PUBLISHING
HOLLOWEARTHPUBLISHING.COM

www.ingramcontent.com/pod-product-compliance
Lightning Source LLC
Chambersburg PA
CBHW061514020726
47502CB00006B/2070